I0822509

# ONLY COLD DEPTHS

A GALACTIC BONDS BOOK

JENNIFER ESTEP

# ONLY COLD DEPTHS





ISBN: 978-1-950076-46-8



Published in the United States of America

*To all the readers who wanted more Galactic Bonds books—this one is for you.*

*To my mom—for everything.*

*To myself—for trying something different and writing a book of my heart.*

*Only you know what lurks*
*in the cold depths of your own heart.*

*—AUTHOR UNKNOWN*

# PART ONE

## RUNAWAYS

# ONE

## VESPER

Sometimes in life, you must hide who you really are to survive.

Like slink through a marketplace in the morning, avoid bounty hunters at noon, and escape from a planet before midnight.

I had been hiding who I was for the last few weeks. I might be surviving, but I wasn't any safer now than when I started—

A woman with wavy, dark red hair bumped into me. The sharp, unexpected motion knocked me off-balance, and I staggered to the side of a narrow, cramped aisle. My shoulder smacked into the corner of a polyplastic booth, and the trinkets on the display table rattled in an ominous warning, like vipers about to bite me.

My heart kicked up into my throat, and I whirled around, expecting an attack. My hand dropped to my black leather belt, reaching for my stormsword, but my fingers only skimmed over empty air. I silently cursed my own forgetfulness. I hadn't wanted to wear such a distinctive weapon, so I'd slid the sword into the long, oversize shopping bag hanging off my left forearm.

My right hand darted down into the bag, and my fingers curled around the three eye-shaped sapphsidian jewels embedded in the sword's silver hilt. Smaller pieces of sapphsidian winked along the silver crossguard, which curled out in opposite directions, although the two end points perfectly aligned like the halves of a yin-yang symbol. More prongs of silver curled up to touch the lunarium blade, which glimmered with an opalescent sheen.

My fingers tightened around the sword, but instead of attacking, the woman kept going. She didn't even glance back, and her red cloak streamed out behind her like a long scarlet ribbon. The woman quickly vanished into the bustling crowd roaming through the marketplace.

I hissed out a breath, released the sword, and rubbed my throbbing shoulder. No one had noticed my awkward landing except the booth's owner. I ignored her angry glower and glanced around, my gaze skipping from one person and booth to the next.

This marketplace on Tropics 44 was as bright, vibrant, and colorful as the rain forest that covered the planet. The booths ranged from tall and wide to short and squat, and each one was painted a different color, from ocean blue to flamingo pink to electric purple. Even the hibiscus-shaped cobblestones underfoot were painted with brilliant hues, making me feel as though I was walking on a bed of blossoms.

Large, stiff plastipaper pennants topped many of the booths. Some bore cutesy graphics of bananas and coconuts, while others featured images of clothing, jewelry, and tools. In between the booths, food vendors cooked everything from brown-sugar-crusted pineapple chunks and juicy mango kabobs to spicy chicken wings and balsamic-glazed filet mignon bites over open flames. The sweet smells of caramelized fruits mingled with the deeper, smokier scents of the grilled meats, and my mouth watered at the delicious aromas.

"Well?" the booth owner demanded in a sharp voice. "Are you going to buy anything? Or are you just going to stand there gaping like a fool? You almost knocked all my lovelies off my table!"

I turned to apologize and caught sight of myself in a glass mirror standing on the table.

Dirty-blond hair, purple eyes, a long lumpy nose, a thin white scar slashing across my chin. I blinked a few times, not recognizing the face staring back at me. Then again, it wasn't really *my* face.

My hand crept up, and I traced my finger over the small, eye-shaped bobby pin nestled in my hair. The polyplastic pin was a miniature colorizer that changed someone's hair without the need for messy dyes. One of the many inventions I'd been working on at Quill Corp before I'd been forced to abandon my company, leave everything behind, and go on the run.

Still staring at myself in the mirror, I kept tracing my finger over the bobby pin, and the ends of my hair darkened from their colorized dirty blond to their natural brown. I dropped my hand. The colorizer was still a work in progress, and fiddling with it drained the solar charge. Plus, the purple contacts and the sculpted bits of plastipaper that made up the rest of my disguise were itching. Time to get back to the ship.

I hoisted the straps of my cloth bag onto my left shoulder so both my hands were free. I'd already bought fresh mangoes, tomatoes, and cucumbers, along with beef jerky, potato hash, and other freeze-dried staples.

"Well?" the booth owner demanded again. "Are you going to buy anything?"

I didn't want to buy anything, but the woman was pissed, and I didn't want to give her any more reasons to remember me, so I studied her goods.

The woman was selling rose quartz, amethyst geodes, and other pretty stones. A few silver-framed mirrors perched on the table, along with white velvet trays bristling with jewelry. Nothing useful or edible like the food in my bag, but I needed to buy *something* . . .

A tiny rainbow of blues caught my eye, and I leaned down and focused on a butterfly brooch nestled among a row of necklaces and bracelets. Unlike the rest of the chunky jewelry, the brooch was made of delicate, curving swirls of silver. Blue opals gleamed on the butterfly's wings, while sapphsidian chips formed the creature's eyes and antennae.

I picked up the brooch. The midmorning sunlight made the blue opals spark with inner fire and brought out the true, deep blue of the sapphsidian chips. The brooch reminded me of the mammoth butterflies lazily flapping their wings in a netted petting zoo I'd passed earlier.

"I'll take this."

The booth owner's anger melted away, replaced by a sunny smile. "My lady has excellent taste! That piece was designed to match a hairpin that Lady Vesper Quill wore during the recent Regal midnight ball."

I flinched at the sound of my own name. My fingers went cold and numb, and I almost dropped the brooch.

The booth owner frowned, suspicion crinkling her face. "Is something wrong?"

I forced myself to shrug. "Of course not. I just didn't realize the brooch was modeled after . . . her."

"Oh, yes," the woman chirped. "Everyone follows the Regal trends, but items from that night have been particularly popular. I can barely keep them in stock . . ."

The woman prattled on about Regal fashions, gesturing at several other pieces of jewelry, along with a rack of gowns stuffed into the booth. I tuned out her words and studied the brooch even more carefully. It *was* a replica of the butterfly hairpin I'd worn during the midnight ball, although the original hairpin had been more of a small dagger.

That hairpin had been a bit of good luck. Maybe this brooch would bring me more of the same. And if it didn't, well, I could always pry out the opals and sapphsidian chips and melt down the silver and use them in my inventions.

I held the brooch out to the booth owner. "Will you wrap it up for me, please?"

She took it from me. "Of course! House Zimmer is always happy to serve its customers."

This time, my entire body went cold and numb, as though I'd been transported from this warm Tropics planet to an icy Frozon moon. My head slowly lifted, my neck cracking with the motion. I stared up at the booth's gray plastipaper pennant, which was emblazoned with a large stylized ice-blue *Z*—the sigil for House Zimmer.

Tropics 44 was officially controlled by the Erzton, although it was on the border of Erzton and Imperium territory and featured a mix of people and businesses. More than one booth boasted a sigil for an Imperium Regal family, although I hadn't noticed the House Zimmer symbol until now.

House Zimmer was run by my, well, *family*, if you could call them that. Beatrice, my grandmother, was the head of the House, while my father, Wendell, was her second-in-command. And then there was Zane, my older brother, who was also the head of the Arrows, the Imperium's elite warriors.

Nerezza Blackwell, my mother, had abandoned me when I was seven, and I'd never had any clue as to my father's identity until a few weeks ago. Ever since I'd discovered that Wendell was my father, I'd been struggling with my simmering anger and deep disgust at the Zimmers for hiding my existence for the last thirty-seven years.

"Here you go," the booth owner chirped again. "I wrapped it up all neat and pretty."

I mumbled my thanks and used my tablet to transfer the appropriate credits into the booth owner's account. She charged me an outrageous amount for the brooch, far more than what it was worth, but I paid without complaint. The second the transfer went through, I snatched the tiny ice-blue box out of her hand, shoved it into my bag, and hurried away.

I moved past booths filled with everything from porcelain tea sets to fresh flowers to swords, blasters, and other weapons. A few people shot me curious looks, clearly wondering why I was wearing a long gray cloak over my dark blue jacket, shirt, cargo pants, and boots instead of the colorful short-sleeved shirts, shorts, and sandals most folks were sporting in the sticky heat. I ignored them and kept going, hefting my bag onto my shoulder. Maybe it was my imagination, but the House Zimmer butterfly brooch felt heavier than all the food stuffed inside the cloth.

*Vesper? What's wrong?* a deep voice murmured.

I flinched again at the sound of my own name. My heart galloped up into my throat, and my gaze zoomed from side to side like an out-of-control spaceship. Then I remembered the voice was only in my mind and no one here knew I was Vesper Quill, Regal lady and Imperium fugitive.

*You feel . . . upset*, the voice continued.

For the third time, I flinched, although my expression quickly morphed into a small, rueful smile. I was still getting used to Kyrion Caldaren telepathically talking to me, especially when a considerable distance separated us.

I was in the marketplace, but Kyrion was in the nearby spaceport, on board the *Dream World*, his blitzer, waiting for me to return with the supplies.

*Vesper?* Kyrion asked again, concern sharpening his voice. *What's wrong?*

*Nothing*, I finally replied. *I just spotted a House Zimmer booth. It took me by surprise.*

*Ah, I see.* The words rumbled through my mind, and a wave of soft, warm sympathy washed over me as though I was standing in a Tropics ocean that was the perfect temperature. Even without our truebond, the psionic connection that let us share thoughts, feelings, skills, and more, Kyrion still would have known about my conflicted emotions regarding my long-lost family.

*I should have been the one to go to the marketplace*, Kyrion continued, his crisp Corios accent becoming more pronounced.

My smile widened. He always worried whenever I left the ship. After being on my own for so long, it was nice to have someone who cared, especially as much as Kyrion did.

*We've talked about this a dozen times. You were the leader of the Arrows and have been a staple on the Regal gossipcasts for years. You are* far *more recognizable than me, even with a disguise.*

*We're both pretty recognizable now, thanks to Holloway and his bounty*, Kyrion replied, a sour note creeping into his voice.

The sticky cobweb that was Kyrion's psionic presence in my mind bristled with anger, as though the strands had morphed into tiny spears, and the same sensation prickled my skin with its tingling intensity. Our truebond was still so new that it was often difficult to tell whether some of the emotions I experienced were my own, Kyrion's feelings, or a combination of the two.

*Don't worry. I'll be back soon, and then we can make the final pinpoint jump to Sygnustern.* I paused. *And eat a meal that doesn't come out of a plastic wrapper.*

Soft laughter drifted through my mind. *I'll be waiting, and so will my taste buds.*

*Good, because I bought some delicious-looking fruit for dessert.*

*Oh, I had something* else *in mind for dessert. Something* far *more pleasurable and satisfying than fruit.* The low, silky purr of Kyrion's voice made anticipation skitter down my spine.

An image bloomed in my mind: Kyrion and me in bed, my

hands digging into his back, pulling him closer as he thrust inside me. Once again, I wasn't sure if it was my thought or his or a shared memory of all the things we'd done last night, but heat flooded my cheeks, and desire spiked through my body.

*Dessert for two is a marvelous idea*, I replied, my voice husky with longing.

A satisfied rumble echoed through the bond, along with a light, feathery touch, as though Kyrion was trailing his fingertips down my spine. More desire spiked through me, and my steps quickened. The sooner I got back to the ship, the sooner we could forget about the rest of the galaxy and focus on each other again.

Kyrion didn't telepathically speak to me again, but I could still feel his presence in my mind, just as I knew that he could feel me in his. When our truebond had first formed when we'd been trapped together on a broken ship, I'd *hated* the feel of him, all those tight, tiny knots that tied us together, and Kyrion had despised the unwanted connection just as much. But now, after everything we'd been through, his presence comforted me, like an anchor that was always there to steady me. The bond also added another level of heady sensation to the already amazing chemistry we shared.

Still smiling, I reached the edge of the marketplace, which sprawled across an open square lined with palm trees. I stopped and glanced back over my shoulder. The last thing I needed to do was lead someone back to our ship—

A pop of neon pink caught my eye, and a woman with short, spiky pink hair and pale skin stepped out of an aisle, her head swiveling back and forth as though she was searching for someone. She was dressed in a tight tactical tank top, cargo pants, and boots, all in a dull, durable brown. A blaster was nestled in a holster on her right thigh, while a shock baton and a pair of polyplastic handcuffs dangled from her metal belt.

A blaster, a shock baton, and handcuffs—all the tools of a bounty hunter.

Given all the near misses Kyrion and I had had with bounty hunters over the last few weeks, I'd gotten good at recognizing them. Just looking at the woman made the hair on the back of my neck stand up, and my seer magic whispered an extra warning, adding to my screaming instincts. I stepped to my left to duck behind a tree out of her line of sight.

Too late. The woman's dark brown gaze settled on me, and she lifted her hand to her ear and said a few words, talking to someone through a comms device. Then she dropped her hand, yanked her shock baton off her belt, and strode in my direction.

I muttered a curse. Somehow the woman had seen through my disguise and locked on to me like a heat-seeking missile.

Forget hiding. It was time to run for my life—again.

I whirled around and sprinted away from the pink-haired woman. Several side streets branched off from the square, all going in different directions like the spokes on a transport wheel. I picked the first street I came to and hurried along it. My boots smacked out a quick, frantic rhythm on the painted cobblestones, and people ambling along the sidewalk jumped out of the way as I hurried past.

*Vesper?* Kyrion's voice sounded in my mind again. *Vesper, what's wrong?*

*A bounty hunter is chasing me! I'm headed your way! Get ready to leave as soon as I get back to the ship!*

Kyrion growled, and his fury crashed over me like an icy river, cold enough to make my teeth chatter.

I made one turn after another, moving closer toward the spaceport, but I couldn't shake my pink-haired pursuer. Every time I zigged, she did the same, and even when I circled around and doubled back, her footsteps pounded in the distance.

Frustration spiked through me, but I picked up my pace.

By this point, most folks would have been gasping for air, but I had an oxygen optimization, or O2, enhancement. A special liquid had been injected into my lungs that greatly increased their capacity and functionality, so I didn't need as much air to breathe as other people, even when I was exerting myself.

With every breath I drew in, an answering amount of fresh, steady energy flowed through my body—Kyrion's energy. Even with my O2 enhancement, my legs would have given out, and I would have been forced to stop running a few streets ago. But the rogue Arrow was in amazing physical shape, and our truebond was letting me tap into his strength and endurance—even if I wasn't quite sure how I was doing it.

Then again, desperation helped people do all sorts of unexpected things.

I kept running. Four streets later, I glanced back over my shoulder. I didn't see the bounty hunter or hear her footsteps anymore, so I darted down an alley, sprinted to the far end, and ducked behind a large trash bin. The stench of rotting food and other garbage wafted through the air, and I twitched my nose to hold back a sneeze.

I dropped my bag of food onto the grimy cobblestones and ran my hands over my clothes. Someone in the marketplace must have realized who I was and tagged me with a tracker. That was the only explanation for how the pink-haired bounty hunter had followed me through all these twists and turns.

My hands skimmed first one piece of fabric, then another . . .

*There.*

My fingers brushed across something that felt like a small button. I ripped the piece of metal off my cloak, dropped it to the ground, and crushed it with the heel of my boot. Next, I reached up and tapped three times on the colorizer bobby pin still nestled in my hair. The bounty hunter had already seen me as a blonde, but maybe she would overlook me if I was suddenly a redhead.

I yanked a piece of my hair forward, but instead of red, my locks were now their regular dark brown with a few auburn highlights. Drat. The bobby pin was out of juice.

Even worse, sweat was streaming down my face, and the salty drops had loosened the sculpted pieces of plastipaper that formed my fake nose and scarred chin. I peeled off the papers and popped the itchy violet contacts out of my eyes and tossed them all aside.

The only thing I could do now to change my appearance was get rid of my cloak, so I ripped it off and threw it down. Maybe the bounty hunter would be looking for the long gray garment instead of my blue clothes.

I scooped up the shopping bag from the ground. My fingers itched with the urge to pluck my stormsword out of the dark depths, but carrying the weapon would be akin to having a bright red sign flashing over my head. *Look at me! I have a stormsword! I'm Vesper Quill!*

I left the sword hidden inside the bag, threw the straps over my right shoulder, and hurried forward. I needed to get out of the alley before the bounty hunter zeroed in on the tracker's last location.

As if my thought had summoned her, the pink-haired woman stepped into view at the front of the alley. I stopped in my tracks. She let out a low whistle, and footsteps smacked on the cobblestones, growing louder and closer.

Four men ran into the alley and skidded to a stop. The men yanked blasters off their belts and leveled the weapons at my chest, while the pink-haired bounty hunter twirled the shock baton around in her hand again, making it glimmer a bright, warning silver.

I glanced behind me, but the alley was a dead end, and the twenty-foot wall was as smooth and slick as glass. Even with Kyrion's strength, I couldn't climb it.

I was trapped.

# TWO

## VESPER

I held my position. My fingers curled around the shopping bag straps still on my shoulder, and a sharp corner poked into my upper arm. I glanced down. The ice-blue box with the butterfly brooch was jutting up out of the bag.

I glared at the offending box. Why had I ever thought that anything to do with House Zimmer could be a good-luck charm? It was more like a blasted curse, and it had already sunk its claws into me.

*Vesper?* Kyrion's voice sliced through my mind, his tone rough with worry. *Where are you? What's happening?*

*The bounty hunter and her friends caught up with me. We're in an alley about a mile from the spaceport.*

*On my way*, he growled.

More of Kyrion's icy fury crashed over me, and I had to grit my teeth to keep them from chattering again.

"Are you sure this is her, Rina?" one of the men asked. "She doesn't look nearly as pretty and polished as she did on the gossipcast footage of the Regal ball."

"Oh, it's definitely her," Rina, the pink-haired woman, replied in a tart tone. "I didn't notice you at first, but one of my special friends spotted you right away."

Special friends? Who was she talking about?

Rina clucked her tongue in mock sympathy. "Given the enormous bounty, I thought you'd have a *much* better disguise than bleached hair, colored contacts, and a fake nose."

I shrugged off her taunt. "Everyone's a critic. How did you and your friends spot me?"

I needed to keep her talking to give Kyrion time to get here, but I was also genuinely curious. As a lab rat, someone who toiled away in the Quill Corp research-and-development lab, I specialized in designing appliances, weapons, and spaceships. Basically, I figured out how things worked and especially how to make them better, faster, and more efficient and powerful.

And this was far more important than tweaking the temperature settings on a new brewmaker or upping the voltage on a blaster. I wanted to know what had drawn the bounty hunter's attention so I wouldn't make the same mistake again. I *couldn't* make the same mistake again, not if Kyrion and I were going to stay free.

Rina shrugged back at me. "I spend my days finding people who don't want to be found. Desperation comes with a variety of signs—lowered heads, hunched shoulders, furtive movements, always looking around and jumping at every loud noise. You had all the classic tells, along with that ridiculously large shopping bag. People only slink around and carry bags like that when they need to stock up on supplies and return to their hiding spots as fast as possible."

She gestured at my discarded cloak lying on the ground. "Plus, you tried to hide your body with that cloak because you either didn't want someone to recognize your outfit or you didn't have anything else to wear."

She was right. All the garments on the *Dream World* matched my current Arrow uniform, and I had wanted to hide my clothes since the dark blue color might make someone think of House Caldaren.

"Either way, no normal vacationer would be dressed like that. Even the most expensive tempered silk is no match for this sweltering humidity."

Once again, she was right. Tempered silk might adjust to the wearer's body temperature, along with the surrounding environment, but I was still sweating, thanks to the sun beating down on my head. I was starting to despise Tropics planets almost as much as Magma ones.

I stabbed my left index finger at her hair, which was brighter than any tropical hibiscus. "You're one to talk. Neon-pink hair doesn't exactly make you incognito."

Rina ran a hand over her locks, but the spikes sprang right back into place. "I don't care about being incognito. I *want* my targets to know I'm coming." A cruel grin spread across her face. "I love the thrill of the chase."

She tilted her head to the side, studying me even more closely. "Even with all your tells, I still wasn't sure it was you, Lady Vesper. At least, not until you bolted like a snow rabbit being chased by a Frozon wolf." She jerked her thumb over her shoulder. "That's when I called in my men, and now here we are, about to score the biggest bounty ever offered in the Archipelago Galaxy."

The air beside her shimmered, and the image of another Rina appeared. The second Rina rubbed her hands together in glee, then plunged them into a bag brimming with old-fashioned gold coins. Rina lifted her hands, letting the coins trickle through her fingers and drop back down into the bag. Maybe it was a quirk of my seer magic, but I could hear every *clink-clink-clink* of the coins clattering together.

I blinked. The second Rina vanished, along with the bag of coins, like a hologram that had abruptly cut off, leaving only the real woman in front of me. I grimaced. My seer magic was useful in a variety of ways, but I could have done without the visions it often showed me of other people's goals.

"What is the going rate for my capture these days?" I asked, once again genuinely curious.

"For you? Ten million credits," Rina replied, her dark eyes gleaming with greed. "Twenty million for Kyrion Caldaren. Thirty million for the two of you together."

Annoyance shot through me that Kyrion's bounty was so much higher, although I should have expected it. Kyrion Caldaren was a powerful psion, someone with mental abilities like telekinesis, telepathy, and telempathy. He was also one of the most notorious assassins in the galaxy, an expert warrior who'd been the head of the Arrows for years. Of course Callus Holloway would offer more for Kyrion's capture, but the glaring disparity still irked my pride.

"Ten million credits? Is that all?" I said, as though the amount didn't make me want to clutch my chest in shock. "Holloway is low-balling you. Ten million credits isn't *nearly* enough to risk your lives trying to capture me."

Rina let out a merry laugh, and her men joined in with hearty chuckles.

Since they weren't intimidated by me, I tried a different tactic. "Like you said, I'm a Regal lady. The head of a powerful, wealthy corporation. I'm sure we can come to some arrangement. Something that's a lot more rewarding than ten million credits."

Rina laughed again. "Nice try. You've been a Regal lady for about three seconds. I seriously doubt you have ten million credits to toss out to every bounty hunter who crosses your path."

I opened my mouth to try again, but she cut me off.

"Where is your other, more lucrative half?" Rina scanned the alley. "An experienced warrior like Kyrion Caldaren would *never* let his truebonded partner get too far away, especially a seer like you."

More annoyance shot through me at her snide tone. As a seer, I was also considered to be a psion, a catchall term for spelltechs, siphons, and anyone else with extraordinary abilities. Some folks even referred to such abilities as magic, since no one had ever been able to figure out where psionic powers came from or how to consistently replicate them with science and technology.

Magic or not, most folks scoffed at my seer abilities, especially when I told them how silver flares of light often appeared around people or objects that were going to be important, useful, or even harmful to me in some future way. Or how I could often just look at a faulty brewmaker or a misfiring blaster and immediately see how to fix it. Or how I sometimes saw memories of things people had done in the past or things they might do in the future or even the objects they desired the most, like the vision I'd had of Rina and that bag of coins.

My seeing things simply wasn't as visually impressive—or, admittedly, as cool and deadly—as a psion like Kyrion using his telekinesis to send his stormsword spinning through a roomful of enemies and skewering them one after another. Even calling my seer abilities magic didn't make them any more respected.

"Caldaren letting you out of his sight is a good way for you both to get killed," Rina continued.

I grimaced at the reminder. A truebond might make two people much, much stronger, but in some ways, it also made them exceedingly vulnerable, especially when it came to experiencing each other's pain and injuries.

I had no desire to die and kill Kyrion in the process, and if Kyrion died, I selfishly didn't want to perish from a broken heart, as was the common notion when it came to couples who had a romantic truebond. But I had accepted our bond, and so had Kyrion, and it was one of the many risks that went along with all the power we were supposed to have—power I could have used to escape the bounty hunters, if only I could figure out how it worked and especially how to tap into it on a regular basis.

"So where is he?" Rina asked, an eager note creeping into her voice. "Where is Kyrion Caldaren?"

"We split up weeks ago. For all I know, Kyrion Caldaren is on a Frozon moon on the other side of the galaxy."

Rina rolled her eyes. "You're even worse at lying than you are at disguises."

She shoved her shock baton back onto her belt, then jerked her head. The four male bounty hunters surrounded me.

Another cruel grin spread across Rina's face. "Bring her."

The bounty hunters forced me to leave the alley and step back out onto the street. Rina led the way, while the four men kept their blasters trained on me, and we quickly made it back to the main square where the marketplace was.

One of the bounty hunters shoved me toward a path that led into the rain forest, but Rina punched him in the shoulder.

"No!" she barked out. "Not that way."

The bounty hunter frowned. "But what about—"

"Forget them!" she barked out again. "Change of plans. Let's go. Double time."

The male bounty hunters eyed the rain forest, but once again, they forced me to follow their boss.

I glanced back over my shoulder, but I didn't see anyone or anything moving in the thick, dense greenery. Why had the bounty hunters changed direction?

Rina skirted around the marketplace, then moved through several streets. The tourist shops and restaurants quickly vanished, replaced by squat, grimy buildings, and the few people in this area either studied us with open suspicion or ducked back into their businesses, clearly wanting no part of whatever trouble I was in.

While we walked, I reached out with my magic and touched

the sticky cobweb of Kyrion in my mind. *Kyrion? Can you hear me? We're moving into the industrial part of the city.*

No response. I could still feel Kyrion, but I couldn't hear his thoughts anymore. I also couldn't tell where he was or what he was doing, and I couldn't access any of his telempathy, telekinesis, or other abilities.

*Kyrion? Kyrion!*

Still no response. His icy fury was a nugget buried deep in my mind, and no matter how much I hammered at it with my own magic, I couldn't crack through the cold, hard shell. It was like having a stone in my boot that constantly scraped across my skin but that I could do nothing to remove.

I chewed on my lip, even as needles of worry and dread pricked my heart. Why couldn't I communicate with Kyrion? Was something wrong with the bond? Was something wrong with *me*?

"Here we are," Rina drawled. "Home sweet home."

She'd stopped in front of a metal gate at the end of a deserted street. Rina punched in a code on a keypad, and the gate rattled back. She stepped through to the other side, and the other bounty hunters shepherded me forward.

Like the marketplace, this area was also a large square, but instead of booths and trinkets, rusty transports and broken engines filled the space, and buckets of nails, bolts, and screws glinted like metallic diamonds in the noon sun. Tumbleweeds of snarled wires listed back and forth in the breeze, and the scents of machine oil and smoky exhaust greased and clouded the humid air.

Despite the danger, I perked up. Most people would have called it a junkyard, but to me, it was a trove of treasures just waiting to be discovered—and potential weapons I could rig together to escape.

"This way," Rina called out, heading deeper into the junkyard.

We went down one aisle after another, moving past busted machines and castoff pieces that were jammed together like a jigsaw puzzle and piled higher than my head. The bright Tropics sun reflected off all the metal, making the junkyard as hot as a Quill Corp smelter.

Rina skirted around a low concrete building in the center of the junkyard and headed to the back side of the structure. Here the transports and engines had been pushed to the sides to make way for a crude landing pad, and a small blitzer was parked on the hard-packed dirt, close to a dilapidated Regal carriage that squatted on a tower of cracked blocks instead of wheels, like a ragged wooden queen perched on a crumbling cement throne.

Unlike everything else, the blitzer was in excellent condition, and the cargo-bay ramp was lowered, as if it was just waiting for passengers to board.

Rina spun around and held her arms out wide like a salesperson showing off a brand-new spaceship on a factory floor. "Welcome to your new home, Lady Vesper. This is my blitzer, the *Tempest*. I'm sure it's not *nearly* as big and fancy as whatever Regal ship you've been traveling on, but you won't have to suffer our cramped accommodations too long. My ship will have you back on Corios in a few days."

Dread punched into my heart. My seer magic surged up again, and the image of another blitzer shimmered in the air—*Pretty Boy*, Zane's ship. My brother had taken me back to Corios, the Imperium's home planet, so that Callus Holloway could tap into my truebond with Kyrion. Even now, all these weeks later, I could still feel the greedy siphon's power blasting over me like hundreds of robotic needles stabbing deep into my body, then abruptly, painfully retracting and sucking out my magic, along with my life.

I shuddered and shoved the memory away. The second ship vanished, leaving only the *Tempest*. Dread punched into my heart again, although it was quickly drowned out by my pounding anger.

"I'm not going back to Corios. And unless you release me right now, you and your men won't be going anywhere but into the great beyond."

Rina laughed at my threat. "It's been a long time since I've had the pleasure of getting Regal blood on my hands. Normally, I would give you a sporting chance to get the better of me, but I'm in a rush."

*I suppose I wanted to give you and Kyrion a sporting chance.* Zane's voice drifted through my mind.

Even more anger pounded through my body. My arrogant jackass of a brother had said that was the reason he'd slowed down Adria and Dargan Byrne when the three Arrows had been hunting me. Well, I didn't need anyone to give me a sporting chance. I was more than capable of making my own luck.

My fingers tightened around the straps of the shopping bag still hanging from my shoulder. The bounty hunters hadn't bothered to search me, and my stormsword was still hidden inside the cloth—

A silver light flared around Rina. The brief flash of my magic was the only warning I had before the bounty hunter swung her fist at my face.

She was probably trying to knock me out with one quick, decisive blow, but I whipped to the side, and her punch plowed into my right shoulder instead of my jaw. Pain erupted in my upper arm, radiating down past my elbow. I staggered back, and the shopping bag slipped off my shoulder and dropped to the ground.

Blast it. That had *hurt*. Rina must have strength and speed enhancements just like so many of the other bounty hunters Kyrion and I had dodged over the last few weeks.

I shook out my arm, waiting for the pain to die down. Rina grinned and raised her fist for another strike—

"I told you *not* to damage her," a cool, light, feminine voice cut in.

Rina whirled around, as did the four male bounty hunters. I also turned around.

Two more people now stood in the junkyard. Like Rina and her men, the two newcomers looked to be in their late thirties, the same as me.

The first was a tall man with dark blond hair, dark brown eyes, and ruddy skin. His biceps and thigh muscles bulged against his tight gray tactical shirt and cargo pants, and his broad shoulders and sculpted chest made him look like he was carved from solid stone. He was clutching a long, oversize hammer in each hand, with the heads pointing down at the ground, and he idly swung the hammers back and forth and back and forth, like they were the hands of an enormous clock counting down the seconds until he could use the weapons.

The hilts of the hammers were gold, but the actual weapons were crafted from lunarium, a precious mineral that could enhance psionic abilities and transform them into physical elements like fire, ice, lightning, and wind. Even more curious was the shape of the hammers. One side of each weapon was flat, like a regular hammer, and lined with jagged teeth like a saw, while the opposite side featured a large, sharp spike. All the edges glinted with a razor-sharp sheen. Not regular hammers—war hammers, instruments of death and destruction.

The second person was the woman with wavy, shoulder-length, dark red hair who had bumped into me in the marketplace. She was still wearing that long red cloak, and the garment ebbed and flowed around her like a scarlet wave. Given her confident stance, I got the sense the woman wore the cloak because she wanted to, not because she'd been trying to hide her clothes like I had been.

The woman's skin was pale, but her eyes were a deep, dark green studded with bright flecks of gold. Just like the man, she too was dressed in a gray tactical shirt and cargo pants, but her clothes were much finer and embellished with green ribbons and gold buttons. A dagger with a gold hilt and a long, curved lunarium blade hung from her belt.

The four male bounty hunters tensed, their hands tightening around the blasters still in their hands.

Rina wet her lips, then stepped forward, held her arms out wide, and plastered a bright smile on her face. "Esmina! I was just getting ready to signal you."

Esmina tilted her head to the side like a Tropics tiger lazily studying its prey right before ripping it to shreds. My seer magic erupted like a Magma volcano, and a blaze of silver light flared around the other woman, gilding her from head to toe. I winced against the harsh glare, quickly blinking it away, but a telltale chill slithered down my spine. Rina and her bounty hunters might be dangerous, but Esmina was the true threat here.

"Well, how serendipitous we found you instead," Esmina drawled.

Her sardonic tone made her faint accent a bit more pronounced. It was similar to Kyrion's crisp, proper Corios tone, but I couldn't quite place it.

"Pollux and I were at the rendezvous point, but you and your men never appeared," Esmina continued. "Then the tracker I planted on Lady Vesper went offline, as though it had been destroyed."

A sheen of sweat popped out on Rina's forehead that had nothing to do with the suffocating heat. "I don't know anything about your tracker being destroyed. Lady Vesper must have disabled it."

Esmina kept her icy gaze on the bounty hunter. "It doesn't matter who destroyed the tracker. You were supposed to bring Lady Vesper to *me*, not here to your own ship. Unless, of course, you were thinking about taking my credits *and* trying to cash in on Vesper's bounty."

So Esmina and Pollux had hired Rina and her men to capture me, but Rina had decided to double-cross her employers and keep me—and all the credits I was worth—to herself. Bold but risky.

"Your vision was right. This bounty hunter scum betrayed us the second she got the chance," Pollux rumbled in a deep voice. "You should have just let me bash her skull in like I wanted to."

He hefted one of his war hammers onto his left shoulder, even as he twirled the other weapon around in his right hand. My seer magic also painted him in a silver light, although the glow wasn't as bright and strong as it had been around Esmina.

I frowned at his words. What vision? What had Esmina seen about this moment?

Rina's arms plummeted to her sides, although she kept the smile on her face. "Esmina had a vision? How wonderful! She must have seen us all here together."

Pollux snorted in disbelief. We could all hear the lie in Rina's high, nervous tone. Whoever Esmina and Pollux really were, the bounty hunter was afraid of them. No wonder she'd wanted to hustle me onto her ship and get off-planet.

The man closest to me shifted on his feet, his finger curling around his blaster trigger. I eased away from him. Any second, he was going to lose his cool, raise the weapon, and fire.

"Now," Esmina said in a bored voice.

I tensed, expecting telekinesis or some other psionic power to surge off her, but instead, Pollux snapped his right hand forward, throwing his hammer. The weapon streaked through the air like a shooting star and slammed into the forehead of the bounty hunter who'd been about to fire his blaster.

*Crack!*

The bounty hunter's skull split open like a ripe melon. Blood sprayed everywhere, and the man dropped to the dirt without making a sound. Pollux jerked his arm back as though he was pulling on an invisible rope, and the hammer yanked free of the dead man's skull and zipped back over into his waiting hand.

Pollux was an extremely strong telekinetic, maybe even stronger than Kyrion. As soon as the war hammer settled into his palm, he started swinging the weapon back and forth in the same eerie motion as before. Bits of bone and brain matter dripped off the hammer's head, every soft, sickening *plop* as loud as a drum banging in the shocked silence.

Beside me, the dead bounty hunter's blood sluiced across the ground. I shuddered, then looked past the crimson stream. The man's blaster had slid out of his hand and landed a few feet away. The weapon was much closer than my stormsword, which was still tucked away in my shopping bag.

Rina and the three remaining bounty hunters were gaping at their friend's body, so I sidled toward the blaster.

Esmina let out a soft laugh and looked at me. "I wouldn't do that if I were you."

I froze.

Esmina's eyes were even darker than before, more black than green, although the gold flecks in her irises were much brighter now and sparking with magic. Before meeting Kyrion, I had never paid much attention to other psions' abilities. They had power, and I didn't, and that was all I needed to know. But this woman . . . magic just rolled off her like the heat blazing off the Tropics sun above.

Esmina had more raw magic than any psion I had ever met, except maybe Callus Holloway. Somehow she had known that I was going to reach for the bounty hunter's blaster almost the second the thought entered my mind. Was she a siphon like Holloway? Or something else? Something even more dangerous?

"Don't bother, Vesper," Esmina purred. "I know *exactly* what you're going to do even before you do it."

She strode forward. Rina and the three remaining bounty hunters scuttled back, leaving me standing alone. Esmina stopped in front of me. Even more of her magic surged over me, scraping against my skin like a razor. Sweat prickled the back of my neck, and another cold chill slid down my spine.

"Oh, yes. I can feel it now. Your power—or, rather, lack thereof." She shook her head as though she had just revealed some sad, devastating fact. "You're the weak link, destined to be broken."

*Weak link?* Her words slapped me across the face, and I jerked back in shock. She was talking about my truebond with Kyrion. My hands balled into fists, and fury exploded in my chest, punching the air out of my lungs. She didn't know *anything* about me or Kyrion or our connection or how we felt about each other.

"Don't bother denying it," Esmina continued. "You've already sensed it. How much weaker you are than Kyrion. How fragile and vulnerable you make him. How you're going to be the death of him, one way or another."

She tilted her head to the side again. The gold flecks in her eyes brightened even more, and her gaze burned into mine like a cold laser, cutting straight to my core. A knowing smile curved her lips. "Ah, I see. You've already started having problems with your bond. How very sad Kyrion has all that magnificent power, and you don't know how to use it."

The fury in my chest died, choked to nothingness by sharp thorns of worry and doubt that burrowed deep into my heart. Kyrion *was* a much stronger psion and far more skilled with his stormsword, whereas I was still struggling to figure out how my seer magic worked and trying to play catch-up with him as a warrior.

Esmina's lips curled back into a disgusted sneer. "That's the trap of truebonds. The weak *always* drag down the strong."

Those thorns burrowed even deeper into my chest,

crystallizing into jagged shards of icy dread. Somehow she was peering into the darkest recesses of my mind and heart and dragging out my deepest secrets and most terrifying fears—that I was going to get myself killed and doom Kyrion along with me.

Esmina shrugged, as if my lack of power was of no real concern. "Still, you are supposed to be useful in other ways, small though they may be."

I flinched, but I finally found my voice again. "Not that small. You can get a lot of *use* out of ten million credits."

She laughed. "Whoever said I was here for the bounty?"

Another chill zipped down my spine, stronger than the others, and morphed into an ocean of ice that surged out into my arms and legs. Having a bounty on my head was bad enough, but far worse fates were lurking in the cold depths of the galaxy.

Harkin Ocnus had shown me that.

The sadistic scientist was the son of General Orion Ocnus, one of the leaders of the Techwave, a terrorist group that wanted to topple the Imperium and become the main ruling force in the galaxy. Several weeks ago, on his father's orders, Harkin had kidnapped me and cuffed me to a table in his medical lab. The cruel bastard had cut me with a scalpel, then used skinbonds to heal my injuries. Harkin had tortured me over and over in hopes of forcing me to fix the Techwave's new hand cannon, a deadly weapon capable of cutting through psionic and other defensive energy shields.

My seer magic surged up. This time, instead of a double image or a blinding silver light, the ends of Esmina's scarlet cloak oozed down and started dripping, just as my blood had dripped off the table in Harkin's lab.

I shuddered at the unwanted vision. "If you're not here for the bounty, then what do you want with me? Are you working for the Techwave?"

"The Techwave?" A mocking laugh tumbled from Esmina's

lips. "Please. Don't insult me. I have far bigger goals than ordering around a bunch of mechanized soldiers."

"I wouldn't mind crushing a few Black Scarabs," Pollux chimed in. "They make such odd noises when you smash them."

He kept swinging his hammer, and another shudder rippled through my body at his casual dismissal of the Techwave's dangerous automated troops.

"Forget it," Rina growled. "I stole Lady Vesper from you fair and square. *We're* collecting the bounty, not you."

Rina plucked her blaster out of its holster and aimed the weapon at Pollux. The three male bounty hunters did the same thing.

I eased to the side, getting out of the potential cross fire, and a small flare of light appeared. I tensed, thinking it was more of my seer magic, but the light was coming from the long dagger on Esmina's belt. She wasn't even touching the dagger, and the lunarium blade was still glimmering a faint gold in a reflection of her magic. I'd never seen a weapon light up like that without a psion's touch, which was just another confirmation of how powerful she was.

Rina waggled her blaster at Pollux, although her gaze flicked over to Esmina. "Tell your lapdog to stand down, and we won't kill you."

Pollux snorted at her lie. "Really? You and what army? All I see are buckets of bolts and piles of metal."

Rina puckered her lips and let out a high, sharp whistle. All around the junkyard, the buckets of bolts and piles of metal shifted to the sides, smoothly skating along hidden tracks embedded in the dirt. A series of secret doors opened, and more than a dozen bounty hunters poured out of the hiding spots. Clever.

The bounty hunters spread out and aimed their blasters at Pollux and Esmina.

Rina grinned. "What were you saying about an army?"

# THREE

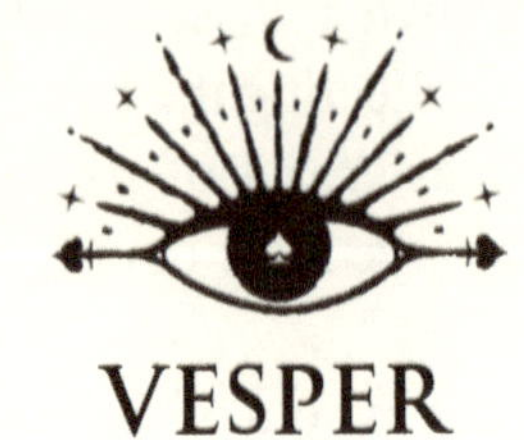

## VESPER

This situation had quickly gone from bad to worse to catastrophic, like a blitzer spinning out of control and about to crash into the ground.

Esmina sighed, as if the reinforcements bored her. Pollux grinned and kept swinging his hammer back and forth.

"You're surrounded and outnumbered," Rina crowed. "Now what you are doing to do, you arrogant bitch?"

Esmina blinked a few times, and the gold flecks in her eyes brightened again. Her lips puckered, and a sour look crinkled her face. "Nothing."

Rina blinked in surprise, as did the other bounty hunters. Me too. Usually, these sorts of standoffs involved more threats and posturing until someone escalated things to their inevitable bloody conclusion.

"So . . . you're . . . surrendering?" Rina asked in a bewildered voice.

Esmina scoffed. "Please. I *never* surrender, but this fight is already over."

"Are you sure?" Pollux asked. "It won't take me long to kill them all."

Rina tensed, as did her men. Even when facing down more than a dozen armed enemies, Pollux was still certain he could win, and my seer magic was whispering that he was right.

"You know I'm always sure, and I'm always right," Esmina replied in a chiding tone.

Pollux shrugged, but he stopped swinging his hammer.

I frowned. Esmina and Pollux might be severely outnumbered, but I had no doubt they could still kill the bounty hunters and capture me. So why was Esmina acting like the battle was already lost?

*Boom!*

A bright green blast of energy zinged through the junkyard, hitting the bounty hunter closest to me. The man screamed and dropped to the ground, his chest sparking and smoking with deadly electricity.

My head snapped up, tracking the blast's trajectory. A tall man clutching a silver hand cannon stood on top of the building in the center of the junkyard. A dark blue jacket stretched across his broad shoulders, while his tactical shirt and cargo pants outlined the rest of his muscled body. A lunarium sword with a silver hilt dangled from his black leather belt, and a silver blaster was holstered to his right thigh.

My gaze traced over his features, which were as familiar to me as my own. Longish black hair with a hint of a wave. Pale skin. High cheekbones. A long, sharp nose. A strong chin. And eyes that were such a dark blue they bordered on black, just like the sapphsidian chips in the butterfly brooch I had bought in the marketplace.

Kyrion Caldaren looked every inch like the Regal lord, rogue Arrow, and elite assassin he was. The cold, hard nugget of him in my mind pulsed with even more icy fury, but to me, it was as comforting as a warm blanket. My heart quickened, my breath caught in my throat, and a smile spread across my face.

Kyrion fired the cannon four more times, hitting another bounty hunter and forcing a third man to dive behind an old furnace. He released the cannon, which was attached to the silver bandolier slung across his chest, then spun the bandolier around so that the cannon was on his back and out of the way. The second his hands were free, Kyrion plucked his blaster out of its thigh holster and took aim.

*Pew! Pew! Pew!*

He dropped three more bounty hunters in rapid succession, causing the others to scatter around the junkyard.

"Return fire! Return fire!" Rina screamed, ducking behind a stack of broken transport wheels.

She sent several bolts shooting up at Kyrion, as did the other bounty hunters. He ran forward, leaped off the roof, and dropped down behind a pile of junk.

One of the bounty hunters lunged forward and latched onto my arm. "Come here—"

I snapped up my hand and punched him in the throat. The bounty hunter staggered back, coughing and gasping for air. He tripped over the first man Kyrion had killed with the hand cannon and went down in a wheezing heap on the dirt.

I crouched down and scuttled in the opposite direction, heading toward my shopping bag, which was still lying on the ground. I shoved my hand into the dark depths, searching for my stormsword among the fruits, vegetables, and other items. Where was it? Where was it?

*There.*

My hand closed around the silver hilt, and I yanked the sword free of the cloth. The lunarium blade pulsed with a dark blue light in a reflection of my seer magic and my connection to Kyrion.

Off to my right, Rina whipped around, aimed her blaster at me, and pulled the trigger.

*Pew!*

I threw my body down and to the right. The red bolt zinged past me and slammed into a tin can full of nails. The small, sharp projectiles shot out in all directions, pelting my arms, legs, and back, cutting through my clothes, and scratching my skin. So much for taking me alive.

I hissed at the stinging pain, scrambled back up onto my feet, and darted forward, ducking behind the cement blocks that propped up the Regal carriage.

*Pew! Pew! Pew!*

Rina fired a few more bolts in my direction. The corners of the cement blocks cracked, and stone chips flew out and pelted my cheeks. I hissed again, but I held my position, lifted my sword, and blinked through the tears running down my face.

*Pew!*

Rina fired another bolt at me, then broke cover and headed toward the blitzer parked at the back of the junkyard. Saving her own skin must have been worth more than my bounty.

The remaining bounty hunters hunkered down behind broken transports and piles of metal and kept firing their blasters.

Still crouching behind the cement blocks, I turned to the left, and my gaze locked onto the pile of junk Kyrion had taken refuge behind. *Kyrion? Kyrion!*

That cold nugget in my mind finally cracked wide open, and his voice and presence rippled through me. *I'm here. Get ready to move.*

Before I could ask what he was planning, a swirl of scarlet caught my eye. Across the junkyard, Esmina jerked her head to the side, spun around, and strode away. Pollux scurried after her.

Kyrion popped into view and hurled a small metal ball through the air. The ball arced up, then down, and landed in the exact spot where Esmina and Pollux had been standing.

*Boom!*

The explosion ripped through the air, the force knocking some of the bounty hunters off their feet, but Esmina kept walking forward at a slow, steady pace. Pollux kept moving right beside her, backpedaling all the while, and the two of them headed away from the battle and toward the front of the junkyard.

I frowned. Esmina had known *exactly* where the device was going to land and detonate even before Kyrion had thrown it. How was that possible?

The bounty hunters scrambled back up onto their feet. Some of them fired at Kyrion, while others targeted the retreating Esmina and Pollux.

Esmina never turned around, but Pollux used the lunarium heads on his war hammers to send several bolts shooting right back at the bounty hunters, who screamed at the brutal impacts.

A man stood up, aimed his blaster at Esmina, and pulled the trigger.

*Pew! Pew! Pew!*

Bright blasts of energy streaked through the air toward her. Pollux spun in that direction, but he was too far away to deflect the bolts with his hammers, and Esmina was directly in the line of fire.

My seer magic surged to life, and time slowed down, as though I was viewing everything one frame at a time on a holoscreen. The blaster fire zinging through the air. The streaks sparking and crackling with deadly electricity. The colorful bolts painting Esmina's scarlet cloak in an eerie glow . . .

I blinked, and time snapped back to its normal speed and flow.

At the last instant, right before the bolts would have slammed into her back, Esmina stepped smoothly to the left, then to the right, and then to the right again. She easily avoided all the bolts, which punched into the piles of junk around her. Sparks and smoke spewed up into the air, even as several engines crashed down, blocking the aisle behind her and Pollux, but Esmina didn't duck for cover. Instead, she just kept walking forward as though she was strolling along a garden path instead of away from a dangerous battle.

My jaw dropped. How could she avoid blaster bolts when her back was turned? When she couldn't even *see* the danger zipping her way?

Esmina stopped and glanced over her shoulder, her gaze locking with mine. *I see* everything, *Vesper. Don't worry. We'll meet again soon, and then we'll see how useful you* really *are.*

Her smug voice and thought stabbed into my mind, as clear, sharp, and bright as if she had just punched her lunarium dagger into my skull. Pain exploded in my head, and white starbursts erupted in my eyes, blotting out everything else. Her words echoed in my brain, and her magic was so strong that every syllable felt like a splash of acid burning everything it touched.

I sucked in a breath, too stunned to even scream. My left leg buckled, throwing me off-balance, and I couldn't stop myself from staggering forward, away from the relative safety of the cement blocks and out into the middle of the junkyard for everyone to see—and target.

For a moment, all I was aware of were the psionic echoes of Esmina's magic jangling through my mind like a bad song blaring on repeat. A second passed. Maybe two or three or even ten. I staggered back and forth the whole time, listing dangerously from side to side like a space cruiser about to crash into a skyscraper.

*Pew! Pew! Pew!*

More blaster fire rang out. Bolts zinged through the air all around me, the bright streaks of color adding to the starbursts still exploding in my eyes. I snapped up my stormsword and whipped it back and forth in a wild motion, trying to stop the bolts from hitting me.

*Pew!*

A bolt slammed into my right bicep. Electric agony erupted in my arm, as though someone had stabbed me with a red-hot knife. I screamed and crumpled to the dirt, my stormsword tumbling out of my twitching fingers.

*Vesper? Vesper! Hang on! I'm almost there!*

Kyrion's frantic voice sounded, cutting through some of the pain, and I latched onto the sticky cobweb of him in my mind. The cool, silky threads helped me push away some of the electric pain, although my arm continued to burn and burn, like a chemical fire that refused to be extinguished.

I sucked down one breath after another, and the starbursts faded from my vision. Somehow I had stumbled past the cement blocks and ended up close to the blitzer at the back of the junkyard. Blaster fire zinged through the air behind me as Kyrion battled the remaining bounty hunters. I needed to help him, so I got up onto my hands and knees and focused on my stormsword, which had landed a few feet away.

My right arm was still burning from the blaster bolt, so I stretched out my left hand, trying to use the truebond and Kyrion's telekinesis to make the sword lift off the ground and zip over into my waiting fingers.

Nothing happened. No bond, no telekinesis, no sword spinning through the air.

I growled and tried again with the same useless result. I didn't have time to figure out what was wrong, so I crawled forward. I reached out with my left hand again, and my fingers finally closed around the hilt—

Footsteps scuffed on the dirt, and a shadow fell over me. I froze and raised my head.

Rina loomed over me, her blaster leveled at my chest. "Why couldn't you just come along quietly?" she snarled. "This should have been the biggest, easiest score of my life, and you *ruined* it."

"Yeah," I rasped. "I tend to ruin things for people."

Fury flared in her dark eyes, although it quickly gave way to a cold, calculating look. "I get ten million credits if I bring you in alive. Only a million if you're dead." She paused. "But I'll take the million."

Once again, my seer magic roared to life, and everything slowed down. Rina's eyes narrowing in concentration, her lips drawing back into a feral grin, her index finger curling around the blaster trigger.

Even worse, I also felt like *I* was moving in slow motion and doing everything at half speed. Once again, I reached for Kyrion's telekinesis to toss Rina aside or rip the blaster out of her hand, but my arm kept burning, and I couldn't quite grasp the silky threads of Kyrion's power.

"Vesper? Vesper!" This time, Kyrion's voice cut through the air instead of sounding in my mind, and everything snapped back to its normal speed.

I quit reaching for the truebond. Instead, I curled my fingers even tighter around the stormsword's hilt, then heaved it up and slashed it forward.

It was a desperate, awkward blow, but the lunarium blade clipped Rina's right leg and sliced a deep gash across her shin. She screamed and pulled the blaster trigger.

*Pew!*

I jerked to the side. The bolt zipped past my head and smacked into the dirt, so close the acrid stench made my eyes water.

"Vesper!" Kyrion yelled again. "Vesper!"

He was using his stormsword to cut down and deflect blaster bolts at the remaining bounty hunters, but he was too far away to help me. Kyrion's worry surged through the bond and clawed against my skin like razor-sharp talons, but I shut the sensation—shut him—out of my mind.

Rina was cursing and staggering around, so I surged up onto my knees and lashed out with my stormsword again. This time, the blade sliced across her left knee. She screamed again and tumbled to the ground beside me.

She was still clutching her blaster, and she lifted her arm to aim the weapon. I tightened my grip on my stormsword, raised the blade, and propelled myself forward.

For the third time, everything slowed down. Rina's blaster arcing toward my body. My stormsword zooming toward her chest. The glint of her silver weapon mirroring the gleam of the opalescent lunarium blade . . .

*Crunch.*

Time snapped back to its normal flow. My sword punched into Rina's chest, and one of her ribs cracked under the sharp blade. She screamed and tried to aim her blaster at me again, so I shoved the sword deeper into her chest.

Rina's gaze locked with mine. She opened her mouth, but this time, no sound escaped. She stared at me for a heartbeat longer, then slumped to the ground, still clutching her blaster.

I yanked my sword out of her chest, then got to my feet. Sweat rolled down my face, and my breath puffed out in ragged gasps, despite my O2 enhancement. My stormsword was as heavy as an anvil, and I couldn't hold it upright. The tip dug into the dirt, and I leaned on it like a walking stick to keep from toppling over. All the while, my right arm kept burning and burning.

*Pew! Pew! Pew!*

A few more blaster bolts zinged through the air behind me. A man screamed, and then everything was still and quiet.

Footsteps smacked into the dirt, and a tall shadow engulfed me. I forced myself to straighten up and hook my stormsword to my belt.

Kyrion's gaze flicked over me. Concern creased his forehead, and his hand tightened around the hilt of his blood-covered stormsword. "You're wounded."

"Just a few bumps and bruises." I rasped out the lie. "I hardly feel them."

"Well, *I* can feel them too, remember?"

Drat. I'd forgotten that Kyrion could sense my injuries through the truebond, the same way I could sense when he was wounded. Sometimes our injuries would even physically appear on each other's bodies, like a few days ago, when I'd cut my hand on a piece of metal, and a smaller, shallower slice had popped up in the same spot on Kyrion's hand.

I scanned Kyrion from head to toe, but he didn't seem to be in any pain or mirroring my injuries this time. Good. Although some wounds appearing while others didn't was another mercurial quirk of truebonds that aggravated my scientific, results-based, lab-rat heart to no end.

Kyrion slid the sword onto his belt. He started to take hold of my injured arm, then grimaced and dropped his hand. More of his worry surged through the bond, and the sticky cobweb in my mind vibrated with a mixture of icy fury and chest-tightening fear.

I glanced down. The blaster bolt had obliterated most of the right side of my jacket and my shirtsleeve and severely burned my skin underneath. Mountains of blisters had already formed around the deep hole the bolt had punched into my bicep, and my entire arm felt tight, like it would burst open if I so much as breathed on it. Electricity was still burning through my muscles, and my heart throbbed out a painful rhythm I could sense all the way down in my fingertips. My stomach roiled at the gruesome injury, and I swallowed a mouthful of hot, bitter bile.

"I'm fine." I repeated my earlier lie. "Just a little charred."

Kyrion's lips pinched into a thin, grim line at my black humor. "In addition to sensing your injuries, I can also tell when you're lying."

"So our truebond is nothing but a giant tattletale?" I muttered. "Wonderful."

He stabbed his finger at my burned arm. "Bond aside, anyone could see that your skin is more than *just a little charred.* Hold still."

Kyrion pulled his silver bandolier of supplies from his back around to his chest. He plucked a skinbond injector out of one of the slots, then plunged it into my arm, right above my elbow where the burn stopped.

A skinbond did just what its name implied—it stitched cut, bruised, broken, and otherwise injured skin, muscles, and bones back together. A cool wave of chemicals flooded my veins, soothing the intense burning. I sighed with relief. Some of the redness faded from my skin, although the blisters, tightness, and throbbing remained, as did the deep puncture wound.

"You're still hurting," Kyrion murmured, his voice lower and more concerned than before. "Here. This should help."

He gently cupped my left cheek in his right hand, and his thumb stroked over my skin, making me shiver, despite my injuries. Kyrion's dark blue eyes glimmered like stars, and the sticky cobweb of him in my mind surged, pulsed, and expanded, until I was securely wrapped in the threads of his magic. A strange sensation flowed through my body, as though I was being bundled into a cool cocoon, and each new smooth, silky layer lessened my pain.

I glanced down again. My burned arm looked the same as before, and I could still feel the tightness and throbbing, but the sensations were muted, as though they were on the outside of the cocoon that was protecting my mind and body from the stark, vivid pain.

"What did you do?" I asked, staring up at Kyrion.

"I created a psionic shield to help you block out the pain. A trick my father showed me. Chauncey would do the same for Desdemona whenever Holloway took my mother's power." Kyrion grimaced and dropped his hand from my cheek as though his right arm was suddenly hurting him as much as mine had been hurting me.

My eyes narrowed. "Wait. Did you just take my pain for your own? Psionically absorb it so that *you* would experience it instead of *me*?"

He shrugged, but it was a guilty, uncomfortable motion.

"You didn't have to do that, Kyr," I protested. "*I* got caught and injured by the bounty hunters, so *I* should be the one suffering the pain and consequences, not *you*."

His face softened, and he gently brushed my hair back over my shoulder, his fingers skimming along my collarbone and making me shiver again.

"I *wanted* to do it," Kyrion countered in a low, fierce voice. "I will always protect *you*, Vesper, no matter what the cost is to *me*."

My heart soared at his words, even as guilt stabbed into my chest like a sharp needle pinning a flapping butterfly to a display board. If only I'd been smarter, faster, and stronger, then neither one of us would be hurting.

"Besides, I've had far worse injuries as an Arrow. I know how to erect psionic shields to numb the pain until I can get medical treatment." The corner of Kyrion's mouth quirked up into a rueful expression. "Although I'm not nearly as good at creating shields as Zane is. He could take a mortal wound and keep fighting, at least until his power gave out and his psionic shield finally cracked."

My heart lurched at the mention of my brother, but I shoved Zane out of my mind. Instead, I looked out over the bounty hunters. Smoke wafted up off their burned bodies, and the acrid stench of blaster fire lingered in the air like a cloud of death.

"Don't feel sorry for them," Kyrion growled. "The bounty hunters brought this on themselves. They didn't have to chase after you."

"You're right. I *know* you're right. It's just . . ."

"What?"

I blew out a breath. "I hate that people are dying because Holloway put that bounty on us."

"I hate it too," Kyrion replied in a soft voice. "But it was either them or you, and I will choose you every single time."

Once again, my heart soared, but before I could tell him I felt the same way, sirens blared in the distance. We both flinched at the high-pitched screeches.

Kyrion cursed. "Someone must have heard the explosion and blaster fire and alerted the authorities. We need to find another way out of here."

He moved past Rina's blitzer and ran toward the back of the junkyard. I limped over to my shopping bag, dropped to my knees, and scooped the wayward fruits and vegetables back into the cloth. We still needed fresh food, and I wasn't about to leave a single mango behind.

My fingers brushed up against the ice-blue box with the butterfly pin. I considered leaving the cursed thing behind, but I couldn't risk the purchase being traced back to me, so I shoved it into the bag as well.

I glanced around, making sure I hadn't missed anything, and my gaze landed on Rina's body. Her mouth was frozen in a pain-filled grimace, and her sightless eyes glared at me in accusation. Blood was still trickling out of the ugly wound in her chest, and the drops had already formed a dull, rusty pool underneath her body.

"Vesper!" Kyrion called out. "Back here!"

I slung the shopping bag onto my left shoulder and got to my feet. The abrupt motion made the pain of my burned right arm flare up again, like a stream of scalding lava oozing through the cool cocoon Kyrion had built around my mind. An instant later, more of Kyrion's power surged through the bond, rebuilding the cocoon and numbing the hot, jagged edges of my injury.

Tears of anger and frustration pricked my eyes, but I blinked them away and trudged toward the back of the junkyard. I just hoped Kyrion couldn't sense all my emotions through the bond and that he didn't realize how much of a failure I was at being his partner.

Kyrion had adapted to our new situation with ease, and he wielded his psion power as strongly and effortlessly as he had before. Me? I couldn't even make it through a simple trip to a marketplace without getting cornered by bounty hunters, and my seer magic had been useless against Rina and her men.

This battle was just an example of a larger problem. Every time I thought I finally had a handle on my magic—and my combined power with Kyrion—it either didn't do what I wanted or didn't work at all.

*You're the weak link, destined to be broken.* Esmina's mocking voice zipped through my mind. This time, I didn't feel the pain of her telepathically speaking to me, but I couldn't ignore the uncomfortable truth of her words.

A truebonded pair was only as strong as its weaker member, and if I didn't figure out how to wield my magic soon, then I was going to wind up dead—and kill Kyrion as well.

# FOUR

## KYRION

Vesper limped into view. Weariness vibrated along the velvety ribbon of her in my mind, but she kept trudging forward, a large bag hanging on her shoulder. Even after everything she'd been through, she'd still grabbed the supplies we needed. Pride warmed my heart, along with more than a little frustration at her stubbornness.

My gaze dropped to the horrific wound in her arm, and the pain of Vesper's injuries boiled up in my own body. My right arm pulsed with a vicious, staccato rhythm, the skin so raw and sensitive the mere touch of my tactical shirt made me grimace. As an Arrow, I'd been shot with a blaster more times than I cared to remember, but it was always a miserable experience, and Vesper's wound was worse than most.

"Now what?" she asked in a tired voice.

More of her pain boiled up in my mind, and I swallowed a snarl. I might have absorbed the worst of Vesper's agony, but I *hated* the fact she had been injured—and that I had been too slow and too far away to protect her.

I cleared my throat and gestured to the right. "This way."

Vesper followed me over to the fence that cordoned off the back of the junkyard from the rain forest. I used my stormsword to slice through the rusty metal links and then my telekinesis to peel them back and create an opening. I also held out my hand. Vesper sighed, but she passed me the shopping bag.

More sirens blared, the sound coming from the front of the junkyard. Vesper grimaced and ducked through the opening. More of her pain rippled through my mind, and I swallowed another snarl.

We plunged into the rain forest, moving from one tree to the next and heading back to the spaceport. It took us almost an hour, but we made it to the landing strip where our ship was parked without incident.

I drew my blaster and made Vesper stay behind me as we approached the blitzer, which was shaped like an old-fashioned arrow. The flight deck formed the sharp, triangular tip, then came a long shaftlike corridor that comprised the body of the ship. The corridor, in turn, flowed into the cargo bay, which spread out like a tuft of feathers at the back of the blitzer.

I reached out with my telepathy, but no thoughts twinged my power, and I didn't sense anyone lurking on board with my telempathy. "We're clear."

I exchanged my blaster for my tablet and entered the access code to lower the cargo-bay ramp.

"I hate that you had to paint over the name," Vesper murmured.

The gray hull used to boast large, dark blue letters that spelled out *DREAM WORLD*, but after we'd fled from Corios, I'd replaced them with *VK4EV3R* to match the ship's fake registration.

Vesper's eyes twinkled with merriment. "I rather enjoyed having a ship named after my mindscape."

I huffed, as though greatly annoyed, but I couldn't stop a teasing tone from creeping into my voice. "As I've told you countless times, I had to name the blitzer *something*. The fact that I once called your mindscape a dream world is entirely a coincidence."

"Keep telling yourself that, my lord," Vesper replied in a smug voice. "Maybe one day you'll actually believe it."

"I will believe anything you tell me to, my lady," I drawled back.

She opened her mouth but then grimaced, and more of her pain boiled up in my mind. Even with my psionic shield, Vesper was still feeling her injury. More fury hammered in my chest. If I could have, I would have killed the bounty hunters all over again for hurting her.

"Come on," I said in a gentle voice, taking hold of her uninjured arm.

Vesper didn't protest as I helped her up the ramp and into the cargo bay. I hit a button on the wall, and the ramp lifted and closed behind us. I put her shopping bag on a counter, then unhooked the cannon from my bandolier and set it aside.

"The modifications you made to the Techwave cannon worked," I said, trying to focus on something positive. "I got off five shots this time before it started to overheat."

"Mmm. Yes, the cannon will fire a few times with my new solar magazines before it overheats again, but I haven't figured out how to truly *fix* it," Vesper murmured in an absent voice, swiping through screens on her tablet. "The local gossipcast is already reporting about the bodies at the junkyard, but so far, there's no chatter about who killed them. Looks like we got away clean." A frown creased her face. "As did Esmina and Pollux."

"Who are you talking about? All the bounty hunters are dead."

Vesper shook her head. "They're not bounty hunters. The woman wearing a long red cloak and the guy clutching two war hammers. You threw that ball of explosives at them."

"Those two? I just got a glimpse of them, and I thought

the explosives killed them. Besides, they weren't my main objective. I just wanted to cause a distraction so I could pick off more of the bounty hunters and get closer to you."

Vesper's frown deepened. "But if you weren't targeting them, then how did Esmina know to move out of the way?"

She chewed on her lower lip, and her fingers drummed on the corner of her tablet, making the screen flicker. I knew that look. Esmina and Pollux, whoever they were, had presented Vesper with a challenge, a puzzle, and she wouldn't give up until she solved the mystery.

Vesper's fingers stilled. "Ask Daichi to hack into the security footage from the marketplace. Esmina bumped into me there, and Pollux was probably lurking nearby."

Daichi Hirano was my chief of staff and extremely skilled at ferreting out information. If anyone could track the elusive Esmina and Pollux, it was Daichi.

Vesper tapped on the arrow streaking upward through a cluster of stars that was stitched onto her jacket right over her heart. "And we can download the footage from the spy camera in my jacket. That should also help Daichi identify them."

The arrow and stars were the sigil for House Caldaren, so the same symbol was stitched into my own jacket, and the same spy camera was also hidden in the fabric.

"I'll send the footage to Daichi. Which means you can take a break and get healed. Your arm still looks awful, despite the skinbond injector."

I'd given Vesper a strong dose of chemicals, but they hadn't helped her nearly as much as I would have liked. Neither had my psionic shield, and the pain of her injuries kept slipping from my mind and body back into hers.

Vesper glanced down at her arm, and her nose crinkled with disgust. "It looks like I've been run through a meat grinder, doesn't it?"

"Yes," I growled, stabbing my finger at a long rectangular

table near the front of the cargo bay. "Which is why you need to get on the medtable. *Right now.*"

Vesper raised her uninjured arm and snapped off a salute. "Aye, aye, captain, sir!"

I rolled my eyes. "Your mockery is duly noted."

"As is your bossiness," she quipped back.

"I thought you liked it when I was bossy. I certainly didn't hear any complaints last night."

A blush exploded in Vesper's cheeks. Her eyes glittered with heat, and the velvety ribbon of her in my mind arched, hummed, and vibrated with pleasure. A memory erupted in my mind: Vesper writhing on the bed last night while I loomed over her, kissing, licking, and tasting every single inch of her soft, delectable skin. My dick hardened, and a different kind of throbbing coursed through me.

I blinked, and the image vanished. Had that been my memory—or Vesper's recollection? Now that we had both accepted the truebond, I could tap into her psionic powers just as she could mine. Over the past few weeks, more than one silver flare of light and lifelike vision had filled my eyes, but the odd surges of Vesper's power seemed completely random. As a Regal lord and especially as an Arrow, I had been trained to use my telekinesis, telepathy, and telempathy to their utmost ability, but I had no idea how to access seer magic, much less wield it like a weapon the way Vesper could.

Vesper set her tablet down on a counter. She sauntered over to me, then reached out and toyed with a button on my jacket. "Well, if that's the kind of bossy you have in mind, then I say boss away, my lord."

"I'd like nothing more, my lady," I murmured in a husky voice.

I bent my head as though I was going to kiss her. Vesper licked her lips and rose up on her tiptoes. I lowered my head a little more . . . and a little more . . . and then I leaned down and scooped her up into my arms, careful of her injury. I crossed the cargo bay in a few long strides and set her down on the medtable.

"You're no fun." Vesper pouted.

"I am exceedingly fun—when your arm doesn't look like raw sausage. Now, let the table heal you. Consider it an order from your bossy lord and ornery captain."

Vesper snapped her hand up in another mock salute. Still being careful of her injury, I helped her peel off her ruined jacket, then used a dagger from my bandolier to cut off her right shirtsleeve, leaving her injured arm bare from her shoulder down to her fingers. Vesper's grumbles faded away, replaced by one pain-filled grimace after another, and she laid down on the medtable.

I hit a button, and a clear piece of polyplastic slid out of its hiding spot, arced up over the table, and sealed itself shut on the other side. Oxygen hissed into the hyperbaric chamber, while robotic needles popped up out of the tabletop and danced around Vesper, administering skinbonds, antibiotics, and other medicines. She jerked and let out a muffled cry that pierced my heart, but her body relaxed as the sedatives took effect, and her eyes fluttered shut.

"Severe burns detected, along with a deep puncture wound and significant nerve damage. More skinbonds needed," a feminine voice chirped in a chiding tone, almost as if the medtable blamed me for Vesper's injuries.

Well, that made two of us, because I was certainly blaming myself.

I gripped the table and watched while the robotic needles quickly, expertly sloughed off Vesper's burned, blistered skin and repaired the blaster hole in her arm. The overhead lights brought out the russet strands in her dark brown hair, which framed her face in wavy wisps. Her skin was paler than usual, and a few tiny freckles stood out on her cheeks like a star map I could spend hours studying. Even covered with blood and grime, Vesper still took my breath away.

My fingers twitched with the urge to smooth back her silky hair and feel her warm skin against my own, to wake her up and see the silver flecks glimmering in her dark blue eyes like pinpoint moons reflected in the surface of a beautiful lake. But I didn't dare interrupt the medtable's work, so I contented myself with devouring her with my gaze.

Vesper remained unconscious, a dreamy smile on her heart-shaped lips. She was probably in her mindscape, which was filled with doors that showed everything she had ever seen, done, and experienced. I hoped Vesper was viewing a happy memory instead of this disaster of a day.

My fingers curled a little tighter around the table. The metal edge dug into my palms like a dagger about to slice my skin, but I welcomed the discomfort. It gave me something else to focus on besides the dread and fear that had gripped me ever since Vesper had been cornered by the bounty hunters.

No, that was a lie. My dread and fear had started a few weeks ago, right after we'd escaped from Crownpoint Palace. I'd been lying on the medtable, just as Vesper was right now, when Adria Byrne had revealed her presence on the *Dream World*. Adria and her brother, Dargan, were among the most skilled, powerful, and vicious of the Arrows, and they had helped Zane capture Vesper on Tropics 33 and take her back to Corios.

In the throne room, Vesper and I had fought Adria and Dargan, who also had a truebond. Vesper had killed Dargan to save me, and Adria had gone mad with grief at the loss of the connection with her brother.

Adria had snuck onto the ship determined to kill us both, but Vesper had killed Adria instead by purging all the oxygen out of the cargo bay. Despite her O2 enhancement, Vesper would have died too, if I hadn't used our truebond to enter her mindscape. I still wasn't sure how I had done that, only that it had brought Vesper back to me.

Once we'd recovered, Vesper and I had admitted our feelings

for each other, and we'd spent the next few magnificent days lost in each other's arms.

But all too soon, we'd had to set our happiness aside and deal with the rest of the galaxy, and we'd set a course for Sygnustern. So far, our long, circuitous route had kept us away from Zane and the other Arrows, and we'd been able to avoid trouble—until today.

As soon as Vesper had told me about the bounty hunters, as soon as I'd sensed her worry and felt the distance between us increasing through the bond, I'd left the ship and tracked her down as fast as I could. But it had been far more difficult than I'd expected, far more difficult than it *should* have been.

When we had battled the Imperium soldiers and Bronze Hand guards to escape from Crownpoint Palace, using our truebond had been so *easy*. Vesper's thoughts, feelings, and psion power had flowed freely into me, just as my thoughts, feelings, and power had flowed freely into her. We had been like two Regals whirling around the dance floor, and we had moved, attacked, and defended ourselves and each other in perfect rhythm, tempo, and harmony.

That same easiness had flowed through the bond this morning, right up to when Vesper had been taken. After that, all I had been able to sense was my own cold fury and razor-sharp dread. The smooth, velvety ribbon of Vesper in my mind had thinned into a fragile, brittle strand that frayed and crumbled a little bit more every time I tried to grab it.

I'd used all my psion power and instincts to find Vesper, and even then, I'd almost been too late.

The image of the pink-haired bounty hunter clutching a blaster and towering over Vesper flickered through my mind, and fresh dread chewed through my gut like a plasma torch. If Vesper hadn't used her stormsword to defend herself, the bounty hunter would have killed her.

After my parents had died when I was thirteen, I had been

largely on my own. Oh, I had been surrounded by the other Regals, and Callus Holloway had me trained as an Arrow to further his own agenda.

After considering almost everyone an enemy for the last twenty-five years, I had finally found Vesper. I had finally found someone who looked past all my dark deeds, someone who accepted all the awful things I'd done to survive, someone who understood and embraced me, inner monster and all.

I had finally found someone to love, and my greatest fear was that the galaxy was going to take her away.

Oh, I would happily die to protect Vesper, but the galaxy would *never* let a monster like me off that easily. No, the worst would happen, the way it always did, and then I'd be forced to confront what life without Vesper would be like.

Truebond or not, it was going to destroy me.

I *knew* it was, and yet, every single day, I cared about Vesper a little more. Her smile, her laugh, her kindness and intelligence and blazing determination. They all drew me in like a mammoth butterfly hovering over a laser, unable to veer away from the bright, tempting light that would inevitably burn its fragile wings to a crisp.

When Vesper had been shot . . . well, I hadn't just wanted to kill the bounty hunters. I'd wanted to strew bloody bits and pieces of them all over the junkyard as a warning for anyone who even dared to *think* about hurting her. Even now, my inner monster growled with the desire to rip and tear everything around me to shreds.

But even louder was the bitter, jaded voice in the back of my mind that kept muttering that I was destined to lose Vesper regardless. That eventually, she would come to her senses, realize I was no good for her, and get fed up with constantly being in danger just because she had the misfortune of having a truebond with me.

Oh, yes. Even if the galaxy didn't take her away, Vesper still had plenty of reasons to leave me behind—and I wouldn't blame her if she did. She was a blue moon shining her beautiful light on everyone, while I was a black hole, sucking people into my orbit until they were utterly destroyed.

But wallowing in my doom and gloom wasn't helping anything, certainly not Vesper, so I forced myself to straighten up and release the medtable. I grabbed her ruined jacket from the counter, along with the shopping bag and the Techwave cannon, and turned to leave the cargo bay—

A bright silver light flared, and a woman shimmered in the air in front of me like a hologram. Strawberry-blond hair, gray eyes, rosy skin, a stormsword dangling from her hand.

I jerked back, and it took me a gut-clenching moment to realize that I was only seeing a memory of Adria Byrne, a psionic echo of when she'd snuck on board the ship.

I glanced over at Vesper on the medtable. Her eyes were still closed, but her easy, dreamy smile had vanished, and her brow was furrowed. Was she seeing the same disturbing image I was? Had her seer power conjured up this vision of Adria? Or was this related to my thoughts of the dead Arrow?

*You killed Dargan, so I'm going to kill Kyrion. Maybe then you'll know how it feels. Maybe then you'll know how much it* hurts.

Adria's voice hissed through my mind. She'd said those words to Vesper, but right now, her gaze was focused on me, as though she was taunting me with my own secret worry and dread.

I squared my shoulders and strode forward. The memory melted like a shadow, but Adria's hysterical howls of laughter echoed in my ears, and her words chased after me like a ghost I couldn't escape.

I didn't have Vesper's seer power, but I couldn't help but feel like this had been much more than a memory from our past—more like a vision of my future.

# FIVE

## KYRION

I stepped out of the cargo bay, entered the long corridor that made up the center of the blitzer, and went to the flight deck at the front of the ship. I dropped into the pilot's seat, fired up the engines, and took off from the spaceport. A few minutes later, the *Dream World* was rocketing through space, on course for Sygnustern. No proximity alarms sounded, and no other ships were tracking us. Good.

I left the flight deck and headed into the kitchen. I put away the food Vesper had bought in the marketplace, then entered a room I'd turned into a miniature version of my library at Castle Caldaren. A large table stood in the center, while wooden cases flanked the walls, each shelf filled with real paper books, which Vesper loved to smell for some strange reason. Comfortable chairs were stuffed into the corners, and a window in the far wall offered a view of the glimmering stars in the distance.

I might be expecting the galaxy to take Vesper away, but until the worst happened, I was going to do my best to protect her, especially from Callus Holloway. The greedy bastard wanted to siphon off our truebond power and take it for his own, just as he'd done to my parents. Holloway had eventually taken too much of my mother's power, causing Desdemona's wasting sickness and death. My father, Chauncey, had gone mad with grief at the loss of my mother, and he had attacked me in a drunken rage, forcing me to kill him in self-defense.

Cold fury flooded my body, drowning out the faint echoes of Adria's mocking laughter. My inner monster roared with determination, and I slapped Vesper's ruined jacket and the Techwave cannon down onto the table hard enough to scatter some plastipaper schematics lying there.

We were *not* going to end up like my parents.

I waved my hand over the table, activating the embedded holoscreen. While it downloaded the battle footage from the camera in Vesper's jacket, I called up *Celestial Stars*, a popular gossipcast that covered the Imperium. I flicked through one story and video after another, tracking the sightings of the Arrows, but none of them were close to Tropics 44. A small but welcome favor. Right now, I would take every single favor and scrap of luck the galactic gods deigned to toss my way.

After I mapped out the Arrows' latest locations, I searched for information on another enemy: Nerezza Blackwell.

During the midnight ball, Vesper had outed Nerezza as a Techwave spy, thus ruining her mother's standing among the Regals. No one had seen Nerezza since she had fled from Corios, but according to the gossipcast reports, she had emptied out the House Blackwell accounts, which meant she had more than enough credits to go anywhere she wanted.

Since there was no news on Nerezza, I moved on to yet another enemy: the Techwave.

A few weeks ago, several of the Techwave's mechanized Black Scarabs had rampaged through the summer solstice celebration at Castle Rojillo in the Corios countryside. None of the Regals, servants, or guards had been killed, but a Techwaver named Silas had infiltrated the castle, stolen some temperature-shielding technology created by Lord Jorge Rojillo, and sent the data to General Orion Ocnus.

Asterin Armas, an Erzton lady, had been at the solstice celebration, along with Tivona Winslow and Leandra Ferrum, our other friends. Asterin had snuck into the main research-and-development lab inside the castle, and she had sent us copies of the temperature-shielding technology, which was designed for people to wear like an old-fashioned wristwatch to cool and heat the air around them. Vesper had studied the schematics, but so far, she hadn't figured out what the Techwave wanted with something so seemingly simple—or how they were planning to weaponize it.

I watched one gossipcast after another, but each theory was wilder than the last, and no one had any concrete intelligence about Nerezza or the Techwave. I let out a frustrated growl and swiped my hand across the holoscreen, cutting off the feeds.

A soft *ding* sounded. The battle footage from Vesper's jacket was ready, so I watched it, grimacing when Vesper was shot. The footage rewound and started playing again, but this time, I froze it, stuck my fingers into the hologram, and focused on Esmina and Pollux.

As an Arrow, I'd dealt with scores of terrorists and criminals, but neither one of them was familiar. I'd been taking cover behind a pile of junk, so I hadn't gotten a good look at the pair. My throwing a ball of explosives at them had been a lucky break—or perhaps an unlucky one, since it hadn't killed them.

I flicked my fingers, unfreezing the footage and studying how Esmina and Pollux moved, communicated, and attacked.

Pollux was obviously a psion like me, and I was willing to bet he also had strength and speed enhancements. You didn't carry around big, heavy weapons unless you had the skill to wield them to their fullest, deadliest potential.

I froze the footage again and zoomed in on one of his war

hammers. Long hilt, flat head, spike on one side, razor-sharp edges all around. The lunarium weapon matched those used by the Hammers, the elite warriors of the Erzton, although Pollux's weapons were larger than normal. With his psion power and strength enhancements, bashing in skulls was child's play, and he could probably crack open a mountain with those hammers if he wanted to.

Being the head of the Arrows meant spying on the Hammers, but Pollux's face had never appeared on any rosters or missions I'd reviewed. Still, I was willing to bet he either had been part of the Hammers at one time or had been trained by the warriors. Either way, Pollux was just as dangerous with his war hammers as I was with my stormsword.

Next, I focused on Esmina, who was also obviously a psion. I couldn't figure out what powers she had, but she was definitely the leader, and thus more dangerous. An alpha warrior like Pollux wouldn't follow anyone who wasn't stronger than himself.

I watched the footage a few more times, but no more clues presented themselves. Two new enemies had just dropped out of the sky and landed on top of the mountain of people already chasing us. Terrific. Just bloody terrific.

I swiped my hand across the holoscreen, cutting off the battle footage. For several seconds, I glared at the empty air where the hologram had been. Then I raked a hand through my hair, exhaled, and bent down over the table.

I sent Daichi the footage, then straightened up. I needed to check on Vesper—

A soft *ping* sounded, then repeated itself in rapid succession. *Ping-ping-ping*.

I glanced back down at the table, but the alert wasn't coming from the encrypted group channel that Vesper and I used with our friends. No, the *pings* were emanating from a channel used on an Arrow mission last year, and only one other person knew about it.

If I ignored the alert, the cocky bastard would just keep trying to make contact. He could be annoyingly persistent, so I waved my hand, activating the holoscreen again. I hit a few buttons, and a man popped into view.

Longish blond hair, ice-blue eyes, and skin that was somehow always perfectly tan, despite the amount of time he spent in the black void of space. An ice-blue jacket stretched across his broad shoulders, and the curlicued *Z* of House Zimmer was stitched on the fabric, right over his rotten heart, if he even possessed such an organ.

"Finally," Zane Zimmer drawled. "I was starting to think you were *never* going to answer."

I glowered at him, but Zane grinned, laced his hands behind his head, and leaned back in his chair.

I studied the hologram, but there wasn't much to see. Just Zane, a desk, a chair, and a small, round window in the background. I squinted. What were those flickers of light rushing by in the distance? I couldn't tell, but the Arrow wasn't in his tower library in Castle Zimmer on Corios.

"Nothing to say, Kyr?" Zane drawled again. "I didn't reach out just to watch you brood in stony silence."

*Kyr.* When Vesper called me that, it was a lovely endearment. Coming from Zane, it was a mocking curse.

"What do you want? Because I have far better things to do than listen to you crow at me."

Zane sniffed. "Please. I haven't even *begun* to crow at you yet."

"That's debatable."

He waved away my snarky words. "Pish-posh. We both know when I'm crowing, and this is not it." A sly smile split his lips. "Not yet, anyway."

My eyes narrowed. "Why do you look so smug?"

Zane's smile widened. "According to some people, namely you, I *always* look smug."

"Smug and annoying. Has anyone ever mentioned you have a very punchable face?"

"Frequently," he chirped. "And yet it's usually the other person who ends up getting punched."

"That's not what happened during the summer solstice attack. Hard to miss the giant black hole in your jacket from where that Techwaver shot you point-blank with a hand cannon."

Zane ran his hand down his jacket, right over the *Z* stitched into the fabric. His face remained calm, but his left eye twitched as if he found the reminder he'd almost died as unpleasant as I found the fact he'd managed to survive. "Yes, well, that Techie is dead, and I'm not, so I got the better end of that deal."

"Yes, well, from what I hear, the entire evening was an unmitigated disaster. Let me guess. Lady Halecia didn't want you to cut down any of her prize pink-star honeysuckle bushes, and Lord Jorge didn't implement any of your security suggestions, thus allowing the Techwavers' attack to succeed." I clucked my tongue in mock sympathy. "Such things wouldn't have happened if *I* was still the head of the Arrows."

Zane's eye twitched again. "True, but you threw away your position the night you and Vesper escaped from Crownpoint. *I'm* the head of the Arrows now, for better or worse."

"Oh, it's definitely for worse. I'm sure the Regals who attended the summer solstice ball would agree with me." I snapped my fingers. "Oh, wait. They *have* been agreeing with me. Loudly and repeatedly on the gossipcasts."

Zane's nostrils flared with anger, but he quickly smoothed out his features again. "Be that as it may, I'm calling to speak to my little sister. Where is Vesper?"

I stiffened. Of course he would call *now*, when Vesper had been injured. Sometimes I thought bad timing was one of Zane's special skills. "Vesper is sleeping."

"*Sleeping*?" he snapped, his voice sharp with suspicion.

"Funny how that seems like another word for *wounded.* What happened?"

"None of your business. And why would you care, anyway?"

Zane's face remained calm, but something flickered in his pale eyes. The emotion was gone in an instant, but the fact that it had been there at all made me even more wary.

Callus Holloway had ordered Zane to find Vesper and me, and the other Arrow had tracked us to Tropics 33, where we had gone to help Asterin fight off a Techwave attack at her lunarium mine. Zane had helped Adria and Dargan Byrne subdue Vesper and deliver her to Crownpoint.

Of course, Zane hadn't known Vesper was his sister back then, but even after I'd told him the truth, he had still watched while Holloway siphoned off my magic, and he'd chased after Vesper and me to try to keep us from escaping.

Oh, yes, Zane had done everything he was supposed to that night, but I couldn't help but feel like he had also done *other* things—like deliberately lowering his guard and letting me cut him with my stormsword while we'd been fighting in the throne room. The injury had severely hampered Zane, and it was one of the reasons he'd been unable to capture us.

Vesper didn't think Zane was capable of such a selfless action, but I'd known Zane Zimmer our entire lives, and family meant *everything* to him. The Arrow might be a monster, the same as me, but he was a monster who would do anything to protect his father and grandmother. Would that same protectiveness extend to a sister he never knew existed until a few weeks ago? I didn't know, but the answer would go a long way toward determining Vesper's fate, along with my own.

"I care what shape Vesper is in because it's my duty to return her to Corios," Zane replied. "Along with you, dear reckless, rebellious Kyrion."

Icy bits of anger swirled up in my chest like a blizzard roaring to life. "I've seen your press conferences vowing to bring Vesper and me before Callus Holloway so we can face Imperium justice." I let out a derisive snort. "As if Holloway knows the slightest thing about *justice*. He just wants to use Vesper and me as his battery."

"Holloway is rather determined to doom you to the same gruesome fate as your parents, but that's not my concern."

I put my hands down on the table and leaned forward. "What *is* your concern?"

"Are you really trying to intimidate me through a holoscreen?" Zane chuckled, rocked forward in his chair, and dropped his hands to his sides. "You couldn't intimidate me in person, Kyrion. Don't waste your time and energy trying to do it when you are millions of miles away."

His eyes narrowed. "My concern is Vesper. How badly was she wounded? None of the Arrows has reported sighting you, so I'm assuming you tangled with some bounty hunters. Several, from the looks of it."

"Why would you think that?"

"Because your jacket and sword are covered with blood."

I glanced down. The bounty hunters' blood had sprayed across the dark blue fabric like raindrops, and even more of it had dried on my stormsword, turning the pale lunarium blade a rusty red.

Zane smirked at me. "Made you look. But that just confirms my suspicions. You and Vesper ran into some bounty hunters, and she was wounded. I will ask again: How badly was she hurt?"

I crossed my arms over my chest. "And I'll ask my question again: Why do you care?"

"I can't very well deliver Vesper to Holloway if she's hurt—or dead." Zane snarled out the last few words, and his hands curled into fists on the desk. He was far more invested in Vesper's health than he wanted me to know.

"You won't be delivering Vesper anywhere. If you come near us, I *will* kill you, Zane."

He flicked his fingers, dismissing my threat. "Please. Any

true fight between us would be a toss-up at best. You might kill me, but I could just as easily kill you."

"So our fight in the throne room wasn't a *true* fight?" I countered. "Why would you say that? Unless, of course, you deliberately dropped your guard and let me wound you."

Zane laughed again, but the sound was brittle and hollow instead of certain and mocking like before. "Please. I know better than to *ever* drop my guard around you, Kyr. You got lucky that night. Nothing more, nothing less."

Vesper's jacket was still lying on the table, and an idea popped into my mind. I hesitated, wondering if I should give in to my foolish notion, but I needed more information about who was hunting us. That was the only way I was going to keep Vesper safe.

"Have you ever heard of a woman named Esmina? Red hair, pretty features, hangs out with a guy named Pollux who carries two war hammers."

Zane's eyes narrowed again. "Is that who hurt Vesper?"

"Not exactly." I hesitated again, but I'd already told part of the story, so I decided to confess the rest. "They hired some bounty hunters to corner Vesper, but they weren't interested in the credits. I don't know who they are or what they want."

"You've only been on the run a few weeks, and you already have mysterious new enemies chasing you and Vesper?" Zane shook his head. "You're really excelling in your new station in life. Kyrion Caldaren, rogue Arrow and fugitive extraordinaire."

My hands clenched into fists. I hated it when he was right.

Zane smirked at me a moment longer, then his face turned serious. "You didn't answer my question: How badly was Vesper hurt?"

"That's because it's none of your bloody business. You have made your feelings about Vesper and me quite clear on the gossipcasts."

"Oh, yes, my feelings about you are crystal clear, dear

Kyrion. I despise you, and you despise me, and proper Regal lords we both be."

I rolled my eyes. "Even for you, that's a shitty bit of poetry."

Zane grinned. "Aw, you think I'm a poet? And I didn't even know it."

I waited for him to make a similar quip about Vesper, but he didn't. Strange. The Zane Zimmer I knew would never hesitate to talk trash and spout off a bad rhyme about anyone. Perhaps the fact that Vesper was his sister had made him grow a sliver of a conscience. Doubtful, but I hoped so, for her sake.

Vesper kept insisting she didn't care about Zane, but I could hear the wistfulness in her voice and feel the same emotion rippling through the bond every time she talked about him. Thanks to Nerezza's abandonment, Vesper had never had a real family, but the idea still meant everything to her. Another way in which she and Zane were eerily alike.

Zane gave me a look that was almost pitying. "You can't protect her forever, Kyrion. Eventually, someone will be a tiny bit smarter, stronger, or luckier than you, and Vesper will suffer the consequences."

"Don't you think I know that?" I snapped back. "Don't you think that is my greatest bloody *fear*?"

The words tumbled out of my mouth before I could stop them, and I had to grind my teeth to keep from spewing out all my worries about how I was going to fail Vesper, sooner rather than later.

"Then surrender, and let me bring you both in," Zane replied.

For a moment, I considered it. I'd come so close to losing Vesper today. Even now, I could still see the bounty hunter shooting her, still hear Vesper's cry of pain, still feel her agony pulsing through the bond. Like it or not, Zane was right. Eventually, our luck *was* going to run out, and then one or both of us would wind up even more seriously injured—or dead.

Zane leaned forward, his gaze locking with mine. "Come

on, Kyrion. Prove your truebond with my sister is about more than just the psionic power the two of you have. For once in your miserable life, do the right thing—for Vesper's sake."

More cold fury swirled through my body, and I stiffened as though someone had shoved a shock baton into my back. "I will do *anything* for Vesper's sake. And if I have to kill every bounty hunter in the galaxy, then so be it."

Zane shook his head. "You stupid, stubborn fool. You're going to get yourself killed, and her along with you."

"Perhaps," I admitted. "But I'd rather be dead than be Holloway's battery or wind up in some Techwave lab, and I'd rather die fighting for Vesper than anyone else."

"I *will* catch you," Zane snarled. "And then the two of us are going to have a reckoning."

"Do your worst, Zane." I snapped my fingers again. "Oh, wait. You actually have to *find* us first, something you are failing at miserably."

"The two of you have led me on a merry chase, but all good things come to an end."

I eyed him, but Zane stared right back at me, his face calm. As with many strong psions, his telepathy and telempathy often canceled out my own abilities, and I couldn't tell if he was bluffing or if he really did know where Vesper and I were going. The other Arrow had always had an excellent poker face, and I had never been able to read him as well as I wanted to.

A faint noise sounded on Zane's end of the holoscreen, and he looked at something I couldn't see. After a few seconds, Zane focused on me again.

"Duty calls," he drawled. "Tell my little sister I hope she recovers quickly from whatever injury you inflicted on her with your stubbornness."

"Fuck off," I snarled.

Zane smirked back at me. "See you soon, Kyr."

He sliced his hand over his holoscreen, cutting the connection.

For several seconds, I glared into the empty space where his smug face had been. Then I shrugged off my anger, hit some buttons, and ran a diagnostic scan on the encrypted channel he had used. Zane was nothing if not clever, and it would be just like him to bait me into a conversation so he could try to track the signal back to the *Dream World* and get a lock on the ship's location.

The scan came up clean, thanks in large part to all the security measures Daichi had installed. But Zane hadn't even tried to trace the signal, which made me even more wary.

Did Zane realize we were going to Sygnustern? But how could he possibly know that? Vesper and I didn't have any obvious allies among the Erzton, and the group's leaders would be reluctant to take us in, since that could severely damage the Erzton's relations with Callus Holloway and the Imperium.

Still, Zane's parting words indicated he had *some* plan to find us. The other Arrow had always been a tricky enemy, and in some ways, he was the most devious and dangerous person I had ever met. Zane's cleverness was another thing he had in common with Vesper.

But what annoyed—and worried—me the most was that he was right. Vesper was in danger every single moment she was with me, and sooner or later, someone would get the better of us. Zane, the other Arrows, another group of bounty hunters, some criminal conglomerates looking for a quick payday. Then Vesper and I would be captured and shipped back to Corios, to suffer Holloway's wrath.

I just wondered how much longer Vesper and I could keep running—and what would happen when our luck finally ran out.

# SIX

## VESPER

I didn't like being healed by a medtable. It was awkward and uncomfortable and a giant hassle to just lie there, trying to be still, while dozens of tiny robotic needles stabbed into my body and stitched everything back together. Plus, this particular table was equipped with a smug feminine voice that seemed to enjoy trapping me in a plastic bubble like a mammoth butterfly and then cheerfully listing my many injuries.

"Severe burns detected, along with a deep puncture wound and significant nerve damage. More skinbonds needed . . ."

But the one good thing about the medtable was its truly excellent and extremely effective drugs. It injected me with skinbonds, antibiotics, and other medicines, including some anesthesia that sent me straight to dreamland—or at least, my version of it.

One moment, I was lying on the medtable, staring up at Kyrion's worried face, and trying not to let him sense just how much my injured arm was hurting. The next, I was standing in a long corridor in an old-fashioned castle—Castle Caldaren, Kyrion's home on Corios.

Relief rushed through me, along with another round of cool, soothing chemicals. I had been dreaming about Kyrion's castle ever since I was a child, long before I had ever met him or set foot in the real-world Castle Caldaren. Despite all my visits, I always found something new to admire, from the crystal chandeliers sparkling overhead, to the elegant tables and chairs made of real wood, to the dark blue rugs underfoot that featured silver arrows and stars stitched in beautiful paisley patterns.

A grandfather clock bellowed out the hour like a stodgy butler. I ran my fingers along the wooden case, and the bellowing faded away, replaced by a steady, easy *tick-tick-ticking* that pleased my engineer's heart. A few months ago, the clock hadn't worked, but I had used my seer magic to repair it, the way I did so many broken things.

Too bad I could never seem to fix myself, especially when it came to my magic.

My mood soured, and I dropped my fingers from the clock and trudged onward.

Despite the beautiful furnishings, the castle seemed frozen in time, as though it was holding its breath and waiting for Kyrion to return home. Right now, our plan was to stay on Sygnustern until we figured out how to defeat Callus Holloway, but I had no idea how long that might take.

Holloway controlled the full weight, strength, and resources of the Imperium, including the support, however reluctant, of the Regals, along with the Imperium soldiers and his own personal Bronze Hand guards. Plus, he was an extremely powerful siphon who could absorb energy from a variety of sources, including blasters and other weapons.

Kyrion and I needed our own weapon to defeat Holloway—like the Techwave cannon, which could cut through a psion's magic and body in brutal, horrific fashion. I was hoping that if I fixed the cannon, it might be powerful enough to nullify Holloway's siphon ability and let Kyrion and me finally kill him.

I entered the library, my favorite room in the castle, and trailed my fingers over the spines of the real paper books that lined the shelves. Despite all the years I had been dreaming about the castle, I had never been able to read the books' titles until Kyrion and I had accepted our truebond. My gaze skimmed over the gold, silver, and copper foil words stamped on the spines. Kyrion had eclectic tastes, although the books leaned toward the action-packed and fantastical—fairy tales, stories about clever animals, even one about a talking sword.

Smiling, I moved over to a silver-framed portrait hanging above the fireplace. On the canvas, a man with black hair and eyes and tan skin beamed at a woman with blond hair, blue eyes, and pale skin. Chauncey and Desdemona Caldaren, Kyrion's parents. A young Kyrion was also featured in the family portrait, glaring sourly at the artist while his parents rested their hands on his shoulders.

I stared up at the painting, waiting for what I knew was coming next. After a few seconds, an eerie, invisible force swirled through the air, like a ghost ruffling my hair. In the portrait, Desdemona's head swiveled to the front, and she peered down at me.

Just like with the book titles, I had never been able to see the faces in the painting until I had met Kyrion. But now, every time I came in here, Desdemona turned her head and stared at me. When it first happened, I had screamed and jumped like a kitten scared of its own shadow, but now the Regal lady's movements were yet another puzzle I needed to solve.

"Where do I know you from?" I asked. "What are you trying to tell me?"

Desdemona Caldaren was one of the most famous people in

the Archipelago Galaxy, and countless gossipcasts had covered her fairy-tale romance, wedding, and marriage to Chauncey Caldaren. But over the last few weeks, I'd had the growing, nagging sense I actually *knew* Desdemona, that I had seen or met or even spoken to her once upon a time, although I couldn't remember when or where or why. Something that greatly confused me, since I was a seer who supposedly never forgot anything I saw, heard, or experienced.

A secretive smile slowly curved Desdemona's lips. I waited for the better part of a minute, but the Regal lady didn't do anything else, so I moved away from the portrait.

At my approach, a door appeared along the wall and swung open, revealing a tight, narrow staircase. I went down the spiral steps, skimming my fingers over the sigils carved into the dark stone banister.

The sigils were something else I had never been able to make out until I had accepted my bond with Kyrion. Some were butterflies with flapping wings that stirred the air, while others were stormswords that shimmered, sparked, and crackled with cold, heat, and even small bursts of lightning. But many of the sigils were still indecipherable, as were the whispers they emitted, as though I was walking through a group of invisible people murmuring secrets I couldn't quite hear.

I reached the bottom of the stairs and stepped into the large round room that was the foundation of my mindscape, the place deep inside my mind, heart, and body where my seer magic resided. According to the books I'd read on psionic theory, each mindscape was unique to its seer and reflected something about their personality, powers, and experiences. I had been coming here since I was seven years old, but even now, thirty years later, I was still trying to figure out what my mindscape said about me.

Thick black vines snaked along the floor and climbed up the wall, while pale blue flowers scented the air with a sharp but sweet aroma that reminded me of the spearmint candy sticks I had loved as a child. According to Kyrion, the flowers were blue-moon peonies, which also bloomed in his mother's garden at Castle Caldaren. The flowers were another odd, unexpected connection between Desdemona and me, although I didn't know what, if anything, they meant.

The vines and peonies draped over arched doors set into the wall. The doors were different shapes and sizes, some tall and wide, others short and narrow. Some of the doors were closed and locked, and I had no idea what lay behind them, but several were open, and images flickered on the other side, like videos playing on a holoscreen.

All the memories of everything I had seen, done, and experienced in my life—good, bad, and undeniably ugly.

In the smallest door, which was just large enough for a child to walk through, a woman with pale skin, long dark brown hair, and dark blue eyes glared at another woman who could have been her twin. My mother, Nerezza, and her cousin, Liesl, facing off the day the Imperium academy instructors had told my mother that my seer magic was too weak to waste time training me to properly use it.

The memory played out just as it had in real life, and Nerezza's sharp voice boomed out of the door.

*I should be back on Corios. I should be part of the Regals, not rotting away on a useless planet trapped in a useless life with an utterly useless child.*

Even though this had taken place thirty years ago, I still flinched. No matter how much time passed, my magic never let me forget my mother's deep disdain and casual cruelty, and this memory was always lurking in here, ready to wound me again.

Sometimes I really hated being a seer.

In the doorway, Nerezza stormed away. Liesl looked up at the stairs where I was hiding, opened her mouth, and stretched out a hand as if to comfort me, but the seven-year-old version of me clutched a book and ran away crying.

The memory rewound and started playing again. I rubbed my chest, trying to massage the dull ache out of my heart. Reliving that moment was bad enough, but the worst parts were the witnesses to my misery. I wasn't alone in my mindscape. Not really.

Not while the eyes followed my every movement.

Dozens and dozens of wide, open, unblinking eyes stared at me from the doors, the walls, and even the low ceiling. Many of the jeweled eyes seemed to be a dull, flat black, but a closer look revealed their true, deep blue color. The eyes were all made of sapphsidian, and sparkling black flecks swirled through their blue depths, like comets constantly spinning around and around deep inside the winking facets.

I plucked my stormsword off my belt, carefully gripped the lunarium blade, and held the weapon up to one of the eyes. The three sapphsidian jewels embedded in the silver hilt were a perfect match to the eyes in my mindscape, although I didn't know how they all might be connected. I excelled at figuring things out, but these days, I had far more questions than answers, especially when it came to my seer magic.

How was I supposed to help Kyrion when I couldn't even master my own magic? Much less how my power worked with his and how they worked together as part of the truebond.

I sighed, slid my sword back onto my belt, and moved on. Near the back of the room, I stopped in front of a door that featured a large stylized *Z* made of alternating pieces of sapphsidian and blue opals that sparkled with inner rings of fiery color. Even in my mindscape, I couldn't escape the cursed sigil for House Zimmer—or my brother.

A few weeks ago, I had been in my workshop on the *Dream World* watching Zane give a press conference about the summer solstice attack, when I'd fallen asleep and entered my mindscape. This door had appeared and flung itself open, showing a cozy, cluttered tower. I'd been so curious that I'd done something I'd never tried before: I'd walked through the door and ended up in Zane's library in Castle Zimmer on Corios.

Even stranger was the fact that Zane had actually been able to *see* me, as though I was really there and standing right in front of him, and we'd had a tense conversation about Beatrice, his grandmother, hiding my existence from Zane and his father, Wendell.

Astral projection, Zane had dubbed this new ability. He'd speculated that either my magic was growing or Kyrion's power was pushing mine to new heights. Or maybe it was a combination of the two. Either way, it was yet another frustrating question with no obvious answer.

Ever since, I'd been replaying our threat-filled talk in my mind, parsing Zane's words and analyzing every quirk of his lips and arch of his eyebrows. Despite my anger and disgust, I still wanted to know what Zane truly thought about me, beneath all his Regal bluster and Arrow bravado, and I couldn't stop a sliver of my heart from longing—*hoping*—that he might view me as his *real* sister someday, and not just a grave mistake by his father.

My fingers twitched, and my hand crept toward the knob. I considered opening Zane's door and trying to spy on him, but dread washed over me, and my arm dropped to my side. I had no desire to see Zane talking about how I would never be a part of his family.

Zane wasn't even my brother, not really, not in any way that truly *mattered*, but I was still afraid he was going to hurt me just as badly as Nerezza had.

I was such a paranoid, broken fool.

I shook off my troubled thoughts and moved over to a door on the opposite side of the room. This door also featured a familiar symbol: an arrow streaking upward through a cluster of stars.

I traced my fingers over the House Caldaren sigil. The sapphsidian arrow was shaped like a spade from an old-fashioned tarot or playing card, and it was as cold as ice, but the sensation wasn't an unpleasant one. I liked Kyrion having a door in my mindscape, liked this connection to him, even if I still didn't understand much about our abilities.

Kyrion said that everything about the bond felt easier now. That he could sense my thoughts, feelings, and magic much more readily and deeply than before and that my seer ability even showed him things from time to time.

In some ways, I felt that same connection. Kyrion's thoughts and feelings were much easier to sense now. Most of the time, we had no problems communicating telepathically, but I still couldn't use his other psion powers, especially his telekinesis, with any regularity. I also couldn't form a psionic blade, a weapon made of pure mental energy, on a consistent basis like Kyrion could. And neither one of us had been able to replicate the incredible lightning storm of psionic power we'd unleashed when we'd first accepted the truebond and decimated the Crownpoint throne room.

Oh, yes, a few things had gotten easier, but all the big, important things—the abilities that would actually help and protect us—had gotten much more difficult, and I had no idea why.

Frustration spiked through my body, and I stalked away from Kyrion's door and moved over to the final door in the very back of the room. The Door, as I always thought of it. My door, the one that led into the true, hidden heart of my seer magic.

Beautiful carvings of crescent moons and stars swirled across the stone, but the centerpiece was a large upside-down sapphsidian eye that sparkled just a bit more brightly than all the other jewels. I waved my hand, and the sapphsidian eye turned right side up. A lock clicked, and the door opened. Unlike the other doors with their endless loops of memories, wisps of blackness spilled out of this opening, curling up like fingers beckoning me closer, and I strode forward.

Over the last few months, I had thoroughly embraced my own inner darkness, along with all the cold, cruel, calculating things I'd done to survive. Like exposing Rowena Kent's scheme to crash Imperium ships on command for the Techwave. Fighting and killing Julieta Delano, the traitorous Arrow who'd been working with Rowena. Tricking and then killing some soldiers so I could escape from the Techwave facility where Harkin Ocnus was torturing me. Then, later on, shoving my stormsword into Harkin's chest. Battling the Imperium soldiers and Bronze Hand guards who'd tried to keep me away from Kyrion during the midnight ball.

Sometimes I couldn't believe how drastically my life had changed. I'd gone from being a lowly lab rat toiling away in obscurity, to a Regal lady and the head of a corporation, to an infamous fugitive. I didn't know what the future held, but maybe I could get a glimpse of it here in my own inner darkness.

I plunged deeper and deeper into my mindscape. The blackness was so thick and absolute that I couldn't see anything, not even my hand in front of my face, and the only sound was the soft scrape of my boots on the stone. Slowly, in the distance, the darkness receded, and rays of light bloomed like a flower unfurling its petals one by one.

More time passed. It might have been a few seconds, it might have been a few minutes. But from one moment to the next, I stepped from the absolute blackness into a pool of silver light, as though I had been transported into the middle of a Frozon moon.

The light illuminated a slab of stone that resembled an altar, and the entire thing was shaped like an oversize eye, just like the jewels out in the main part of my mindscape. The top of the altar was made of sapphsidian, but instead of being static, the stone rippled like a deep, dark blue lake. Lunarium eyes were also embedded in the stone, staring up at me like silver stars.

Down below, the altar's curving sapphsidian legs were mounted on sturdy pieces of lunarium shaped like arrows, and lunarium arrows also glimmered in the sapphsidian lake like sparkling treasure just waiting to be brought to the surface. Despite the disparate parts, the pieces of stones flowed seamlessly into each other, as though each bit was intricately connected to the next, and they were all an integral, inextricable part of one another, and the whole.

The eye-shaped altar was a psionic nexus, a visual representation of a psion's power, the place deep inside them where their magic, abilities, and instincts resided. I'd first stumbled across my nexus a few weeks ago, when I'd been trapped at Crownpoint Palace and was recovering from Holloway draining off my magic. Kyrion had also found me here when I was more dead than alive from sucking all the air out of the cargo bay on the *Dream World* in order to kill Adria Byrne.

According to Kyrion, I had been lying on the altar like a mermaid floating on an ocean wave, although I didn't remember that or him picking me up, returning to the main part of my mindscape, and carrying me through his door and back out into the real world. One moment, I had been drifting along in a peaceful black void. The next, I'd heard Kyrion calling my name, demanding I come back to him. I'd drawn in a breath to tell him I was trying, and I'd woken up on the medtable, with Kyrion cradling me in his arms.

I smoothed my hand over the nexus. The sapphsidian rippled a little more vigorously, causing the lunarium eyes and arrows to bob up and down like shimmering water lilies. The nexus was cool to the touch, although I could have sworn a bit of heat was lurking in the dark depths.

My fingers sank a little deeper into the stone, and I held

my breath, wondering if I might finally unlock the nexus's secrets . . . but nothing happened.

No flares of magic, no sparks of power, nothing.

I'd come to my psionic nexus several times, trying to figure out how it worked, but the slab of stone never *did* anything. It just stood here, in the darkness of my heart, like a glowing beacon I couldn't quite understand or access.

I swallowed an angry snarl and kept trying, but nothing happened, and my frustration built and built with every soft slide of my hand across the stone. Nothing was going right today, especially when it came to my magic.

My frustration boiled up, and my fingers itched with the urge to throw something. I didn't even really think about what I was doing. I just reached down, plucked one of the lunarium eyes out of the sapphsidian surface, and hurled it away as hard as I could.

As soon as the eye left my fingertips, I clasped my hands over my mouth in horror. I grimaced, waiting for the telltale *tink* of the eye hitting the stone somewhere in the darkness, but everything remained quiet. Weird. Then again, everything was a bit weird in here. What did that say about me and my magic?

A bright flare of silver appeared in the distance, streaking toward me like a shooting star. I ducked, and the lunarium eye whistled past my head before arcing back around like a boomerang. I ducked again—

The lunarium eye stopped in midair and dropped back down into the nexus like a stone plummeting into a lake.

*Plop.*

Eyes wide, I peered at the altar. Had I just broken my own mindscape? An annoyed huff tumbled from my lips. Well, wouldn't that just be the cherry on this shitshow sundae of a day.

Ripples spread across the surface of the stone, and the lunarium eye bobbed back up to the surface of the sapphsidian. After a few seconds, it settled back down into place, floating alongside the other eyes and arrows.

I exhaled, but my relief boiled away in the simmering stew of my frustration. I could look at a faulty brewmaker, a misfiring blaster, or a malfunctioning spaceship and know how to fix it in minutes, sometimes even seconds. So why couldn't I figure out my own magic? What was *wrong* with me?

I stared down at the rippling sapphsidian, my reflection weak, watery, and wavering, just like my seer magic. More frustration scorched through my body, and I whirled around and stormed away. The silver light around the nexus abruptly vanished, like a moon that had been eclipsed by a sun, but I kept going, trudging through the darkness.

A minute passed, maybe two or five or even ten. I could never tell how long I had been in here or how much time had passed out in the real world. I was probably still lying on the medtable, but right now, I yearned to wake up, no matter how painful the robotic needles stitching my arm together might be.

Finally, I stepped out of the darkness and back into the round room of my mindscape. I stopped and looked at all the vines, flowers, and eyes, but just like the nexus, none of them did anything—

A door to my left threw itself open and banged against the wall.

Esmina's snide voice drifted out of the opening. *You're the weak link, destined to be broken.*

"Yeah, tell me about it," I muttered, even though it was just a memory.

As if my words were a command, the memory rewound and started playing again, stuck on that one sound bite like an old-fashioned record skipping on the same spot again and again.

*You're the weak link, destined to be broken . . .*

A growl erupted from my throat, and I stomped toward the spiral stairs. I had never tried to leave my mindscape before, but everything in here reminded me what a failure I was. Even worse, Esmina's mocking declaration from earlier today mixed with Nerezza's sneering insult from long ago, creating a cackling chorus of derision.

*You're the weak link . . . useless child . . . destined to be broken . . . useless child . . .*

I ground my teeth and walked faster.

In the distance, a loud chime sounded. The voices cut off, and the images in the doorways flickered and faded away.

"Treatment complete. Injuries healed. Life saved," the smug feminine voice of the medtable rang out.

Startled, I blinked and left my mindscape. My eyes snapped open, and I found myself staring up at the medtable's polyplastic bubble.

The table chirped out a few facts about how much of my skin it had repaired and replaced, as if it was giving itself a verbal pat on the back for a job well done. Then the plastic detached itself from one side of the medtable, arched up, and vanished back into its hiding spot.

I slowly sat up, swung my legs over the side of the table, and examined my right arm. No traces of the ugly blaster burn and deep puncture wound remained, and my skin was pink and smooth, as though I had just sloughed it clean with a fancy spa scrub.

My body might be whole again, but my head and heart were still pounding with anger and frustration, and Esmina's and Nerezza's snide voices echoed in my ears.

Even worse was the knowledge that they were right. Until I figured out what my psionic nexus did or meant or how to fully use my seer magic, I *was* the weak link, destined to be broken—and in danger of dragging Kyrion down with me.

Still haunted by my turbulent thoughts, I went into the bathroom and took a hot shower to wash away the blood, sweat, and dirt of the fight with the bounty hunters. Then I changed into some clean clothes and went in search of Kyrion.

He was in the library, glaring down at the holoscreen embedded in the table like he wanted to smash it to pieces with his fists.

"What happened? Did the local gossipcasters realize we were on Tropics 44?"

"No, nothing like that." Kyrion sighed and raised his gaze to mine. "Zane contacted me."

Shock swept over me in a cold, numbing wave. "When? How? Why?"

"While you were getting healed. He used a private channel that was part of an old Arrow mission." Kyrion hesitated. "I recorded our conversation. You can watch it—if you want."

More of that cold, numb shock swept over me, even as my heart hammered in a quick, painful rhythm. I jerked my head in agreement. Kyrion hit a few keys, and Zane popped into view.

I watched my brother carefully, cataloging and analyzing his every word, breath, twitch, and gesture, but Kyrion's conversation was similar to the one I'd had with Zane in his tower library a few weeks ago, and I didn't glean any new information from his taunts.

Kyrion waved his hand, cutting off the recording. His shoulders were tense, and the sticky cobweb in my mind pulsed with anger, worry, and more than a little dread.

"Don't pay any attention to Zane," I said. "He's all bluster and bravado. We've heard all his threats before, and no doubt we'll hear them all again—and again and again, thanks to the gossipcasts. Sometimes I think he's the only reason they have enough ratings to stay in business. They might as well rename *Celestial Stars* the *Zane Zimmer Adoration Channel*."

Kyrion smiled a little at my dark humor, but the expression

quickly vanished. "Zane is right about one thing. We can't run forever. Sooner or later, someone is going to get the drop on us. And when that happens, I'm afraid . . ."

He paused and cleared his throat. When he spoke again, his voice was much lower and rougher than before. "I'm afraid I won't be able to protect you and that you'll get hurt again—or worse, end up in Holloway's clutches."

The grim, haunted look in his eyes made my own heart crack in commiseration. I stepped forward and rested my hands on his shoulders. "Neither one of us is going to end up in Holloway's clutches. We're going to protect each other, just like we've been doing. Don't give Zane another thought."

"He's always been able to get under my skin, ever since we were children."

"I thought I was the only one who got under your skin," I teased, trying to lighten the mood.

The anger in Kyrion's eyes flared up into something hotter and more intense. His hands settled on my waist, and he pulled me closer so that my body was flush against his. Then he leaned down, his breath skimming against my ear.

"If you want to get under me, all you have to do is ask," he murmured.

I hummed my agreement and wrapped my arms around his neck. Kyrion lifted his head, his eyes burning like blue suns. He lowered his face toward mine. I hummed again and stood up on my tiptoes to meet him halfway—

A chime sounded. Kyrion and I both froze, our lips inches apart. I tensed, then looked over at the flashing holoscreen. "Do you think Zane is calling again?"

Kyrion let out a regretful sigh and dropped his hands from my waist. "If he is, he won't give up until we answer."

He moved over to the holoscreen and started tapping buttons. After a few seconds, his shoulders relaxed. "Not Zane. Daichi and Tivona."

Kyrion entered several long codes to access the private group channel. The holoscreen flickered a few times, processing the information, then two people popped into view.

The first was a man with short black hair, dark brown eyes, and golden skin who was wearing a House Caldaren uniform, just like Kyrion and me. The second was a woman with dark brown hair, dark brown eyes, and ebony skin who was clad in a sleek gold business suit.

Daichi Hirano arched an eyebrow at us. "The two of you have certainly been busy."

"Oh, yes," Tivona Winslow chimed in. "The story just got picked up by the Regal gossipcasts. Multiple dead bodies found in a junkyard on Tropics 44. No one knows who killed the bounty hunters or why, but even without the battle footage from Vesper's jacket, Daichi and I knew right away it was the handiwork of Team Truebond."

Despite her light, teasing tone, I grimaced. I'd only taken down Rina, and only with a lucky blow. Kyrion had killed most of the bounty hunters, and if not for him, I would be a prisoner. Not much of a team effort on my part.

"They were trying to get Vesper onto a ship," Kyrion replied.

Daichi's eyebrow arched a little higher. "And you stopped them the way you stop everyone—permanently."

Kyrion shrugged. "Once an Arrow, always an Arrow."

Daichi snorted, but it sounded suspiciously like a laugh, and Kyrion's lips twitched up into an answering grin.

I gestured over at my ruined jacket, which was lying on the table. "What about Esmina and Pollux? Did you find any info on them?"

Daichi nodded and hit a few buttons. Several documents popped up and floated over the holoscreen, along with some photos.

"Meet Esmina Reston and Pollux Lamont. I haven't found

out much about their personal lives yet, but the two of them have made quite a name for themselves as corporate mercenaries."

"Corporate mercenaries? Fuck," Kyrion muttered.

My thought exactly.

Almost every large corporation employed its own private army of mercenaries—skilled fighters who provided security and executed missions to increase a corporation's resources, power, wealth, and influence. In some ways, these corporations were even more dangerous than the Imperium, Erzton, and Techwave. Those groups had rules, structures, and leadership that provided some semblance of checks and balances, but a corporation was an entity unto itself and usually controlled by a handful of people who would do anything to achieve their goals.

A few months ago, Rowena Kent had sent some of her corporate mercenaries to capture me. The mercenaries had forcibly boarded this very blitzer and shot me with a blaster before Kyrion and I had killed them. I rubbed a spot above my left hip, which ached at the memory.

When I'd taken over Kent Corp and rebranded it as Quill Corp, I'd discovered just how many mercenaries Rowena had employed. Given the regime change, most of the mercenaries had left, but I'd kept several on staff, although I didn't trust or use them in any capacity. I'd been so busy dealing with the day-to-day running of the R&D lab and the production plants that I hadn't had a chance to figure out what to do with my own personal goon squad. Although now I supposed they were Tivona's goon squad, since she was running Quill Corp in my absence.

Daichi hit some more buttons, and a couple of dossiers popped up. "Esmina and Pollux aren't your typical mercs who float from one job to another. They have their own corporation—Serpens Corp—which specializes in high-risk operations. Assassinations, kidnappings, prisoner exchanges, even hostile takeovers of other corporations. They have an extremely high success rate and are extremely well compensated for their time, skills, and expertise."

He paused. "These are the kinds of people you hire when money is no object, and you don't care how big or bloody a mess they leave behind."

Kyrion muttered another curse. "Of course they are."

I thought of the way Esmina had strolled away from the battle, easily dodging one blaster bolt after another, even though her back was turned and she couldn't see the deadly streaks of electricity zipping in her direction. "Not much risk if you know how things are going to play out."

"What do you mean?" Tivona asked.

I called up the battle footage and pointed out all the times Esmina had known something was going to happen seconds before it actually occurred.

Tivona frowned. "What kind of psion power would let you do that?"

I stared at a photo of Esmina, studying the gold flecks glinting in her green eyes. "She's a seer."

"How do you know?" Kyrion asked.

I hesitated. I wasn't sure how I knew, but as soon as the words left my mouth, I could *feel* the truth of them, and I could have sworn a soft chime of confirmation rang through my mind.

"I just . . . have a feeling that's what she is." I shook my head. "Although I've never heard of a seer having enough magic to predict the future so quickly and accurately. She was adjusting to how the battle was playing out in real time seconds before everyone else was."

Daichi nodded. "Esmina being a seer does seem to be the most logical conclusion. Perhaps if I had more information, I would have been able to learn more about her abilities."

I huffed at the chiding note in his voice. "Sorry. The next time I'm stuck between two powerful psions threatening a bunch of bounty hunters, I'll politely interrupt the hostilities and ask everyone to give me their full names, along with their birth planets, star signs, and favorite colors."

Daichi huffed right back at me.

"Any updates on Holloway?" Kyrion asked.

"Holloway is holed up in the palace like usual," Daichi replied. "Although Zane hasn't given a gossipcast interview in almost three days, even though reporters are camped out in Promenade Park, right across the Boulevard from Castle Zimmer."

He tapped on his holoscreen, and new images appeared, showing a lush green park and a wide cobblestone thoroughfare lined with colorful, quirky castles. The most powerful Regal families all had homes along the Boulevard.

Castle Zimmer was made of a pale blue stone streaked with jagged forks of midnight blue. My gaze locked onto the tower that housed Zane's library. My stomach clenched with a familiar nauseating combination of anger and dread. Would I ever get used to hearing about my long-lost family? Or was I destined to suffer every time someone uttered the Zimmer name?

Kyrion snorted. "The lack of attention must be killing Zane. Perhaps that's why he called me earlier."

Daichi's dark gaze sharpened. "You spoke to Zane?"

Kyrion nodded, hit some buttons, and played his conversation with Zane.

When the recording finished, Daichi shook his head. "Zane is definitely up to something. I'll see if I can find out where he is."

I had no desire to talk about Zane anymore, so I looked at Tivona. "How are things at Quill Corp?" I asked, unable to keep a wistful note from creeping into my voice.

Tivona winked at me. "Everything is running smoothly, thanks to your chief operating officer."

I winked back at her. "I have no doubt of that."

After I had seized control of the corporation, my first order of business had been to install Tivona as my chief operating officer. Tivona was a skilled negotiator who was an expert at legal strategy, public relations, and the hundreds of other details that went into running a Regal corporation. She handled the business side of things, while I ran the R&D lab, working alongside the other lab rats to improve old Kent Corp products and create new cutting-edge designs.

Tivona typed on her holoscreen, and several reports popped up and hovered over the table. "Sales of your new brewmaker have tripled since the midnight ball. Your newfound notoriety has been great for business, and I've been diverting half the funds into your anonymous accounts, as requested."

A sharp finger of annoyance poked into my chest. The influx of credits had proven useful while Kyrion and I were on the run, but I wanted people to buy my brewmaker because it was the best beverage and food fabricator on the market, not because my face was plastered all over the gossipcasts.

"Are the Imperium investigators still giving you problems?" I asked.

After Kyrion and I had fled from Corios, Holloway had dispatched a squad of Imperium investigators, along with several Arrows, to Quill Corp headquarters on Temperate 42. Tivona had played her part to perfection, claiming she didn't know about my truebond with Kyrion, and she'd managed to keep Holloway from seizing control of Quill Corp. I would be forever grateful to my friend for that.

Tivona shrugged. "I haven't heard a peep from the Imperium investigators in weeks. They're too busy dealing with the summer solstice attack at Castle Rojillo to bother with Quill Corp right now."

Relief rushed through me. At least my fugitive status wasn't causing her any more headaches. "Have you learned anything new about Jorge Rojillo's temperature-shielding technology?"

Tivona shook her head, making her gold star chandelier earrings tinkle together like tiny wind chimes. "No. I gave the schematics to Bodie and a few of the other trusted R&D workers, but to them, it's just a personal device, an old-fashioned wristwatch to manage the temperature. The climate-control tech is an improvement over previous iterations—smaller, faster, more powerful—but none of the Quill Corp lab rats has any idea why the Techwave wanted it so badly."

I drummed my fingers on the table. "Tell Bodie and the others to keep working on it."

Tivona nodded. "What about the Techwave cannon? Have you figured out the right amount of sapphsidian and lunarium to make it work properly?"

My gaze darted over to the cannon, which was lying on the table beside my ruined jacket and some plastipaper schematics of the temperature-shielding technology. The silver barrel was sleek, shiny, and intact, but the once-clear solar magazine was now black and brittle. Despite my latest tweaks, the magazine had still overheated and fried itself after Kyrion fired the weapon a few times.

"No. I've run several simulations, but I need some actual sapphsidian to test my theories. More lunarium and solar wiring too."

Frustration surged through me. If I'd had access to all the materials and equipment in the Quill Corp R&D lab, I might already have the answer, but I couldn't return to my lab until Callus Holloway was dead and Kyrion and I had eliminated the bounty on us. Losing my work, my happy place, was something else the Imperium ruler had taken from me and yet another reason I wanted to destroy him.

My frustration vanished, replaced by more wistful longing.

I didn't just miss the R&D lab—I missed how I *felt* in the lab. Strong, smart, confident, capable. Like all I had to do was work long and hard enough, and I could puzzle out the answer to any problem.

"Don't worry, Vesper. You'll figure it out," Tivona said. "I have faith in you."

"Me too," Daichi chimed in.

"Me three," Kyrion murmured, placing his hand on mine and squeezing my fingers.

Warm pride surged off him, along with steady, unwavering belief, but for once, the sensations didn't comfort me, and I had to force myself to smile at him.

Kyrion squeezed my fingers again, then he, Daichi, and Tivona started talking about other things. My gaze strayed back to the Techwave cannon, and the charred solar magazine stared at me like a black hole slowly soaking up all my confidence.

Kyrion excelled at being a warrior, and he knew exactly what he was capable of—good, bad, and deadly. Well, figuring things out was my area of expertise, and sometimes it felt like the *only* way I could contribute to Team Truebond. But right now, I was hitting one dead end after another.

But the worst thing was this snide little voice in the back of my mind that chided me for not figuring things out long ago. And try as I might to ignore it, this nagging feeling and odd stirring of my magic kept whispering that if I didn't start coming up with answers soon, then Kyrion and my friends would pay a terrible price for my failures.

# SEVEN

## VESPER

Kyrion and I made a few more plans with Daichi and Tivona, then signed off. I was lost in my thoughts, as was Kyrion, and neither one of us said much as we left the library and prepared dinner in the ship's kitchen.

Kyrion was quite the chef, and he transformed the fresh vegetables and freeze-dried beef jerky I'd bought in the marketplace into a hearty stew with a side of crispy, cheesy hash browns and a loaf of sourdough oat bread slathered with honey-lime butter. He even made a mango-lemon sorbet topped with a tropical salsa and crystalized ginger that was light, refreshing, and utterly delicious.

After dinner, the two of us went to bed. Kyrion wrapped his arms around me and held me tight like he never wanted to let me go. I hooked my leg over his, drawing him even closer, then buried my face in his neck, drinking in his sharp spearmint scent. His breath was a warm, feathery caress against my skin, and his heart thumped a steady, comforting rhythm under my fingers. We still didn't talk, but his worry rippled through the bond, the emotion as loud, clear, and sharp as my own.

Even if we hadn't been on the run, I still would have been concerned. Kyrion and I had both accepted the truebond, but we hadn't talked about what might happen if we managed to defeat Holloway. We hadn't discussed what the future might hold—or how we really felt about each other.

Ever since the bond had formed, I'd wondered—and worried—how much it was influencing our decisions, especially when it came to our feelings for each other. A few weeks ago, when Kyrion and I had first gotten together on the *Dream World*, I'd claimed I didn't care about the bond anymore since it had given me a chance to find him.

I'd meant what I'd said, but I also couldn't stop myself from analyzing everything that had happened—and was still happening—between us. In some ways, the truebond was like a brewmaker in the R&D lab, and no matter how bright, shiny, new, and wonderful it was, I couldn't stop poking at it and trying to figure out how it worked—and especially how to make it better.

That poking often took part during our sparring sessions. In addition to training with our stormswords, Kyrion and I had also been testing out each other's psionic abilities. He tried to access my seer magic, while I attempted to do the same with his telekinesis, but neither one of us had any consistent success. Our lack of progress frustrated us both, but on the bright side, our sparring sessions usually ended with us working out that mutual frustration by rolling around on the mat, kissing, and yanking each other's clothes off as fast as possible.

I cared about Kyrion, and he cared about me. I could *feel* it through the bond. Our physical chemistry was amazing, as was the sex. But did he love me? Did I love him? In the weeks we'd been on board the *Dream World*, neither one of us had mentioned the word *love*. If we *did* love each other, had it all only happened because of the bond? And would all our feelings and potential love vanish if the bond was broken?

Despite my emotional spiraling down an ever-deepening hole of doubt, I was exhausted from the fight with the bounty hunters, and I fell asleep quickly and didn't hear anything until late the next morning. Kyrion had already gotten up, as was his custom, leaving me to sleep in, since I despised getting out of bed before it was absolutely necessary. Another bit of thoughtfulness on his part, which made me care about him even more.

I took a hot shower to soothe away the last of yesterday's aches and pains. Then I donned some fresh clothes, went to the flight deck, and slid into the copilot's seat next to Kyrion.

"You're just in time," he said, sweeping his hand out at the planet in the distance. "Welcome to Sygnustern."

Relief coursed through me. We should be, well, not completely safe, but *safer* on the Erzton-controlled planet. Holloway couldn't officially send any Arrows and Imperium soldiers here, and I doubted many bounty hunters were looking for us this far from Imperium-controlled space.

"Why does it look so . . . gray?" I asked.

"Apparently, there are lots of mountains, lots of clouds, and lots of fog," Kyrion replied, swiping through a few holograms.

Unlike Tropics planets, which often sparkled like jewels with their aquamarine seas and verdant green rain forests, Sygnustern resembled a dull gray stone suspended in the black ocean of space. The lack of colors was disappointing, but something about the planet made me uneasy, although I couldn't put my finger on exactly what it was.

"What do you think will happen once we get down there?"

Kyrion shrugged. "No idea. Despite all my Arrow missions, I've never visited the Erzton home planet. It's not forbidden, though. Many Regals travel to Sygnustern for business and pleasure."

"Is Asterin still supposed to meet us at her workshop?"

Our friend had suggested we rendezvous there so that she could escort us to the estate owned by her stepfather and mother,

Aldrich and Verona Collier, who were among the leaders of the Erzton. I wasn't sure why Asterin didn't want us going directly to the Collier estate. Maybe it was some Erzton social rule about not showing up uninvited. Or maybe she didn't want to give the Colliers any advance warning that we were coming so they wouldn't have time to figure out how to politely turn down our request for sanctuary.

Kyrion tapped a holoscreen. "Yes. I just confirmed the location and copied everything to your tablet. With Asterin advocating for us, the Colliers should offer us asylum from the Imperium and Holloway."

"And if they don't?"

Kyrion tensed. We'd both asked this question more than once during the last few weeks, and neither one of us had a concrete answer.

"If the Colliers won't shelter us, then we'll find someplace else to stay," Kyrion replied.

His voice was steady, but a muscle twitched in his jaw, and the sticky cobweb in my mind vibrated with worry. We were risking everything by asking the Colliers for refuge. If things didn't work out, we might very well end up captured, dead, or worse.

But I had another reason for coming to Sygnustern: to learn more about truebonds. According to Asterin, truebonds were not uncommon among her people, and Aldrich and Verona Collier had such a connection. I was hoping the couple might give Kyrion and me some insight into how to master our own abilities.

"Are you ready?" Kyrion asked.

"Now or never, right?" I drawled, trying to make my voice light and cheerful.

The corners of his mouth crooked up into a grin, and some of the worry eased out of the bond. "Now or never, and tried and true."

Kyrion set a course for the planet. As the surface zoomed closer, I stared out the windows, wondering if Sygnustern would really be the safe harbor Asterin claimed—or if new dangers and enemies were waiting for us on the planet.

Kyrion punched in the coordinates for a public spaceport, and the blitzer descended. He had been right about the clouds, which quickly enveloped the ship in a thick layer of white. We sat in silence as the blitzer dropped lower . . . and lower . . . and lower . . .

Finally, the clouds thinned out and wisped away, revealing the planet's surface.

Mountains stretched out in all directions, each rocky peak higher and more jagged than the last. Snow capped many of the peaks before giving way to dense forests of gray coniferous trees that jutted up like arrows covering the steep slopes.

Massive waterfalls gushed down many of the mountains, sending up constant sprays of mist. The late morning sun hit the tumbling waters at just the right angles, creating shimmering rainbows that arced from one peak to another. Some of the waterfalls ended in crystal-blue lakes that pooled in the bottoms of the valleys, but some sprays of water plummeted so far down they vanished into the shadows.

The blitzer curved to the right, and a large city loomed into view, sprawling across at least ten different mountain peaks—Gewitter, the capital city of Sygnustern and the seat of Erzton power.

An enormous dome made of different colors of permaglass perched atop the highest mountain peak. A clear spire twirled up from the center of the dome, stretching high enough to tickle the bottoms of the clouds. Similar smaller domes glinted atop the other mountains, as well as farther down on the enormous flat plains that had been carved into the slopes.

The permaglass domes were all deep, rich, vibrant shades—

sapphire blue, amethyst purple, ruby red, emerald green—and they glittered like precious jewels just waiting to be plucked out of the surrounding gray stone. Shops and homes made of permaglass, stone, and wood clustered around the domes before spreading out and running down the slopes.

Gigantic gondolas that were bigger than some spaceships cruised along thick metal cables that connected one mountain to another, along with wide bridges crowded with people. I also spotted a few chairlifts that seemed to be a more private—or maybe riskier—method of transportation, since only a few people were using them.

Many of the gondolas, bridges, and lifts crossed over chasms that were thousands of feet deep, but no one seemed concerned that they could plummet to their death should any of the cables and support beams fail. A few small transports also zipped through the air, moving much faster than the lumbering gondolas and churning chairlifts.

"Not what you were expecting from a Temperate planet?" Kyrion asked. "Given how gray it looks from space?"

"Most of the Temperate planets I've visited have been covered with more buildings than mountains. It's not as breathtakingly beautiful as a Tropics planet, but it's pretty in its own way."

Kyrion flipped the switches to engage the autopilot, then hit a button to start the landing sequence. The blitzer glided down past the gondolas and bridges and docked without any problems. The small spaceport looked like any other—a functional, no-frills building surrounded by rows of docking slots—but cold unease trickled down my spine.

I pulled out my tablet and told Asterin we had arrived, although I didn't mention where we had landed. Despite Asterin's assurances that Kyrion and I would be safe on Sygnustern, I didn't want to put our friend in the awkward position of having to reveal the ship's location to the Erzton authorities in case things went wrong.

Asterin messaged me. *Glad you're here. No mention of you or Kyrion on the local gossipcasts. Waiting at my workshop. See you soon.*

I showed the message to Kyrion, then we left the flight deck and headed to the cargo bay. Kyrion handed me a large duffel bag, then took one for himself, and we both grabbed clothes and other supplies.

Kyrion belted his stormsword to his waist and nestled his blaster into a holster on his right thigh. He also slid a fresh solar magazine into the Techwave cannon so that it was functional again.

Kyrion added a few magazines to his silver bandolier, then tucked the Techwave cannon into the bottom of his duffel bag. I slid my stormsword into a slot on my weapons belt, along with a small blaster.

According to our tablets, the temperature was on the chilly side, so we both donned long gray cloaks over our regular clothes to keep warm and hide our weapons. I'd used up all my supplies making my disguise on Tropics 44, so Kyrion and I couldn't change our hair or eye color, and plastipaper noses and scars would probably freeze to our faces. I didn't like leaving the ship without some sort of disguise, but we didn't have a choice.

We hoisted our duffel bags onto our shoulders.

"You ready?" Kyrion asked.

"Now or never." I repeated my quip from earlier, but this time, he didn't grin back at me.

Kyrion hit a green button on the wall, and the cargo-bay ramp lowered. "Standard operating procedure. If anything feels off, we retreat to the ship and leave."

We strode down to the ground, and then Kyrion hit some buttons on his tablet, raising the ramp and engaging the ship's defensive shield.

The wind slapped me in the face, stinging my cheeks and

whipping my hair around my shoulders. The air was bitingly cold, with a faint metallic tang that hinted that snow was on the way. Even though Sygnustern was a Temperate planet and it was technically late summer, the mountains were high enough that wintry weather was always a possibility. I shivered and tucked my chin down into the top of my cloak, trying to find some extra warmth.

Several other ships had also landed at the spaceport, and we fell in with a line of people entering the main building. Kyrion and I both pulled out our tablets and showed our fake IDs as we moved from one checkpoint to another. Kyrion was masquerading as Baron Christian Alejandro Rowell Evanston, while I was his wife, Baroness Sophie-Anne Parker Linley Evanston.

I held my breath every time a guard scanned our tablets, but the lights flashed green one after another, and the guards waved us forward with bored looks. I sent a silent thanks to Daichi, who had created the new fake IDs. Daichi's work was always impeccable, even if he had given me and Kyrion long, outrageous names taken from the romance serials he watched.

We exited the spaceport and stepped into a busy area filled with transports. Most people had their heads down, their eyes fixed on their tablets, as they hurried toward their next destination, but several folks were lined up along a permaglass railing, taking photos and videos of the stunning views of the surrounding mountains.

Kyrion and I headed in that direction. He pulled out his tablet, pretending to take photos while he scanned the crowd, looking for threats. I used my own tablet to plot a route to the rendezvous coordinates.

"We're supposed to meet Asterin on that mountain." I pointed at a peak directly opposite this one. "Want to try a bridge? Walking might be quicker than taking a gondola."

Kyrion peered over the side of the railing. His face took on a slightly greenish tint, his stomach gurgled, and the sticky cobweb in my mind bristled with unease.

My eyebrows lifted in surprise. "Don't tell me the great Kyrion Caldaren, one of the most notorious killers and feared warriors in all the galaxy, is afraid of heights."

Kyrion straightened up and peered down his nose at me, morphing into the arrogant Regal lord and deadly Arrow I knew so well. "I am *not* afraid of heights. Merely of plummeting to my death from them."

I laughed and threaded my arm through his. A reluctant grin crooked his lips, and he bent down so that his mouth was close to my ear.

"No matter what happens, I'm glad I'm here with you, Vesper," Kyrion said in a low, husky voice.

Emotion clogged my throat, and it took me a moment to respond. "Me too."

Arm in arm, we followed the signs to the nearest gondola station, bought tickets, and climbed on board. Unlike gondolas I had seen on other planets, which were only single cars, this one featured several cars all linked together like a train so passengers could move back and forth between the compartments.

We found some seats in the corner and put our backs to the glass. Several folks eyed us, and my heart rose in my throat, matching the gondola's slow motion. Had someone recognized us?

Across the aisle, a little girl tugged on her mother's sleeve. "Mama, why are their clothes so dull?"

"Shhh!" the mother hissed, shooting us an apologetic look. "Remember, we don't comment on what outsiders wear."

Dull clothes? Outsiders? I glanced around the gondola car. Everyone was bundled up in thick coats or cloaks, along with hats, scarves, and gloves, but Kyrion and I were the only people dressed in dark, drab gray. Everyone else was sporting the same jewel-toned colors as the permaglass domes that topped the mountains. Intricate patterns were also woven into the bright, cheerful fabrics, everything from snowflakes and icicles to cursive letters to hammers, axes, and other tools. Not patterns—sigils, just like the ones the Regals used to distinguish their Houses.

Kyrion and I had wanted to blend in, but our plain clothes made us stick out.

"So much for going incognito," he muttered.

I grimaced, but there was nothing we could do. Not wearing the cloaks would make us even more noticeable, given the chilly temperature.

A few more folks stared at us, but most people focused on either their tablets or the amazing views as the gondola quickly, smoothly climbed over to the neighboring mountain.

Fifteen minutes later, the gondola glided into its station, and the doors slid back. Once again, Kyrion and I fell in with the flow of people. Unlike the section in front of the spaceport, which was clearly for travelers, this was part of the actual city of Gewitter. Most folks were walking to their destination, but some zipped by on vehicles that were a cross between hoverbikes and snowmobiles. Several horse-drawn carriages decked out with silver bells jingle-jangled merrily over the cobblestones, with the passengers in the open-air vehicles wrapped up in blankets to ward off the cold.

I checked my tablet. Still no warnings from Asterin, so I called up the rendezvous coordinates again and pointed to the left. "Asterin's workshop is that way."

"Let's go," Kyrion said, his gaze flicking back and forth, studying everyone around us. "The sooner we get there, the better."

We walked along the main street, skirting around the throngs of people clustered around the busy shops, which were selling everything from clothes and shoes to real paper books and stationery to mouthwatering scones and cakes. Many of the shops were also filled with long glass cases, which contained hunks of stone and chunks of wood resting on white velvet trays.

"Mineral exchanges," Kyrion explained, seeing my curious looks. "Along with wood, stone, and other raw resources. Dealers put out samples of their products so customers can see what quality and grade of materials are available and decide how much to bid on them."

The Erzton controlled hundreds of planets and moons rich in raw resources, and they were always searching for more, just like the Imperium was constantly looking for psionic outliers to add to the Regal Houses and bloodlines. Back at Quill Corp, I'd received dozens of memos about the materials the production plants needed to buy from the Erzton, but those had been abstract numbers, so it was fascinating to see how the process worked here on Sygnustern.

Kyrion and I turned a corner and stepped onto a much quieter side street that led to a massive dome that rose hundreds of feet into the air. The dome was made of enormous panels of emerald-green permaglass connected by thick seams of gold and smaller gold bolts, like it was a giant tortoise shell. *Antiques Emporium* was painted in gold in an elegant cursive script on a dark green wooden sign.

"Asterin's workshop is on the other side of the dome," I said, sliding my tablet back into my pocket.

Kyrion nodded. "Let's cut through the emporium. It should be quicker than going around."

The double doors were open, so we entered the building. A wide corridor circled around the entire dome, so we crossed it and went through another set of open doors. My breath caught in my throat, and Kyrion stopped beside me, his wonder rippling through the bond.

From the outside, the permaglass had looked green, but inside it was clear and offered a magnificent view of the surrounding mountains. More clouds cloaked the sky, and a few flakes of snow were drifting down, making it seem as though Kyrion and I were inside an oversize snow globe.

Thick cables dangled like golden icicles from the curved ceiling, each one ending in a bright golden bulb shaped like a four-pointed star. A much larger, longer green glass spike dropped down from the center of the ceiling like an enormous stalactite. Gold seams glowing with light ribboned around the spike's jagged edges and glittering, sparkling facets.

My gaze flicked from the seams to the spike and then up along the curve of the dome. My seer magic kicked in, highlighting each section in a soft silver flare and showing me how they all worked together. The gold seams and green glass might look pretty, but they had a much more practical purpose: they were solar wiring and panels that provided energy, light, and heat for the structure. Impressive.

Aisle after aisle ran from this end of the dome all the way to the other far in the distance, as well as from side to side. Booths, tables, and carts lined the aisles, along with shelves, bookcases, and glass curio cabinets that held a wide variety of objects: books, clothes, tools, dishes, weapons, even some old brewmakers and other appliances. Almost all the items were made of real stone, wood, and glass, instead of the polyplastic versions I was used to. Some of the items had obviously been well used, but many gleamed as if they had never even been touched.

"I've heard about places like this," I murmured to Kyrion as we strode down one of the smaller aisles. "Places where people buy things that are old instead of new."

He nodded. "The Erzton is much more environmentally conscious than the Imperium. The Erztonians reuse and recycle as many items for as long as possible, whereas the Regals are always throwing out the old in favor of the newest invention."

We moved deeper into the antiques emporium. Several people were browsing through the goods, but no one gave us a second look, as they were all focused on finding whatever hidden treasure they were searching for.

"Touma would love this place," Kyrion said.

A smile curved my lips. Touma Hirano was Daichi's uncle, a spelltech who dabbled in all sorts of illegal things. Touma had a cluttered workshop on Corios that was stuffed from top to bottom with odds and ends. If the spelltech were here, he would be rubbing his hands together in glee and flitting from one booth to the next, searching for the perfect parts and pieces to take back to his workshop.

The smile faded from my lips, and guilt bubbled up in my chest like a Magma volcano about to erupt. No, that was wrong. Touma couldn't go back to his workshop, just like I couldn't return to Quill Corp. The spelltech had helped us escape from Crownpoint, and now he was a wanted fugitive, the same as Kyrion and me.

"There's an open space in the middle of the dome up ahead," Kyrion said. "We'll have to cross it to reach the other side."

I shook off my guilty thoughts, and we headed in that direction.

As we moved deeper into the antiques emporium, the shoppers thinned out, the murmurs of conversation vanished, and an eerie quiet cloaked the air. A finger of cold unease slid down my spine. Maybe I was being paranoid, but I felt like someone was watching us—

*Ding!*

A soft chime shattered the quiet. A woman looking through a display of books pulled out her tablet. She glanced at the message, then looked around. Her gaze landed on us. For a moment, she froze, then her eyes widened, and she scurried around the far side of the booth, moving away from us.

Kyrion quickened his steps, and I hurried to keep up with his long strides.

"Someone knows we're here," he said in a low voice, his

gaze sweeping from side to side. "We need to get out of this building."

I pulled out my tablet and messaged Asterin, saying we had been spotted. My tablet dinged almost immediately with a response.

*On my way!*

I slid my tablet back into my pocket. Asterin might get here in time to help us, but we couldn't count on it.

Kyrion and I walked even faster. This aisle opened into the wide, circular space in the very center of the dome, directly underneath the green solar spike. Up close, it was even more beautiful, and the sharp, gold-pointed tip was only about a hundred feet above our heads.

Kyrion and I stepped into the open space. No one was browsing through the surrounding aisles. The silence was more eerie and absolute than before, but my seer magic kept whispering a warning that we weren't alone.

Kyrion pushed his cloak back, revealing his stormsword. His hand clenched around the silver hilt, which featured small carvings of stars, eyes, and arrows clustered around a large sapphsidian jewel shaped like the House Caldaren sigil arrow. Curls of silver stretched out in opposite directions to form the weapon's crossguard, while other pieces of silver snaked up and wrapped around the base of the lunarium blade.

"No matter what happens, if you see a chance to escape, take it," he said.

"No," I growled. "I'm not leaving you. I will *never* leave you."

Warmth sparked in Kyrion's eyes. The same heat rippled through the bond, but it was quickly followed by a wave of stubbornness. He opened his mouth to argue—

Soft footsteps rasped against the gray stone floor, and a woman rounded a curio cabinet, strode forward, and stopped in front of us on the opposite side of the circular center space.

The woman was our age, late thirties, with light brown skin and long black hair sleeked up into a ponytail. Bright green shadow and liner rimmed her hazel eyes, while pale gold gloss covered her lips. She was wearing an emerald-green tactical jacket over a matching shirt and cargo pants, along with thick black work boots. A delicate gold pendant shaped like a cursive *C* with two hammers crossed in front of it dangled from a thin gold chain around her neck.

But the most eye-catching thing about the woman was the weapon in her right hand. The long gold hilt was topped with a large piece of lunarium that had a familiar shape—a flat hammer head on one side and a sharp, wicked-looking spike on the other. The war hammer was similar to those Pollux had used during the junkyard fight.

My stomach twisted with worry. Was this woman another corporate mercenary?

"She's a Hammer," Kyrion muttered. "I recognize her face from Holloway's files."

The woman hoisted her war hammer up onto her shoulder. Sparks flickered and shimmered deep inside the lunarium, and the weapon started glowing a soft, pale green. Not just a Hammer but also a psion.

Footsteps sounded behind us, and Kyrion and I both spun to the side. Several more people appeared, all clutching war hammers and wearing the same green uniform as the woman. The Hammers formed a loose circle, then stopped and studied us with hostile expressions. My heart sank into the choppy sea of worry churning in my stomach.

We were surrounded.

# PART TWO

## REUNIONS

# EIGHT

## KYRION

I tightened my grip on my stormsword and studied one Hammer after another, trying to find any weaknesses among them.

The men and women all clutched their weapons with easy familiarity, and many of them also had blasters and shock batons holstered to their belts. The lunarium heads on their war hammers all glowed with pale, colorful lights, indicating that each warrior had some sort of psion power. I was willing to bet many of them also had speed, strength, and other enhancements that would make them even more deadly.

In addition to the woman who had first approached us, I recognized several of the warriors' faces from Holloway's files. The Hammers eyed me in return, their hard, calculating gazes flicking from my face to my sword. I hadn't drawn the weapon—yet. I didn't want to kill these people, but I would do it to protect Vesper.

"Bond of two," Vesper called out. "Tried and true."

Asterin had told us to say the code phrase to any Hammers

we met on Sygnustern. Supposedly, the phrase would guarantee us safety on any Erzton-controlled planet, but the Hammers didn't bat an eye at Vesper's words, and none of them lowered their weapons.

"Bond of two, tried and true," Vesper repeated, her voice louder and sharper. Her hand crept over to her stormsword, and worry rippled along the velvety ribbon of her in my mind.

Several more seconds ticked by in cold, contemplative silence, and I used the tense lull to strategize. I would attack the man to my left. His war hammer wasn't glowing nearly as brightly as those of the other warriors, which meant he was weaker in his psion power. If I could cut him down, Vesper could sprint down an empty aisle while I kept the rest of the warriors from chasing after her.

The woman who had first confronted us stepped forward. "I am Siya, head of the House Collier Hammers." She stabbed her weapon at us. "And you are trespassing."

Vesper lifted her chin and gave the other woman a cool look. "We were invited here by Lady Asterin Armas. She's part of House Collier too, is she not?"

Siya's lips puckered into a sour expression, and red-hot anger surged off her and tweaked my telempathy. She was not fond of Asterin, which was a problem for us.

"Not only are you trespassing," Siya continued, "but you also gave false names and a phony ship registration to the guards at the spaceport. No one is allowed to land in House Collier territory with fake credentials."

A low, mocking laugh tumbled out of Siya's mouth. "As if our scanners wouldn't recognize Lady Vesper Quill and Lord Kyrion Caldaren, the two most wanted people in the Archipelago Galaxy. We might not be obsessed with the Regal gossipcasts, but how stupid do you think we are?"

Siya's gaze flicked over to me, and even more anger sparked

in her hazel eyes. She liked me even less than she liked Asterin. Fantastic.

I searched my memory, wondering if I had ever come across Siya before, but I would have remembered meeting her. Unlike the Arrows, many of whom loved to share their exploits on the gossipcasts, the Hammers kept a much lower profile. Even Holloway's spies didn't know much about the Hammers, their members, or their inner workings. But then again, the only thing anyone really needed to know was not to fuck with them.

Siya stabbed her war hammer at us again. "Surrender your weapons, so you can be taken into custody and returned to the Imperium where you belong."

Vesper and I both tensed. We couldn't afford to let the Hammers take us into custody, much less ship us back to the Imperium.

"You didn't finish your threat," I said in a cold voice. "Surrender your weapons or . . ."

Siya shrugged. "Or die where you stand."

The other Hammers shifted on their feet. Their weapons remained up and steady, but some of them looked a little less certain and confident. I might despise the gossipcasts, but sometimes it was good to have a reputation as a ruthless killer.

*You have that look on your face*, Vesper's voice sounded in my mind.

*What look?* I asked, although I never took my eyes off Siya.

*The look that says you are about to kill everyone who gets in your way. It's terrifying.* She paused. *And kind of hot.*

The velvety ribbon of her vibrated with a mixture of amusement, worry, and a thread of desire that made my inner monster preen like a Tropics tiger having its back scratched. Vesper's emotions also hardened my own determination. We had come here seeking shelter, but, if necessary, I would paint the entire dome with the Hammers' blood.

I slid my duffel bag off my shoulder and set it on the floor.

Then I drew my stormsword out of its slot and twirled the weapon around in my hand. The lunarium shimmered with a dark blue light, and bits of ice spewed out of the blade in an eerie match to the snow still falling outside the dome.

Siya's knuckles went white against the gold hilt of her hammer. "Last chance. Surrender peacefully, or suffer the consequences."

"Surrender?" Vesper hissed. "And let you ship us back to the Imperium? Hard pass."

Vesper dropped her duffel bag and drew her own stormsword. Flashes of fire smoked up into the air instead of the ice my blade was spitting out, but her sword glowed with the same dark blue light as my weapon.

"Damn," one of the Hammers muttered. "They really *do* have a truebond."

"That's right," Vesper hissed again. "So maybe you want to rethink your hostility before Kyrion and I cut you all to pieces."

"Big talk for someone who's only been training with that sword for a few months," Siya taunted.

Surprise flickered across Vesper's face.

"Oh, yes," Siya drawled. "I've seen your gossipcast interviews, so I know all about you, Lady Vesper, including the fact that you aren't *nearly* the warrior you pretend to be."

More fire smoked up out of the lunarium blade, but an odd, uneasy emotion pulsed off Vesper. Was that . . . doubt? Why would Vesper be doubting her abilities as a warrior? She'd made amazing progress in the months she'd been training.

"You're right," Vesper replied, a bitter note creeping into her voice. "I haven't been training with my stormsword long, so I guess it's a good thing I've had some excellent teachers." She gestured at me. "Like him. Unless you are doubting Kyrion Caldaren? Because that would be an extremely stupid thing to do."

Once again, some of the Hammers shifted on their feet. Vesper's unwavering confidence and trust made my inner monster purr in satisfaction.

Vesper kept glaring at Siya. "So maybe *you* should think about surrendering."

"Not a bloody chance," Siya snarled back.

"Your loss." Vesper's face hardened. "And your death."

My inner monster purred again, this time with delight, and I couldn't stop myself from grinning. *You have a look on your face too.*

*What look?* Vesper growled.

*The look that says you are about to come up with some invention, solution, or clever trick to kill everyone who gets in your way. It's terrifying.* I paused. *And kind of hot.*

Vesper's laugh sounded in my mind. *We really are a matched pair, aren't we?*

My grin widened. *Absolutely. Cold, cruel, and murderous to the core—and I wouldn't have it any other way.*

Vesper grinned back at me, and the silver flecks in her dark blue eyes sparked with heat and desire. *Me neither.*

I faced our enemies again. "This is your last warning. Let us leave, and no one has to get hurt."

Siya shook her head. "I can't do that, Arrow."

She lifted her hammer into an attack position. I lifted my sword in response and stepped forward, putting myself between Vesper and Siya.

Once again, that cold, contemplative silence dropped over the dome, and the only sounds were the crackles of fire spewing out of Vesper's stormsword and the bits of ice spitting out of mine.

"Attack!" Siya yelled.

I was already moving before the word left her lips. I charged straight at the Hammer and swung my sword at her as hard as I could.

Perhaps it was a quirk of my imagination or a surge of Vesper's seer power, but for an instant, time slowed down, even as everything around me came into super-sharp focus. Siya narrowing her eyes. The green glow of her psion power intensifying on her war hammer. Her weapon rising to meet mine . . .

Without warning, time snapped back to its normal flow. Siya blocked my attack, and my sword glanced off the side of her hammer.

I whirled around for another strike, but Siya was already moving to attack. I dodged her vicious blow, and then, before she could recover, I snapped up my hand and used my telekinesis to throw her back into two other Hammers. All three of them tumbled to the floor.

A bright glow flickered at the corner of my vision, and I spun in that direction. Vesper stabbed out with her sword, making one Hammer scramble back to avoid getting his guts sliced open, but she didn't see another warrior coming up on her blind side.

*Vesper! Behind you!*

I called out a warning with my telepathy, but she didn't respond.

*Vesper! Vesper, behind you!*

She kept attacking the man in front of her instead of turning to deal with the other warrior. I called out for a third time, but all I heard was my own frantic voice, and the velvety ribbon of Vesper went cold and dark, like a candle flame abruptly snuffed out by a winter wind.

Frustration and dread shot through me. Why couldn't I feel her anymore? Was something wrong with our bond?

Siya scrambled to her feet, darted forward, and raised her hammer for another strike. I could block her blow, or I could protect Vesper.

I chose Vesper.

I lowered my sword, leaving myself open to an attack, and

rushed toward Vesper. Siya growled, leaped toward me, and slammed her war hammer into my right shoulder.

Pain exploded in my joint. Shards of ice spewed out of the lunarium weapon and pelted my body, and my entire arm went cold and numb. My stormsword slipped from my nerveless fingers and skittered across the floor, but I staggered forward, gritted my teeth, and kept going.

The man on Vesper's blind side lifted his hammer to hit her. I put on another burst of speed and slammed into the man, knocking him away from Vesper before he could strike her.

The two of us crashed into a booth at the end of one of the aisles. Wood broke, glass shattered, and bits of metal pinged across the floor as our combined weight destroyed the booth and the goods inside.

The Hammer cursed and tried to extricate himself from all the antiques we had just smashed. I jabbed my left elbow into his throat, making him wheeze.

Vesper whirled around, her eyes going wide. "Kyr! Look out!"

Siya was once again storming in my direction. Her lunarium hammer was glowing an even brighter green, and more ice was spewing out of the weapon, along with sharp crackles of wind.

I scrambled to my feet, but the wheezing warrior grabbed my ankle, throwing me off-balance. Siya snarled and raised her weapon high.

But Vesper darted forward, put her shoulder down, and rammed into Siya, and both women toppled to the floor, sliding across the slick stone.

My right arm was still numb and useless, so I snapped my left hand out and reached for my telekinesis. My stormsword zipped up off the floor and flew past two more Hammers, making the warriors yelp and lurch out of the way.

My sword settled in my palm. I wasn't as skilled with my left hand, but I slashed the weapon down. The still-wheezing

Hammer released my ankle and rolled out of the way of the whistling blade.

Vesper and Siya both surged to their feet and snapped up their weapons, circling each other. I hobbled forward and once again put myself between Vesper and the other warrior—

"Enough!" a voice yelled. "That is *enough*!"

A woman darted into the open space between me and Siya. I pulled up short to keep from hitting her, as did Siya.

Unlike the Hammers in their green uniforms, this woman was wearing dark gray coveralls and black work boots. A silver blaster dangled from her belt, along with a matching hammer, but it was a small, delicate instrument, like a jeweler's tool. Her long black hair was piled into a messy bun, and dirt streaked across her pale face.

Lady Asterin Armas slapped her hands on her hips, making dust puff off her coveralls. She glared at Siya, her silver eyes bright with anger.

The leader of the Hammers scowled at Asterin, but she made no further move to attack Vesper or me. The other Hammers also held their positions, and the warriors who had been knocked down quickly got to their feet.

Another round of silence descended over the dome. Asterin glanced at Siya, then Vesper, and finally me. Once she realized we weren't going to start fighting again, Asterin swung her angry gaze back to Siya.

"Lady Vesper and Lord Kyrion are here by my invitation," she snapped. "You had no right to try to detain them, much less attack them!"

Siya matched Asterin's hot glower with one of her own. "I serve House Collier, not you, Asterin. And you do *not* speak for House Collier."

Asterin's hands dropped to her sides and clenched into fists, and she looked like she wanted to punch the other woman.

I didn't know much about Erzton Houses and politics, but

Asterin's mother, Verona, was married to Aldrich Collier, the head of House Collier. That relationship alone should have afforded Asterin a place of honor and respect, but Siya clearly didn't see it that way.

Asterin hissed out a breath, making a visible effort to get her emotions under control. "It doesn't matter whether I speak for House Collier. Vesper and Kyrion have a truebond. Did they say the phrase?"

A faint grimace crossed Siya's face.

"So they *did* say the phrase, and you chose to ignore their plea." Asterin slapped her hands on her hips again, making more dust puff off her coveralls. "Despite the fact that it is a House Collier edict to offer sanctuary to any couple who has a truebond. Looks like you don't speak for House Collier either. At least not when it comes to the rules."

A muscle twitched in Siya's jaw, and an angry flush stained her cheeks a vivid pink. "You want to talk about House Collier edicts? Then perhaps you and I should settle our differences the old-fashioned way, according to House rules. Unless you've forgotten your combat training while you've been off gallivanting through the Imperium."

"Maybe we should," Asterin replied in a cold voice. "I'd be more than happy to knock some of that self-righteousness out of you."

Someone deliberately cleared their throat, more footsteps sounded, and a man stepped up next to Asterin. He was in his fifties, with light brown hair, ruddy skin, and a short, stocky body that was all muscle. He was dressed in an emerald-green tactical jacket, shirt, and cargo pants, just like Siya was, but his clothes were covered with grime, just like Asterin's were. His right hand rested on the war hammer dangling from his belt, and all the other Hammers nodded in deference to him.

I recognized the man. Rigel, an Erztonian who'd attended some Regal balls on Corios with Asterin.

Rigel's dark brown gaze flicked back and forth between Siya and Asterin. "Siya is right," he said in a calm voice. "Asterin does not speak for House Collier."

He shot Asterin an apologetic look. Asterin's face remained blank, but a sharp spike of hurt shot off her and tweaked my telempathy.

Rigel focused on Siya again. "But Asterin is also right. Anyone with a truebond is to be offered sanctuary, according to House Collier rules. As soon as they said the phrase, you should have stood down immediately."

Siya wilted a little under Rigel's cool, steady gaze, and she lowered her weapon. "Fine," she muttered. "We'll continue our patrol."

She jerked her head, and the other Hammers also lowered their weapons. Siya shot me and Vesper one more angry look, along with Asterin, then stepped into one of the aisles. The other Hammers followed her, and they all vanished.

Asterin massaged her temples, as though she had a raging headache, then dropped her hands. "Sorry about that. Siya takes her position as the head of security for House Collier very seriously."

I snorted. That was an understatement.

Rigel cleared his throat again. "Siya is probably informing Lord and Lady Collier about the . . . situation right now. You should escort Lady Vesper and Lord Kyrion to the estate without further delay."

Asterin grimaced, clearly not liking his suggestion, but she nodded. "Rigel is right. I know you've had a long journey and would like to rest." She paused and glanced at my arm. "And get some medical attention."

"I'm fine," I growled.

The numb sensation had finally faded from my fingers, although I probably already had a wicked bruise from where Siya had hit me with her hammer. A skinbond injector from my bandolier would take care of that—later. Right now, I didn't want to show any sign of weakness.

Vesper speared me with a hard look. *You are most definitely not* fine. *I can* feel *how much your arm is throbbing through the bond.*

I quickly walled off the pain behind a psionic shield so it wouldn't keep rippling through the bond to her. *I've had worse. Besides, we need to be careful. Asterin might be a friend, but Siya is not.*

I nodded at Asterin. "I appreciate your concern, but truly, I'm fine. I'm just glad you and Rigel intervened."

"Part of my job is to keep Lady Asterin out of trouble," Rigel said in a dry, sardonic tone. "Along with her friends."

On Corios, I had dismissed Rigel as Asterin's social handler, a glorified bodyguard, but he was clearly much more than that.

"Yes, thank you, Rigel. I appreciate you talking some sense into Siya. You're the only one who can." Asterin muttered the last few words.

A wry smile curved Rigel's lips. "As I said before, it's my job to keep you out of trouble." His smile vanished. "Although someday, you and Siya are going to have to resolve your differences."

Asterin huffed. "There's about as much chance of that happening as there is of the moon dropping out of the sky."

Rigel shrugged, as if he agreed with her sentiment, then strode away.

Asterin watched him go with a pensive expression, then jerked her head to the side. "Come. Let's get you two to the estate."

She headed toward the front of the dome, in the opposite direction from Rigel, Siya, and the other Hammers. Vesper slid her stormsword onto her belt, grabbed her duffel bag, and followed our friend.

I did the same thing, but my gaze moved from one aisle to

the next. I didn't see any of the Hammers, but a presence tickled my telempathy. Siya was still here somewhere, watching us.

Once we'd reached Sygnustern, I'd thought—hoped—we might be able to take a breath, rest, and recuperate while we plotted our next course of action. But once again, I had the uneasy feeling we were surrounded by far more enemies than allies.

# NINE

## VESPER

Kyrion and I trailed Asterin out of the antiques emporium. A horse-drawn carriage was waiting on the street. Asterin climbed into one side of the open-air carriage, while Kyrion and I slid into the opposite seat.

Asterin signaled the driver, who whistled softly. The horse bobbed its head in response, and the silver bells on its collar and harness jingled out a cheerful tune as the carriage rolled along the cobblestone street.

Asterin hit a button on the side of the door, and small metal tubes popped up around the perimeter of the carriage. The tubes were a little longer than my fingers and featured holes that made them look like old-fashioned flutes. A faint purr sounded, and warm air wafted out of the tubes, creating a cozy bubble over the three of us.

Asterin slumped back against her seat. "I'm so sorry. I was hoping if you came to my workshop first, you could avoid running into Siya. As soon as I got your message, I left my workshop, but of course, Rigel and I were too late to stop Siya from doing, well, what Siya *always* does."

"Trying to solve problems with her war hammer?" Kyrion drawled. "Believe me, I noticed."

Asterin's gaze flicked to his injured arm. Kyrion waved his hand, dismissing her concern, but guilt still creased her face.

"Who is she to you?" Kyrion asked. "And how much trouble is she going to cause us?"

Asterin's grimace deepened. "Siya is the daughter of my stepfather, Aldrich Collier. When we were children, Siya and I were the best of friends, until . . ."

Her voice trailed off, and a distant look filled her eyes as though she was seeing something far, far away. Asterin let out a long, tired sigh and focused on us again.

"Don't worry about Siya. My stepfather has the final say on House Collier matters, not her. Aldrich has seen the gossipcast footage of the Regal midnight ball, and he knows about the bounty Callus Holloway has offered for your capture. I'm sure once he meets you, he'll offer you sanctuary."

Kyrion and I glanced at each other. We could both hear the doubt in Asterin's voice, but all we could do now was hope for the best.

Asterin gave us a bright smile and assumed the role of tour guide, pointing out clothing shops, sweets stores, and more. Kyrion listened to her politely, although his gaze kept flicking from one side of the street to the other as he searched for threats. I couldn't fault the Arrow for his vigilance, but Asterin was clearly trying to take our minds off our troubles, so I played along and started asking her questions about the various landmarks.

In many ways, the city of Gewitter was similar to Corios—wide cobblestone streets, colorful buildings with quirky architecture, scores of luxury goods for sale. But unlike the chrome façades and polyplastic coatings on many Corios structures, almost every building here was made of real stone, wood, and glass in a reflection of the raw resources the Erzton controlled. Add in the views of the surrounding mountains and the flakes of snow drifting down from the sky, and it all combined to give Gewitter a quaint, old-fashioned air, as though I had stepped into some long-ago holiday story.

The driver stopped to let another carriage cross in front of us, and my gaze snagged on a building at the end of a nearby side street. Unlike all the other shops with their immaculate, gleaming storefronts, a rusty metal fence cordoned off this building.

"What's that?" I asked.

"An old mining museum that sits atop a series of caverns, along with Stardrop Falls, an underground waterfall. It used to be a popular tourist attraction, but it's been closed for quite a while." Asterin's nose scrunched up in thought. "Years ago, there was an accident. I was off-planet at university at the time, but from what I remember, a young man fell off a bridge beside the waterfall and died. After that, the whole facility was shut down."

The other vehicle moved out of the way. The driver whistled to the horse, and our carriage rolled forward again. Asterin gestured at another building, pointing out the gargoyles on the stone structure, but I glanced over my shoulder at the closed museum.

For a moment, the barred windows glimmered with a silver sheen, winking at me like tall, skinny eyes. I squinted, but I couldn't tell if the glimmer was my seer magic flaring up or simply the afternoon sun glinting off the glass. Either way, a shiver skittered down my spine.

First, Kyrion and I had been attacked, and now, an abandoned building was giving me the creeps. I'd thought we might be able to relax on Sygnustern, but I had a funny feeling we were in just as much danger as before.

The carriage rolled along a few more streets, then rounded a wide curve. The shops and other buildings thinned out, then disappeared altogether, replaced by thick stands of gray coniferous trees. Even through the warming shield, the sharp, sticky scent of sap tickled my nose, and I had to hold back a sneeze.

The carriage climbed a steep hill, and patches of snow appeared, covering the cobblestones. The driver hit a button, and the carriage sank lower to the ground. I leaned over the side, watching in fascination as the metal wheels collapsed, changed shape, and smoothly flattened out, turning into runners on an old-fashioned sleigh. An engine also hummed to life on the undercarriage, helping the horse pull the vehicle up the slope.

I let out a whistle of admiration. "I've seen transports that can go from land to water, and vice versa, but I've never seen one where the wheels changed into something else entirely."

"One of my father's inventions," Asterin replied, pride rippling through her voice. "A few years ago, I applied it to all the House Collier carriages since we often have snow year-round."

"I didn't realize your father was an engineer."

A wide smile stretched across her lips. "My father wasn't an engineer or an inventor, not like you are, Vesper. But if Urston needed a new tool or device for one of his mines, he usually made it himself. He was very good at figuring out how to solve problems." Her smile cracked, then vanished completely. "At least, before he died."

Asterin clearly didn't want to talk about her father anymore. My tongue itched with questions, but I swallowed them, sat back in my seat, and watched the passing scenery.

We rounded another curve and crested the steep slope, and a sprawling estate appeared. In many ways, it reminded me of the Regal castles that lined the Boulevard on Corios, but instead of being one building, this was a series of castles that rose and fell with the rocky mountainside.

Each structure was made of the same pretty pale green stone, and the smooth surface reflected the surrounding gray trees, making it seem as though the trees were encased in the castles' walls. Diamond-shaped windows studded each level of each castle, and the stone parapets were all shaped like coniferous trees, each one ending in a slender, wicked-looking spike. Not so much a pretty decoration as a defense mechanism.

In between the castles, dense green hedges that had been snipped into the shapes of wolves, foxes, rabbits, and other animals frolicked around flower beds that were still bright with blossoms, despite the chilly air. Instead of gondolas, all the buildings were connected by stone and glass bridges, along with a few of the metal swinging bridges I had seen around the spaceport. People hustled along all the bridges, even the swinging ones, going about their afternoon chores and duties. Emerald-green flags topped all the castles' towers, each one featuring a large gold cursive *C* with two hammers crossed in front of it.

I glanced over at Asterin, but the House Collier sigil wasn't on her gray coveralls, and she wasn't wearing it as a pendant around her neck as Siya had been. How odd. Why wasn't Asterin wearing the symbol and colors of her mother's House?

The carriage stopped beside a stone shack positioned at the end of a massive drawbridge that led into the front of the estate. A guard inside the shack peered through the permaglass window. He was clad in green polyplastic armor, and his hand curled around the blaster on his belt.

*Look over there*, Kyrion's voice whispered through my mind, and he jerked his chin to the side. More guards armed with blasters were posted just inside the tree line.

I frowned. *Surely the Colliers don't think we're going to attack them?*

Kyrion's eyes narrowed as he studied first one guard, then another. *I don't think the guards are for us. Something else has them on alert.*

Asterin waved at the guard inside the shack, who eyed Kyrion and me with suspicion. Asterin waved at the guard again, the motion sharper and more impatient. The guard hesitated a moment longer, then pulled a green lever, touched his ear, and murmured something into his comms device.

The driver whistled to the horse, and the carriage continued onward. A faint crackle of electricity sounded, and the air in front of us shimmered like a heat wave. The carriage rattled onto the drawbridge, and a tingling sensation swept over my body, as though someone was scrubbing my skin with a rough cloth. Beside me, Kyrion tensed, his hand clenching around his sword.

A few seconds later, the tingling sensation vanished, although the bitter tang of copper filled my mouth, as though I had licked an old-fashioned penny.

"A defensive shield," Asterin explained. "It covers the entire estate like an invisible bubble of static electricity. It won't harm people trying to leave, but no one can enter without authorization. Mostly, my stepfather uses it to keep the heat in and the cold out, although of course, it has other benefits."

"Like frying your enemies should they try to breach it?" I asked.

A rueful grin spread across Asterin's face. "Something like that."

The carriage rattled across the drawbridge, through an enormous stone archway, and into a massive courtyard. A ring of fountains bubbled in the courtyard, while several evergreen hedges shaped like hammers loomed over stone planters filled with blue-moon peonies. I drew in a breath, and the peonies' spearmint scent flooded my nose. At least something here was familiar.

The carriage stopped in front of some wide, shallow steps that led up to two green frosted-glass doors boasting the House Collier sigil.

"Here we are," Asterin said. "Home sweet home."

Her words were light and pleasant, but a sad, bitter undertone rasped through her voice. Kyrion raised his eyebrows in a silent question. I shrugged back. I didn't know what to make of Asterin's obvious reluctance to be here.

Asterin hit a button. The warming shield vanished, and the metal pipes slid back into the body of the carriage. Kyrion and I grabbed our duffel bags, then followed Asterin up the stairs and stopped in front of the doors. Green lights shot out from the center of the hammers embedded in the frosted glass. I flinched, as did Kyrion, but the lights only scanned our faces before vanishing. A few seconds later, a soft chime sounded. Asterin strode forward, and the doors automatically opened as she approached them. Once again, Kyrion and I followed her.

We stepped into the main castle. Pale green stone rolled out in all directions, while gold bulbs dropped down from the vaulted ceilings, highlighting dark wooden tables, chairs, and other furniture.

Kyrion and I trailed Asterin up a curving staircase to the third floor. Several servants passed us, holding trays of food and drink, vases of fresh-cut flowers, baskets of clean laundry, and other household objects. Some of the servants bowed their heads to Asterin, but just as many ignored her completely. Not what I expected, given that her stepfather was the head of House Collier. What was going on here?

Asterin entered a corridor and stopped in front of another pair of frosted glass double doors. More green lights shot out, scanning our faces again. After several long seconds, a soft click sounded, and the doors opened. Asterin squared her shoulders, as if preparing for an unpleasant task.

We stepped into an enormous library that took up this corner of the castle. Dark wooden shelves filled with real paper books lined one long wall and stretched up to a second level that could be reached by a spiral staircase in the corner. Several wide, comfortable-looking settees with green cushions were scattered throughout the room, while polished stones of various shapes, sizes, and colors adorned many of the tables, casting rainbow prisms of light onto the floor, walls, and ceiling.

A table along another wall held red clay pots bristling with small topiary trees, along with pruning shears, gloves, and other gardening tools. Many of the topiary trees had already been sculpted into cats, dogs, birds, butterflies, and other small, whimsical shapes. The sharp tang of greenery perfumed the air, along with a pleasant hint of woodsmoke from the flames crackling in the fireplace.

The cozy space reminded me of Kyrion's library at Castle Caldaren. Wistful longing rippled through me, but I couldn't tell if it was my own feeling or Kyrion's emotion reverberating through the bond.

A man and a woman were sitting in matching chairs in front of a large picture window that offered a sweeping view of the lush garden and lawn that stretched out from the back of the estate.

Siya was standing off to the side, her hands clasped behind her back as she delivered some report. Rigel was also here, leaning one shoulder against the wall, his arms crossed over his chest, an unreadable expression on his face. Another man was sitting behind a small desk in the corner, typing notes on a tablet.

Siya stopped speaking, and everyone looked at us. Kyrion slowly set his duffel bag on the floor and straightened up. I did the same thing.

Asterin squared her shoulders again, then strode forward and stopped beside Siya, although she kept a healthy distance between herself and the other woman.

"May I present Lord Aldrich Collier and Lady Verona Collier," Asterin said in a formal voice.

The couple rose to their feet. Aldrich Collier looked to be

in his mid-sixties, with iron-gray hair that jutted up from his head like a layer of spikes. He was on the short side, and an emerald-green jacket stretched across his stocky chest. Seams of gold piping ran down the jacket sleeves, as well as the legs of his matching pants, while his black wing tips were polished to a high gloss.

Aldrich had the same light brown skin, hazel eyes, and straight nose as Siya, and the resemblance between the father and daughter was obvious. A large gold pendant dangled from a thick chain around his neck, and the round disk featured a *C* made of glittering emeralds with two diamond hammers crossed in front of it.

Verona Collier was a few years younger than her husband, with long black hair and pale skin that made her look like an older version of Asterin. Her pantsuit was a pretty mint green, and she wore a smaller, more feminine version of the House Collier pendant. Her blue eyes were kind, and a welcoming smile creased her face.

The man sitting at the small desk finished his typing and got to his feet. He also looked to be in his sixties, with light brown eyes and pale skin. Thick seams of silver ran through his wavy, dark brown hair, giving him a distinguished air. He was dressed in an emerald-green jacket, shirt, and pants just like Rigel, but the cut of his uniform was much sleeker and more tailored, and not a hint of a wrinkle or a speck of dirt marred his garments.

"This is Leland," Asterin said. "The House Collier chief of staff."

Leland tipped his head to us.

"And this is Lady Vesper Quill and Lord Kyrion Caldaren." Asterin finished the introductions.

We all murmured greetings, although an awkward silence quickly descended over the library.

The only other people I'd been around who had a truebond

were Adria and Dargan Byrne, so I reached out with my seer magic and studied the Colliers a little more closely. The Byrnes' bond had looked like jagged gray veins of energy crackling between the siblings, but the Colliers' magic was softer and smoother, like pale green waves of power constantly flowing between them.

The married couple didn't have the raw force the Byrnes had possessed, but Aldrich and Verona were still powerful psions. Even more impressive, the Colliers' magic felt as warm, solid, and sturdy as the floor under my feet, and I couldn't help but contrast it to the icy walls, hard knots, and wide gaps that sprang up between Kyrion and me whenever we needed our power the most.

A bolt of envy punched deep into my heart. The Colliers' connection seemed so simple, so effortless, so *easy*. What did they know that Kyrion and I didn't?

"Once again, I will state my objection to this ridiculous plan." Siya crossed her arms over her chest. "We have no business offering sanctuary to Imperium fugitives. We should send them back to Corios at once, not let their unwanted presence drag House Collier into a galactic incident. Relations with Callus Holloway are already tricky enough without us openly courting disaster by harboring fugitives."

"Yes, everyone knows your stance on such things," Asterin said. "Which is exactly why I asked Vesper and Kyrion to come to my workshop first, instead of here to the estate."

"Please," Siya scoffed. "You just wanted to tuck your friends away with the rest of the projects in your dusty old workshop while you sweet-talked my father into your scheme, instead of risking them being immediately turned away."

"My workshop is *not* dusty," Asterin snapped back.

"The dirt on your face and coveralls suggests otherwise," Siya countered.

Asterin stiffened and swiped a hand across her cheek,

smudging said dirt. "You're just pissed Vesper and Kyrion were getting the better of you. Exactly how many of your Hammers did my friends knock on their asses at the antiques emporium?"

Siya's glare burned even brighter than before, and fury surged off her, hot enough to warm my cheeks. "My Hammers and I were only trying to subdue the fugitives. If we'd wanted them dead, then dead they would be."

"Subdue us?" Kyrion let out a low, mirthless chuckle. "Funny how I distinctly remember you threatening to kill us where we stood."

Siya turned her angry glare to him. "I can still make that a reality, Arrow."

Kyrion stared down his nose at her. "As could I, Hammer."

"Enough!" Aldrich Collier said in a deep baritone voice. "Threatening each other is a waste of time, oxygen, and energy."

Siya fell silent, but she kept glaring at Asterin, Kyrion, and me in turn.

Aldrich strode forward and stopped in front of Kyrion, inspecting him from head to toe. Verona also moved forward, doing the same thing to me. The couple circled around us, moving in opposite directions, although their steps rang out at the same steady, measured pace.

Something soft brushed up against my body, like a feather tickling my skin. A shimmer of green caught my eye, and I reached out with my seer magic again. Waves of power were ebbing and flowing between Kyrion and me, but it wasn't *our* power. Somehow the Colliers were using their own truebond and telempathy to explore the similar connection between Kyrion and me.

I stiffened, as did Kyrion, and the sticky cobweb of him in my mind pulsed with wariness. The waves kept ebbing and flowing, as though Kyrion and I were caught in two different, but connected, ocean currents. I held my breath. Kyrion and I might be strong in our magic, but the Colliers had a level of finesse we didn't, which made them extremely dangerous.

The Colliers finished their slow, circling inspection and stopped in front of us. The invisible waves of their magic dropped away and vanished completely.

"Curious," Aldrich said in a thoughtful voice. "Their connection is quite powerful, one of the strongest bonds I've ever sensed, but it's . . . unstable."

I frowned. *Unstable?* What did that mean?

"My assessment exactly," Verona murmured. "Kyrion's power is a cold blue moon, while Vesper's is a white-hot star. Complementary and close together but not truly connected—yet."

The married couple shared a look, although I couldn't hear what thoughts they were whispering to each other with their telepathy. More soft green waves of power flowed between them, but their magic was now distant and self-contained, as though I was peering at it through a sheet of permaglass.

Seeing and feeling the Colliers' magic was nothing like my experience with Callus Holloway. The siphon's power had stabbed into my body like enormous needles plunging all the way down into my bones, then ruthlessly retracted, sucking out my life, energy, and magic. But even when the Colliers had been testing Kyrion's and my connection, their magic had remained smooth and fluid, touching but not taking anything in return.

Kyrion shifted on his feet, his gaze flicking back and forth between the Colliers. A shadow passed over his face, and I didn't need to feel his sadness rippling through the bond to know he was thinking about his parents. I wondered if the Caldarens' truebond had felt the same to him as the Colliers' connection did.

"We will offer you sanctuary, as Asterin has requested," Aldrich said.

Siya's arms plummeted to her sides. "But Father—"

Aldrich waved his hand, cutting off her protest. "They have a truebond, Siya, and thus, we must honor our own laws. Plus, Lady Vesper and Lord Kyrion helped Asterin save a great many Erztonian lives when they thwarted the Techwave attack at the Regenwald Resort on Tropics 33."

Siya bit her lip, but after a few seconds, she dipped her head in agreement.

Aldrich turned back to Kyrion and me. "For now, the two of you may stay at the estate as our guests. You can come and go as you like in House Collier territory, but I would advise you to be cautious, given your notoriety."

I snorted. "You mean you won't interfere if some bounty hunters come after us."

"I have little control over bounty hunters," Aldrich replied.

"And what about Callus Holloway?" Kyrion asked.

Aldrich shrugged. "I have even less control over the Imperium ruler. Holloway can lodge a complaint and try to revoke your sanctuary status through the proper Erzton channels, but that will take quite some time."

Kyrion let out a bitter laugh. "Holloway doesn't care about *proper channels*. Sooner or later, he'll send people to try to capture us, no matter how many Imperium and Erzton treaties it violates."

Aldrich shrugged again. "Which is why I suggest you be cautious."

I could hear what he wasn't saying. The Erzton lord wouldn't turn us over to bounty hunters or Holloway, but he wouldn't help us defeat our enemies either.

Aldrich's thoughtful gaze hardened into a stern expression. "The two of you might have a truebond, but it has not fully solidified. That makes it a danger to everyone in House Collier, and it could be deadly to the two of you."

How could our bond not be solidified? Kyrion and I had tapped into our collective power to escape from Crownpoint, and since then, we'd spent practically every waking moment of the last few weeks together. We'd trained and sparred and tried to use each other's abilities dozens of times. Not to mention all the thoughts and feelings we'd shared, along with our bodies. We'd solidified *plenty* of things in that time.

And what made the bond unstable? My fumbling with my magic? Or something else?

"What do you mean, *deadly*?" Kyrion asked in a sharp voice. "I thought the only danger to a truebonded pair was if one person died."

Aldrich clasped his hands behind his back. "That is often true. If one person in a bond dies, then the other usually soon follows." His gaze cut to Verona for a moment. "Once a truebond is formed, severing it has devastating consequences for everyone involved."

Everyone involved? He was making it sound like it was possible for *more* than two people to share a truebond, to share a psionic connection, but I had never heard of such a thing. The Regal gossipcasts concentrated almost exclusively on romantic truebonds, and none of the books I'd read about psionic theory mentioned more than two people being involved in any kind of bond, whether it was between lovers, siblings, friends, or strangers.

"As long as your truebond is unstable, you will never have full control of your power," Aldrich continued. "And you will never be able to protect yourselves from other psions, especially siphons like Callus Holloway."

"So you know what Holloway does to truebonded couples," Kyrion said. "How he takes their power over and over again like they're his own personal batteries."

"Oh, yes. The members of the Erzton ruling council, myself included, have our spies in the Imperium, just as Holloway has his spies in the Erzton," Aldrich replied. "We have been aware of Holloway's actions for quite some time—ever since he started taking your parents' power roughly thirty years ago."

Kyrion jerked back as though the other lord had just punched him in the throat. A muscle twitched in Kyrion's jaw, and his hands clenched into fists. Siya drifted closer to Aldrich, her hand dropping to the hammer hanging off her belt. Rigel remained along the wall, although his eyes narrowed, like he was calculating whether he could tackle Kyrion before the Arrow attacked the lord.

Kyrion ignored the other warriors, his icy gaze squarely on Aldrich. "You *knew* what Holloway was doing to my parents?"

The lord nodded. "I did."

Kyrion's fists curled a little tighter, his knuckles standing out like white knots against his skin. His cold, dark fury vibrated through the bond, stealing my breath and chilling me to the bone.

"You could have offered my parents sanctuary. You could have offered them the same chance you are giving Vesper and me. You could have given them some bloody *hope*."

Even though he was much shorter, Aldrich still managed to peer down his nose at Kyrion. "Hope has nothing to do with truebonds, and it has absolutely no place in politics. Business is business, and it's a mistake to attach personal feelings to such things. The Erzton does not get involved in Imperium matters, and vice versa."

"And yet here you are, offering us sanctuary," I cut in. "So what's changed between then and now?"

Aldrich looked at me. "You helped my stepdaughter save Erztonian lives and property. The Caldarens did none of those things. You are also standing here before me, on Sygnustern, not halfway across the galaxy on Corios."

"So what you're really saying is if we hadn't helped Asterin defend the Regenwald Resort, you wouldn't be offering us shelter now?" Kyrion laughed, but it was a low, ugly sound. "Funny how Erzton law is so very flexible."

Aldrich's eyes narrowed, but Kyrion glared right back at him.

"What happened to your parents was a tragedy, Lord Kyrion. Truly," Verona said in a serious voice.

"But?" he growled again, turning his icy glower to her.

"But don't compound it by refusing our help now. The past is the past. We cannot change it, no matter how much we might wish to." Verona's face softened with sympathy. "All we can do is move forward together into a brighter future, but the choice is yours."

"And what is this *choice* going to cost us?" I asked.

Verona arched an eyebrow at my snide tone. "We don't charge credits, if that's what you're asking." She paused. "But future favors are always appreciated."

I huffed. In other words, the Colliers would help us now, with the true cost to be determined later as they saw fit.

Kyrion looked at me. *I don't trust the Colliers.*

*I don't trust them either.* I hesitated, but I finally gave voice to the thought that had been haunting me for the last few weeks. *But we both know something is wrong with our bond. We need help if we're to have any chance of stabilizing our connection. If we don't master our magic, we'll* never *be able to stop running.*

Some of the icy fury trickled out of the bond. Kyrion's fists loosened, but his stance remained tense and watchful. Together we faced the Colliers again.

"Excellent," Verona chirped in a bright voice. "I'm glad all that unpleasantness is settled. The two of you must be exhausted after your long journey. I'll show you to the guest wing, and you can get something to eat and rest up. You are both also invited to attend the marriage mart House Collier is hosting tomorrow night."

"What's a marriage mart?" I asked.

"A long-standing Erzton tradition, although this year, my

father is hoping to bribe someone from another House to marry Asterin," Siya said in a snide voice. "Since my stepsister didn't manage to snare a husband while she was flitting about all those Regal balls on Corios."

Asterin bristled, and a hot blush scalded her cheeks, although I couldn't tell if it was from anger, embarrassment, or both.

Verona ignored the tension between her daughter and her stepdaughter and turned to Leland. "Has everything been prepared for our guests?"

The chief of staff nodded. "Yes, my lady."

"Good." Verona gestured at us. "Lady Vesper, Lord Kyrion, please follow me."

The Erzton lady swept out of the library. Asterin glared at Siya a moment longer, then followed her mother. Siya remained behind, along with Leland and Aldrich, and the three of them huddled together and started speaking in soft voices. Rigel also remained behind, still leaning against the wall. He hadn't moved or said a word the entire time we'd been in the library.

Kyrion grabbed his duffel bag off the floor, spun around, and headed after Verona and Asterin. I picked up my own bag and followed him, trying to tamp down my growing sense of dread.

Bounty hunters, corporate mercenaries, Zane Zimmer, Callus Holloway, and a whole host of other enemies might be waiting outside the Collier estate, but I had a sinking feeling that just as many dangers were lurking inside this bright, glittering castle.

# TEN

## KYRION

Vesper and I followed Lady Verona and Asterin through the castle.

We passed several servants going about their chores, along with more guards, who were stationed in almost every corridor. The guards were clad in green polyplastic armor and equipped with blasters and shock batons, just like the warriors I'd spotted outside the estate. A few Hammers were also roaming around, all armed with traditional war hammers.

Something was wrong.

Nervous energy surged off the servants and saturated the air like a storm cloud, and far more guards and Hammers were on duty than were necessary to secure the estate. I'd been an Arrow a long time, and I knew all the warning signs.

Aldrich Collier was worried his home and people might be targeted.

I noted the placement of each guard, along with each entrance and exit, creating a mental map of the castle. If the worst happened and someone attacked, I wanted to be able to escape as quickly as possible.

I didn't keep up with Erzton politics, so I didn't know who might be threatening House Collier, and I didn't care. Not after Aldrich had revealed he'd known *exactly* how Holloway had been torturing my parents.

As an Arrow and a Regal lord, I could understand why Aldrich hadn't helped my parents. Galactic incidents and all that. Plus, Holloway would *never* have let both of my parents leave Corios at the same time, and even on the off chance they could have escaped, Holloway would have done everything in his power to drag my mother and father back to the Imperium planet.

Vesper touched my arm. *Are you okay? You feel . . . upset.*

I forced myself to nod. *Fine. Just getting the lay of the land, so to speak.*

She eyed me, clearly not believing my lie, but she didn't send me another thought. For once, I was grateful for the quiet.

Lady Verona stepped through an archway into the open air. More snow fluttered down from the clouds, although the flakes hissed away to nothingness the instant they touched the estate's defensive shield.

"Do you ever lower the shield?" Vesper asked, staring up at the shimmering air a hundred feet above our heads.

"Sometimes," Lady Verona replied. "If there is a heavy snow, we'll lower the shield so that it piles up enough for the servants' children to build snowmen and go sledding. Asterin and Siya used to love playing in the snow when they were young."

A wistful note crept into Verona's voice, but Asterin flinched, as though the memories weren't as fond as her mother made them out to be.

We followed the Erzton lady across a wide stone bridge, went through another archway, and stepped into a slightly smaller castle.

"This is the guest wing," Verona said. "If you need anything, just tap one of the holoscreens in the walls, and the servants will come and assist you."

Lady Verona flitted from one corridor to another, a cheerful note in her voice as she talked about the kitchen, the libraries, and the other amenities. Her conversation was probably meant to put us at ease, but I ground my teeth at the social niceties.

The Colliers might have granted us sanctuary, but our position here was clearly tenuous. Perhaps even tenuous enough for one of the Erztonians to sell us out to our enemies.

Lord Aldrich had said it himself. Business was business, and right now, there was no better business and especially no richer reward to be had than turning Vesper and me over to Callus Holloway. I didn't think Aldrich and Verona would renege on their promise, but Siya didn't want us here, and she might decide to try to subdue us in hopes of shipping us off-planet to protect House Collier. And the thirty million credits Holloway had promised for our capture would be enough to tempt even the most loyal servant or guard.

We had come here seeking refuge, but I couldn't help but feel like the sooner Vesper and I left this place, the safer we would be.

Lady Verona stopped in a long corridor and opened a door, revealing a luxe suite. "Vesper, Kyrion, these are your chambers." She gestured at another door farther down the corridor. "Asterin's suite is right over there."

I glanced at Asterin, who had an unreadable expression on her face. She was Verona's daughter, so why was she staying in the guest wing instead of the main castle?

"You can leave your bags in your suite, then head to the south terrace for some refreshments. Normally, I would join you, but Aldrich and I have some business to finish regarding the marriage mart." Verona's gaze flicked to Asterin, who remained stone-faced. "We are currently engaged in several sensitive negotiations."

"Of course," Vesper murmured. "We appreciate your kindness."

A smile spread across Lady Verona's face. "Once Siya told us you were coming, I had the servants put some spare clothes and toiletries in your suite. If you need something else, just let one of the servants know."

She nodded at us, then went down the corridor, rounded a corner, and vanished.

"Mother's right," Asterin chirped in a bright voice that was eerily similar to the one Lady Verona had just used. "Let's drop your bags in your suite and head to the south terrace."

We did as she asked, then followed her down another corridor, through an archway, and onto a large stone terrace that arced out like an enormous half-moon and connected the guest wing to the main castle. The terrace overlooked a garden filled with topiary trees and hedges, along with blue-moon peonies, pink-star honeysuckles, and other colorful flowers I recognized from my mother's garden at Castle Caldaren.

Several tables covered with food were clustered along one side of the terrace. Asterin grabbed a plate and filled it high, and Vesper and I did the same. Then the three of us sat down and dug into our food.

The House Collier chefs had prepared a spread that rivaled anything I'd ever eaten at a Regal ball. A thick, rich pumpkin soup with a dollop of fresh cream and just a hint of cinnamon. A warm salad of greens, dried cranberries, apples, and roasted sweet potatoes tossed with a tangy honey-mustard vinaigrette. Toasted pumpernickel bread topped with a light, refreshing lemon chicken salad that was covered with melted sharp white cheddar cheese.

I might not trust anyone at House Collier, but the food was delicious, and Vesper and I both went back for seconds and thirds.

For dessert, we all inhaled several pieces of a pumpkin roll with a sweet cream-cheese filling and studded with dark chocolate chips and toasted marshmallows. We washed everything down with a crisp apple punch.

Asterin quickly finished her food, but Vesper and I were still eating when Leland stepped onto the balcony, tapping buttons on his tablet, which was cradled in the crook of his arm. The motion reminded me of Daichi.

Guilt churned in my gut, souring the wonderful meal. If Daichi and Touma were caught on Corios, Holloway would execute them for helping Vesper and me. Or worse, Holloway would stick Daichi and Touma in the Crownpoint medical labs and let his scientists conduct horrific experiments on them.

Leland hit another button, then looked up at the three of us. "I just wanted to make sure you and your guests had everything you needed, Lady Asterin. I had the chefs prepare some of their best dishes."

"It was excellent," I replied. "One of the best meals I've eaten."

Vesper also murmured her thanks, and a pleased smile spread across the chief of staff's face.

Leland focused on Asterin. "I'm sorry I couldn't meet you at your workshop earlier, as you requested. I had some other House Collier business, although if I'd known your friends were coming, I would have assisted you." He grimaced. "I should have been there to smooth things over with Lady Siya."

Asterin laid her hand on his arm. "It's not your fault, Leland. You know how much I appreciate everything you've done for me, not just today but over the years. You were such a huge help to my father, and Urston would be so happy to see how well you're doing as part of House Collier."

Some emotion flickered in the chief of staff's eyes, but it vanished in an instant, and he smiled at Asterin. "If there is nothing else, I will leave you to your guests."

Asterin smiled back at him. "Thank you, Leland."

He nodded to us all, then left the terrace.

As soon as Leland was gone, Asterin's smile vanished, replaced by an odd, wistful expression. After a few seconds, she toasted us with her glass. "The chefs might have prepared the food, but the apple punch came straight out of the latest Quill Corp brewmaker. Vesper, if you ever get tired of inventing things, you should become a cook. Your appliances make everything taste better."

Vesper laughed, and I relaxed, just a bit. I still didn't know what to make of House Collier's people and politics, but for this moment, we were safe, and I was going to enjoy it while it lasted.

We sipped another round of punch, while Asterin pointed out one colored permaglass dome after another on the surrounding mountains. "The Erzton is currently made up of twelve major ruling Houses, including House Collier. All the Houses deal in minerals, metals, coal, timber, and the like. Each dome on each mountain represents a different House, all connected by the gondolas and bridges to form the city of Gewitter."

"I thought Sygnustern was a mining planet," Vesper said. "I didn't expect it to be so charming."

"Oh, there are plenty of mines on Sygnustern. The Houses just built their city on top of the mines." Asterin gestured at the mountains in the distance. "Hence all the cliffs and chasms."

"There are actual, working mines in the bottoms of the chasms between the mountains?" I asked.

"Oh, yes. And they are the ever-grinding, ever-deepening heart of the planet," Asterin replied in a wry tone.

I might not like heights, but the thought of going to the dark depths of one of those chasms, and then even farther underground, made my gut churn. Vesper also looked a bit pale at the notion.

"Home sweet home, eh? Although things are clearly not sweet between you and Siya." The history lesson was nice, but I wanted to know exactly what problems were brewing in House Collier.

Asterin twisted her glass around on the table. "Things are usually not this . . . tense. Most of the time, I ignore Siya and she ignores me."

"But she can't do that while Vesper and I are here. Because our very presence threatens the safety of everyone she's sworn to protect as the head of the House Collier Hammers."

"Something like that," Asterin admitted. "Although Siya and I have been at odds for a long time, ever since . . ."

"What?" I asked. "What happened between the two of you?"

Vesper shot me a sharp look, but I was tired of dancing around the truth. I wanted to know exactly how dangerous Siya Collier was—and what lengths she might go to in order to protect her House.

Asterin's fingers dropped away from her glass. "House Armas, my father's House, used to be among the major Houses."

"Until?" Vesper asked in a soft, sympathetic voice.

Asterin sighed, the sound full of aching regret. "Until there was an accident at one of my father's mines. At the time, Siya and I were both thirteen and loved to explore the mine. We had gone up to the surface to fetch some tools for my father, and we were headed back inside when a massive explosion ripped through the mine. We were only knocked down, but dozens of people were seriously injured."

She slumped back in her seat, as though all the strength had left her body. "My father was killed, along with Irzin Collier, Siya's uncle and Aldrich's brother. Siya adored her uncle, and she was devastated by his death."

Vesper squeezed Asterin's hand. "I'm so sorry."

Asterin gave her a wan smile. Then she cleared her throat, pulled her fingers out of Vesper's light grip, and straightened up. "My father was found to be at fault for the accident. The victims' families sued House Armas and took everything my parents had. Leland was my father's business partner, and he lost everything too."

Sadness surged off her and tweaked my telempathy, along with a surprising amount of anger.

"But I thought you owned the mineral rights on several Frozon moons that are rich in lunarium deposits," I said.

That's what Callus Holloway had claimed a few months ago, back when he wanted me to marry Asterin in order to get his hands on all that lunarium. Of course, I had already been bonded to—and was falling for—Vesper at the time, so no romantic feelings had ever sparked between Asterin and me.

"I do own those mineral rights, along with many others," she replied. "My father put the rights in a trust for me a few months before he died, so they weren't included in the House Armas assets after his death."

More anger surged off Asterin, and power sparked in her eyes. Despite dancing with her at a Regal ball and fighting side by side with her against the Techwave, I'd never been able to figure out what kind of psion she was or exactly what abilities she had. She had helped rescue Vesper from Crownpoint, and I considered her a trusted friend, but in some ways, Asterin Armas was still a complete mystery.

"But?" I prompted, wanting to know the rest of her story.

"But lunarium is only worth something when it's out of the ground, not buried beneath hundreds of feet of ice and snow." Asterin muttered the last few words.

Asterin Armas might seem like another wealthy, privileged member of Erzton society, but in reality, she was penniless. Hers was a common story among the Regals, especially those with relatives who had made risky investments or gambled away a House's credits and resources.

"So that's why your parents want you to find a Regal husband. You need someone with a big enough fortune to finance your mining operations," I said.

"More or less. My mother and stepfather also have other reasons." Asterin grimaced, but after a few seconds, her expression smoothed out. "But at least Zane Zimmer is out of the running. My mother and stepfather were *very* upset about the Techwave attack at the summer solstice ball." Another grimace twisted her face. "Even though Zane saved my life that night."

Vesper fidgeted with her fork. "I've been studying the schematics for Jorge Rojillo's temperature-shielding technology, but so far, I can't see why the Techwave thinks it's so valuable."

Asterin shrugged. "I haven't had any luck either. I was hoping we could work on it together while you're here. Maybe tomorrow, at my workshop?"

Vesper's entire body perked up. "I would love that!"

A sword of guilt stabbed deep into my chest. Vesper hadn't looked that excited in weeks. The stress of being hunted by practically everyone in the galaxy had taken a much bigger toll on her than I'd realized. It had taken a toll on me too, but Vesper was the one who'd had to give up her corporation and her beloved R&D lab.

All I'd given up was my place in Regal society, which was uncomfortable at best, and being the head of the Arrows, a job I'd never wanted in the first place. And while I missed Castle Caldaren, it hadn't been a real home since my parents died.

Sometimes I wanted to ask Vesper if being a fugitive was worth giving up the life she'd fought, bled, and almost died for—if *I* was worth all that trouble, danger, and misery—but so far, I hadn't found the courage.

I couldn't bear to see her face or feel her pity through the bond if the answer was no.

Asterin beamed back at Vesper. "Excellent! We'll go to my workshop in the morning."

The two of them started talking about the temperature-shielding technology again, along with the Techwave cannon that Vesper wanted to fix—

A spike of anger slammed up against my telempathy, stabbing into my side like a red-hot poker. Asterin and Vesper kept chatting, not sensing the strong emotion, but I looked to the left.

Siya Collier was standing on a bridge that led into the main castle about fifty feet away. She was once again clutching her war hammer, and the lunarium head was glowing a pale green in a reflection of her psion power. A sharp, predatory grin split Siya's mouth, and she raised her hammer and twirled the weapon around and around.

Siya twirled the weapon faster and faster, and the green glow of the lunarium intensified, until it looked like she was twisting lightning around in her bare hand. Just as quickly, she stopped the twirling motion and stabbed the hammer toward me.

*Better watch your step, Arrow*, Siya's voice sneered in my mind. *I wouldn't want you to slip off a bridge and fall to your death.*

As far as threats went, it was pretty mild, so I didn't bother responding.

Siya lowered the weapon and strode away, whistling a jaunty tune. She stepped through an archway and vanished, but her anger lingered in the air, and her threats echoed in my mind.

We'd only been on Sygnustern a few hours, and we had already made a dangerous new enemy.

By this point, the sun was setting, painting the sky in darkening shades of twilight gray and purple, and it was growing quite chilly outside, even with the warming shield. The three of us went back into the guest wing. Asterin led us to our suite, then bade us good night and disappeared into her own rooms.

Vesper stepped into our suite, and I shut and locked the door behind us.

The front part of the suite was a large sitting area with several tables and settees, along with cushioned chairs arranged in front of a stone fireplace. Flames were crackling behind the black iron grate, which featured the House Collier sigil, while thick, fuzzy blankets were draped over the backs of the chairs in case extra warmth was needed.

Just like in the main castle, all the furniture was obviously well made and extremely expensive, given the gold, silver, and colored glass accents. Still, despite the finery, I felt like a Frozon wolf that had just stepped into a trap and was about to get crushed by its sharp jaws.

Vesper went over to her duffel bag, rummaged around inside, and pulled out a device that looked like two halves of a broken tablet tied together with thick strands of solar wiring that snaked up and ended in a sharp, antenna-like point. She hit a button on the device, which started whirring, then moved through the sitting area and the attached bedroom and bathroom.

A minute later, Vesper returned to the sitting room, set the device down, and gave me a thumbs-up. "The suite is clean. No hidden cameras or listening devices."

I nodded, although the lack of spy technology didn't ease my worry. "Good. Because we need to leave. Right now. Slip out of the guest wing, get off the estate, return to the *Dream World*, and get off this planet."

Vesper frowned. "Why? Because Siya doesn't want us here?"

"That's one issue."

I tilted my head, and she followed me over to a permaglass wall that overlooked the same central garden we'd seen from the terrace earlier. Down below, golden hoverlights bobbed up and down in midair, illuminating the House Collier guards patrolling through the topiary trees and hedges.

I stabbed my finger at the guards. "There's the second issue.

The Colliers have an incredible amount of security. The only reason you have that many guards on duty is if you're worried about an attack."

Vesper's gaze moved from one guard to the next. "You pointed out the guards when we first reached the estate, but surely Asterin would have told us if the Colliers were in some sort of trouble."

"Perhaps. Or perhaps Asterin doesn't know anything about it. Either way, we have enough enemies without getting caught up in House Collier's problems."

Vesper held her arms out wide. "Say that we leave the estate and return to the *Dream World*. Where do we go? Because the way I see it, we're out of options."

I ground my teeth. She wasn't wrong, which only added to my frustration.

Vesper lowered her arms. "House Collier might be in trouble, but Aldrich and Verona have promised to shelter us, and I seriously doubt Verona would break that promise to her daughter. From everything I've read about Erzton society, honor is *everything* to them. Once Erztonians give someone sanctuary, they are duty-bound to maintain that sanctuary, no matter what threats or repercussions they might face themselves."

"I trust other people's honor as much as I trust Callus Holloway. Which is to say, not at all. We're not safe here. *You're* not safe here."

"I'm not safe anywhere," Vesper snapped back. "And neither are you."

We glared at each other, and emotions crackled back and forth through the bond like lightning scorching us both. Vesper's anger. My frustration. Her determination. My worry.

Vesper blew out a tense breath, and her face softened. "But I'm safer with you, Kyr, than anywhere else in the galaxy."

For once, her saying my nickname only added to my misery, as did her unwavering faith in me. "You weren't safe yesterday when those bounty hunters cornered you, along with Esmina and Pollux. Or today at the antiques emporium when Siya and the Hammers tried to capture us."

Her eyes narrowed. "Wait. Is that why you made such a reckless charge toward the Hammer that was coming up behind me? Because you thought I didn't see him, and he was going to hurt me?"

I stiffened. "Far better for me to be injured than you."

Vesper's eyes narrowed a little more. "Really? Because it sounds like you didn't trust me to defend myself." Despite her hot, angry glare, more than a little hurt rasped through her voice. "I am *not* a weak link."

"I never said you were," I replied, my voice harsher than I intended. "And of course I trust you. It's just . . ."

"What?"

"I tried to warn you with my telepathy, but you didn't respond. I also couldn't . . . feel you anymore. Through the bond. It was . . . troubling."

Some of the anger trickled out of Vesper's face. "I couldn't feel you either. The same thing happened on Tropics 44. You were talking to me through the bond, but after the bounty hunters abducted me, I couldn't reach you anymore. It's like . . ."

"What?" I asked, my voice losing some of its previous heat.

"It's like you were on one side of an icy wall, and I was on the other," Vesper replied. "And no matter how hard I pounded on the wall, I couldn't break through the ice. I couldn't break through to *you*."

A tense, awkward silence sprang up between us. Even though Vesper was standing right in front of me, she seemed distant and far away through the bond, as though the velvety ribbon that connected us was stretched to its breaking point.

"It's not just shelter we need," Vesper said in a soft voice. "It's help. With our bond."

*We both know something is wrong with our bond.* Her earlier thought whispered through my mind, and each word was like a dagger to my heart.

I hadn't wanted to admit it, but she was right. Something *was* wrong with our bond, and I had a sinking suspicion it had everything to do with me. If only I had found a way to kill Callus Holloway years ago, we would have had all the time in the galaxy to figure out our bond. The blame for our current predicament was mine and mine alone, and I was terrified Vesper was going to pay the ultimate price for my mistakes.

"The Colliers have had a truebond for years," Vesper continued. "You heard what they said about how our bond hasn't solidified and isn't stable. Maybe they can help us fix that. Maybe they can help us figure out how to use our respective magics and truebond abilities."

She stepped forward and grabbed my hand. "Tried and true, remember, Kyr?" A wry smile twisted her lips. "I think maybe this is the *trying* part. Either way, I want to figure it out. Don't you?"

Her determination rippled through the bond, making my own chest squeeze tightly in response. Even if the bond hadn't connected us, I would have done anything to keep Vesper safe.

Before I met Vesper, I had been living in the dark, like some creature trapped in a cave who never saw the sun. She had brought so much joy and wit and humor and warmth into my life in such a short time, and if anything happened to her . . . well, it would destroy me, regardless of our psionic connection.

"Very well," I said, forcing my voice to stay level and even. "We'll stay here—for now. But as soon as we figure out what's wrong with the bond and you fix the Techwave cannon, we're leaving. Once Holloway gets word that we're on Sygnustern, he'll start plotting to revoke the Colliers' protection. Holloway won't care how badly he damages relations with the Erztonians so long as he gets us in the end."

"I know," Vesper replied in a low, strained voice. "But figuring out how to fully use our bond is the only thing that's going to keep us safe from Holloway, the Techwave, and everyone else who might be targeting us."

The silver flecks in her dark blue eyes brightened, glimmering like pinprick stars, and Vesper's gaze became dreamy and unfocused, as though she was looking at something far, far away. Psion power surged off her and curled against my skin, even as the velvety ribbon of her vibrated in my mind.

"I also feel like we *have* to stay here," she murmured in an absent voice. "Like there's something important we have to do or see or experience before we go anywhere else."

"What do you think that is?" I asked in a soft voice, not wanting to interrupt her vision.

"I'm not sure." Vesper stared into the distance a moment longer, then shook her head. When she looked at me again, her eyes were clear. "But the only way we're going to figure it out is together."

She squeezed my fingers again, and I nodded, hoping she couldn't feel the clamminess of my skin or the anger, guilt, and dread still coursing through me.

"Together," I echoed, even as I vowed in the cold depths of my heart that I would do whatever was necessary to keep Vesper safe from Holloway, the Techwave, and all the other monsters in the galaxy.

Including myself.

# ELEVEN

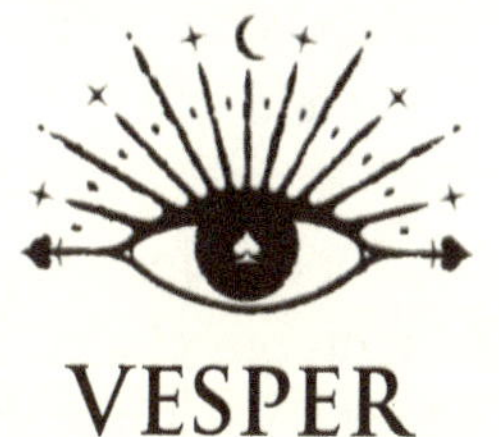

## VESPER

Kyrion and I unpacked our clothes and weapons, then checked in with Daichi and Tivona.

Daichi hadn't found out where Zane was, and he hadn't learned anything new about Esmina and Pollux, although he promised to keep digging. Tivona updated me on a few things at Quill Corp, then our friends signed off.

Once that was done, I headed into the bathroom and closed the door. Somehow I resisted the urge to bang my head against the sturdy wood to release some of my frustration. That would be pointless, just like us running away to another planet would be pointless.

Sooner or later, Kyrion and I would have to make a stand against our enemies. If the Colliers couldn't help us with our bond, maybe Asterin and I could fix the Techwave cannon or at least figure out why the Techies had gone to such great lengths to steal Jorge Rojillo's temperature-shielding technology—and especially how they planned to use it against the Imperium.

Either way, the lovely, private, romantic bubble Kyrion and

I had been in for the last few weeks on the *Dream World* was gone, and we both needed to deal with the ugly realities we were facing.

I moved away from the door, stripped off my clothes, and stepped into the shower. Like everything else in the suite, the shower was the epitome of luxury, with heated tiles, a steam-bath feature, and a plethora of nozzles that sprayed water in all directions. I stayed in the shower a long, long time, listening to the steady hiss of the water and letting the hot spray beat down on my body.

By the time I turned off the water and put on some silk sleep clothes I found in the bathroom closet, I felt a smidge better. My steps and mood lighter, I went into the bedroom.

Kyrion had taken off his jacket and shirt, revealing his bare, muscled chest. He was standing in front of a full-length mirror, studying the mottled black-and-blue bruise that covered his upper right arm like a macabre tattoo.

My steps faltered. "Is that from where Siya hit you with her war hammer?"

I'd felt his injury through the bond when it had happened in the antiques emporium, but his pain had quickly vanished. Kyrion must have used a psionic shield to keep me from realizing just how badly he'd been hurt.

"It's fine," he said in a low voice. "I just gave myself a skinbond. That should take care of it."

Even as he said the words, the bruise faded away. Kyrion flexed his fingers and rotated his arm, and the sticky cobweb in my mind twinged with pain and soreness. Guilt churned in my stomach. He'd been hurt because he'd been trying to protect me, and I'd been annoyed and upset at him for it.

I moved forward, held out my hand, and opened my mouth to apologize, but Kyrion stepped back and tossed the used skinbond injector into a recycler in the corner. I stopped, my hand plummeting to my side.

He smiled, as though everything was fine, but his eyes were dull and tired, and his shoulders sagged with exhaustion. "I'm going to take a shower. Try to get some sleep, okay?"

Before I could respond, Kyrion went into the bathroom. The soft *click* of the door closing made me flinch, and more guilt churned in my stomach.

Even though Kyrion was only on the other side of the wood, and I could still sense him through the bond, right now he felt a million miles away. Even worse, I had no idea how to fix the awkward distance that had suddenly sprung up between us.

I crawled into bed and pulled a cozy, weighted blanket up to my chin. I wanted to stay awake until Kyrion got out of the shower so we could talk, but the stress of the day caught up with me, and I fell asleep. I didn't wake up until the next morning, when a sharp knock sounded on the main suite door.

I rolled over and stretched my hand out, but my fingers only met cool sheets. My eyes popped open. Kyrion was gone.

I sat up, my gaze darting around the bedroom. His stormsword was also gone, along with his bandolier of supplies.

*Kyrion?* I called out through the bond.

He didn't answer me, but the sticky cobweb of him was calm and still, and I could sense he was on the estate . . . somewhere. Kyrion normally got up before I did, but he was always quick to come find me when he realized I was awake.

I waited a minute, but I didn't sense him moving any closer. Why wasn't he returning to the suite? Did he want to avoid me because of our conversation last night? Hurt spiked through me at the thought.

Another knock sounded, a little louder and sharper. I groaned, wanting nothing more than to dive back under the blankets, but I got out of bed, threw on some clothes, and slid my stormsword into its slot on my belt.

A third knock sounded, and I opened the door to find Asterin in the corridor, dressed in a clean pair of gray coveralls. She was holding a large paper bag in one hand and a travel mug in the other.

"Where's Kyrion?" I asked.

"I ran into him a few minutes ago when he was leaving your suite. I offered to have a servant make him breakfast, but he muttered something about exploring the estate and reviewing the security."

I snorted. "I'm sure Siya will love that."

Asterin let out an agreeing chuckle, although her laughter quickly faded away. "You and Kyrion *are* safe here, Vesper. You don't have to wear disguises and hide who you are anymore. The estate and the rest of the mountain are all House Collier territory. Holloway can't touch you here, and even a bounty hunter would think twice about attacking. Plus, my mother and stepfather would *never* go back on their word to shelter you, and neither would Siya. The honor of House Collier means everything to her, and she would never disobey a direct order from Aldrich."

I thought about all the guards Kyrion had pointed out last night. "Is something going on with House Collier? Some dispute or trouble with another House?"

"Not that I'm aware of, but I haven't been here much over the last few months. I've been too busy husband hunting on Corios." Asterin's mouth puckered with disgust, but after a few seconds, her eyes narrowed. "Wait. Why would you ask that?"

"No reason," I lied. "I guess I'm just looking for trouble everywhere these days."

Asterin's face softened with sympathy. "Do you still want to visit my workshop? I understand if you would rather stay here and rest."

For a moment, I considered doing just that. Closing the door, getting back into bed, and pretending the rest of the galaxy didn't exist. But that wouldn't help me, and I was tired of running and hiding like I had done something wrong when Callus Holloway's lust for truebonds was to blame for this whole messy situation.

"I would love to see your workshop. Just give me a few minutes to get ready."

Asterin followed me into the suite and handed me the bag and mug. "You can eat while you finish."

I took a cautious sip. A delicious apple cider with subtle notes of orange and a warm touch of cinnamon exploded on my tongue. I hummed with pleasure, then opened the bag, which contained several chocolate-apple scones.

My stomach rumbled, and I crammed a scone into my mouth. Buttery, flaky crust. Big chunks of sweet apple. Bigger chunks of chocolate. All of it drizzled with a vanilla-bean sugar glaze. Mmm-mmm-mmm.

"You're a good friend." I shoved another scone into my mouth.

Asterin grinned. "I know."

I quickly scarfed down all the scones, along with the cider. Then I brushed my teeth and pulled my dark brown hair back into a ponytail. I also grabbed the Techwave cannon, along with some of the solar magazines Kyrion had packed.

Asterin and I left the guest wing and went to the courtyard in front of the main castle. Instead of the open-air carriage-slash-sleigh we'd used yesterday, a mechanized transport was waiting. The door hissed open, and Asterin ducked inside.

A tingling awareness swept over me, and I glanced up and spotted Kyrion on one of the guest-wing balconies. I considered trying to talk to him through the bond, but I had no idea what to say, especially given how tense and awkward things had been between us last night. So I just waved instead.

Kyrion's expression was blank and unreadable, and I didn't

sense any emotions rippling off him. After a few seconds, he lifted his hand and waved back.

"Vesper? You ready?" Asterin called out.

I looked at Kyrion a moment longer, then stepped into the transport. As much as I wanted to figure out what was going on between Kyrion and me, maybe spending the day apart would give us both some perspective.

The transport lifted off the ground, crossed the courtyard, and sailed over the drawbridge, heading down the mountain toward the city streets.

I peered through the window. People riding in transports and carriages, other folks strolling along the sidewalks, carts selling food and drinks. Everything was normal. I didn't doubt Kyrion's instincts when it came to sensing danger, but maybe we would be safe here, at least for a little while.

Several minutes later, the transport stopped in front of the emerald permaglass dome that housed the antiques emporium. I followed Asterin down a long street, which ran by an enormous area filled with cranes, forklifts, and other heavy machinery.

In the distance, a crane operator lowered a massive magnet onto a stack of metal rods that was almost as large as the *Dream World*. The magnet clamped onto the rods, then the crane operator hoisted them onto a hoverpallet with a wide, flat bed. The pallet lifted off the ground and zoomed away.

"This is the House Collier shipping yard," Asterin called out, raising her voice to be heard above the cranking, clanking machines. "Metals, ores, and other materials are brought up from the House Collier mines, then refined, processed, loaded into containers, and sent to their buyers."

Asterin steered clear of the machinery and headed to the right, where a short, blocky building of silver chrome and green permaglass faced both the street and the shipping yard. "This is the main mineral exchange where House Collier goods are displayed for people to bid on."

We stepped through an archway and entered the first floor of the mineral exchange, which featured row after row of clear glass counters. The workers standing behind the counters were wearing House Collier uniforms, along with green velvet gloves, and they carefully pulled out one bit of metal and chunk of ore after another, showing off the items to customers as though they were baubles in a high-end jewelry store.

Asterin exited out the far side of the mineral exchange. She skirted around the edge of the shipping yard and ended up in front of a small building made of dull gray stone at the end of a street that circled back around to the antiques emporium.

Given its cracked bricks and grimy windows, this building had seen better days, and it had a quiet, still, abandoned air, as if few people bothered to come here anymore. Two interlocking *A*s were carved into the battered door, and the words *House Armas* stretched across the weathered wood in chipped, faded silver paint.

Asterin punched in a code on a keypad. A lock clicked, the door opened, and we stepped through to the other side.

"And this is my workshop," Asterin said, flipping on the lights. "I spend most of my time here whenever I'm on Sygnustern."

Dark wooden shelves filled with polished stones, jagged chunks of ore, and a variety of tools ran across the back of the workshop, while blasters, shock batons, and other weapons hung on metal racks on the side walls. Each item had its own little space and was clearly, neatly labeled.

Tables featuring terminals and holoscreens clustered in the center of the room. Larger pieces of machinery squatted in the corners, although thin patches of dust coated some of them, as though they hadn't been used in ages. The small workshop was a far cry from the acres of sterile white tile at Quill Corp, but a pang of longing shot through my heart all the same.

The harsh stench of melted plastic and scorched metal filled the air, but the scent comforted me, and I breathed it in like a sweet perfume. It smelled like *home*, given how much time I had spent in R&D labs over the years.

Asterin went over to the tables. I followed her and set the Techwave cannon down on an open space, along with the extra solar magazines. Thick gray tarps covered some of the tables, hiding the objects underneath, but a splash of white caught my eye.

I drew a tarp aside, revealing something that looked like an air purifier. "What's this?"

Asterin's fingers twitched like she wanted to shove the device back underneath the tarp. "Something for a different project."

Her fingers twitched again. I didn't like it when people studied my unfinished projects in the Quill Corp lab, so I slid the tarp back into place.

Asterin turned toward a table and waved her hand over the embedded holoscreen, and the schematics for Jorge Rojillo's temperature-shielding device popped into the air. Asterin enlarged the hologram, then we both studied the schematics.

"They don't even look that impressive, but these schematics almost cost me my life," she said in a wry voice. "If I'd known the Techwave was targeting Lord Jorge, I would have steered clear of his R&D lab during the summer solstice ball."

"Sometimes the smallest things can be the most dangerous."

Asterin arched an eyebrow. "Like a navigation sensor that overheats and crashes a ship?"

I grimaced at the reminder of the design flaw I'd found in Rowena Kent's spaceships. Only it hadn't been a design flaw but, rather, a calculated effort on Rowena's part to destroy Imperium ships on command for the Techwave.

"Exactly like that. Sometimes I can't believe my figuring out the sensor was faulty caused all of these events to happen."

Asterin's gaze strayed back to the air purifier, which was

still peeking out from beneath the tarp. "Sometimes all it takes is one small spark to ignite a raging fire."

We both fell silent, lost in our thoughts.

Asterin reached underneath another tarp, grabbed a glass box, plucked out the device inside, and placed it on the table. The device resembled an old-fashioned wristwatch—a wide silver band that wrapped around a small holoscreen that featured tiny bits of lunarium and sapphsidian.

I let out a low whistle of appreciation. "You built one of the temperature-shielding watches? When?"

"Turns out husband hunting takes up an inordinate amount of time. Once my mother and stepfather asked me to return to Sygnustern, I had plenty of time to work on the watch."

"Well, I certainly had the time to build one, since Kyrion and I have basically been trapped on board the *Dream World* for the last few weeks, but I didn't have all the materials," I groused.

Asterin smirked. "Oh, I'm sure you and Kyrion were working on *other* things."

A hot blush scalded my cheeks. "I have no idea what you're talking about."

"Please. I was at the midnight ball, remember? I saw how hard you and Kyrion fought to reach each other, and now the two of you have been traveling together on a blitzer for the last few weeks. It's like an episode of a romance serial." Asterin let out a loud, dramatic sigh and clutched her hands to her heart, as though she was about to swoon.

My blush burned a little hotter. "What about you?" I asked, desperate to change the subject. "Do you admire any of the Erzton lords?"

Asterin's smirk vanished, replaced by a sour expression. "Nope. Most of them are as puffed-up, pompous, and self-important as all the Regals on Corios. All the Erzton lords are interested in is forging a connection with House Collier or exploring the mineral rights I own. None of them cares about me as a person."

She shrugged as though the knowledge didn't bother her, but a sad, wistful note rasped through her voice. I had a sneaking suspicion Asterin Armas's tough exterior was hiding a dreamy, romantic heart.

"But focusing on alliances and resources is pretty common when it comes to Erzton marriages, just like it is in Regal society," Asterin continued. "That was certainly my experience with House Zimmer, and especially with Zane. That pompous jackass only cares about himself."

Her lips curled back in revulsion, but after a few seconds, she winced. "Sorry. I keep forgetting Zane is your brother."

I mimicked her earlier shrug, trying to slough off all the uncomfortable emotions that scraped my insides raw whenever someone mentioned Zane. "He's my brother in DNA only. If Zane catches me, he'll shock me into submission, slap some plasticuffs on my wrists, and drag me back to Corios."

Even as I said the words, a bit of hope flared in my heart like a match trying to sputter to life in a rainstorm. Despite everything Zane had done, a teeny-tiny part of me still wanted to believe my being his sister actually *meant* something to Zane, even though he was the very epitome of an arrogant Regal lord.

"I'm sorry," Asterin said. "I didn't mean to stir up bad memories."

"It's not your fault. Unfortunately, bad memories are all I have when it comes to my family."

Asterin's gaze strayed back over to the air purifier. "I have a lot of bad memories too," she confessed in a low, strained voice. "But sometimes I think the good memories are the hardest ones to bear because they just remind you of everything you lost, everything that was taken away in an instant."

My seer magic stirred to life, and another image of Asterin appeared, shimmering in the air like a hologram. The second

Asterin was also wearing gray coveralls, but she was a teenager, with long black braids trailing down over her shoulders. She was slumped against one of the workshop tables, clutching a cracked, grimy miner's helmet.

Tears streamed down young Asterin's face, and her choked sobs rang in my ears, even though I hadn't even been here when she had been crying in real life. Her grief and heartbreak were so strong they made my head spin and my chest tighten, and I had to clutch the table for support.

"Vesper?" Asterin asked in a concerned voice. "Are you okay?"

I blinked. The younger, sobbing version of Asterin vanished, and the dizziness and tightness also faded from my body.

I straightened up. "I'm fine. Let's get to work."

Asterin hesitated, then waved her hand, activating the holoscreen, which scanned the temperature-shielding wristwatch. She fell silent, but her long-ago sobs continued to ring in my ears like a bell chiming out a mournful song.

I knew that kind of pain all too well, and I couldn't help but wonder what had really happened to Asterin's father—and why my seer magic kept whispering a warning that my friend was headed for even more heartbreak in the future.

# TWELVE

## VESPER

The holoscreen finished scanning the temperature-shielding wristwatch. Asterin dug her fingers into the resulting holograms, enlarging each image. We looked at every single piece of the wristwatch, along with the accompanying schematics, and started tossing out ideas about what the Techwave might do with the climate-control tech.

Asterin might claim she wasn't an inventor or engineer, but she was just as smart, skilled, and insightful as any of the Quill Corp lab rats, and she came up with several theories I hadn't considered.

"Why are you smiling?" she asked. "We haven't figured anything out yet."

"I've missed this." I gestured at the shelves and machines. "Being in a lab and trying to figure out how to fix something. Especially since I haven't made much progress stopping the Techwave cannon from overheating."

My gaze zipped over to the cannon, which was lying on another table, then back down to the temperature-shielding watch. Silver flares of light glimmered around each device, and my mind started humming with ideas.

"Vesper? What are you thinking?" Asterin asked. "You have a really strange look on your face."

I stared at the Techwave cannon again. "Sometimes overheating isn't such a bad thing. Sometimes it can be quite useful."

Asterin also glanced over at the cannon, her forehead crinkling with confusion. She didn't understand, but I could *see* the possibilities.

Excitement coursed through me. "I need some solar wiring and a set of jeweler's tools."

An hour later, I put down my tools and swept my hand out in a grand gesture. "May I present the new and improved House Rojillo wristwatch."

I'd added two new components to the original design: a small knob on the side and thin threads of solar wiring, which I'd painstakingly wrapped around the bits of lunarium and sapphsidian already embedded in the device. Basically, the watch looked as though I'd laid a silvery spiderweb over the holoscreen.

"Ready to test it?" I asked.

Asterin grinned. "You do the honors."

I picked up the watch, turned the knob, and pointed the holoscreen away from my body. The solar wiring flared to life, growing brighter and hotter, as did the pieces of lunarium, although the sapphsidian chips darkened, turning more black than blue.

"Come on," I muttered. "Come on . . ."

I turned the knob again and again, as though I was physically winding up the wristwatch . . .

*Zing!*

A tiny bolt of white electricity sizzled out of the device, zipped across the room, and slammed into a bin of nails, shooting hot sparks everywhere.

I pumped my fist in the air in triumph, then quickly spun the knob in the opposite direction. The light faded from the solar wiring, and the lunarium and sapphsidian returned to their normal hues.

Asterin clapped her hands, and I bowed to her applause.

"I can't believe you turned what was essentially a personal thermostat into a miniature shock baton," she said. "I would have never thought of that."

"Thanks, but the credit goes to Jorge Rojillo." I waved the wristwatch in the air. "Because I never would have thought to make something this small and compact."

Asterin started typing on a holoscreen. "Well, Lord Jorge isn't satisfied with the watch being small and compact. He's planning to scale up the device so it can be wrapped around individual trees and bushes in Promenade Park to help maintain each plant's desired temperature."

Several holograms appeared, flickering in midair. I set the watch aside and studied the images. "These are updated schematics. How did you get them?"

Asterin gave a modest shrug. "I planted a few lines of code in the House Rojillo servers when I broke into the R&D lab during the summer solstice ball. Now I automatically receive copies of every project Lord Jorge and his lab rats work on."

"How did you become such an accomplished spy?"

"Ah, that, I'm afraid, is a House Armas trade secret," she replied in a teasing tone.

I started to ask another question, but my stomach growled. We'd been working for hours, and the morning had sped by.

Asterin waved her hand, cutting off the holograms. "Let's get some lunch."

We left her workshop, went through an alley, and stepped out onto another street. From this angle, I could see the green dome of the antiques emporium, along with the shipping yard and the mineral exchange. An enormous square connected all three areas, and cobblestone paths crisscrossed every which way.

Several food carts had set up in the square, and the heady smells of sizzling meat and baking bread wafted through the crisp air. Dozens of people were waiting to place their orders, while even more folks were already sitting at chrome benches and tables that were nestled in between topiary trees like the ones on the Collier estate.

Asterin headed toward a cart with one of the longest lines. "This place has amazing shock bacon sandwiches."

"What, exactly, is *shock bacon*?"

Her eyes glimmered with anticipation. "Bacon that's so blasted good it shocks your taste buds. I'll get you some different flavors to try. Why don't you find us some seats?"

"Thanks," I replied in a wary voice. "I'm sure my taste buds will love it, even if my arteries don't."

Asterin laughed and got in line. I wandered around the square. More than one cart was selling shock bacon, along with Magma s'mores and erupting apple pies. I didn't know if I was ready for such violent-sounding desserts, so I veered away from the carts and started looking for an empty table—

A figure stepped out from behind a topiary tree and headed toward the shipping yard entrance. Like everyone else, the person was wearing the emerald green of House Collier, including a long hooded cloak that covered their head. I couldn't tell if it was a man or a woman, but their smooth, confident stride was strangely familiar. I stopped and looked at the figure, but they entered the shipping yard and vanished.

Curious, I went over to the shipping yard entrance. All the workers must have been taking their lunch breaks, because the area was deserted. No machines or hoverpallets were moving, and the only sounds were the faint murmurs of conversation and sizzling of food from the square behind me.

A finger of unease tickled my spine. Why would someone enter a shipping yard when all the workers were gone? Was the person a spy like Asterin? Someone here to steal House Collier secrets?

I glanced back over my shoulder. Asterin was still in line, too far away for me to call out and get her attention, so I pulled my tablet out of my pocket and sent her a message. I waited, but Asterin was chatting with another woman, and she didn't reach for her own tablet. She must not have heard the alert. If the mysterious figure was up to something, then I was the only one who might be able to see what it was—and stop them.

I hesitated a moment longer, then shoved my tablet back into my pocket and slipped into the shipping yard.

Even though Asterin had shown it to me earlier, the shipping yard was much, much larger than I'd realized, and heavy machinery, stacks of metal rods, and hoverpallets stretched out in all directions. Searching for the intruder was like looking for a star in the proverbial galaxy, but maybe I could change that.

I stepped into an open space between two metal bins heaped high with coal. Then I stopped, reached for my seer magic, and looked around again. The hulking shapes of the machinery, rods, and hoverpallets remained the same, but I searched for the smallest speck of color or movement among all the dull gray metal—

*There.*

A bit of green fabric rippled low to the ground around a forklift, like a snake slithering deeper into the shipping yard. I yanked my stormsword off my belt and headed in that direction. Every instinct I had was whispering that I needed to follow this person, even if I had no idea who they were and what they were doing.

The sounds of conversation and frying food dimmed, then

faded away altogether, and all I could hear were my own soft footsteps on the hard-packed dirt—

*Gurp!*

Up ahead, a muffled cry rang out, although it abruptly cut off. I hurried in that direction, then eased up to a pile of pipes and cautiously peered around the side.

The mysterious figure in the green cloak had gone through the shipping yard and was standing at a back entrance to the mineral exchange. The figure was clutching a sparking shock baton, and a guard wearing a House Collier uniform was twitching on the ground.

The intruder slipped their shock baton back onto their belt. Then they reached up and drew back the hood of their cloak, revealing their features. Wavy red hair, pale skin, green eyes, a straight nose, and a rounded chin.

Shock zinged through me just like the electricity still zipping through the unconscious guard's body. It was Esmina Reston.

My shock vanished, replaced by a rising sense of dread. What was the corporate mercenary doing here? Had she tracked Kyrion and me to Sygnustern? Had I foolishly followed her straight into a trap?

Esmina whirled around. Her eyes narrowed, and her gaze darted back and forth, as if sensing my lurking. I froze, not even daring to breathe. A cool breeze whistled past my face, ruffling my ponytail, and I silently cursed the unwanted motion.

Esmina's sharp, searching gaze passed right over me. Why hadn't she spotted me? Another breeze whistled past, making my gray cloak flap around my ankles. The dull fabric must be letting me blend in with the surrounding metal and machinery. I sent a silent thanks to whatever galactic gods might be listening that I'd worn the plain cloak instead of the green House Collier garment that had been in my suite.

Esmina touched her ear, talking to someone through a comms device. In the distance, a grinding vibration filled the air, quickly growing louder and louder, like a dentist's drill reverberating through my skull. What was that awful noise?

A small, nimble blitzer rose out of the chasm at the edge of the shipping yard, zipped over the stone wall, and landed close to the back of the mineral exchange. The instant the blitzer touched down, a door on the side slid back, and more than two dozen men wearing black polyplastic armor and carrying blasters erupted out of the dark depths. The men were all wearing helmets with black visors, so I couldn't see their faces, but their quick, precise movements reminded me of the corporate mercenaries Rowena Kent had employed at Kent Corp.

A final man hopped out of the transport. He was clutching a hand cannon, but unlike the rest of the mercenaries, he wasn't wearing a helmet, so I could clearly see his blond hair, brown eyes, ruddy skin, and square chin. Pollux Lamont.

Pollux and the other mercenaries headed straight for the mineral exchange. One of the mercenaries placed a small, round black device on the back door, then scurried away. Pollux hit a button on the holoscreen strapped to his left forearm, and the device exploded, taking the door along with it.

"Move! Move! Move!" Pollux yelled. "We have three minutes to get in and out!"

The mercenaries swarmed into the mineral exchange like a horde of killer bees. Pollux hurried in after them, but Esmina followed at a leisurely pace, as though she had all the time in the galaxy before someone came to investigate the explosion.

Esmina, Pollux, and their crew weren't here to capture me—they were here to rob the mineral exchange.

For a moment, my mind went completely blank, and I just stood there, gaping like a fish out of water. Then my brain sputtered back to life, and I stepped forward. I had to stop Esmina, Pollux, and their Serpens Corp mercenaries before they hurt anyone else—

*Pew! Pew! Pew!*

The high-pitched sounds of blaster fire erupted inside the building, and streaks of color shimmered through the clear glass walls.

*Asterin!* I yelled. *Asterin, can you hear me?*

Only a faint, buzzing silence filled my mind in return, and I didn't get any sense that Asterin had heard my telepathic call. Once again, despite my truebond with Kyrion, I couldn't tap into his power. Why? Why couldn't my magic just *work*?

Anger shot through my body, but I tried again. *Asterin! Asterin, can you hear me?*

Still no response. A low, frustrated snarl spewed from my lips, but I forced myself to draw in a deep breath and let it out. Then I tried again, this time focusing on the person I had the best chance of reaching.

*Kyrion! Thieves are breaking into the House Collier mineral exchange! I'm going to try to stop them!*

I waited, but his voice didn't sound in my mind. Another snarl rose in my throat. Why couldn't I reach him?

A hot, stinging jolt of awareness shot through the bond and punched into my chest like an arrow. I gasped and staggered to the side, banging my shoulder against a metal bin.

Kyrion's voice didn't sound in my mind, but the sticky cobweb of him pulsed with icy fury. Kyrion had definitely heard me, but he was still miles away at the Collier estate.

*Pew! Pew! Pew!*

More blaster fire zinged through the mineral exchange, and surprised shouts rose in the distance. The workers eating lunch in the square must have finally noticed the sounds of the battle.

I took a few steps toward the blown-out door of the mineral exchange, then made myself stop. As much as I wanted to help the House Collier workers, I was no match for a swarm of mercenaries armed with blasters. Not to mention Esmina and Pollux and their psionic abilities. I might occasionally be impulsive, but I wasn't completely reckless.

So how could I stop the mercenaries? And I *had* to stop them. Esmina and Pollux showing up the day after Kyrion and I landed on Sygnustern *could* just be a coincidence . . . if I believed in such things. But I didn't. Not anymore. Not since my truebond with Kyrion had formed.

No, this attack had something to do with Kyrion and me. I was *certain* of it—just as I was certain that Siya would blame us for the mercenaries' appearance.

I spun away from the mineral exchange and looked out over the shipping yard. Even if I had been able to get a grip on Kyrion's telekinesis, the metal rods were all far too big and heavy to move. I wouldn't be able to pick up a single rod with my mind, much less throw it at the mercenaries. The same thing went for the machinery, especially since some of the cranes were bigger than the *Dream World* . . .

My gaze snagged on the crane closest to the mercenaries' blitzer, and my seer magic surged to life, outlining the machine in that familiar silver light. Relief rushed through my veins, morphing into a wave of determination. I might not be able to figure out how to fully use my truebond with Kyrion, but my own magic hadn't deserted me, and for once, I knew exactly what my power was trying to tell me.

I slid my stormsword back into its slot on my belt, then sprinted toward the crane.

# THIRTEEN

## KYRION

Watching Vesper get into a transport and leave the estate was more difficult than I'd imagined, especially since all I wanted was to follow and make sure she stayed safe.

The velvety ribbon of Vesper unspooled in my mind, the strand growing thinner and thinner the farther away the transport moved. My hands tightened around the balcony railing at the unsettling sensation, and it took all my willpower not to frantically grab onto that strand like a belligerent child who refused to relinquish a beloved toy. My inner monster grumbled, unhappy with my decision to stay behind, but I grumbled right back at it, and the moody bastard finally shut up.

I watched until the transport was out of sight. Then I released my grip on the railing and went back inside the guest wing to continue my reconnaissance.

I prowled from one level to another, studying every single area, from small libraries filled with paper books, to larger rooms boasting hoverbilliards and other gaming tables, to hidden alcoves that were only large enough for a single rocking chair. I even swept through a kitchen with a well-stocked fridge and pantry and a servant waiting to make whatever I desired, instead of having a brewmaker or some other food fabricator spit it out.

Oh, yes. The guest wing featured everything I would expect in a noble's home—except security cameras. I didn't see a single camera embedded in the ceiling, hidden inside a light fixture, or attached to a glittering geode sculpture on the walls.

The Colliers were placing a lot of trust in Vesper and me *not* to be spying on our every movement. But I supposed when your society was largely based on notions of honor and etiquette, eavesdropping on your guests would be considered very bad form indeed.

I wound up on the ground floor, stepped through a pair of double doors, and stopped in front of the large, central topiary garden. Like everything else, the garden was securely ensconced below the estate's energy shield, so the air was pleasantly cool without a hint of the stiff breeze that was currently whistling around outside the shield.

House Collier guards armed with blasters were standing at the garden entrance, but they didn't try to stop me as I stalked past them. I moved from one sculpted tree and hedge to the next, making mental notes of where all the paths led and which trees and hedges were large enough to provide cover from the guards' blasters. I might not have gone with Vesper into the city, but I could make certain the estate was secure for her return.

Eventually, I reached the center of the garden, which opened into a wide circular area that featured several stone benches and small bubbling fountains. Thick stands of blue-moon peonies ringed the area, perfuming the air with their sweet spearmint aroma. A few mammoth butterflies were hovering over the blossoms, their shimmering black-and-blue wings making peony petals drift through the air like scented snowflakes.

Unexpected longing spiked through my chest. The area reminded me of my mother's garden at Castle Caldaren . . .

The air shimmered, and suddenly, Desdemona appeared, sitting on a bench and pruning stray leaves off some peonies. My mother looked up, and for a moment, her gaze bored into mine. Then she looked to her right, and another vision appeared: me as a thirteen-year-old boy.

In the vision, I stormed over to my mother and started yelling at her. Not such a happy memory after all, especially given the cruel things I'd said that day. I grimaced and spun away from the sight. As much as I cared about Vesper, I could have done without the odd visions her seer power showed me from time to time.

Lady Verona was sitting at a table in the middle of the circle, sipping tea and swiping through screens on her tablet. A single place setting was laid out across from her, as though she had been expecting me, while silver platters heaped with food covered the rest of the table.

From Holloway's research into the Colliers, I knew Verona and Aldrich were both psions, and I'd seen them telepathically communicate with each other in the library yesterday, but Verona anticipating my arrival was a tad unsettling.

Verona looked up at me, a wide smile splitting her face. "Hello, Kyrion. Care for some breakfast?"

"Of course," I murmured the automatic response.

I might be an Arrow, a monster, and a ruthless killer, but my mother had drilled good manners into me since I was old enough to walk. Desdemona had been a stickler for following protocol, although she'd also had a sly, subtle habit of bending societal niceties to her own will. More bittersweet longing spiked through my chest. So many horrible things had happened with my mother that I had almost forgotten how clever and devious she could be, even when she and my father had been under Holloway's thumb.

I fixed a plate of food and sat down across from Verona. Cranberry scones, apple pancakes topped with sweet vanilla-bean cream, decadent egg frittatas filled with vegetables, crispy bacon covered with a tangy, blood-orange glaze. Everything was delicious, and I found myself relaxing.

I also gently, carefully checked my connection to Vesper, and a hum of happiness rippled back to me. Whatever she was doing in Asterin's workshop was pleasing her. Good.

I dropped my napkin onto my empty plate. "Thank you. The food was excellent. My compliments to your chefs."

Verona set down her tablet, lining it up perfectly with the edge of the table. "I'm glad you enjoyed it. I hope your suite is also to your liking."

"Everything has been lovely so far," I replied, matching her politeness.

To my surprise, Verona let out a loud snort. "Except for my stepdaughter's rude welcome yesterday in the antiques emporium."

"I have received far worse welcomes, my lady."

She snorted again and waved her left hand, making an emerald ring sparkle on her finger. "Verona, please. We are not nearly so formal as you Regals are."

"I will try to keep that in mind, my lady."

Verona picked up her teacup and studied me over the rim. "You want to know if Aldrich and I are going to betray you to Callus Holloway. If we are plotting your capture at this very moment. That's why you've been prowling around the guest wing all morning, giving the servants and guards fits."

"If they were true guards, they wouldn't have such fits," I countered. "But yes, those thoughts had crossed my mind."

A delighted laugh burst from her mouth. "I can see why Asterin likes you, Kyrion. You don't mince words, do you?"

"Words are meant to be used, not minced, my lady."

She laughed again. "Well said, but let me reassure you

anyway. Aldrich and I would never do anything to harm you or Vesper. We gave you our word and our order of protection. Unlike Regal society, words mean a great deal to Erztonians."

Her voice rang with sincerity, and the same emotion twinged my telempathy. A tight knot of tension unwound in my chest. I didn't care so much about myself, but knowing Vesper would be safe here lifted a heavy weight off my shoulders.

"But safe shelter isn't the only reason you came here." Verona set down her teacup. "You also want to know what's wrong with your truebond with Vesper."

"Yes." I saw no reason to lie, especially given my awkward conversation with Vesper last night.

"Well, I hate to disappoint you, Kyrion, but nothing is wrong with your bond."

I frowned. "What do you mean, nothing is wrong? You and Aldrich both said the bond hadn't solidified and wasn't stable. That it was a danger to Vesper and me and everyone around us."

"Each truebond is unique to its individual couple. What works for one couple might not work for another. And yes, your bond is new, so it hasn't fully solidified yet. And yes, it is a danger, but not in the way you think." Verona gestured at the garden. "The two of you won't suddenly lose control of your collective magics and decimate the estate with psionic lightning the way you did the Crownpoint throne room."

"But?"

She dropped her hand. "But the bond will only solidify once you and Vesper figure things out."

"What *things*?" I growled.

"A truebond is about more than just trust. It's also about balance." She paused. "And conquering your fear."

I stiffened in my seat.

Verona leaned forward, her blue gaze frank and assessing. "I can *feel* your fear, Kyrion. It wafts off you like the cold fog rises off these mountains each morning. You're afraid you're going to lose Vesper to Callus Holloway."

Once again, I saw no reason to lie, even if the confession cracked something deep inside me. "Yes, I'm afraid I'm going to lose Vesper, and I'm bloody *terrified* that I'm not strong enough to protect her. Not just from Holloway and the bounty hunters but everyone else who might come after us."

I scrubbed a hand through my hair, trying to put my frustration into words. "I have to be smart and strong and capable all the time. I can't slip up or make a mistake. Not even *once*, not for one bloody *second*, because that could mean the difference between Vesper living and dying."

I drew in a breath and let it out, along with the rest of my dark confession. "And even if I manage to protect Vesper, I could still end up killing her. Because if I die, then she dies too."

Another laugh erupted out of Verona's mouth, startling me. She waved her hand again. "Sorry! I'm sorry! But I just can't help myself when people say such ridiculous things. You Imperium Regals really do have some odd ideas about truebonds, but I suppose that's only natural, given all the dreck on your gossipcasts." Her face softened. "As well as what happened to your parents."

I stiffened in my seat again. Out of the corner of my eye, the vision of my mother reappeared, along with my teenage self yelling at her. "And how, exactly, is being worried about my own death and thus killing Vesper by proxy ridiculous?"

Verona shrugged. "It is patently ridiculous to worry about things that might never happen. Besides, not every truebond automatically ends in death."

"What are you saying? That one person can actually *survive* a truebond even if the other person dies and the connection is severed? How is that possible?"

"No one really knows," Verona replied. "But one person

dying in a truebond can have a variety of effects on the remaining partner."

Her shoulders drooped, and sadness rippled off her and twinged my telempathy. A memory bubbled up in my mind. Information from a file Holloway had given me on Verona, back when he'd been trying to force a truebond between Asterin and me.

"You had a truebond with your first husband, Urston, Asterin's father."

"Yes, I did. Urston and I were childhood sweethearts, and we got married after we both graduated from universities here on Sygnustern. Falling in love, getting married, having a truebond, it was all a slow, easy, natural progression."

A smile crept across Verona's face, and her eyes brightened. For a moment, I got a glimpse of the beautiful young woman she had been—and just how much she had loved her first husband.

But just as quickly, her smile snuffed out, and her gaze darkened with weary grief. "But then Urston died."

I remembered what Asterin had said about the mining accident that had claimed her father's life. "But you survived. How?"

"I had a heartbroken teenage daughter to care for, myriad lawsuits to settle, and mountains of debt to dig myself out of, quite literally. I didn't have time to *die*." Verona's voice sharpened with every word. Her hands balled into fists, and her body vibrated, as if she was bracing herself to face an old, familiar enemy.

Questions swirled through my mind, but I held my tongue. Talking about this was obviously difficult for the Erzton lady, so why was she baring her soul?

Verona sighed out a breath and loosened her fists. "Not everyone involved in a truebond will end up like your parents, Kyrion. Some people can survive the severing of a bond." A sour note crept into her voice, and her nostrils flared with disgust. "Some people even thrive on it."

How could someone thrive on losing such a deep connection to another person? I had never heard of such a thing, much less imagined it was possible. No, everything I had seen, especially with my parents, had led me to believe a severed truebond equaled a slow, miserable death for the remaining partner.

Verona's tablet chimed, and she scooped up the device and got to her feet. "Duty calls. I must go help Aldrich and Leland prepare for the marriage mart tonight. You and Vesper are still welcome to attend as House Collier guests."

I also got to my feet and bowed to her. "Of course, my lady. Thank you for breakfast . . . and your advice."

Verona reached up and patted my cheek. The gentle motion reminded me so much of my mother it made my chest ache, and for the third time, I spotted that vision of Desdemona out of the corner of my eye. If only I could go back to that moment, I would have done so many things differently.

Verona dropped her hand, strode away, and disappeared into the garden, but her words kept echoing through my mind. With just one brief conversation, the Erzton lady had made me question everything I knew about truebonds.

Perhaps more important, she had also given me the tiniest ember of hope that I wouldn't end up getting myself and Vesper killed.

Servants came to clear away the remains of the breakfast. Shouts rose in the distance, along with several distinctive *thwacks*. I followed the noise through the garden and over to a large training ring that butted up against the main castle.

Unlike the rest of the lush landscaping, not a topiary tree was in sight, and the ground was hard-packed dirt. Hoverpallets covered with towels, drinks, and other supplies sat off to the side, along with targets bristling with spears, daggers, and other sharp, pointed weapons. At the back of the ring, a permaglass wall jutted ten feet into the air, cordoning off this section of the estate from the dangerous drop below.

Siya paced back and forth along the edge of the training ring, watching two Hammers expertly batter each other with wooden staffs. The House Collier Hammers were the match of any Arrow I had ever trained with, except for Zane. As much as I hated to admit it, Zane Zimmer was an exceptional warrior—when he could control his own ego and end a fight without stopping to show off.

One woman knocked the other down, and the sparring match ended. The warrior who had landed flat on her back lifted her head and saw me. She let out a muttered curse, but I didn't care if the Hammers realized I was cataloging their strengths and weaknesses. We might not be outright enemies, but we certainly weren't friends.

One of the warriors nudged Siya, who looked in my direction.

"Well, well, we have an audience. Care to test your luck against some real warriors, Arrow?" Siya called out in a sarcastic voice.

I considered walking away. I was long past the point of letting an enemy goad me into a fight, except for Zane, who always slithered under my skin no matter how hard I tried to ignore him.

Siya kept smirking at me, as did the other Hammers. They wanted to fight? Well, I would be more than happy to oblige them. Perhaps my kicking their asses would make the warriors think twice about attacking Vesper and me again. Plus, my talk with Lady Verona had unsettled me more than I cared to admit, and taking my frustration out on someone else was always an excellent way of ignoring my emotions. My inner monster licked its chops in anticipation.

"I would be delighted to participate in your sparring session."

Siya's black eyebrows lifted in surprise, but she crooked her finger in a clear invitation. I walked through the center of the training ring, right past all the other warriors, eyeing them just as they were eyeing me.

The Hammers were a mix of men and women of all shapes and sizes. The youngest looked to be in his early twenties; the oldest was a woman in her sixties. I had never sparred with any Hammers, but Callus Holloway had spies everywhere, and from time to time, he showed me, Zane, and the other Arrows secretly recorded footage of the warriors' training. And of course, the Hammers had had a few skirmishes with the Techwave's mechanized Black Scarab troops that had aired on both the Erzton and the Imperium gossipcasts.

Rigel was here, leaning up against the castle wall just as he had done yesterday in Aldrich's library. He nodded to me, and I returned the somewhat friendly gesture.

Siya gestured at a hoverpallet. "Pick your poison, Arrow."

An impressive spread of wooden practice weapons covered the surface—swords, daggers, staffs, crossbows, and, of course, hammers. I was still wearing my stormsword, so I took it off and laid it on an empty spot on the hoverpallet, along with my blaster. Then I picked up one war hammer after another, testing their weight and balance. Even though the hammers were made of wood, their solid heft could still inflict serious damage.

I found a hammer I liked, then strode over to the center of the training ring and crooked my finger at Siya, mocking her earlier gesture. She growled, grabbed a wooden hammer, and stepped into the ring. The other warriors gathered around, except for Rigel, who maintained his relaxed position by the wall.

"The great Kyrion Caldaren." Siya sneered, circling around

me. "According to the Regal gossipcasts, you're the best warrior in the Imperium and deal out death on a daily basis. I'm disappointed with the reality."

I matched my steps to hers as though we were two vipers trying to bite the other's tail. "What is the old saying? Never meet your heroes."

"Oh, you're no bloody hero. Just another Arrow assassin running around the galaxy and doing Callus Holloway's bidding."

"Like you aren't doing the same thing for Lord Aldrich?"

Anger sparked in Siya's hazel eyes, making them burn a bright, glimmering gold. "Aldrich is my father, and this is my House. It is an *honor* to serve my people, and I will give my life to defend them. Can you say the same about any of your fellow Arrows?"

No, I could not. I had never been close to any of the other Arrows, given the Regal politics and constant jockeying for position that permeated the group. The other Arrows had simply been tools to ensure my own survival and avoid Holloway's wrath, and I had certainly never cared about any of my fellow warriors the way Siya cared about her people.

Siya shot me a knowing smirk. "I didn't think so."

Without warning, she lunged forward, swinging her hammer and trying to catch me by surprise. I snapped up my own weapon to block her attack, and the force of her blow reverberated all the way up my arm.

My eyes narrowed. "You have a strength enhancement."

A wicked smile curved her lips. "Among other things."

She lunged forward again, and the battle began in earnest. Around and around the training ring we went, with Siya slamming her hammer into mine over and over. In addition to being strong, she was also fast—much faster than I expected—and she managed to break through my defenses and smash her hammer into my left ribs.

Even though we were fighting with wooden weapons, pain

still erupted in my body, and the hard blow punched the air out of my lungs. I wheezed and staggered away.

"Not so tough without your stormsword, eh, Arrow?" Siya mocked.

The other warriors let out loud, approving claps and jeers, except for Rigel, who maintained his silent, watchful stance.

I ignored the taunts and drew in one deep breath after another, even as I slumped my shoulders and lowered my hammer, just a bit, as though I was more injured than I truly was. Siya took the bait, darted forward, and swung her weapon high overhead.

I might not be as proficient with a war hammer as she was, but I had learned a long time ago that I didn't always need to be quicker or stronger than my opponent—just smarter. So even as Siya brought her hammer down, trying to break my collarbone, I went low, dropped to one knee, and spun past her. Then, before she could recover, I used my hammer's long hilt like a wooden staff and swept Siya's legs out from under her.

The other warrior landed flat on her back. The hard fall stunned her, and the hammer tumbled out of her grasp. I rose to my feet, twirled the hilt of my own hammer around in my hand, and pressed the spiked end up against her throat.

Siya froze. Even with a wooden practice weapon, I could easily crush her windpipe and kill her. The other Hammers froze as well, and their mocking jeers cut off. A tense, charged silence dropped over the training ring, and the only sounds were Siya's raspy breaths.

"Do you yield?" I asked in a soft, dangerous voice.

Fury sparked in Siya's eyes. She surged up, trying to use her speed to slip away, but I pressed the spike a little more firmly against her throat.

"Do . . . you . . . yield?" I asked again, deliberately drawing out each word.

All around me, the other Hammers crept forward, hefting

their practice weapons, and mistrust crackled through the air like psionic lightning about to vaporize us all. I hoped Lady Verona was right about Vesper being able to survive the true-bond even if I died. Because one wrong move, and my death would become a fact instead of an eventuality—

*Kyrion! Thieves are breaking into the House Collier mineral exchange! I'm going to try to stop them!* Vesper's voice rang through my mind as clear and loud as an alarm blaring in my ears, and the velvety ribbon of her vibrated with determination.

*Vesper? Vesper, wait for me!*

I tried to send a thought back to her, but I couldn't tell if she had heard me. Worry shot through me, morphing into cold claws of fear that stabbed deep into my heart.

I lifted the hammer from Siya's throat and stepped back. She scrambled to her feet and grabbed her weapon to continue our fight, but I stabbed my hammer at her.

"Where is the House Collier shipping yard?"

Siya blinked at the abrupt change in topic. "What?"

"Where is it?" I growled. "Vesper is there, and she says thieves are breaking into the shipping yard."

Siya's eyes widened, and she looked over at Rigel, who pushed away from the wall and yanked his tablet out of his pocket.

"Not the shipping yard," he muttered, swiping through screens. "The mineral exchange."

Concern surged off both Siya and Rigel, the emotion strong enough to break through my own cold worry and tickle my telempathy like hot, needling fingers. All around the training ring, the other Hammers snapped to attention.

Siya's gaze flicked back over to me. "The shipping yard is in the city. Close to the antiques emporium."

"Take me there," I growled again.

She glanced over at Rigel, and the two of them shared a look I couldn't decipher.

"Take me there right *now*, or I will find it myself." I stabbed my hammer at her again. "But if I get there too late, and Vesper is dead, then I will hold *you* accountable. Understand?"

Siya flinched at my cold, deadly tone. Wariness flickered across Rigel's face, and all the other Hammers tensed.

After a few seconds, Siya jerked her head in agreement. "We'll take a transport. Rigel, contact security at the shipping yard and mineral exchange, and see if you can find out what's going on."

Rigel nodded and started typing on his tablet. I strode over to the hoverpallet, dropped the wooden war hammer onto the surface, and scooped up my stormsword and blaster. Siya and the other warriors also hustled over to the hoverpallet and exchanged their practice weapons for the real things.

As soon as we were all armed, Siya raised her hand in the air and made a circular motion with her index finger. "Let's go. Move! Move! Move!"

The other Hammers rushed out of the training ring and sprinted into the topiary garden.

"There's a transport garage on the other side of the garden," Siya said. "You'd better be right about this, Arrow."

"And Vesper better not be dead, Hammer," I growled right back at her.

Siya's eyes narrowed at my icy tone, but she plunged into the garden. I followed her, worry thrumming through my body with every quick step.

# FOURTEEN

## VESPER

I sprinted through the shipping yard, heading toward the crane I'd spotted earlier.

*Pew! Pew! Pew!*

More blaster fire zinged through the air. I ducked my head, but no bolts came close to me. The mercenaries must still be fighting the House Collier guards inside the mineral exchange.

I skidded to a stop beside the crane. Up close, the machine was much, much larger than I'd realized, and the metal crawler tracks alone were more than twenty feet tall. My gaze roamed over the crane for several seconds before I spotted a ladder that stretched up to the operator's cab.

I glanced back over my shoulder, but I didn't hear or see any more blaster fire. The mercenaries must have already overpowered the guards, which meant I was running out of time.

I hurried over to the ladder and started climbing. The rungs stretched up and up . . . while the ground got farther and farther away. Maybe Kyrion was right about heights not being the best thing in the galaxy. I shuddered and forced myself to climb faster.

A few seconds later, I reached the final rung of the ladder and swung my body into the cab that topped this part of the machine. I dropped into the operator's seat and stared at the holoscreens, levers, and buttons on the dashboard. The workers in the Quill Corp production plants used similar cranes to move large pieces of metal, especially when building spaceships, but as a lab rat, I had never operated such a machine.

Frustration simmered in my chest. I couldn't use the crane to stop the mercenaries if I couldn't even turn the blasted thing on, and the seconds just kept ticking by.

*Think, Vesper, think!*

I drew in a deep breath and slowly let it out. Then I leaned forward and stared at the numbers and letters next to the holoscreens, levers, and buttons, trying to figure out what each one controlled . . .

My gaze snagged on a large green button on the right side of the dashboard. Green almost always meant go or start, so I punched the button.

One after another, the holoscreens powered up, and an engine rumbled to life deep inside the crane. I pumped my fist in the air in triumph, then swiped through screens and menus until I found a hologram that showed the dashboard. I stuck my fingers into the hologram, enlarging it, then flicked it off to one side and studied the information.

Next, I started pulling levers and punching buttons. Slowly, the operator's cab swung around, and the long arm of the crane came into view in front of me. I leaned to the side, making sure the enormous magnet was still attached to the bottom of the arm. Then I hit some more levers and buttons, and the cab, arm, and magnet all started moving.

After about fifteen seconds of slow, steady turning, I was facing the mercenaries' blitzer, which was still parked close to the mineral exchange. I studied the dashboard hologram again, making sure I knew which button I should use next, but

I didn't do anything else. Not yet.

Thirty seconds later, the Serpens Corp mercenaries ran out of the mineral exchange. Each man was still armed with a blaster, and heavy, bulging packs were now strapped to their backs, although I couldn't see what they had stolen.

Pollux appeared, still clutching his hand cannon, with a large pack strapped to his own back. Esmina followed him, and the two of them headed toward the blitzer at a more leisurely pace than the running mercenaries.

My eyes narrowed. *Come on, you thieving bastards. Get on your transport and try to fly away, just like you planned.*

Esmina abruptly stopped and lifted her hand. Pollux also stopped, but the other mercenaries kept hurrying forward.

I ground my teeth. Esmina had heard my thoughts. That was the only reason the psion had stopped moving.

*Stupid, stupid, Vesper!*

I grimaced and cut off the rest of my chiding words. That had been stupid too.

Esmina's head snapped up, and she spotted me in the operator's cab. "Stop!" she yelled. "Stop running! Get away from the transport!"

The other mercenaries skidded to a halt and whipped around, not sure what was happening.

Esmina stabbed her finger up at me. "Shoot her! Shoot her now!"

The mercs raised their blasters, but Pollux was quicker, and he lifted his hand cannon, aimed it at the crane, and pulled the trigger. I ducked down.

*Boom!*

The permaglass windshield shattered, and chunks of safety glass cascaded all around the operator's cab in a tinkling, musical rain.

*Boom!*

Another blast of cannon fire zipped through the shattered

windshield and punched into the wall behind me, scorching the metal. Hot sparks and noxious smoke boiled up, stinging my skin and eyes and making me cough. Tears streamed down my face, but I blinked them away, leaned forward, and punched the green button on the dashboard again.

With a loud snap, the magnet broke free of the cable attaching it to the arm of the crane. The magnet plummeted downward like a meteor barreling toward the earth . . .

*BOOM!*

The magnet smashed into the top of the blitzer, crumpling the ship and pinning it to the ground like an aluminum can. I grinned. The mercenaries weren't getting away so easily now.

*Pew! Pew! Pew!*

Blaster bolts pinged into the sides of the operator's cab, making me duck down again. I was an easy target up here, so I hit another button, and the cab swung around, turning away from Pollux and the other mercenaries who were still firing at me.

The instant the cab stopped, I slid out of the operator's seat and quickly climbed down the ladder to the ground. Then I plucked my stormsword off my belt and ran to the end of the crane, heading toward the spot where I'd last seen Esmina, Pollux, and their men.

I might be outnumbered, but I couldn't let them escape. I wanted—*needed*—answers about why the mercenaries were here and what, if anything, stealing from House Collier had to do with me.

"Vesper!" a voice yelled.

I skidded to a halt and glanced to my right. Asterin was crouching down beside a metal bin. A small, compact silver blaster glinted in her right hand, and she was clutching a tablet in her left hand.

"Attack!" Asterin yelled into the tablet. "We are under attack at the shipping yard! At the back of the mineral exchange!"

She shoved the tablet into her pocket, then ran over to my position. A grim expression filled her face. "We have to keep the thieves in the shipping yard until Siya, Rigel, and the Hammers arrive. We can't let the thieves escape into a public area and start targeting civilians."

The two of us crept to the end of the metal crawler tracks. Asterin looked at me, and I nodded back. Together the two of us moved around the tracks and sprinted forward, heading toward the mercenaries.

*Pew! Pew! Pew!*

Red blaster bolts zipped through the air as the mercenaries fired at us. Asterin returned fire with her own blaster, while I snapped up my stormsword and whipped it back and forth in the rapid patterns Kyrion and Leandra Ferrum had taught me. Using the lunarium blade, I managed to deflect some of the blaster bolts back at the mercenaries.

One of my rebound bolts punched into a merc's chest, and he screamed and tumbled to the ground. Beside me, Asterin kept firing her blaster, and she dropped another merc. The others broke ranks and scrambled for cover.

I rushed forward, with Asterin running along beside me. We moved from one bin and stack of metal rods to another, using them for cover as we kept attacking the mercenaries.

Pollux backed up, firing his hand cannon at us, but his shots went wide. Esmina shook her head in disgust, then spun around on her bootheel and strode away.

*Pew! Pew! Pew!*

Asterin fired her blaster at the psions. Pollux ducked one of the bolts, but Esmina never turned around. Instead, she stepped to one side, then the other, smoothly and easily avoiding the deadly bursts of electricity just as she had during the battle with the bounty hunters. Once again, she knew *exactly* where the bolts were going even before they were fired.

I snarled and gripped my sword even tighter, and hot blue

sparks sizzled off the lunarium blade, mirroring my frustration. If I didn't do something drastic, Esmina and Pollux were going to escape again, just like they had on Tropics 44.

"I'm going after the leaders!" I yelled at Asterin. "Cover me!"

She nodded, rose up from behind the bin, and fired her blaster. While the other mercenaries were distracted, I skirted around the far side of the container, then darted across an open space and behind another container. I hurried along the side and rounded the corner, still chasing after Esmina and Pollux—

A mercenary lunged forward, his fist whistling toward my head. I ducked the blow, then spun around and lashed out with my stormsword. The lunarium blade easily sheared through the merc's polyplastic armor and ripped into his stomach, and he screamed and staggered back against the bin. I drove my sword into his chest, and he grunted and flopped to the ground, already more dead than alive.

The mercenary landed on his stomach, his bulging backpack sticking up into the air. I crouched down and used my sword to slice through the thick fabric. Several large chunks of blackish stone spilled out and landed at my feet. I grabbed one and held it up to the afternoon sunlight, and the warm rays brought out the stone's true dark blue color.

"Sapphsidian?" I muttered.

Why would the mercenaries steal sapphsidian when far more valuable things were stored inside the mineral exchange? I didn't know, but I shoved the stone into my pocket to study later. Then I eased up to the container and peered around the side.

Several mercs had taken cover behind some forklifts. Every few seconds, a merc would pop out and fire their blaster at Asterin, who returned fire, but I didn't see Esmina or Pollux.

More frustration filled me, but I kept scanning the shipping yard. In the distance, a ripple of green caught my eye, and I spotted Esmina entering a building I hadn't noticed before.

*Pew! Pew! Pew!*

Asterin fired at the mercs again, making them duck down, then scurried over to me.

I stabbed my finger at the mystery building. "The leaders went that way. What's in there?"

"The refinery," she replied. "Where the raw ores are melted down and shaped for shipping."

"Why would they go in there? The mercenaries should be trying to get out of the shipping yard, not moving deeper into it."

Asterin let out a curse. "There's an exit on the far side of the refinery that comes out close to the antiques emporium. If the mercs get into the emporium, they could go out several different exits and get lost in the city streets." Worry creased her face. "Or they could start taking the emporium shoppers hostage and use them for human shields."

My hand tightened around my stormsword, and the lunarium blade glowed a little brighter in response. "Then let's stop them."

Asterin hesitated. "Are you sure? The thieves obviously don't care about collateral damage, including us."

I nodded. "I'm sure."

Asterin nodded back at me. We both lifted our weapons a little higher, stepped around the container, and ran toward the refinery.

To my surprise, no blaster bolts zinged in our direction, and Asterin and I made it to the refinery without encountering any resistance.

The enormous double doors were standing wide open, so Asterin and I slowed our pace, softened our steps, and cautiously crept inside.

In many ways, the refinery reminded me of the Techwave facility where I'd been held on Magma 3, and the first floor was basically a giant factory with humming machinery and conveyor belts running in all directions. Along the walls, a metal grate opened and closed like the jaws of some massive monster, swallowing one chunk of ore after the other and gulping them all down into red-hot furnaces and smelters. The acrid stench of melted metal filled the air, and the intense heat made sweat bead on my forehead and trickle down my spine.

Asterin and I moved quickly and quietly, but we didn't spot Esmina and Pollux among the machinery and conveyor belts. A minute later, we reached another set of double doors at the opposite end of the refinery. They too were standing wide open.

"The thieves must already be outside," Asterin said.

Together we stepped through the opening. This part of the shipping yard was filled with neat stacks of metal rods and other materials fresh from the furnaces, and they all gleamed like newly minted coins. Asterin and I crept from one stack of materials to another. In the distance, the emerald-green dome of the antiques emporium jutted up like an enormous hill a couple of streets over.

"They're not here," Asterin muttered. "They must have already slipped out of the shipping yard and headed into the emporium."

She moved forward, rounding some cement blocks, and a silver light exploded around her. For an instant, time slowed down—or maybe it sped up. I wasn't quite sure. But suddenly, I could see a blast of green cannon fire zinging through the air, slamming into Asterin's chest and knocking her backward even though she was still moving forward right beside me. Even worse, I could smell the sizzle of her fried flesh and see the light leaking out of her eyes . . .

In the next heartbeat, time snapped back to its normal flow, and the images vanished, although not the dread they left behind.

"No!" I yelled. "Asterin, stop!"

I lunged forward, dug my hand into Asterin's coveralls, and yanked her back behind the blocks—

*Boom!*

Green cannon fire zipped through the air where Asterin had been and slammed into a pile of pipes behind us, scorching the metal's shiny finish.

Asterin's eyes widened, and her face went white with shock. "How did you know they were going to fire at me?"

I shook my head. "I'm not sure. I just knew something bad was going to happen."

I'd never had that kind of sudden, screaming warning from my magic before. Was my power growing? Or was this another sign of my unstable truebond with Kyrion?

*Boom! Boom! Boom!*

More cannon fire erupted, causing Asterin and me to hunker down.

*Pew! Pew! Pew!*

Blaster bolts joined the cannon fire, coming from different dircctions. In an instant, we were pinned down.

*Boom! Boom! Boom!*

*Pew! Pew! Pew!*

The cannon and blaster fire continued, and each bolt obliterated a little bit more of our cover. Just when I thought the mercs were going to shoot right through the cement blocks, and us too, the shots abruptly stopped, although the electric aroma of the bolts lingered in the air like a smoky, suffocating cloud.

"Come out!" Pollux commanded. "Or we'll blast those blocks to pieces, and you along with them!"

Asterin and I slowly stood up, weapons still in our hands, and stepped around the broken blocks.

More than a dozen mercenaries armed with blasters were standing in front of us. Esmina was in the center of the men, with Pollux by her side.

Esmina glanced at Asterin a moment, then focused on me.

The gold flecks in her green eyes shimmered, and her magic curled through the air, slithered around me like a boa constrictor, and slowly tightened, as though each twist around my body was squeezing out more of my secrets.

"Did you follow me and Kyrion here?" I demanded.

Asterin looked back and forth between me and the mercenaries, clearly confused about what was happening.

Esmina let out an amused laugh. "I have no need to follow you and Kyrion anywhere. I told you before, Vesper, I know *everything* you're going to do before you even do it. Even without my psion power, I still would have known you were coming here. Truebonded couples *always* come to Sygnustern for refuge." She shook her head. "What a bloody joke."

Bitterness colored her last few words. My magic surged up, and suddenly, I was seeing another image of Esmina. This younger version looked to be in her early twenties and was a bedraggled mess, with long, dirty hair, a grimy face, and torn, tattered clothes, as though she had tumbled down a cliff.

I blinked, and the image vanished, although questions crowded into my mind.

"Oh, yes," Esmina said in snide voice. "I was once just like you, Vesper. Trapped in a truebond."

I blinked again. Had she just seen what *I* had seen? But how was that possible? Was Esmina using her seer magic to tap into my own power?

"Why are you stealing from my family?" Asterin asked.

Esmina clucked her tongue. "They're not really *your* family, are they, Asterin? You're just a poor relation when it comes to House Collier. A castoff from your own once-great House now dependent on others' generosity."

An angry flush stained Asterin's cheeks. "Who are you? What do you want?"

"You don't recognize me? If you did, then you would know *exactly* what I want."

Confusion creased Asterin's face. She had no idea what Esmina was talking about. Well, that made two of us.

"I suppose your ignorance is to be expected, since you've always been much more concerned with other things." Esmina tilted her head to the side, and the gold flecks in her eyes glimmered again. "Like finding out what really happened to your father. Poor little lost girl, trying to restore her dead daddy's honor."

A muscle twitched in Asterin's jaw, but she didn't respond to the other woman's taunt.

Esmina smirked at Asterin a moment longer, then crooked her finger at me. "Come along quietly, Vesper, and I'll let your friend live."

Pollux aimed his hand cannon at Asterin. His finger curled around the trigger, and his dark eyes gleamed with anticipation.

"Okay!" I said, sliding my stormsword into its slot on my belt. "Okay! I'll come with you, but you let Asterin go first."

"No!" Asterin said. "I'm not leaving you, Vesper."

"You don't have a choice. Besides, they're not going to kill me. They've gone to too much trouble to capture me. Go."

Asterin wavered, torn between staying with me and escaping to find help—

"Fuck!" Esmina snarled. "We need to leave. Now!"

She whirled around and sprinted toward the part of the shipping yard that butted up against the street. Pollux immediately spun around and followed her, but the rest of the mercenaries hesitated, clearly confused about why their bosses were fleeing when they had captured Asterin and me.

An engine roared, and a transport zoomed into view, dropped down, and hovered over the shipping yard. The door on the side slid back, and a series of ropes unspooled out of the dark depths. Several figures stepped out of the transport and slid down the ropes, firing blasters as they zoomed toward the ground.

*Pew! Pew! Pew!*

Kyrion fired his blaster over and over, as did Siya, Rigel, and the other Hammers. By the time their feet touched the ground, several of the mercenaries were dead, and the remaining men were running for cover.

"Hammers!" Siya yelled, exchanging her blaster for the war hammer on her belt. "Attack! Attack! Attack!"

The Hammers rushed forward, taking the fight to the mercenaries. Kyrion cut down a couple of enemies with his stormsword, then hurried over to me, wrapped his arm around my waist, and yanked me close. The sticky cobweb of him in my mind bristled with worry, although the sharp, spiky edges quickly smoothed out into cool relief. I curled my fingers into his jacket, soaking up the warmth and strength of his physical body, along with his nearness through the bond.

"Vesper! Are you okay?" Kyrion asked, his concerned gaze locking with mine. "I heard you call out, and I came as fast as I could."

More of his relief surged through the bond, along with softer emotions that made a knot of answering feelings clog my throat. I basked in the sensations a moment, then released his jacket.

"Esmina and Pollux are here. We have to find them!" I said, heading in the direction the other two psions had gone.

Kyrion let out a loud curse, but his footsteps pounded on the ground behind me.

I sprinted through the shipping yard, moving past one pile of metal after another. Even though I couldn't see Esmina and Pollux, I knew I was going in the right direction. Maybe it was weird, but I could have sworn that I could actually *see* Esmina's magic, and every time I thought I'd lost her, another spark of green would flare in my field of vision, as though her power was a trail of psionic breadcrumbs only I could see and follow.

To my surprise, Esmina and Pollux had veered away from the street that would take them to the antiques emporium and had doubled back around to the middle of the shipping yard where I'd used the giant magnet to crush the mercenaries' transport. My steps slowed, and my head whipped around, but I didn't see Esmina or Pollux anywhere. The feel of her magic had also vanished.

Anger and frustration beat through my body in a sharp staccato rhythm. Once again, the mercenaries had escaped.

A flutter of movement caught my eye, and I whirled in that direction. One of the mercenaries wasn't as dead as I thought. He staggered up and onto his feet and aimed his blaster at Kyrion. Once again, that strange slow motion filled my eyes, and I saw the merc firing and the bolt punching into Kyrion's back . . .

I opened my mouth to scream a warning, but I felt like I was deep underwater, and everything was moving slowly . . . so damn slowly . . .

Kyrion spun toward me, sensing my distress through the bond. I snapped up my hand and focused on the mercenary, trying to use Kyrion's telekinesis to knock the blaster out of his hand, but once again, my magic—our magic?—wouldn't cooperate, and it all trickled through my fingers like raindrops.

Desperate, I sprinted forward to shove Kyrion out of the way, even though I already knew I was going to be too late to stop the mercenary from shooting him—

*Pew!*

A pale blue bolt zinged through the air, slammed into the mercenary, and knocked him back five feet. Smoke boiled up from the merc's chest, and he was dead before he hit the ground.

Asterin lowered her blaster and hurried over to Kyrion and me. "Are you both okay?"

Before I could answer her, footsteps pounded in this direction, and Siya and the other Hammers appeared.

Siya's gaze flicked from one dead mercenary to another, then her eyes widened as she noticed the smashed transport with the giant magnet still sticking out of the top.

A loud groan sounded, along with a screech of metal, and the round magnet teetered off the top of the transport, landed on its side, and rolled away like an oversize coin before finally stopping and clattering to the ground.

Silence descended over the shipping yard. Then Siya slowly turned to me, anger darkening her face.

"What in all the bloody moons happened here?" she snarled.

I sighed and looked at Asterin, who grimaced. We had a lot of explaining to do.

# FIFTEEN

## VESPER

The Hammers made sure all the mercenaries were either dead or taken into custody, then did a thorough sweep of the shipping yard, the mineral exchange, and the surrounding area.

The mercenaries had only stunned the guards and workers inside the mineral exchange, so no innocent people had been killed. Since most of the mercs were dead, the Hammers were able to recover the majority of the stolen House Collier materials, but Pollux had been wearing a large backpack, and he and Esmina were long gone with those goods.

Two hours later, I was back at the Collier estate. Asterin, Kyrion, and I were in the library, along with Aldrich, Verona, and Leland. Siya and Rigel were also here, and more Hammers were standing guard outside the doors. We were all clustered around a table that featured a large holoscreen.

"Three mercenaries are still alive and are currently being questioned," Leland said, scrolling through screens on his tablet. "But none of them knows anything useful. They were contacted, hired, and paid to break into the mineral exchange through anonymous channels. We're trying to trace the payments, but so far, they're all a dead end."

Aldrich rubbed his temples. "What were they after?"

"They targeted the jewel repository."

Leland swiped his finger across his tablet, and a couple of holograms appeared. The first image showed a heavy-duty vault with its door intact, while the second showed the same vault with its door peeled back like the lid on a tin can.

"The mercenaries took out the security cameras first, so there's no footage of them entering the shipping yard or the mineral exchange," the chief of staff said in an apologetic voice. "It appears the mercenaries neutralized the House Collier guards, then went straight to the jewel repository, disabled the anti-theft measures, and cut through the vault door with a plasma torch. They grabbed all the jewels they could stuff into their backpacks and left the mineral exchange."

Leland cleared his throat. "Although the mercenaries didn't get very far, thanks to Lady Vesper using the crane magnet to destroy their transport."

He smiled at me, but the expression didn't quite reach his eyes. Then again, no one here had any reason to smile. Not given the mercenaries' attack.

Verona frowned at the holograms. "Why would they break into the jewel repository? Why not steal from the lunarium reserves instead? Lunarium is much more valuable than diamonds, sapphires, and the like."

Leland swiped his tablet again, making the vault holograms disappear. "I'm not sure, my lady. Perhaps the thieves simply couldn't breach the lunarium repository given its thicker vault and more extensive security measures. If you ask me, this whole thing has the feel of a slapdash, smash-and-grab operation." The chief of staff let out a little sniff, as though greatly affronted by such low-class, common thievery.

Nothing about this had been slapdash, and the Erztonians were focusing on the wrong things or, rather, the wrong people.

"Forget why the mercenaries broke into the mineral exchange. Has anyone spotted Esmina Reston?" I asked.

Leland froze, as did Verona. Aldrich blinked in surprise, Siya sucked in a startled breath, and even Rigel frowned in a rare show of emotion.

"How do you know that name?" Aldrich asked in a sharp voice.

"Kyrion and I ran into Esmina Reston on Tropics 44. She's working with a man named Pollux Lamont, and they hired some bounty hunters to kidnap me."

Siya sucked in another breath. Rigel's frown deepened, and his hand curled around the hilt of the hammer hanging off his belt.

"Pollux Lamont?" Siya asked, her voice just as sharp as her father's. "Are you sure?"

"Of course I'm sure. Here. See for yourselves."

I pulled out my own tablet and called up the footage of Esmina and Pollux confronting the bounty hunters. I stopped on a clear image of the two mercenaries, placed my device on the table, and flicked the footage up into the air so everyone could see it.

A heavy blanket of silence dropped over the library, and the air practically dripped with tension, like water oozing out of a sodden towel.

"What do you know about Esmina and Pollux?" Kyrion asked. "Who are they to you?"

Aldrich and Verona looked at each other. Magic surged off them, along with the whisper of a telepathic conversation, although I couldn't hear what they were saying.

"Your facility was breached by two very powerful psions," Kyrion continued, his voice growing more suspicious. "This is no time to keep secrets."

The couple looked at each other again.

"If Esmina and Pollux are back on Sygnustern, then today's attack is even more serious than we realized," Verona said. "Kyrion and Vesper deserve to know, as does Asterin."

"Deserve to know what?" Asterin asked.

Aldrich grimaced. "Esmina Reston is an Erztonian. So is Pollux Lamont." The lord hesitated. "They are both originally from House Collier."

Shock jolted through me, zipped along the bond to Kyrion, and bounced back. Asterin frowned at her stepfather, but then her confusion slowly cracked away, and her eyes widened in growing recognition—and horror.

Aldrich waved his hand at Leland. "Show them the files."

The chief of staff hesitated. "Are you sure, my lord?"

Aldrich nodded, a resigned expression on his face. Leland swiped through a few screens on his tablet, causing more holograms to appear. More shock jolted through me. The images showed a younger version of Esmina glaring at the camera with a sour expression.

Aldrich stared at Esmina's photo. "Esmina's father, Stefanos, was one of my best friends, and they were both part of House Collier. When she was twenty, Esmina formed a truebond with Micah Dilson, a twenty-year-old who also belonged to the House."

"I remember hearing about that," Asterin said. "Didn't House Collier throw a party for them?"

Verona nodded. "We did, although you were away at university at the time."

Kyrion frowned. "I've never heard of a truebond being formed at such a young age. Most truebonds don't form until people are in their late twenties, after their psion power has fully matured."

Verona gave him a grim smile. "Neither had anyone else in the other Erzton Houses. We all thought it was a marvelous blessing." Her smile vanished. "But Esmina did not."

"What happened?" I asked.

"Even back then, Esmina was an extremely strong psion." Verona's gaze flicked over to me. "A seer."

*Like you.* Verona didn't say the words, but they whispered through the air anyway.

Aldrich picked up the story. "Micah was also a seer, although he wasn't nearly as strong as Esmina. The two of them were at Stardrop Falls with some other young people from House Collier. Esmina had climbed down to take pictures of the waterfall when her safety rope snapped. She tumbled down the cliff face several feet and would have fallen to her death if Micah hadn't grabbed the rope and caught her. That's when the truebond formed."

His words sank into my mind, and my magic surged to life. Suddenly, I could see it all happening. Esmina and Micah on a jagged cliff face studying the waterfall. Esmina's rope snapping. Micah reaching out to catch it. The two of them staring at each other, even as pale gold magic sparked, hissed, and curled around them . . .

I blinked, and the vision vanished, although the young couple's power kept crackling around me like static electricity.

"At first, everything was fine," Verona said. "Even before the bond formed, Micah had feelings for Esmina. The two of them had grown up together, and he was thrilled to be connected to her."

"But?" Kyrion asked.

Verona sighed. "But Esmina was not thrilled. She wanted to explore the galaxy and already had plans to attend a university on another planet. Micah offered to go with her, and we thought the matter was settled."

"What did she do?" Kyrion asked, his voice sharper than before.

Aldrich nodded at Leland, who hit more buttons on his tablet.

The image of a young man hovered over the table. Dark splotches of blood covered his chest, and his legs were broken in multiple places and twisted at impossible angles. His mouth gaped, and his sightless gold eyes bored into mine in a silent, frozen plea. My stomach roiled with nausea.

"Esmina killed him," Aldrich said in a flat voice. "She lured Micah to the waterfall where he had saved her and shoved him off a bridge. He fell into a deep chasm."

Once again, my magic surged to life, and I could see everything playing out as though I had been there. Esmina smiling and crooking her finger at Micah. The two of them admiring the waterfall. Then Esmina sliding to the side and shoving her hands into Micah's chest, pushing him off the bridge. His terrified screams ringing out even louder than the falling water. And then the sharp, sickening *crack* of his body hitting the bottom of the chasm . . .

I flinched at the phantom sound, and Micah's screams continued to echo in my mind. "Micah fell, but he didn't die right away."

Aldrich and Verona shared a surprised look. Then the lord shook his head. "No, the fall didn't kill Micah."

My magic surged up again. Micah's screams cut off, and everything went dark. Then light flared, and Esmina appeared. She unhooked herself from the rope she'd used to climb down to the bottom of the waterfall, then crouched down beside Micah. Tears streamed down his face, and his chest rose and fell in a frantic rhythm as he struggled to breathe.

*Help . . . me . . . please . . .*

Micah was too injured to speak, but his telepathic thought rasped through my mind, making me flinch again. Esmina stared down at him with a cold, dispassionate expression. Then she drew a lunarium dagger off her belt, leaned down, and cut his throat.

Blood spewed everywhere, coating the dagger, and the

lunarium blade started glowing with a bright golden light that was the same color as Micah's eyes. Esmina tightened her grip on the dagger, and gold sparks exploded in her green eyes. Magic coiled around her, and a satisfied smile slowly spread across her face . . .

"Esmina killed Micah," I whispered. "She killed him so she could take his magic."

My words startled Aldrich and Verona, who shared another surprised look.

"Yes, Esmina took Micah's magic," Aldrich said. "How do you know that?"

I shook my head. The awful vision faded away, but the coppery tang of Micah's blood flooded my nose and slithered down my throat, adding to my nausea.

Shock pulsed off Kyrion and whipped through the bond to me. "Esmina *took* Micah's power? How is that even *possible*? I thought only siphons could take another psion's power for their own."

Verona gave a helpless shrug. "We don't know, exactly. But Esmina broke her truebond with Micah and took his magic."

"I thought if a truebond was broken, it was almost impossible for the other person to survive." Asterin looked at her mother. "Unless the remaining partner had an extremely strong reason and the determined will to live."

"Not if you break the bond yourself," I murmured.

As soon as I said the words, I could *see* how it all worked. Esmina and Micah's bond had formed, but it hadn't solidified, and it wasn't stable. Maybe Esmina's seer magic had whispered the truth to her, or maybe she'd discovered it another way. But somehow Esmina had figured out the same thing I just had: if you severed the bond *yourself*, then the loss of the connection wouldn't kill you like the romance serials, fairy tales, and folk legends claimed. Instead, the other half of the bond would flow to you—and make you even *stronger*.

The hard truth slammed into my heart like a meteor hitting the ground and leaving a devastating crater behind. Everything Kyrion and I thought we knew about truebonds was *wrong*.

The bond wasn't an inevitable, undeniable thing that just happened because of karma or destiny or fate or whatever label you wanted to use to explain the mysteries of the galaxy. That was certainly part of the connection, but having a truebond was also a *choice*—and Esmina had made a very cruel choice indeed.

Leland swiped through some screens on his tablet. Micah's bloody, broken body vanished, replaced by current photos of Esmina, but these shots had all been taken from a distance through security cameras.

"After she killed Micah, Esmina fled from the city," Aldrich continued. "The House Collier Hammers chased after her . . ."

"But she was always one step ahead of us," Rigel said, his voice a low, angry growl. He glared at the images of Esmina, and his fingers twitched, as though he wanted to strangle the holograms.

Aldrich nodded. "Eventually, we received reports Esmina had developed a new ability that let her see danger coming before it actually reached her."

His words made the gears grind in my mind, and once again I could see how it all worked and just what kind of magic Esmina had. She was a seer like me—and so much *more*.

"Precognition," I said, looking at Kyrion. "Esmina can see things before they happen. That's why she retreated on Tropics 44. She knew you were coming to help me and that we would kill the bounty hunters."

Kyrion frowned again. "Precogs are extremely rare, and the number of visions they have often overwhelms them and drives them mad. How has Esmina managed to control her power?"

"We don't know," Verona replied. "For the most part, Esmina steers clear of Sygnustern, as there are still warrants out for her arrest. This is the first confirmed sighting of her on-planet in more than three years."

Asterin stared at the holograms. "So whatever Esmina is planning, it's important enough to risk returning here and being captured by the Hammers."

"Or someone is paying her enough credits to take the risk," Siya muttered.

The two women shared a look. They were now standing shoulder to shoulder, but for once, they didn't move away from each other.

"What about Pollux?" Kyrion asked. "How does he fit in?"

Leland flicked his fingers. More images appeared, showing a younger version of Pollux, grinning wide, clutching two war hammers, and standing with a group of people wielding similar weapons.

"Pollux was a Hammer," Kyrion muttered.

"One of the best Hammers in all the Erzton Houses. I trained him myself." Rigel's lips curled back in disgust, and his fingers twitched again as he glared at his former pupil. "Pollux and his sister, Derissa, were in a transport crash, and they were trapped for more than a day before they were pulled from the wreckage. During that time, Pollux and his sister each formed their own truebond with two other survivors."

"Let me guess," Kyrion said. "Pollux killed the person he was bonded to and absorbed their power just like Esmina did to Micah."

Rigel jerked his head in confirmation. "Pollux was friends with Esmina. We think she told him how to do it, and he fled with her."

Siya drifted over to Rigel's side in a silent show of support.

"Eventually, Esmina and Pollux started hiring themselves out as mercenaries," Rigel continued. "And they've bloody *excelled* at it. Thanks to Serpens Corp, they have enough credits, weapons, men, and resources to go anywhere and do anything they want."

"So why have they returned to Sygnustern?" Asterin asked. "Why now? They couldn't have possibly known Vesper and I would be at the shipping yard. Not even a precog could see that far into the future . . . could they?"

Her words triggered a memory in my mind. "Asterin is right. Esmina *was* surprised to see me. She didn't realize I was at the shipping yard, at least not until I dropped the magnet on the mercs' transport . . ."

Kyrion finished my thought. "Which means Esmina and Pollux were there to steal from House Collier first and foremost. Why steal from your House? Surely there are other mineral exchanges that aren't as well fortified and heavily guarded."

Aldrich cleared his throat. "Thanks to Serpens Corp, Esmina has become quite wealthy and powerful. Our spies have heard rumors she wishes to return to Sygnustern and use Serpens Corp to establish her own House."

Asterin frowned. "But Erzton law dictates there can only be a certain number of major Houses. How could Esmina establish her own House without usurping one of the established Houses? Without destroying . . ."

"Without destroying *our* House?" Siya answered the question in a flat voice. "She can't."

A tense, heavy silence filled the library, and worry crackled through the air.

"So Esmina wants to destroy House Collier and replace it with her own House." Kyrion glanced at Rigel. "Well, that certainly explains all the guards on the estate."

Rigel grunted in response.

Asterin turned to Verona. "Mother, why didn't you tell me about this?"

"Perhaps if you'd come home once in a while instead of gallivanting around the galaxy chasing ghosts, you would be more up to date on House Collier enemies," Siya replied in a sarcastic voice.

Asterin's eyes glittered with anger. She opened her mouth, but Verona shook her head. Asterin swallowed her harsh words, but she kept glaring at Siya.

Leland delicately cleared his throat. "My lord, perhaps we should cancel tonight's event. The gossipcasts have already gotten wind that something happened at the shipping yard. I've been spinning the story as an industrial accident, but the reporters won't stop digging until they uncover the truth. Stories about Serpens Corp mercenaries breaking into the House Collier mineral exchange will only embolden Esmina and her supporters among the other Houses."

Aldrich squared his shoulders and lifted his chin. "All the more reason we should proceed as though nothing is wrong. Besides, Verona put a lot of time and effort into the marriage mart, and I don't want it to have been for nothing."

"Oh, no," Siya piped up again. "We wouldn't want to scare off any of Asterin's potential husbands."

Asterin shot her stepsister another angry look.

"Enough!" Aldrich barked out. "You both know tonight's event is a tradition, one that House Collier is honored to host this social season." He looked at Kyrion and me, cold calculation sparking in his gaze. "The two of you are more than welcome to attend."

Leland blinked in surprise. "My lord, are you sure that's wise?"

Aldrich waved his hand, dismissing his chief of staff's concerns. "As I said, we need to proceed as though nothing is wrong. Besides, having Lady Vesper and Lord Kyrion attend will give the gossipcasts something else to focus on besides what happened at the shipping yard."

My eyes narrowed. "You want to use us as a distraction while you search for Esmina and Pollux."

Aldrich nodded. "Absolutely."

"Bloody Erzton games are just as bad as Regal ones," Kyrion muttered.

Verona gave us a deceptively bright smile. "I was hoping you would attend the marriage mart as our honored guests, so I already made the preparations. You will find appropriate clothes and everything else you need in your suite."

Kyrion crossed his arms over his chest. He didn't want to attend the Erzton event. Neither did I, but we were at our hosts' mercy. I would much rather play along with the Colliers and return to the relative safety of their estate than go on the run again. Besides, if an Erzton ball was anything like a Regal one, then everyone would be gossiping about everyone else, and I wanted to see what information we might discover about Esmina and Pollux and their feud with House Collier.

Leland cleared his throat again. "We need to discuss a few final details about the marriage mart, and I'm sure Siya and Rigel would like to update the security plan."

Verona turned her bright smile to her daughter. "Asterin, I sent some things to your suite too. You should go get ready."

Asterin stiffened, but she tipped her head to her mother, then stalked out of the library. Kyrion and I followed her. None of us spoke as we left the main castle and headed toward the guest wing, but thoughts swirled through my mind like a kaleidoscope shifting from one enemy to another.

I'd thought Callus Holloway was the most dangerous psion in the galaxy, but Esmina Reston had the full power of a truebond running through her veins. She had all the strengths and none of the vulnerabilities of being connected to another person. Plus, she'd had years to learn how to wield her magic. So had Pollux.

I couldn't see as far and as clearly into the future as the other seer could, but dread vibrated through me that Esmina and Pollux were going to be the death of me and Kyrion.

# SIXTEEN

## KYRION

"Bloody Erztonians," I muttered. "I can't believe they're going ahead with their event as though nothing happened. As though two defectors from their own House didn't breach their defenses, steal their resources, and waltz away without a scratch."

I stalked from one side of the bedroom to the other. "Siya, Rigel, and the other Hammers should be locking down the city and scouring the streets for Esmina and Pollux. Not worrying about security at a ball."

"So you've been saying for the last hour, ever since we returned to the suite." Vesper's voice drifted out from behind a wooden dressing screen in the corner.

I quickened my pacing. "The Colliers aren't using us as a distraction. We're the *bait*."

"You think once the gossipcasters realize we're at the marriage mart, word will get back to Esmina and Pollux?" Vesper called out. "And Aldrich will set a trap hoping the mercenaries try to kidnap me again?"

"Yes," I growled. "Because that's exactly what I would do."

Vesper let out an agreeing murmur, and fabric rasped behind the dressing screen. I yanked at my shirt collar, which was choking me, then stomped over to a mirror on the wall.

As if using us as bait wasn't bad enough, our outfits for the marriage mart bordered on the ridiculous. I was dressed in a dark blue tailcoat over tight black leggings and black boots that stretched up to my knees. The front of the coat stopped at my waist, where my stormsword was belted, but the back dropped away in two long, wide pieces that plummeted to my ankles, making me feel like an oversize penguin with two flapping silk tails. Such tailcoats were common attire at Regal events, but the House Collier tailors had paired this one with a silver shirt with frills that spilled down my chest like an ocean of stiff, puffy silk.

I yanked at my shirt collar again. I despised frills, and my fingers itched with the urge to rip off the puffy pieces of fabric and toss them aside like I was molting feathers.

"Any word from Daichi yet?" Vesper asked.

"No," I said, spinning away from the mirror. "I sent him all the info we learned, but he hasn't come up with anything new, and he hasn't identified who Esmina and Pollux might be working for."

"Maybe they aren't working for someone," Vesper called out. "Maybe Esmina and Pollux want to destroy House Collier all on their own and think I can somehow help them."

"Perhaps. Daichi also doesn't know what the mercenaries wanted with the jewels they stole from the mineral exchange."

"Asterin promised to get me a list of everything the mercs targeted," Vesper replied. "Maybe seeing the full list will give us some more insights into their plans."

My gaze flicked over to the chunk of sapphsidian sitting on a table that Vesper had recovered from one of the mercenaries' backpacks. Perhaps Vesper was right, and Esmina and Pollux simply wanted to destroy House Collier, but I couldn't shake the uneasy feeling the mercenaries had a much bigger—and deadlier—goal.

Vesper stepped out from behind the dressing screen. "Well?" she asked, spreading her arms out wide. "How do I look?"

My breath froze in my throat, and my heart tumbled every which way inside my chest. I had seen Vesper in formal gowns before, but the Erzton garment was truly a work of art.

The gown was predominantly silver, the same silver as my frilly shirt, and the layers of gauzy fabric clung to Vesper's body, highlighting her strong curves. Each layer was covered with glittering black crystals, along with tiny pieces of sapphsidian nestled together in the shape of mammoth butterflies.

The shimmering mosaic pattern started at the top of the scalloped neckline, and tiny butterflies dotted the tight, sleeveless bodice before morphing into larger creatures that covered the long, flowing skirt. Vesper shifted from side to side on her silver heels, and the layers fluttered, making it look as though the butterflies were flitting all around her.

Vesper's dark brown hair had been set into loose waves that brushed her shoulders, and small silver butterfly pins glinted in her locks. She'd threaded a larger silver butterfly brooch studded with blue opals and sapphsidians onto a black velvet ribbon and was wearing it as a choker around her neck. Dark blue shadow and silver liner brought out those same colors in her eyes, while her lips were a pale, frosted, silvery blue.

"Does speechless mean I look good?" Vesper teased.

I stepped forward so that I was looming over her. "You are utterly breathtaking."

A pleased blush pinkened her cheeks, and the same emotion rippled along the velvety ribbon of her in my mind.

"You don't look so bad yourself." Vesper flicked one of the puffy frills on my chest. "Nice shirt."

"For a bloody penguin," I grumbled.

She laughed, and the sound warmed me from head to toe. I stepped even closer, captured her waist with my hands, and lowered my mouth to hers.

Even though I had kissed Vesper hundreds of times before, awareness coursed through me. The electric touch of her lips against mine. The quickening pulse in the hollow of her throat. The rise and fall of her chest. The sweet, soft scent of spearmint soap clinging to her smooth skin.

Vesper hummed with pleasure, stood up on her tiptoes, and wrapped her arms around my neck. She deepened the kiss, her tongue flicking out against mine. More electricity jolted through me, and I growled, every part of my body stiffening with desire.

Our tongues stroked together, fast and hard, then slow and soft, and I lost myself in the heady sensations of her.

After the better part of a minute, we broke apart, both of us breathing hard. I leaned down and rested my forehead against hers. "I have a splendid idea. Why don't we skip the marriage mart and stay here? No enemies, no agendas, nothing but the two of us."

Heat shimmered in Vesper's eyes. "Oh, I think we would both have an agenda."

She sighed and drew back. "As much as I would love to stay here and peel that frilly shirt off you, the Colliers want us to attend the marriage mart. Our position here is precarious enough without pissing off our hosts."

Vesper bit her lower lip. "Besides, I feel like it's important we go to the marriage mart."

"Why? Are you seeing something with your power?"

The silver flecks in her eyes brightened like matches flaring in the dark. Then her gaze dimmed, and she shook her head. "No, I'm not seeing anything. It's more of a . . . feeling. It's hard to explain." Her face twisted into a bitter expression. "Maybe I *could* explain it, and maybe I could actually see *something*, if I was a precog like Esmina."

"You don't have to be a precog. You told me about your vision. How you saw what Esmina did to get her power. How she killed that boy, her friend, like it was *nothing*."

Vesper shuddered. "It was awful. Truly. But with that kind of magic, with that much power . . ." Her voice trailed off for a moment. "Well, it would keep us both safe. From Holloway, the Techwave, and everyone else who might be targeting us."

My fingers tightened around her waist. "We keep each other safe, and we don't need any power other than what we have together. Tried and true, remember?"

"Always." Vesper smiled at my echoing her words from last night, but her cheerful expression swiftly melted away.

She pressed a kiss to my lips, then stepped out of my arms, grabbed a small silver blaster off a table, and slid it into a hidden pocket in her skirt.

Not for the first time, I cursed Esmina for targeting Vesper—and all the doubts the other seer had created about our bond and psion powers and whether they would be enough to protect us from our many enemies.

Vesper and I left our suite and went to the courtyard in front of the main castle. Just like me, Aldrich, Leland, and Rigel were dressed in formal tailcoats with frilly shirts, although their garments were the emerald green of House Collier. Verona and Siya were wearing lovely similarly colored gowns trimmed with gold thread and sequins, while Asterin was clad in a gray gown studded with bits of lunarium.

The Colliers climbed into a transport, along with Leland, Siya, and Rigel. I helped Vesper and Asterin into a second transport, while several guards armed with blasters boarded a third vehicle. Lord Aldrich might be using Vesper and me as bait, but he wasn't taking unnecessary chances.

The transports glided out of the courtyard, away from the estate, and down the mountain into the city. About twenty minutes later, the vehicles dropped us off in front of the antiques emporium. Strings of gold lights were draped over the emerald dome, and the structure gleamed even more brightly than the silvery Frozon moon in the night sky.

Throngs of people dressed in glittering gowns and sleek tailcoats were heading into the dome, but I didn't spot Esmina and Pollux. What I did spot were several squads of House Collier guards and Hammers. Still, I couldn't help but wonder if Esmina had already seen the extra security measures with her precog power and figured out a way to thwart the guards. Time would tell.

Lord Aldrich and Lady Verona walked along a green carpet that ran by an area filled with gossipcast reporters. The couple waved and smiled for the cameras that were clicking, flashing, and recording their every movement. Siya, Rigel, and Leland followed the Colliers, but Asterin held out her hand, stopping Vesper and me.

"I don't know about you, but I have no desire to preen for the cameras," she muttered. "This way."

Asterin skirted around the perimeter of the dome and led us to a side door that wasn't mobbed by reporters. The guards stationed there waved her on through, although they eyed Vesper and me with suspicion before letting us pass.

We walked along a corridor, then went through another door to enter the dome. Vesper stopped, her eyes widening in wonder. I stopped too, also awed by the transformation.

Yesterday the emporium had been filled with aisle after aisle of antiques, but those objects had been removed and replaced with topiaries similar to those on the Collier estate. But instead of evergreen trees or hedges, these sculptures were composed of smooth, polished, glittering crystals in every color imaginable—green, blue, red, purple, pink. Scores of gold lights dripped down from the ceiling, hitting the crystals and painting rainbows on the floor.

Even more impressive was the fact that part of the dome's wall had been removed, revealing a hidden topiary garden. Trees, hedges, and more crystal sculptures stretched out into the open air, although a warming shield kept the cold wind and flakes of snow from gusting into the dome itself.

My gaze roamed over the rest of the dome. Tables filled with food, musicians strumming instruments on a hoverdais, people whirling around the dance floor to the lively tune. It was eerily similar to a Regal ball and yet distinctly different, especially when it came to the decorations—or lack thereof.

Instead of flowers, fountains, or pretty streamers, one entire wall was filled with glass shelves lined with chunks of lunarium, sapphsidian, coal, wood, and more raw materials. Other shelves boasted miniature models shaped like castles, spaceships, production plants, and even Frozon moons.

Men and women of all ages were walking past the shelves, peering at the contents, and snapping photos with their tablets. Every few feet, holoscreens flashed names, locations, and other pertinent facts, as though we were at a museum instead of a society event.

*Lady Asterin Armas . . .*

Off to the right, a holoscreen flashed her name, then scrolled through a list of items. Lights flickered on and off, highlighting the corresponding items on the nearby shelves. *Lunarium on Frozon 3 . . . Sapphsidian on Tropics 29 . . . Coal mines on Temperate 13 . . .*

The list of mineral rights and mines went on and on, but no one gave Asterin's holoscreen a second glance. All the Erztonians strolled past her station to peer at the screens of other lords and ladies to see what resources they had to offer. Some people even stopped and tapped in information on the screens, which let out soft chimes of confirmation.

"Isn't it charming?" Asterin said in a bitter voice. "How my net worth is on display for everyone to see, comment, and bid on?"

Two older women heard her words and clucked their tongues in reproach, even as they moved on to the next display.

"So people look at your . . . dowry?" Vesper asked in a puzzled voice. "And then bid on . . . what, exactly?"

Asterin's mouth twisted. "Whether they want the opportunity to court me."

Vesper's nose crinkled in disgust. "Ugh! That's awful."

I shrugged. "Similar practices are common among the Regal Houses, although such negotiations are not quite so . . . public."

Vesper's nose crinkled with more disgust. "But what about being attracted to someone? Or loving them? Or having a chance at happiness?"

Asterin let out a low, bitter laugh. "Attraction, love, and happiness don't last *nearly* as long as mineral rights and mines do."

Her words matched my own jaded views, especially since so many Regals had tried to engage me in relationships—romantic, business, and otherwise—in hopes of getting their hands on the Caldaren fortune.

Asterin's gaze landed on the holoscreen flashing her name, and her mouth twisted again. "I need a drink."

"I'll join you," Vesper said. "Kyr, you want anything?"

"No, thanks. I'm going to wander around."

Vesper gave me a knowing look. "You're going to double-check the security and see if Esmina and Pollux have managed so sneak into the ball."

I grinned. "You know me too well." My grin vanished. "Be careful."

"You too," she murmured.

While Vesper and Asterin headed over to the refreshment

tables, I did a lap around the perimeter of the dome, studying all the people smiling, talking, laughing, drinking, and dancing. Lord Aldrich and Lady Verona might be using us as bait, but that didn't mean I couldn't go hunting on my own terms. If Esmina and Pollux showed up, then I wanted to spot them before they spotted Vesper.

More than one person eyed me as I stalked past, and whispers trailed along in my wake.

"That looks like Kyrion Caldaren . . ."

"Why would he be here . . ."

"House Collier must be offering him sanctuary from the Imperium . . ."

Many of the Erztonians recognized me, and some pulled out their tablets, their fingers flying over the screens, while a few of the bolder lords and ladies snapped photos. I grimaced. It wouldn't be long before news of my and Vesper's attendance hit the local gossipcasts, but everyone at the Collier estate already knew we were on Sygnustern, so there was no point in hiding.

Sooner or later, one of the Regal gossipcasts would pick up the story, which would eventually make its way to Callus Holloway. No doubt, the Imperium ruler would immediately start formulating a plan to wrest Vesper and me away from the Colliers' protection, but that was a problem for tomorrow. Tonight I needed to find Esmina and Pollux, figure out why they were targeting Vesper, and eliminate them.

I didn't spot the mercenaries among the gossiping crowd, and eventually, I ended up right back where I'd started, beside the holoscreen displaying Asterin's name. No one had entered their information on her screen, although several names had been typed in on the surrounding screens, even though those lords and ladies didn't have nearly as many mineral rights and mines. Curious. With her resources and connection to House Collier, Asterin should have been one of the shining stars of

Erzton society, but instead, she was as unwanted as a lump of coal on winter solstice morning.

"My poor stepsister can't even bribe someone to court her," a familiar voice drawled.

Siya sashayed over to me. She scanned the other screens around Asterin's, and her nostrils flared with a mixture of anger and disgust, almost as if she was offended on Asterin's behalf.

"Asterin is a lovely person," I said, defending my friend. "Smart, strong, capable, kind, generous. Any lord, Regal, Erzton, or otherwise, would be lucky to court her."

Siya tilted her head, although I couldn't tell if she was agreeing or not. "Care for a drink?"

I eyed the clear crystal mugs in her hands. Each one was filled with a dark brown liquid topped with a thick layer of frothy white foam. "Is it poisoned?"

An amused chuckle erupted from her lips. "Sadly, no. You are under my father's protection, so I can't poison you. Besides, I would never stoop to such weak tactics. I would kill you myself, Arrow."

"Good to know, Hammer."

I took the mug, then toasted her with it. Siya returned the gesture, and we downed our drinks.

The frothy white foam misted down my throat like marshmallow-flavored frost, but it was quickly followed by a tide of intense dark chocolate, along with a hint of raspberries and a tang of blood orange.

"This is delicious. Are you certain it's not poisoned?"

Siya laughed at my dry humor. "It's Frozon hot chocolate, a specialty of the House Collier chefs."

I sipped the wonderful drink and ambled along the wall, looking at the minerals, models, and other objects. Siya sipped her own drink and matched my steps, and for once the silence between us was comfortable rather than hostile.

"You handled yourself well during the shipping yard attack,"

Siya said. "You cut through those mercenaries with your storm-sword like they were plastipaper targets."

"And you did the same with your war hammer. I've never seen Hammers fight in person. Your squad is very impressive. Well trained and well disciplined."

She tipped her head, accepting the compliment, and we kept ambling along.

"Where is your holoscreen and list of resources?" I asked.

"I don't have one."

"Why not?"

"Because someday I will be the head of House Collier. All the assets of all the major Houses are public record and very well documented. Anyone who decides to court me will know *exactly* what they're getting." A rueful smile curved Siya's lips. "I'm in the rare position of being able to choose a match for love, unlike many of the Erzton nobles."

"In other words, you don't need anyone else's money, mineral rights, or mines since you have plenty of your own."

Siya's smile widened, and humor danced in her hazel eyes. "Something like that."

"Asterin doesn't have that same luxury?"

The humor snuffed out of Siya's eyes, and her smile vanished. "No. But Asterin has something far more valuable."

"What?"

"Freedom," Siya replied in a soft voice. "You're the head of a House. You know what an enormous responsibility it is to have so many people depending on you."

Uncomfortable memories floated through my mind, and the hot chocolate soured in my stomach. After my mother had died and my father had drowned in his grief and brandy, it had fallen to me to try to keep House Caldaren afloat, even though I was only thirteen at the time. I'd tried my best, but it hadn't been enough—*I* hadn't been enough.

Understanding flickered through me, along with a surprising

amount of sympathy. The weight of others' expectations was yoked to Siya's shoulders just as it had been yoked to mine, and it was a hard, heavy burden to bear, no matter how great—or not—your House was.

"Asterin can cavort around the galaxy chasing ghosts all she wants," Siya said, envy creeping into her voice. "But I am bound to House Collier, and it is bound to me. Everything I do is supposed to serve, protect, and advance my House. Sometimes I think there is only my House and nothing else, nothing left of *me*." Her voice sharpened on the last few words.

"Is that why you dislike Asterin so much? Because she can do as she pleases?"

"Asterin is . . . challenging," Siya replied, sidestepping my questions. "We were best friends—until her father died. My mother had passed away the year before, so I knew how much Asterin was hurting. I was hurting too, since my uncle Irzin was also killed in the mine explosion. For a time, Asterin and I grew closer. Verona even started working for House Collier as my father's chief of staff to try to pay down the massive debts relating to the lawsuits against House Armas."

"And then?"

"And then the truebond started forming between my father and her mother." Siya's mouth puckered as though she'd tasted something rotten. "Suddenly, Asterin and I were stepsisters and supposed to exist in the same space, to just accept what was happening, even though both of us were still mourning our relatives. We've never been able to get past it. Especially Asterin. She can't let go of her father's accident, and she'll never stop trying to prove Urston wasn't at fault."

*Chasing ghosts.* Siya's earlier words whispered through my mind. I knew what that was like all too well. After my parents had died, I'd spent countless hours wondering if I could have done something to save them. If I could have found a way to stop Holloway from taking too much of my mother's psion power or said the right words to rouse my father out of his grief and convince him just how much I needed him. Chasing those ghosts had brought me nothing but misery, and they still haunted me.

Siya fell silent. Whatever else she knew about Asterin's father, she wasn't going to share it. Perhaps Siya cared more about Asterin than she realized—or wanted to admit.

I had started to ask Siya another question when an odd emotion crashed over me—a strong, strange mix of anticipation and dread that slammed into my chest like a pair of spears. The emotion faded away as quickly as it had appeared, but my own unease roared up in response.

Something was wrong.

I spun away from Siya and scanned the crowd. Whose emotion was that? Were Esmina and Pollux here?

Out of the corner of my eye, I spotted a glimmer of light. I couldn't tell if it was from the bulbs above or the telltale flare of Vesper's seer power, but I turned in that direction. My gaze landed on two people standing about fifty feet away—a man and a woman scanning the crowd just as I was.

No. That couldn't be right. They shouldn't be here. Had Siya poisoned me after all? Was I hallucinating?

"Kyrion?" Siya frowned. "What's wrong? What are you looking at?"

I blinked, wondering if I had just imagined the man and woman. The crowd parted, giving me an even better look at the pair, and the sight of their faces made my blood run cold.

Vesper was in danger.

# SEVENTEEN

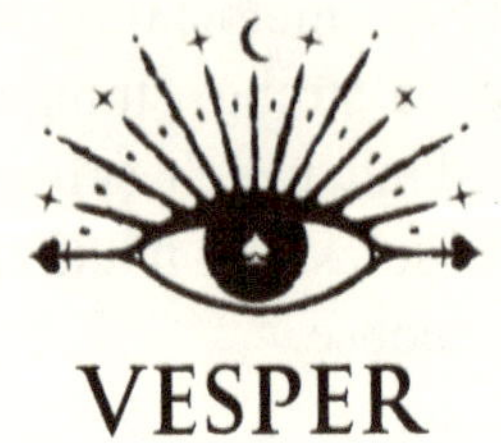

## VESPER

Asterin and I went over to the refreshments tables, and she handed me a mug filled with a dark brown liquid topped with a thick white layer. The beverage started out as a cold cream coating my tongue, but then it rapidly heated up and morphed into a delectable hot chocolate that warmed me from the inside out.

I hummed with pleasure. "This is amazing!"

Asterin clinked her mug against mine. "Frozon hot chocolate has always been my favorite." A shadow passed over her face. "It was my father's favorite too."

Before I could offer my sympathies, a woman came up and engaged Asterin in conversation. Neither one of them was paying attention to me, so I drifted away. Asterin had other duties besides chaperoning me, and I didn't want to ruin her chances of landing a husband . . . or whatever the Colliers were hoping to accomplish with the marriage mart.

I finished my hot chocolate, then wound my way through the crowd, smiling and nodding at everyone I passed. At first, people frowned, wondering where they had seen me before. Then they did double takes, and then their mouths gaped in surprise as they finally realized who I was—Lady Vesper Quill, Imperium fugitive.

Whispers sprang up in my wake, and I did my best to listen to them all.

"She's not nearly as pretty in person . . ."

"Wonder how long it will be before the Colliers ship her back to the Imperium . . ."

"Well, the Colliers could certainly use the bounty credits, along with Callus Holloway's support, especially given how tenuous their own position and House are right now . . ."

Similar murmurs sounded, and I ground my teeth in frustration. I wanted—*needed*—information about Esmina and Pollux, not my own notoriety.

I kept strolling through the crowd, but I didn't see Esmina and Pollux. Even if the mercenaries had been lurking around, I doubted I would have spotted them through the throngs of people clustered around the glass shelves. Folks were standing three and four deep in places, waiting to sign their names to court whichever lord or lady had a dowry that caught their eye—or appealed to their financial bottom lines.

I couldn't decide if the Erztonians' practice of showing their assets in such a public manner was a disgusting display of wealth—or the severe lack of it, in some cases—or an admirable example of efficiency. At least this way, everyone was putting their proverbial cards on the table, even if such a thing reduced relationships to business transactions.

Leland stopped beside me. "Are you having a good time?" he inquired in a polite voice.

"Of course. Are you?"

"It's not my job to have a good time. Just to make sure the marriage mart runs smoothly."

"I'm sorry. That must be tiring."

The chief of staff shrugged. "It is what it is. I've learned to play my part." He nodded at a couple who were taking pictures of me with their tablets. "As have you, it seems."

"Something like that," I muttered.

Leland gave me an encouraging smile. "Don't worry. The gossips will move on to something else soon enough. They always do. Sometimes I think the scandals and Houses rise and fall faster than the ocean waves on a Tropics planet."

His gaze darted over to Verona, who was standing in the middle of a large crowd. Verona gestured with her hand, telling a story, and everyone laughed.

"Although some Houses fall farther and faster than others," Leland murmured. "Even as the people in them rise and rise again."

I eyed him. Was he talking about the fall of House Armas? Or something else?

Leland fiddled with a gold button on his emerald-green tailcoat, which was stamped with a plain bold *L* instead of the cursive *C* of House Collier.

The chief of staff's tablet dinged, and Leland looked at the message. His lips pinched together in annoyance, but he gave me an apologetic look. "Please excuse me."

"Of course," I replied.

Leland tipped his head to me, then disappeared into the crowd. The chief of staff had been nothing but polite, but something about his words bothered me. Then again, I supposed he was right, and we all had our parts to play tonight.

I once again wove through the crowd and searched for Esmina and Pollux, but I didn't spot them. The psions could be wearing disguises, modifications to change their hair and eye color like I had done on Tropics 44, but that didn't seem like Esmina's style. Earlier today, she had strolled right through the middle of House Collier territory and into the shipping yard with only a cloak to obscure her features. She probably thought her precognition magic made her invincible, even against all the guards here tonight.

I was worried she was right.

But the longer I moved through the crowd, the more certain I was that Esmina and Pollux weren't here. The mercenaries might want to topple House Collier, but they were too smart to waltz into a building crawling with guards. Once again, Esmina was three steps ahead, and she was probably relaxing and having a drink while she laughed at us.

A headache throbbed to life in my temples. I should find Kyrion and Asterin and tell them I wanted to leave. My time would be much better spent trying to figure out why Esmina had stolen jewels from the mineral exchange than aimlessly wandering around letting snooty strangers stare at and gossip about me.

I had turned around to find my friends when I spotted Aldrich leaving the dome and slipping into the garden. Curious, I followed him.

This side of the dome was open, although an energy shield like the one at the Collier estate separated the guests from the night air and kept the cold at bay. Smooth paths made of round green tiles spiraled out into the garden in intricate patterns, while strings of gold lights gleamed in the topiary trees and hedges.

Aldrich ambled along the main center path. He stopped in front of a large bush, plucked off a blue-moon peony, and twirled it back and forth in his fingers. Then he turned and held the flower out to me.

I hadn't meant to be quite so obvious in my spying, but I lifted my chin, walked over, and took the blossom from him. The peony's spearmint scent tickled my nose, and a smile lifted my lips. The aroma always reminded me of Kyrion.

Aldrich tucked his hands into his pants pockets. "Verona had this garden built onto the antiques emporium just for me, so I can have a little escape whenever I need a break from all the events we host here. From all of *that*." He jerked his chin at the people inside the dome.

"That was very kind of her."

Aldrich's face softened, and his hazel eyes crinkled with warmth. He obviously adored his wife, and my heart gave a painful wrench. The Colliers made having a relationship and a truebond look so blasted *easy*. I envied them.

"You don't say much, do you, Lady Vesper? By this point, most people would have tripped over themselves to flatter me in hopes of winning some favor from House Collier."

"I've never seen the point in flattering people I don't know."

"And people you don't trust?" Aldrich asked in a chiding voice. "Like me and Verona?"

I shrugged, not even bothering to deny his accusation. "I don't trust many people—although your stepdaughter is one of them."

Aldrich smiled again. "Asterin speaks just as highly of you, Vesper. She doesn't trust people lightly either. I put a great deal of stock in my stepdaughter's opinion. Verona and I wouldn't have offered you and Kyrion our protection if Asterin hadn't vouched for you."

"I appreciate that more than you know." I sighed. "I'm just sorry Kyrion and I have added to your troubles. If we had known Esmina and Pollux were targeting House Collier, we would have gone elsewhere. Maybe the mercenaries wouldn't have attacked the mineral exchange if Kyrion and I hadn't come to Sygnustern."

Aldrich waved his hand, dismissing my concerns. "Someone is always after something that doesn't belong to them. The Erzton has its share of greedy villains, just as the Imperium does."

The two of us rounded a row of blue-moon peonies and moved deeper into the garden. Several guards patrolled the paths in the distance, keeping an eye on Aldrich, but they didn't approach him.

"But talking about societal vipers isn't the reason you followed me out here," Aldrich continued.

"No. I wanted to ask you about truebonds—and how Kyrion and I can stabilize and solidify ours."

He nodded. "Yes, Verona told me she had a similar conversation with Kyrion this morning. I will tell you the same thing she told him. A truebond is about trust and balance, and right now, you and Kyrion are both out of balance with each other—and especially with yourselves."

"Out of balance? What do you mean?"

"What do you think I mean?"

I huffed in annoyance. "I really hate it when people answer a question with another question."

He laughed. "We must be building some trust for you to say something so blunt."

I pinched my fingers close together, not quite touching them. "Just a bit."

Aldrich laughed again, and I found myself smiling back at him. "How am I out of balance?"

"I think you already know," he replied.

I hesitated, wondering if I should tell him what was bothering me. But I'd come out here in search of answers, and I wasn't going to get them by keeping secrets. "When I first met her, Esmina said I was the weak link in the truebond between me and Kyrion." I sighed again. "And I'm worried she's right."

"Why is that?"

I made a face at his question, then blew out a breath. "Because no matter what I do or how hard I try, I can't get a grip on my new abilities. Ever since I met Kyrion, my seer magic has been growing, expanding. Sometimes it works when and how I need it to."

"And other times?" Aldrich asked.

"And other times, my magic has a mind of its own. I also can't use Kyrion's telepathy or telekinesis with any consistency." I blew out another breath. "It's like my magic is a galactic lottery, and I never know which ability will pop up next—or if my magic will pop up at all."

"And you think it's because you're weak, like Esmina said?" Aldrich challenged.

"Isn't that the reason?" I said, a peevish note creeping into my voice.

"Needing some time to figure things out isn't being weak, Vesper. It's natural. It takes time to adjust to a truebond, especially one as strong as what you and Kyrion share." Aldrich paused, and when he spoke again, his voice was pitched much lower than before. "It also takes time to adjust to the other person, no matter how much you care about them. I imagine that is especially true in your case."

"My case?"

"Asterin told me about your childhood. About how your mother . . . treated you."

He was trying to be kind, but his gentle words sliced into my heart like a dagger. My fingers curled around the peony still in my hand, crushing the stem and making the sticky sap spurt onto my skin. The blossom's spearmint scent intensified, reminding me of the similar peonies in my mindscape. The familiar aroma comforted me, although several more seconds ticked by before I was able to swallow my simmering emotions.

"Nerezza Blackwell is one of the main reasons I don't trust people. Hard to trust anyone when your own mother abandons you because you don't have enough psion power for her liking." Bitterness flooded my voice. I could never be completely calm when talking about Nerezza.

Aldrich gave my arm a reassuring pat. "I'm truly sorry. No child should have to go through that."

"But?" I asked in a guarded tone, wary of his sympathy.

"But don't let Nerezza's cruel actions or Esmina's harsh words affect your bond with Kyrion—or especially your belief in your own abilities," Aldrich replied. "Your seer magic is yours alone, Vesper. As is your bond with Kyrion. No one else gets to judge it or use it or decide how right or wrong it is."

This time, his voice was the one with the bitter note.

"Did people think your truebond with Verona was wrong?"

Aldrich stuck his hands in his pockets again and rocked back and forth on his heels. "My wife, Opal, had died the year before. Some people thought it was too soon for me to care about someone else, to fall in love with someone else. Especially the widow of the man responsible for my brother Irzin's death."

I wondered if Siya and Asterin were two of those people, but I didn't ask.

"Verona and I were both grieving the spouses we had lost," Aldrich continued. "We were kindred spirits, and eventually, that understanding led to other things."

*Kindred spirits.* I'd said similar things to Kyrion in the past, how the pain, anger, and darkness inside him perfectly matched those same emotions inside me. Maybe our truebond troubles had less to do with learning to use our respective magics and more to do with our feelings, not just about each other but all the hurt we'd endured over the years and all the wounds—small and shallow, large and gaping—we still carried in the cold depths of our hearts.

Aldrich's tablet pinged, and he pulled it out of his pocket and read the message. "I must return. Leland says it's time for Verona's and my speech thanking everyone for attending."

"Of course. Thank you for talking to me."

"Anytime," he replied. "Don't stay out here too long. Even with the energy shield, a chill can sometimes creep into the warmest places."

Aldrich bowed to me, then strode away. As if summoned by

his words, a bit of a chill breezed through the air, but I stayed where I was, idly twirling the blue-moon peony between my fingers.

Aldrich was right. I shouldn't let Nerezza have any more power over me. I thought I had finally sloughed off my mother's hurtful actions during the Regal midnight ball, but Esmina snidely calling me a weak link had brought all my old fears rushing back to the surface. That I wasn't smart enough to figure out my new seer abilities or strong enough to use my magic to protect Kyrion.

I didn't know how to get rid of those fears or banish the memories bouncing around inside my mind and heart. Ignoring Nerezza's scorn and Esmina's mockery was easier said than done.

Soft footsteps sounded behind me. Aldrich must have doubled back to check on me.

I plastered a smile on my face and turned around. "Really, my lord, please return to the marriage mart. I'm fine—"

The rest of my words died on my lips, replaced by a surge of stomach-churning dread.

A man stood before me. He was a little more than a year older than me, and his mane of longish blond hair glinted like spun gold underneath the soft lights. Just like every other man here, he was wearing a tailcoat and a ruffled shirt, both a pale blue that matched his eyes. A stormsword dangled from his belt, and all the tiny *Zs* carved into the silver hilt gleamed at me like silent, mocking eyes. The sigils were a perfect match to the *Z* on the pommel of my own stormsword, which I'd left in my suite at the Collier estate.

Zane Zimmer smirked at me, his teeth a blinding white against his tan skin. "Hey there, little sister."

My big brother had finally caught up to me.

# EIGHTEEN

## KYRION

For a moment, I remained rooted in place, shocked by the appearance of the man and woman, who were the very last two people I'd expected to see.

The man was in his early sixties, and a few silver threads glinted in his blond hair. His skin was tan, but his eyes were a familiar ice blue that matched his tailcoat and frilly shirt. The woman was older, in her eighties, with rosy skin and silver hair that was piled on top of her head. She too had ice-blue eyes that matched her sequined gown, and the resemblance between her and the man was obvious.

Wendell Zimmer, Vesper's father, and Beatrice Zimmer, her grandmother. What in all the stars were they doing here? But as soon as the question popped into my mind, I knew the answer.

They were here for Vesper—and they weren't alone.

Wendell caught sight of me. "Kyrion!" he called out. "Kyrion!"

Wendell started winding his way through the crowd toward me, as did Beatrice. If the Zimmers were here, then Zane was here too.

Shock, dread, and anger whipped along the velvety ribbon of Vesper in my mind. A dagger of worry plunged deep into my gut. Zane had already found her.

I spun around and focused on the bond, letting it point me toward Vesper. Then I started running.

The dome was even more crowded than before, and I didn't run so much as I shoved people out of my way, threading through the throngs of Erztonians who were talking, laughing, drinking, and dancing as though they didn't have a care in the galaxy.

"Hey!"

"Watch where you're going!"

"So rude!"

Annoyed shouts rose in my wake, but I didn't care. All that mattered was getting to Vesper before Zane . . . did whatever he had come here to do. Given how mercurial Zane was, that could be anything from mocking Vesper, to demanding she leave his family alone, to gifting her a bottle of the Galactic Suds for Studs shampoo he was currently hawking on the gossipcasts. But given the fact that Zane had been publicly vowing to bring us to Imperium justice for weeks, I was betting he was here to capture Vesper—or worse.

I finally broke free of the crowd. I picked up my pace, still following the vibrating ribbon of Vesper in my mind. I ran right past a couple of Hammers. The warriors gripped their weapons and stared at me with open suspicion, but they didn't follow me, probably because I was heading away from the guests.

I burst out of the back of the open dome and plunged into a large garden filled with those topiary trees and hedges the Colliers loved so much. I took the first path I came to, winding my way deeper and deeper into the shadowy landscape.

"Vesper!" I yelled. "Vesper!"

"Over here!"

I quickened my pace and rounded a bend. The trees and

hedges fell away, revealing Vesper standing in an open space, a single peony clutched in her hand. My frantic heart slowed down a few beats. Perhaps Zane hadn't found her yet—

"No! Kyr! Wait!" Vesper threw her hand up in warning.

I skidded to a halt . . . and a fist erupted out of the darkness and slammed into my face.

My nose broke with a loud *crunch.* Pain exploded in my jaw and radiated out through my skull, and a warm gush of blood dripped over my lips and streaked down my chin. I staggered back, trying to blink the flashing white stars out of my eyes.

Fuck, that hurt.

I blinked a few more times, and a man came into view. Blond hair, tan skin, ice-blue eyes, insufferable smirk.

"By the stars, that was satisfying!" Zane crowed.

I growled, stretched out my arms, and lunged toward him, but he spun to the side and skipped away.

Zane spun back around, that smug smirk still on his face. "Aw, Kyr, let's not fight. I would hate to get your blood all over my spiffy new tailcoat. Fergus, the House Zimmer tailor, worked extra hard on it, making sure it conformed to Erzton standards. It's a thing of beauty, don't you think?"

He planted his feet and held his arms out wide as though he was preening for the gossipcast cameras.

"I don't care about your tailcoat," I snarled. "I'm going to rip you apart with my bare hands."

I moved forward, putting myself between Vesper and Zane. I also scanned the garden, expecting to see a squad of Arrows converging on this position, but no other warriors appeared. Had Zane come here alone? And why had he only punched me instead of slicing my guts open with his stormsword?

Zane looked over at Vesper. "I told you he wouldn't listen to reason. That he wouldn't believe I came here in peace. You've shackled yourself to quite the monstrous beast, little sister."

Vesper stepped up beside me. The peony slipped through her

fingers and fluttered to the ground. "*Do not* call me that."

Footsteps smacked on the tiles, and another voice rang through the air. "What in all the moons is going on here?" Lord Aldrich demanded, striding into the garden.

Asterin hurried in after him, along with Leland, Siya, and Rigel. Verona followed them at a more sedate pace, as if she already knew exactly what was happening and wasn't overly concerned about it.

Wendell and Beatrice also hurried into the garden and stopped beside Zane, who kept right on smirking at me. My hands clenched into fists, and my nose throbbed in time to my pounding heart.

Lord Aldrich glanced at me, Vesper, and the Zimmers all in turn. "What is going on? Why are these people here?"

"I invited them," Lady Verona said, coming to stand beside her husband.

Asterin gaped at her mother. "You *invited* the Zimmers here? After everything that happened at the summer solstice ball? You practically ordered me to return to Sygnustern because Corios was no longer safe from the Techwave!"

Verona gave a delicate shrug. "And I stand by my assessment. The Techwave has already launched an attack on Corios. It won't be long before they do so again. But Lady Beatrice made several convincing arguments about why House Collier should continue to explore an alliance with House Zimmer."

"*Invited* is a strong word," Zane drawled, jumping into the conversation. "Your mother made us pay through the nose for the privilege of coming to this shiny little marriage slaughterhouse."

Asterin slapped her hands on her hips. "Marriage *mart*. It's an Erzton tradition."

Zane waggled his fingers. "Call it what you wish, but I know grasping treachery and desperate deception when I see it. If they could, all the Erzton lords and ladies would eliminate their rivals and take what they wanted, rather than going through the tedious, torturous rigamarole of marrying their offspring together."

"You were right about one thing," Siya chimed in. "He's certainly a jackass. I don't envy you, sister."

Asterin gave her a sharp look, but Siya grinned back, merriment dancing in her eyes.

I looked at Vesper. *Are you okay? Did Zane hurt you?*

*I'm fine*, she replied, her voice soft and dull in my mind. *I can't believe* he's *here. I can't believe the three of* them *are here.* Why *are they here?*

Her heartache rippled through the bond, along with sparks of anger.

Wendell held his hands out in a placating gesture. "Vesper, we came here alone. No Holloway, no Arrows, no one else. All we want is to talk. Can we do that? Please?"

An earnest plea filled his voice, and even more heartache rippled off Vesper. This was the first time she'd seen and spoken to Wendell since they'd both learned that he was her father.

A third wave of heartache rippled through the bond, but Vesper crossed her arms over her chest and gave Wendell a cool look. "We have nothing to discuss."

Beatrice stepped forward, her long skirt rustling with the movement. "We have everything to discuss."

Vesper gave her grandmother the same cool look she had given her father. "The last time I checked, I wasn't a member of House Zimmer, so you can't order me to do anything."

Several seconds ticked by in tense silence. Then Beatrice cleared her throat. "Wendell is right," she said in a much softer voice. "All we want to do is to talk, Vesper. Please."

Vesper kept glowering at her grandmother, but doubt crept into her eyes, and her stern expression softened just a bit.

"You might as well give in and say yes," Zane piped up. "We've come halfway across the galaxy to see you, and I, for one, am not leaving until we have a proper conversation."

He grinned at Asterin. "Although I'm sure I can find all *sorts* of things to amuse myself with on Sygnustern while I wait for my sister to grant us an audience."

Asterin's eyes narrowed in commensurate measure to Zane's grin growing wider. He really was an arrogant, insufferable jackass, but unfortunately, he meant every word. I'd seen Zane dig himself in and be far more obstinate about far less important things than the long-lost sister he never knew he had.

Vesper glanced at me, and I shrugged back. It was her choice, and I would support whatever she decided.

"*Fine.*" Vesper ground out the word. "Let's talk."

She crossed her arms a little more firmly over her chest, almost as if she was shielding herself from whatever the Zimmers had come here to say. I stepped closer to Vesper, letting her feel that I was right beside her, no matter what happened.

"Well?" Vesper snapped. "You wanted to talk, so get on with it."

"Not here," Zane replied. "Too many prying eyes."

He jerked his thumb to the side. Several Erztonians had gathered at the edge of the garden, peering in this direction. Zane was right. This wasn't a conversation to have in front of an audience.

"*Fine*." Vesper ground out the word again. "Where do you suggest we talk?"

Zane perked up, as if she'd asked a question he'd been just dying to answer. "Lady Verona was kind enough to offer us some suites at the Collier estate."

I bit back a curse. Not only was Zane on Sygnustern, but he'd finagled his way onto the estate. This just kept getting worse and worse.

Asterin whirled around to her mother. "You invited the Zimmers to stay with you? That breaks all sorts of marriage mart protocols!"

Verona shrugged again. "I thought it would be the simplest and easiest solution to have everyone in the same place. Especially given the complicated matters Vesper, Kyrion, and the Zimmers need to discuss."

Asterin threw her hands up in exasperation. Siya, Rigel, and Leland frowned, as did Aldrich, all clearly confused about Vesper's connection to the Zimmers.

"*Fine.*" Vesper ground out the word for a third time. "Let's leave the antiques emporium, return to the estate, and discuss how House Zimmer has denied my existence for the last thirty-seven years. That will be a pleasant chat, don't you think?"

Wendell flinched at her harsh tone, while Beatrice's lips pressed together into a tight line.

"Excellent!" Zane said, seemingly undisturbed by the simmering tension and angry accusations. "I'm so glad you're finally listening to reason."

"There's no reasoning with you," Asterin muttered.

Zane winked at her, then tilted his head at Wendell and Beatrice. The two of them nodded at Vesper, then left the garden.

Zane turned to me, another smirk on his face. "Broken noses really hurt, don't they, Kyr? You'd better wipe the blood off your chin, put some ice on your face, and give yourself a skinbond. I wouldn't want to ruin your dark and dashing good looks that my sister finds so appealing."

My fists squeezed even tighter, but somehow I resisted the urge to pummel the other Arrow. A few weeks ago, Zane had insulted Vesper while the two of us had been sparring in my training ring at Castle Caldaren, and I'd broken his nose to shut him up. Zane had vowed to pay me back, and he'd finally found a way to get his revenge and hurt Vesper in the process.

Zane smirked at me a moment longer, then strutted away.

"Excellent!" Lady Verona chirped in a cheerful voice as though nothing was wrong. "I've arranged for transports to take you all back to the estate."

"Zane gave you his word that he isn't here to capture Vesper?" I asked in a sharp, suspicious voice.

Verona nodded. "He did, and I made sure Lord Zane realizes he will see the inside of an Erzton prison—or worse—if he attempts something so foolish."

Her voice rang with sincerity, easing some of my worry.

Verona gave us all a bright smile. "Aldrich and I will be along later. Give you all some time to sort things out."

Vesper shook her head. "There's nothing to sort out."

Her face was calm, yet more heartache rippled through the bond. Vesper tipped her head to the Colliers, along with Siya, Rigel, and Leland, then strode past them. I fell into step beside her, with Asterin trailing along behind us.

Vesper didn't say anything, but thoughts whipped around in her mind like a whispering whirlwind, and one emotion after another streaked off her like stars shooting through the night sky—shock, confusion, anger, hurt.

Zane might not have captured Vesper, but in his own way, he had already wounded her. He was going to pay for that. So were Wendell and Beatrice if they dared to do the same thing.

My inner monster roared with rage, but for once, I couldn't help Vesper. There were no Imperium soldiers to escape, no bounty hunters to cut down, no mercenaries to battle.

No, right now, Vesper was being confronted by the most dangerous enemy of all: family.

# NINETEEN

## VESPER

Kyrion, Asterin, and I left the antiques emporium, got into a transport, and returned to the Collier estate.

Asterin's tablet chimed with a message. "The Zimmers are staying in some suites on the ground floor of the guest wing. They're waiting for you in the main library. I'll take you there."

The three of us crossed the courtyard and entered the guest wing. Asterin led us through several corridors before stopping in front of a set of closed doors.

She laid a gentle hand on my arm. "I'll give you some privacy and make sure no one disturbs you."

I nodded, and she disappeared around the corner. I should have reached for the knob, twisted it open, and entered the library, but instead, I stood there, frozen in place, my body numb.

Kyrion looked at me, his face soft with sympathy. The same emotion pulsed through the sticky cobweb in my mind, bringing a much-needed spark of warmth back to my body. "Are you okay?"

A harsh, bitter laugh spewed from my lips. "No, of course not. I can't believe they just showed up here. How did Zane even track us to Sygnustern?" Worry shot through me. "Do you think he told Holloway where we are?"

Kyrion shook his head. "No. Zane is a lot of things, but he would *never* put Wendell and Beatrice in danger. I'm guessing he didn't tell Holloway where he was going or what he was really doing."

"Why would he do that?"

Kyrion hesitated. "If there is one thing that sets House Zimmer apart from the other Houses, it's their devotion to family. The other Regals might crow about the importance of family on the gossipcasts, but the Zimmers truly *believe* it. Family first, House second, and then to the bloody stars with everyone else. The importance of family has been drilled into Zane's head since he was a child, and he would do *anything* to protect his father and grandmother. That's why I told him you were his sister before the midnight ball. I thought the knowledge might sway him to help us."

Surprise flickered through me. "You still think Zane let you cut him with your stormsword so we could escape?"

Kyrion nodded. "Yes. I think he did other things as well, although I can't prove it."

We'd had this conversation more than once, and we'd reviewed everything that had happened during the ball. Every time Kyrion claimed that Zane had helped us, a tiny spark of hope flared up in my heart like a star trying to be born.

I'd had the same spark of hope when I was being held in the Techwave lab and Nerezza had said that her daughter was dead. For one brief, shining moment, I'd thought maybe *that* was why my mother had never tried to see, find, or check on me in the last thirty years. But in the very next breath, Nerezza had said my supposed death was a wasted opportunity since she couldn't use her dead daughter—*me*—against her enemies.

And just like that, my hope had snuffed out, shriveled up, and blown away like bitter ash floating in the cracked chasms of my heart.

In some ways, Nerezza had wounded me far worse than Harkin Ocnus had with his sadistic torture. I'd *let* my mother hurt me again, despite all my vows that I was done with her, and I didn't know how to stop Zane, Wendell, and Beatrice from doing the same thing.

In the R&D lab, a brewmaker could only break so many times before it was beyond repair, and my heart was much more fragile than any appliance.

I rubbed my aching head. Like it or not, the Zimmers were here, and according to Kyrion, Zane wouldn't leave without having this conversation, so all I could do now was get on with it.

I dropped my hand, squared my shoulders, and lifted my chin. "Fine. Let's go see what my not-family wants, and then we can be rid of them once and for all."

Kyrion slid his hand into mine. My fingers were ice-cold in his warm grip, and he gave them a gentle squeeze.

"No matter what happens, I'm right here with you, Vesper." He paused. "And if you want me to slice Zane open from gullet to gut, then that's what I'll do."

The dark promise in his words made me smile. I stood on my tiptoes and pressed a kiss to his lips. Kyrion held me close for a few seconds, then let me go, although he remained a strong, solid, comforting presence at my side.

I stared at the doors a moment longer, then twisted the knob and moved forward to confront the family that had never wanted me.

Kyrion and I entered the library. Beatrice was perched primly on a settee in the center of the room. Her back was ramrod straight, and the long skirt of her ice-blue gown was draped perfectly around her body, as though she was the queen of the castle posing for a portrait. Wendell was sitting next to her, and he kept rubbing his hands along his thighs, wrinkling his pants.

Zane was leaning one shoulder against the wall, his arms crossed over his chest, watching everyone with an unreadable expression. Maybe my seer magic was whispering a warning, or maybe it was my own prior bad experiences with him, but somehow I knew Zane was the most dangerous of the three Zimmers and that he could hurt me the worst of all.

I looked past the Zimmers, studying the rest of the library, trying to buy myself a few more seconds to shore up my defenses.

Settees, tables, and chairs made of real wood, stone, and glass filled the room, along with other luxe furnishings. Seeing the Zimmers in the midst of such finery made me feel as though I was back on Corios and had just stepped into Castle Zimmer.

After I'd learned who my father was, I'd scoured the gossipcasts, searching for every single scrap of information I could find about Wendell, Beatrice, and especially Zane. I'd watched dozens of shows about Castle Zimmer and the history of House Zimmer, as if seeing the Zimmers in their natural, ancestral habitat would give me some clue to who they truly were—and why they had never wanted me to be part of their family.

Beatrice gestured at the porcelain green tea set arranged on a gold platter on the low table in front of her. "I asked the servants to bring us some tea. I hope you don't mind."

As the head of House Zimmer, Beatrice was used to being obeyed. She would have done the exact same thing even if I had minded, but I swallowed my snide thought.

Beatrice gestured at the tea set again. "May I pour you a cup?"

I spun away from her and stalked over to a brewmaker sitting on a table along the wall. I popped a pod into the brewmaker and made my own cup of tea, which I then set on the nearby beverage chiller. The simple act of making it calmed some of my nerves.

I took the cup, walked over, and sat down on the settee opposite Beatrice and Wendell. Kyrion leaned against the wall to my right, close to Zane. Kyrion crossed his arms over his chest, mocking Zane's seemingly relaxed posture, and my brother rolled his eyes in response.

Despite my roiling stomach, I forced myself to take a sip of the tea, then set the cup down. "I despise hot tea. I prefer to make it how *I* like it. Not how everyone else *expects* it to be. I've been making my own tea for a long time."

My voice grew colder and harsher with every word. Beatrice's lips pressed into a thin line, but she picked up her own teacup and took a long, slow, deliberate sip before setting it back down. I didn't touch my tea again. Wendell didn't pick up his cup either.

I braced my back against the cushions, letting them prop me up, then waved my hand in an airy motion, as though I didn't have a care in the galaxy. "You wanted to talk, so talk."

Wendell leaned forward. "I'm so sorry, Vesper. About everything. Truly."

"Like pretending I didn't exist for the last thirty-seven years?" A bitter laugh tumbled out of my mouth. "Yes, I imagine you do feel sorry about that. But only now. *After* we all know the truth."

Wendell shook his head. "I didn't even know you existed until the midnight ball when you confronted Nerezza. Truly, Vesper. I had no idea Nerezza had ever been pregnant."

Sincerity rang through his voice, lessening some of my brittle anger. At him, at least. My gaze shifted over to Beatrice. "But you knew, didn't you?"

"Yes. Nerezza made sure I knew she was pregnant with Wendell's child."

Another bitter laugh tumbled from my lips. "You mean Nerezza tried to blackmail you into letting her into House Zimmer because she was pregnant with me."

"Yes, but I refused."

I opened my mouth to snipe back at Beatrice, but she held up her hand. "Please. Let me speak. That's all I ask."

Reluctantly, I bit back my snarky words. Beatrice dropped her gaze to her lap. She laced her hands together, then peeled her fingers apart and twisted her jeweled rings back and forth, as if settling them into just the right position.

"Anytime now," Kyrion growled.

Beatrice arched her eyebrow in a chiding look, which Kyrion returned with an icy glower.

After a few seconds, Beatrice's hands stilled, and she focused on me again. "I'm sure you've done your research on the Zimmer family. Our bloodlines, our psionic abilities, everything. Not many people know this, but seer magic runs through the Zimmer family, although it is an unpredictable ability that often skips a generation or two. My mother was a seer, and I have a touch of that power as well."

"What does that have to do with Nerezza?"

Beatrice's spine stiffened a bit more at my harsh tone. "When Nerezza revealed she was pregnant, I had a horrible, horrible vision. Of Nerezza becoming part of House Zimmer and then using her child—you—to destroy us. One by one, I saw her kill me, then Wendell, then Zane, so that she could take control of our House. I couldn't let that happen, not to my House and especially not to my family. I know you probably won't believe me, but if Nerezza had become part of House Zimmer, she would have murdered us all."

*Even you, Vesper.* Beatrice didn't say the words, but her thought rasped through my mind, and I had to grind my teeth to keep from flinching.

Even worse, my seer magic stirred to life, and the images

Beatrice had described flickered in the open space between us. Nerezza poisoning Beatrice's tea, then doing the same thing to Wendell, then shoving a young Zane in front of a carriage on the Boulevard. The visions bled into each other, then looped around and repeated, as though Nerezza was here and killing the Zimmers one by one by one in front of me.

I shoved the awful visions away. Zane frowned at me, and his eyes narrowed, as if he too had seen his own childish body splattered across the cobblestones.

"I believe you," I said in a stiff voice. "What happened next?"

"Nerezza thought having a child with Zimmer blood would be enough to force my hand, but she was wrong," Beatrice said in a cold, clipped tone. "I started a rumor that her psion power was fading, then paid the headmaster to kick her out of the academy she was attending on Corios. I used every tool at my disposal and every favor I had ever accrued to discredit her."

She shrugged as though destroying someone's reputation was of no consequence.

"Once Nerezza realized she couldn't outmaneuver me, she threatened to go to the gossipcasts with the story unless I paid her off, so I did. I told Nerezza to leave Corios for good." Beatrice paused. "But I knew it was only a matter of time before Nerezza returned, so I started making preparations."

"What sort of *preparations*?" I asked in a wary voice.

"First, I hired your cousin Liesl to look after you," Beatrice said. "I made sure Liesl was by your mother's side from the moment you were born. I knew Nerezza would bide her time until you were old enough to start showing psionic abilities, and I didn't want any harm to befall you before then."

My heart squeezed in on itself. Even though I had always desperately longed for Nerezza's love, Liesl was the one who had taken care of me.

"When I was seven, the Imperium academy instructors told

Nerezza that my seer magic was too weak to bother training me to use it properly. Was that your doing?"

Beatrice shook her head. "No, that wasn't me. Nerezza knew I had interfered with her schooling, and I couldn't risk doing the same trick again with yours."

Sincerity rang through her voice, although her words made my heart sink. In the back of my mind, I'd always thought—*hoped*—the instructors had been wrong about my magic.

*Useless child.* Nerezza's voice hissed through my mind, although it was quickly followed by Esmina's sneer. *Weak link.*

"Why are you talking about your schooling?" Wendell asked.

I had to wait for the voices to fade away before I could answer him. "When Nerezza realized I didn't have enough psion power for her liking, she left me with Liesl. Then, a few weeks later, Liesl took me to a different Imperium academy—a very expensive academy."

Beatrice nodded. "*That* was my doing. Liesl contacted me and said that Nerezza had abandoned you, so I sent Liesl enough credits to enroll you in the best academy available. I might not have been able to do it myself, but I always made sure you were taken care of, Vesper."

Her soft words cracked through the brittle shell I'd erected around my body, and I struggled to keep them from piercing my heart.

"A few months later, Nerezza returned to Corios and married into a small House." Beatrice's lips curled back with disgust. "I knew Nerezza still wanted revenge on me, so I paid Liesl to become your mother's lady-in-waiting. I thought it was the best chance I had of keeping us all safe."

Kyrion snorted. "You mean it was your best chance of spying on Nerezza and staying ahead of her revenge plot."

Beatrice shrugged a shoulder in agreement. "For a while, everything was fine. Nerezza seemed content to keep quiet and keep climbing the Regal ladder. But then . . ."

"What?" I asked.

My grandmother looked at me, sorrow sparking in her eyes. "Then Liesl told me there had been an accident at your academy—and that you had been killed."

Shock sliced through me. Even though Nerezza had claimed she thought I was dead, I had never considered Beatrice might have believed it too.

"And you just believed Liesl? Without any proof?"

"Of course not," Beatrice snapped. "I sent my own investigators to the academy, but they confirmed Liesl's story. There had been an accident in one of the student labs, and a young girl—you—had been killed."

Once again, sincerity rang through her voice. She really had believed I was dead.

Confusion swirled through me. "An explosion in the chemistry lab killed a girl I knew. But why would Liesl lie and say *I* was the one who'd died?"

Beatrice held her hands out to her sides. "My best guess is Liesl was trying to protect you from some plot Nerezza was considering. As soon as I realized you were still alive, I had my investigators go back over everything, but they haven't come up with any answers about why Liesl did what she did."

I thought back to that time. Liesl had been visiting me more than usual, but one day, soon after the lab accident, without any warning, she made me pack my things, leave my friends, and go to a new academy on a different planet. I'd been so upset I'd called Liesl all sorts of awful names, and she hadn't visited me for several months afterward. I had always thought Liesl had stayed away because she was angry, but what if she had been trying to protect me from Nerezza?

Beatrice cleared her throat. "I noticed Liesl's name on the passenger manifest for the *Velorum*. I'm sorry for your loss, Vesper. Truly."

As soon as I'd realized Liesl had been on the *Velorum*, I'd started wondering what she had been doing on the doomed spaceship. Later on, in the Techwave facility, Nerezza had revealed that Liesl had been trying to blackmail her for more money. Nerezza had responded to her cousin's threat by using a Techwave cannon to shoot the *Velorum* out of the sky, killing Liesl and everyone else on board.

"It doesn't really matter why Liesl claimed I died. She's gone, so we'll probably never know the answer." A bitter laugh erupted from my mouth. "I bet you were happy when Liesl told you I was dead. That solved a lot of problems for you."

"No," Beatrice said in a low voice. "I might not have known you, but I still grieved for you, Vesper."

She stared at me, her gaze level with mine, and needles of sorrow shot off her and scraped along my skin. A little more of that brittle shell around my body cracked away, and I bit down on my tongue to steady my emotions.

Beatrice twisted a blue opal ring around her finger. "I saw your reaction to Nerezza during one of the Regal balls. How you tried to hide from her. That's when I first started to suspect who you really were. Then, when Adria and Dargan Byrne brought you back to Corios for the midnight ball—"

"With Zane's help," Kyrion cut in.

Beatrice cleared her throat again. "When you confronted Nerezza at the ball, I finally realized Liesl had lied to me and that you weren't dead."

"How *did* you figure out that Wendell was Vesper's father before the ball?" Zane asked, looking at Kyrion. "I found Daichi's back door into the Regal archives, but he didn't match my DNA with Vesper's until *after* the ball. So how did you know Vesper was my sister?"

Kyrion jerked his chin at Zane's sword. "There's a tiny *Z* carved into the pommel of Vesper's stormsword. It looks exactly like the *Z*s on the hilt of your sword."

Zane's eyes narrowed, and his index finger rubbed over one

of the *Zs*. "In other words, you just guessed."

Kyrion rolled his eyes, and Zane's hand flexed like he wanted to draw the sword and gut the other Arrow with the blade.

"What do you want?" I demanded. "Why are you all here?"

"Because you're my daughter, and I want to get to know you," Wendell said in a soft voice.

"We all do," Beatrice added.

"Speak for yourselves," Zane drawled. "I already know my little sister quite well. Thanks to her relationship with Kyrion, Vesper and I have had several run-ins over the last few months. Vesper and I also had a little chat in my tower library a few weeks ago, via her astral projection."

I studied the three of them in turn. Beatrice cool and aloof, Wendell open and eager, Zane mocking and sardonic. This was my family. The thing I had always wanted most.

After so many years of wondering, they were right here in front of me. It would be so blasted *easy* to just give in, accept them at face value, and trust they were here for the right reasons. But Nerezza had shattered my trust, and thirty years later, I was still trying to put the jagged pieces back together.

I looked at Beatrice again. "Tell me something. If I hadn't confronted Nerezza at the ball, if Wendell and Zane hadn't learned the truth, would the three of you be sitting here? Or would I just be a footnote to you? A mistake that conveniently got lost in the ether of the galaxy?"

Her faint wince was all the confirmation I needed. The Zimmers weren't here by choice, and that made all the difference. That cold, hard truth snuffed out the tiny, fragile spark of hope in my chest, then seeped deep into my bones, but for once, I was grateful for the numbing chill.

"Well, that settles things," I said, grateful that my voice remained calm and steady. "Beatrice was happy to pretend I didn't exist for the last thirty-seven years, and I see no reason to upset the status quo."

Wendell leaned forward again, a pleading look on his face. "But you're my *daughter*. That means something to me."

The sincerity in his voice almost made me reconsider—almost.

I shook my head, shoving away the softness that kept threatening to creep into my heart. "Well, it doesn't mean anything to me." I stabbed my finger at Beatrice. "You knew *exactly* what Nerezza was like, how she would try to use me against House Zimmer, and you left me with her anyway."

She nodded, but her posture slumped, and something that looked like genuine regret crinkled her features. "I understand."

Wendell looked back and forth between the two of us. "But you *don't* understand. You might think we're all monsters, Vesper, and maybe we are, but Zane helped you during the midnight ball, even before he knew who you really were—"

Zane shook his head the tiniest bit. The motion was almost imperceptible, but Wendell abruptly cut off his thought.

"I knew it," Kyrion said. "I *knew* you lowered your guard and let me cut you when we were fighting."

Zane flicked his fingers in an airy, dismissive motion. "I have no idea what you're talking about. You wounded me fair and square, Kyr."

As soon as he said the words, my seer magic stirred to life, and a second image of Zane appeared in the air. The mirror image of Zane fought with Kyrion just as he had during the ball, and I finally *saw* it—the moment when Zane lowered his guard a fraction of an inch.

"That's not all your brother did," Wendell continued.

"Father," Zane warned in a sharp voice. "*Stop talking.*"

Wendell kept pleading with me. "Zane gave one of the servants a hairpin dagger to give to you. The butterfly dagger you wore to the midnight ball." His gaze flicked to my throat. "It looks just like the necklace you're wearing."

Surprise shot through me, and my hand crept up to the

brooch hanging on the black velvet ribbon. My gaze swung over to Zane, who shifted on his feet.

"Were you trying to give us a sporting chance then too? Just like you did when you tripped Adria Byrne in the rain forest on Tropics 33? Or when you turned on the spy camera you found in Kyrion's blitzer so he would know that Holloway had sent you, Adria, and Dargan to track us down?"

Zane didn't respond, and his face remained smooth and calm. That familiar spark of hope flared in my heart again, burning through the icy numbness that gripped my body. Maybe Zane really had done all those things so we could escape . . . but then he'd spent the last few weeks vowing to hunt down Kyrion and me.

I ruthlessly crushed that spark of hope, snuffing it into oblivion, then encased my emotions in a layer of ice. Zane did whatever was easy or convenient or best for him, just like Nerezza always had. Just like Wendell had by never considering the consequences of his relationship with my mother. Just like Beatrice had by letting Liesl take care of me instead of acknowledging my existence and making me a part of House Zimmer, and especially a part of her family.

I'd never had a real family before, and despite my longing for one now, I wasn't going to settle for leftover table scraps, for whatever meager crumbs of affection Zane, Wendell, and Beatrice deigned to dole out. Nerezza had made a fool of me for years, and I would not make the same mistake again.

Never again.

Weariness crashed through my body, along with more of that numbness, but I dug my hands into the thick cushions and hoisted myself to my feet. Beatrice and Wendell also stood up. Zane pushed away from the wall, as did Kyrion.

"Thank you for telling me what happened," I replied, my voice eerily calm. "I understand why you did the things you did. I know better than anyone else how dangerous Nerezza is.

How she will use anyone at any time to get what she wants. She even has a name for her manipulations: social engineering."

An eager look filled Wendell's face. He opened his mouth, but Zane moved forward and laid a warning hand on his father's shoulder.

"But?" Beatrice asked.

"But you still abandoned me, just like Nerezza did, and I don't think I can ever forgive that," I said, even as the ice crystallized and sharpened into spears skewering my heart. "Even more important, I am no one's dirty little secret. Not anymore."

"So where does this leave us?" Zane asked in a low voice.

"Return to Corios and your regularly scheduled lives. If there's any mercy in the galaxy, we'll never have to see each other again."

Wendell clearly wanted to protest, but he chewed on his lower lip and remained silent. Beatrice tipped her head to me, although she didn't look as relieved as I'd expected.

Finally, I turned my attention to Zane. "Make no mistake. This changes *nothing* between us. If you *ever* try to take Kyrion and me back to Holloway, then we will kill you, and your father will have no children left, secret or otherwise."

Wendell gasped. Beatrice's face paled at my threat, but Zane studied me with an unreadable expression.

I stared at my unwanted brother a heartbeat longer, then whirled around on my heel and strode out of the library, leaving my so-called family behind.

# TWENTY

## KYRION

Wendell hurried forward and stretched out his hand, as though he was going to go after Vesper. I blocked his path.

"*Don't*," I warned in a cold voice. "Don't you *dare*."

Wendell's hand wilted to his side.

"Perhaps we should retire to our suites," Beatrice said. "We had a long trip from Corios."

"I don't care where you go or what you do," I said, my voice even colder than before. "Just stay away from Vesper."

Beatrice harrumphed. "You are in no position to tell me what to do, Kyrion. You've made my granddaughter a fugitive, and yourself one too. And your mother would roll over in her grave if she heard the impertinent tone you're taking with a Regal lady."

Icy fury roared through my body at her tossing Desdemona's devotion to manners in my face. "My mother would heartily applaud my tone—and then she would march over there and slap you across the face for abandoning your own granddaughter."

Beatrice's spine stiffened.

"You should be glad my mother's not here, *my lady*, because she was certainly no fan of yours. Desdemona always said you cared more about avoiding scandal than anything else, including your supposed claims about family *always* coming first. My mother saw you for what you truly are—a bloody *coward*."

An angry blush stained Beatrice's cheeks a dark, mottled red, and her hands fisted in her skirt.

"Come," Wendell said in an anxious voice, glancing back and forth between me and his mother. "You're right. We should retire to our suites."

Beatrice lifted her chin and followed her son out of the library.

"That went well," Zane drawled.

I spun around on my heel and strode out of the room. Like Vesper, I'd had more than enough of the Zimmers.

Asterin was waiting in the corridor, a sympathetic look on her face. "Vesper said she wanted a few minutes alone."

I reached out with the bond. Emotions vibrated along the velvety ribbon of Vesper—hurt, anger, confusion, longing. As much as I wanted to find Vesper, put my arms around her, and tell her everything was going to be okay, I respected her desire for privacy, even as a sense of helplessness cascaded over me. Her unwanted family was one hard problem I couldn't solve with my stormsword.

"Let's fix your nose," Asterin said. "Then you can check on Vesper."

The confrontation inside the library had been so tense that I'd forgotten about my broken nose, but as soon as Asterin mentioned it, a fresh wave of pain throbbed through my face.

Footsteps sounded, heading in this direction, and a cool, familiar presence oozed around me like space sludge.

Zane swaggered to a stop beside me. "Your nose is a spectacular shade of blue, black, and green. Not to mention the blood crusted on your face. You *really* should get that looked at, Kyr."

Asterin sighed. "Why don't you do us all a favor and leave, Zane?"

He grinned. "And miss all the fun of watching Kyrion scowl while you wrench his nose back where it's supposed to be? *Never.*" He bowed to her, then held his hand out to the side. "Lead the way, my lady."

Asterin huffed, but she set off down the corridor. I followed her, and Zane fell into step beside me. He studied every door, window, and archway, along with the guards. Zane was making sure he knew where all the entrances and exits were, just like I had done this morning.

Asterin stepped into an infirmary made of pale green tile. Several medtables were spaced throughout the room, while clear polyplastic cabinets along the wall contained vials of antibiotics, skinbond injectors, and other supplies.

Asterin gestured for me to sit on a medtable. I did as she asked, although the table was cranked up so high my long legs dangled off the side, making me feel as though I was a child.

Zane leaned a shoulder against the wall and crossed his arms over his chest, studying everything in the infirmary, although his gaze kept straying back to Asterin. Curious. Perhaps he was worried about Asterin grabbing a laser scalpel and cutting his tongue out of his mocking mouth. The thought had certainly crossed my mind, but I doubted even that drastic action would silence Zane. The clever bastard would no doubt find some new way to torture me.

Asterin grabbed a skinbond injector and stabbed it into my upper left arm. She tossed the used injector into a recycler, then stepped closer to me and flexed her fingers.

"I need to put your nose back into place before the skinbond kicks in. Otherwise, it might heal crooked." Asterin gave me another sympathetic look. "This is going to hurt."

"Just do it—"

Asterin wrenched my nose to the side. I hissed. A few seconds later, the skinbond started pumping through my veins, dulling the bright, sparking pain to a dim, pulsing throb.

Asterin wet a cloth and handed it to me, and I wiped the blood off my face and tossed the soiled linen into the recycler.

"Well, that was entirely too easy," Zane said. "I was hoping Kyrion would scream a bit."

"The only one who's going to be screaming is you," I growled. "Right after I shove my sword into your chest."

Zane clucked his tongue. "Please. We both know you're never going to do that. You *can't* do that now, given that I am your beloved's big brother. Vesper might not like me much, but I doubt she wants me dead."

My fingers twitched with the urge to throttle him, but he was right. Vesper was hurt and angry, but she didn't want any of the Zimmers dead, not even Zane.

"I might not be able to kill you, but you can't kill me either. Vesper would kill you herself for that."

Zane's lips turned down into an exaggerated pout. "Yes, well, your truebond with Vesper is an unfortunate fact we're all going to have to live with. Have the two of you figured out your psion powers yet? Or is my sister still randomly astral-projecting herself into people's libraries?"

His voice was light and breezy, but concern wafted off him and tweaked my telempathy.

My eyes narrowed. "You actually care about her."

A mulish expression tightened his face. "I have no idea what you're talking about."

I wouldn't get a straight answer out of him, so I tried a different tactic. "How did you know we were coming to Sygnustern? You couldn't have possibly tracked us here."

"Oh, that was easy. Asterin told me."

Asterin jerked back in surprise. "I did no such thing!"

Zane cocked an eyebrow at her. "Oh, yes, you did. I saw how chatty you were with Tivona Winslow and Leandra Ferrum during the summer solstice ball. Every time I turned around, the three of you were whispering, and it wasn't hard to figure out you were talking about my dear sister and her unfortunate choice of paramour. Especially since you, Tivona, and Leandra had already helped Vesper and Kyrion escape from Crownpoint."

Asterin sputtered, but Zane waved his hand, cutting her off.

"Don't bother denying it. Scores of Regals and servants recorded the midnight ball on their tablets, as did the gossipcasts. I went through *all* the footage—every last *frame*."

Zane stabbed his finger at Asterin. "You, my lady, tripped some soldiers trying to apprehend Vesper and Kyrion outside the throne room. Daichi and Touma Hirano scrambled the security cameras, while Tivona Winslow and Leandra Ferrum took out some Imperium soldiers and Bronze Hand guards. Thus clearing the way for Vesper and Kyrion to board the *Dream World* and zoom away from the palace."

I'd figured someone would eventually piece it all together, but Zane doing it so quickly didn't surprise me. He might act like an arrogant idiot, but he could be quite clever and dogged when he put his mind to it.

"But little did Vesper and Kyrion know that Adria Byrne had snuck onto their ship." Zane focused on me. "I'm assuming you and Vesper eliminated Adria, since she is nowhere to be found. How did you manage that? I saw Adria after Vesper killed Dargan in the throne room. She was mad with grief at the loss of her truebond with her brother. No way she went down easy."

"No, Adria didn't go down easy," I muttered. "I was getting healed in the hyperbaric chamber on the medtable when she attacked. Vesper has an O2 enhancement, so she purged all the oxygen out of the cargo bay. Adria died. Vesper didn't."

Zane's golden eyebrows shot up. "That must have been hard to watch."

He had no bloody idea. I would never forget how Vesper had struggled to breathe and then crumpled to the floor when she too ran out of air. How she had been more dead than alive when I'd finally freed myself from the medtable. How I'd used a strange combination of luck, along with our truebond, to find Vesper deep in her mindscape and bring her back to me.

"Since the ball, Tivona has been funneling Quill Corp credits into an account owned by a baroness with a ridiculously long name that's clearly an alias for Vesper." Zane snapped his fingers. "Oh, and Daichi and Touma are hiding out on Corios, just in case you and Vesper return home."

I stiffened. "If you hurt *any* of them—"

Zane snorted, cutting off my threat. "Your friends are fine. Tivona is surrounded by Quill Corp guards, who are being whipped into shape by Leandra, and as far as Daichi and Touma know, they are perfectly safe in their little hidey-hole."

I bit back a curse. Zane knew *everything*, and he could whisper a few words into Holloway's ear and have our friends arrested anytime he wanted.

"What do you want, Zane? Because there is always a price for your silence."

"True," he agreed. "But in this case, it's more about what my father wants."

When Wendell had looked at Vesper in the library, a combination of guilt, pride, and hope had boiled off him like steam from a red-hot teapot. Most Regal lords were cold, pompous bastards, but Wendell was the exception to the rule. Even my mother had liked him.

"This was your idea, wasn't it? Bringing your grandmother and your father to Sygnustern so the three of you could have this impromptu family reunion. So your father could try to build a relationship with Vesper."

Zane's eyes glinted with a mixture of fury and disgust. "It's hardly a reunion when no one ever mentioned you had a sister in the first place."

"You feel like *you're* the one who's been wronged because Beatrice never told you about Vesper?" I shook my head. "By the stars, you are even more selfish than I imagined."

A muscle twitched in Zane's jaw, but he quickly smoothed out his expression. "It doesn't matter how selfish I am. Vesper is *my* sister, and *you* are bonded with *her*." He crossed his fingers together. "You and I are stuck with each other, dear Kyrion, glued together by your bloody truebond, whether we like it or not."

"You call Vesper your sister like it actually means something to you."

Even more fury flared in Zane's eyes, making them gleam like icy Frozon moons. "It means *everything* to me, which you damn well know. You told me Vesper was my sister before the midnight ball in hopes I would help you both escape. You were *counting* on it. You think I'm a manipulator? Yes, I am, but you, dear Kyrion, are just as diabolical."

"Not me," I snapped back. "I didn't care what happened to *me*. I wanted you to help *her*. Unlike you, Zane, I will always put Vesper's well-being above my own."

Zane huffed. "It's easy to be self-righteous when your family is dead, and you don't have anyone else to care about—or who cares about you in return."

Asterin sucked in a breath. I glowered at Zane, who smirked back at me. He'd scored a direct hit with that verbal barb, and the worst part was that he was *right*.

Ever since my parents had died, I had been on my own, more or less. Oh, Daichi and Touma had been my friends for years, and now I had new friends in Asterin, Tivona, and Leandra, but Vesper . . .

Vesper was the one I loved.

The knowledge flooded my mind like a sun rising above the horizon, banishing the shadows, and revealing a planet's surface, but my heart had known it for quite some time, like a blue moon that was constant and steady in the sky, even if you couldn't always see it.

Vesper was my blue moon. My sun, my stars, and everything else that was bright and beautiful and lovely in the galaxy.

Perhaps I had fallen for Vesper during the Regal ball when she had outsmarted Holloway by covering the marks on her hand when I had cut my own hand as part of the truebond test. Or perhaps it had happened when we'd shared a quiet meal on the *Dream World*. Or the first time I'd kissed her. Or when I'd pulled her out of the dark depths of her mindscape and back into the real world. Or perhaps I had loved her through all of that and just hadn't wanted to admit it to myself until right now.

But I loved Vesper, which meant Zane was right—the two of us were stuck with each other. Vesper might claim she didn't want anything to do with the Zimmers, but I'd felt her longing in the library. Despite everything Beatrice had done, a small part of Vesper still wanted to give the Zimmers a chance, and I would never deny her that opportunity, even if I deeply despised her unexpected brother.

"What do you want, Zane?" I asked again, tired of his theatrics.

"What does anyone in the galaxy want? Love, peace, happiness, prosperity," he drawled. "Perhaps a basket of corgi puppies and boodle kittens for good measure."

"You really are insufferable," Asterin muttered.

Zane gasped and clutched a hand to his heart. "You wound me, fair lady. Why, I have not *begun* to be insufferable yet."

Asterin's fingers twitched as though she wanted to throttle him, a sentiment I shared.

"As I said before, it's more about what my father wants, and that is a chance to get to know his daughter." Zane waggled his finger back and forth between Asterin and me. "The two of you will *not* interfere with that, so no whispering in Vesper's ear about how horrible we Zimmers are. That might be true for Beatrice and me, but it's not for my father."

Once again, Zane was right. His father had always been courteous, and even kind, to me. And after I'd killed my own father in self-defense, Wendell and Beatrice had been the only Regals who had voted against my being executed.

"You don't know Vesper at all if you think I or anyone else could convince her to have a relationship with your father," I replied. "Vesper makes up her own mind."

Zane tipped his head, conceding my point. "Yes, but for some reason I will never understand, your opinion matters greatly to her. So do us both a favor and keep quiet about how much you hate me, okay?"

I laughed. "I don't need to give Vesper a reason to hate you, Zane. You did that all on your own. Or do you not remember calling her my conquest when we were sparring at Castle Zimmer a few months ago?"

He shifted on his feet. "Yes, well, Vesper retaliated by building a science experiment of a blaster and burning my clothes, so I'd say the two of us are even." He shrugged. "Besides, siblings fight."

*Siblings?* What was he playing at? Was he actually . . . *sincere*? Despite his breezy tone and arrogant smirk, Zane's posture was tight and tense, and he kept rubbing his fingers over the *Z* sigils carved into his stormsword. Even more telling, cold worry kept wafting off him and twinging my telempathy, like a lonely winter cloud spitting out hard bits of snow.

Zane really *did* view Vesper as his sister, and he actually wanted this crazy gambit to work. He truly wanted Vesper to be part of the Zimmer family—*his* family.

"Kyrion isn't the one you should be threatening," Asterin

chimed in, fury rippling through her voice. "You came to *my* planet and invaded *my* mother's home. You have no interest in the Erzton marriage mart or especially in courting me."

"True, but pretending to repair whatever *this* is"—he sliced his hand back and forth between himself and Asterin—"was the only way I could land on this mountainous rock."

Even more fury flared in Asterin's eyes. Her fingers twitched again and curled into fists, and psion power rippled off her, although I still couldn't tell what abilities she had.

"I saw an opportunity, and I took it," Zane continued. "Just like you took the opportunity to break into Jorge Rojillo's lab during the summer solstice ball." He tilted his head to the side, studying her a little more closely. "What *are* you going to do with those designs you stole? What, exactly, does an Erzton lady need with an air purifier?"

A muscle twitched in Asterin's jaw, and it took her a few seconds to swallow her fury. "None of your damn business."

"Ah, but it *is* my business," Zane countered. "Seeing as how your spying and thieving could reflect poorly on me and House Zimmer, if it were to be discovered. Not to mention what your mother and stepfather would say if they were to realize the *real* reason you've been pretending to hunt for a husband is to steal tech from Regal Houses. That would cause *quite* the scandal and probably ruin your chances of *ever* snaring a husband, among either the Regals *or* the Erztonians."

"At least then I wouldn't wind up shackled to you," Asterin retorted.

Zane clucked his tongue. "Temper, temper, fair lady."

Asterin's fingers fisted a little tighter.

"That's enough," I growled. "You've made your bloody point. Leave Asterin alone. This is between you and me."

"Ah, but I can't do that. This is what is called mutually assured destruction." Zane's lips puckered in thought. "Or perhaps triply assured destruction, since three of us are involved in this little triangle of nastiness."

He stabbed his finger at Asterin. "You can't kick my family off the estate lest I reveal your spying and thieving to the Colliers." He stabbed his finger at me. "And you can't give in to your murderous urges and kill me because I'm Vesper's brother. You also can't badmouth my family lest I decide to tell Holloway the real reason I've come to Sygnustern."

Zane was right. Asterin and I were stuck with him, and his family, until he deemed otherwise.

I slid off the medtable, stalked forward, and stopped right in front of him, but Zane didn't back down or back away. He'd *never* done that, not even when we were boys fighting in a Regal schoolyard. He simply had no fear, which was something I'd always admired about him, as aggravating as that was. Curiously enough, he reminded me of Vesper in that way.

"Ah, but there is *your* problem," I countered in a cold voice. "You can't tell Holloway you came here because your father wants to have a relationship with Vesper. Holloway would order his Bronze Hand guards to seize you, along with your family, and he would destroy your House, along with everyone with even a drop of Zimmer blood."

Agreement flashed in Zane's eyes. We both knew how desperate Holloway was to capture Vesper and me—and how severely he would punish Zane for not immediately revealing our location.

"Like I said, we're all trapped in this little triangle of trouble," Zane said. "So let's make the best of it, eh?"

Neither Asterin nor I responded.

Zane let out a loud, fake yawn and stretched his arms high. He stretched a little wider, then dropped his arms to his sides. "All this family drama has worn me out. I'm going to bed. See you in the morning."

With those ominous words, he snapped off a mock salute, then sauntered out of the infirmary.

"Is it just me, or did that sound more like a threat than a good night?" Asterin asked.

"With Zane, everything is always a threat."

Now I just had to figure out how much of a danger he was truly going to be to Vesper. Oh, Zane wouldn't physically hurt Vesper. Family really did mean something to Zane, and Wendell would never forgive his son for harming his long-lost daughter.

No, I was worried how much of Vesper's heart Zane might destroy.

Asterin's tablet pinged. Verona and Aldrich had returned to the estate, so she went to check on them. I didn't ask what she was going to tell them about Vesper, Zane, Wendell, and Beatrice. It didn't really matter in the grand scheme of things.

Zane was right. Anything he, Asterin, and I did to try to free ourselves from this tangled knot of secrets would only end in disaster for all of us.

I returned to our suite and found Vesper in the bedroom, curled up on a long, wide window seat that overlooked the topiary garden where I'd had breakfast with Lady Verona. The Frozon moon and stars were shining brightly overhead, gilding the peonies in a cool silver light.

"A credit for your thoughts?" I asked in a soft voice.

Vesper gestured at the opposite end of the window seat. I sat down on the cushion, but I kept my distance, giving her all the space she needed.

"I'm sorry I ran away," she said. "I just couldn't look at them any longer."

"I understand." I hesitated, then finished my thought. "I used to feel the same way about my parents."

Vesper frowned. "What do you mean?"

I shrugged, although that didn't ease the sudden tension in my shoulders. "When I was a child, I didn't understand what was going on with my parents and Holloway. All I knew was whenever my mother and father went to see him, one or sometimes both would stay in bed sick for days afterward."

"You couldn't have possibly understood the magnitude of what Holloway was doing, how he was siphoning off your parents' magic."

I let out a bitter laugh. "But I *did* understand the magnitude of it. I was ten, maybe eleven, when I realized Holloway was using my parents' truebond against them."

"What did you do?"

I dragged a hand through my hair, hoping Vesper didn't feel my guilt, shame, and embarrassment churning through the bond. I'd come here to comfort her, but now, I was the one who was decidedly uncomfortable.

"I'd heard all the gossipcasts and legends about truebonds being these marvelous, mystical connections no one could break or interfere with. Plus, my parents were Arrows, and they had been on countless missions. It just didn't make sense to me."

"What?" Vesper asked.

"Why they didn't fight back." Even now, all these years later, I couldn't say the words without an angry snarl creeping into my voice. "I asked my parents point-blank why they didn't use their truebond power against Holloway—why they didn't just *kill* him. My parents said they had tried everything, and nothing had ever worked."

A crooked smile curved my lips. "My parents didn't have Vesper Quill with her seer power and genius engineering brain to help them figure out that the key to blocking Holloway's siphon power was to trust in each other's strength and not let their fear get the better of them."

An answering smile curved Vesper's lips, although it was

quickly replaced by a thoughtful look. "I might not have figured it out either, if I hadn't seen Holloway take your magic during the midnight ball. I could *feel* how much he was hurting you, and then how your pain mixed with your fear and amplified his siphon ability. You were so scared." Her voice dropped to a whisper. "I was terrified I was going to lose you that night, and I almost did."

"I was just as terrified that I was going to lose you," I confessed, my voice as low and ragged as hers.

We fell silent, both of us lost in those dark memories.

"My parents felt that same fear, although I didn't understand it back then. As the weeks, months, and years dragged on and on, and Holloway took more and more of their psion power, and Desdemona and Chauncey got sicker and sicker, I grew angrier and angrier."

"What did you do?" Vesper asked.

"I waited until my father left on an Arrow mission, then confronted my mother. I thought if I talked to her alone that she might listen." I drew in a breath and let it out, along with the rest of my shameful confession. "I called my mother weak and cowardly and a dozen other horrible names."

"What did she do?"

My gaze drifted through the window down to the garden, where the peonies were still glimmering in the moon- and starlight. The memory—vision?—of Desdemona that I'd seen earlier flashed through my mind.

"She just . . . let me." I dragged my hand through my hair again. "Desdemona had this dull, resigned look on her face, like she didn't have a choice but to listen to me the same way she didn't have a choice but to let Holloway siphon off her magic."

I had to stop and clear a hard knot of shame out of my throat. "Even when I was yelling at her, I realized what a monster I was being, but I *just . . . couldn't . . . stop*."

Vesper gripped my hand, the silver flecks in her eyes swimming in a sea of dark blue sympathy. "You were just a kid, and you were afraid of losing your parents. Desdemona knew that."

"Perhaps, but I was out of line and out of control. Just thinking about it still makes me feel like a monster. Perhaps that was the day my inner monster was truly born, even before I killed my father."

Vesper tightened her grip on my hand, more sympathy swimming in her eyes.

I cleared another knot of shame out of my throat. "I confronted my mother in the morning. That afternoon, Holloway summoned Desdemona to Crownpoint. That was the day he siphoned off too much of her magic. She died a short time later."

"Oh, Kyr," Vesper murmured, the same ache in her voice that was pulsing through my heart.

"I've always wondered if I had just kept my mouth shut that maybe my mother wouldn't have been so stressed that day," I confessed, my voice low and strained. "If Desdemona might have been strong enough to survive Holloway just a little while longer."

Vesper rocked forward and crawled across the window seat. She stopped right in front of me and gripped both my hands in hers. "I am so, so sorry. But it wasn't your fault, Kyr. *None* of it was your fault. Holloway was too blasted greedy to stop himself from taking too much of your mother's magic. *He* killed her, not *you.*"

A fierce light burned in her eyes, and her red-hot anger sizzled through the bond and curled around my inner monster, making it whimper in relief.

"I'm the one who's sorry. I came in here to ask how you were feeling about the Zimmers, not to bare my soul about my failures with my own family."

Vesper cupped my left cheek in her right hand. "We comfort each other, remember?"

My hands crept up and settled on her waist, anchoring her to me. "How *do* you feel about the Zimmers?"

Vesper stared out through the glass at the garden, but her gaze was distant, as though she was seeing something far, far away. "Part of me understands why Beatrice went to such great lengths to protect Wendell and Zane. When Beatrice was talking in the library, I could *see* it all unfolding just as she described. Nerezza would have killed Beatrice, Wendell, and Zane to take control of House Zimmer." Her voice dropped to a whisper. "Nerezza might have even killed me too."

Vesper shuddered, and I tightened my grip on her waist.

"But no matter how good her reasons, Beatrice still abandoned me. She still sacrificed me to save Wendell and Zane—her *real* family, the people she truly loved."

A tear slipped away from Vesper's dark lashes and streaked down her cheek like a shooting star. I gently wiped the wet trail away with my fingertip.

"What are you going to do about Wendell? He obviously wants to have a relationship with you. I think Beatrice does too." I paused. "And Zane as well."

Vesper chewed on her lower lip. "Part of me wants to try . . ."

"Try what?"

"To be a part of their family."

"But?"

She sighed, the sound full of weary heartache. "But they're still Regals, and I'm still a scandal just waiting to happen to their House."

I thought of all the times Zane had called Vesper his sister and all the lengths he'd gone to in order to get his family here. Lying to Holloway, traveling across the galaxy, paying the enormous fee to attend the marriage mart, sweet-talking Lady

Verona into letting the Zimmers stay at the estate.

Those were not the actions of a man concerned about a potential scandal. But I kept my mouth shut. Zane had told me not to interfere. I didn't care what Zane wanted, but I wasn't going to inflict my own prejudices on Vesper.

This was her family, and it was her choice to accept them—or not. I would abide by her decision, even if it meant I was bound to Zane bloody Zimmer for the rest of my life.

Vesper shook her head, flinging off her painful thoughts. "I don't want to talk about the Zimmers anymore."

"Then what do you want to do?"

"I want to forget about everything but you right now," she whispered. "Make me forget. Please, Kyr?"

She wasn't the only one who wanted to forget the bad memories we'd both dredged up. My hands flexed around her waist, and I drew her closer.

Vesper straddled my lap. She brushed my black hair back from my face, her fingers sliding through the thick strands and her nails dragging across my scalp underneath. The light, simple touch made every part of me vibrate, like an old-fashioned tuning fork pitched to just the right frequency.

I leaned forward and caught her mouth in mine, licking her lips. Vesper opened her mouth, her tongue darting out to stroke mine. She tasted cold and warm, and light and dark, and sweet and rich, like the Frozon hot chocolate at the marriage mart.

The kiss ended, and we both drew back, staring into each other's eyes. I was already hard and aching for her, but I stayed still, letting her set the pace.

Vesper trailed her fingers down my chest. Her nimble fingers quickly undid my belt, then the button and the zipper underneath. Her hand slid into my pants and closed around my dick. Electric arrows of pleasure zinged through me, and my hips bucked up, every inch of me stiffening and straining for more of her touch.

"I love it when you touch me like that," I rasped in a hoarse voice. "I . . ."

*I love you.* I wanted to say the words, but she'd been through so much tonight. I didn't want to add to her stress, or worse, make her feel like she had to say it back. Just because we were bonded didn't mean she had to love me the way I loved her—if someone as beautiful as Vesper could ever truly love a monster like me.

Vesper kept pumping her hand along my length, and I gave myself over to the quick rhythm of her fingers. While she worked me, I dug my fingers into the fabric of her gown, shoving the long skirt up out the way. My shaking hand landed on her smooth thigh, and I quickly slid my fingers up, cupping and rubbing her core through her silken undergarments.

Vesper's breath stuttered, and her fingers stopped their teasing, blissful motion on my dick. Her eyes widened, the silver flecks swallowing up almost all the blue.

"Kyr," she whispered, squirming against my hand the same way I was squirming against hers. "I want you. Now."

I braced one hand down on the floor, then dragged us both off the window seat. My ass hit the cool stone, and Vesper landed on top of me. Our lips and tongues crashed together in one quick kiss after another. She shoved my pants down, while I bunched her skirt around her waist, and we fumbled with each other's undergarments, pushing them out of the way. We both had birth-control implants, which made things much easier.

Vesper rocked forward, straddling me again, then reached down between us and guided me to her entrance. I surged forward, leveraging myself up and thrusting deep inside her.

More electric arrows of pleasure zinged through me. The same hot, pulsing sensations crackled through the bond, shooting from my body into hers and back again.

Vesper leaned forward, her chest brushing mine. She drew

back, then rocked forward again. I groaned and buried my face in her neck, licking and nipping at the rapid pulse in the hollow of her throat.

"*More*," she murmured, her breath a hot promise against my skin. "More, Kyr. *More*."

Vesper quickened her motion, and I clutched her hips and met her thrust for thrust. My groans mixed with her breathy sighs, and those electric arrows coalesced into jagged streaks of lightning, pleasure zipping from me to her and back again, until finally . . .

They exploded.

Vesper shuddered, an orgasm streaking through her like a comet sizzling across the night sky. I thrust into her again, and an answering orgasm ripped through me and reverberated through the bond to her. Or perhaps our release was one and the same. I couldn't tell anymore, and I didn't care.

All that mattered was Vesper and me riding the amazing streaks of lightning we had created—together.

# TWENTY-ONE

## VESPER

Kyrion and I stayed on the floor, shuddering against each other as we both found our release. Sometime later, I rolled off him so that I was lying on my back, the same as him.

"Well, I've discovered something new," I said once my heart rate and breathing had slowed back down to normal.

Kyrion propped himself up on his elbow. "What's that?"

A satisfied smile stretched across my face. "I rather like forgetting," I declared, then crooked my finger at him. "Want to do it again?"

Kyrion gave me a wicked grin. "Absolutely."

His hands went around behind my back, while mine dropped to his chest. Various tugs and yanks and curses ensued on both sides, but neither one of us was having much luck.

"Why does your gown have so many bloody buttons?" he growled, wrestling with the tiny row of them down my back.

"I could say the same thing about your blasted tailcoat," I muttered.

We both struggled for a few more seconds, then Kyrion growled again, got to his feet, and held out his hand. I grabbed his fingers, and he pulled me up from the floor so that we were both back on our feet. I'd taken my heels off as soon as I'd come into the suite earlier, but he was still wearing his boots.

Kyrion stepped back and crossed his arms over his chest, as though he was considering something important. Then he flicked his fingers and used his telekinesis to open all the buttons on the back of my gown in one long, quick, continuous motion.

Cool air hit my bare back, and I laughed with delight. "Show me how to do that with your telekinesis."

"Here I am," Kyrion teased, holding his arms out wide. "Yours for the ravishing. All you need to do is get rid of some simple buttons. Surely you can figure out how to do that, my lady."

"I think we've both already ravished each other, but point taken."

Kyrion's pants were wide open, but his tailcoat was still securely fastened across his chest. I eyed the rows of buttons gleaming on the garment. He was right. The Erztonians used far too many tiny buttons.

"Perhaps you need some more motivation," he said, a low, husky promise in his voice. "For each garment you remove from me, I will reward you in turn."

"What kind of reward?"

He grinned. "Oh, leave that up to me."

My eyes narrowed. He knew I could never resist a challenge. I stepped forward and reached for Kyrion's telekinesis. To my surprise, his magic came to me easily, and I dropped my gaze and focused on his right boot. The top button began to work its way open . . .

But then his magic slipped away, like water trickling through my fingers. I bit my tongue, trying to hide my frustration.

"You can do it, Vesper," Kyrion said. "I know you can."

The sticky cobweb of him in my mind pulsed with confidence. I blew out a breath, tamped down my frustration, and tried again. A fresh wave of his magic poured into me, and the entire row of buttons on the side of his boot popped open one after another.

Triumph flashed through me, and Kyrion pulled off that boot and set it aside.

"Where's my reward?" I demanded.

Kyrion grinned, then stepped around behind me. The back of my gown was still gaping open, and he slid it down my body so that it pooled on the floor at my feet. Kyrion moved forward, so close that the heat of his body mixed with my own, and slid his hand down the curve of my spine in a light, teasing caress. I shivered in response.

Kyrion stepped back in front of me again. "Your turn."

Once again, his telekinesis came to me easily, and I undid the buttons on his left boot. Kyrion took it off, along with his socks, then moved around behind me again. I was still wearing a strapless corset, and once again, he trailed his finger down my back, using his telekinesis to pop those buttons open. The corset joined my gown on the floor, along with the rest of my undergarments.

"Removing my clothes is not a reward," I groused.

"I never said it was." He pushed my hair to one side, then planted a kiss on my neck, making me shiver again.

Kyrion stepped back in front of me. "Your turn."

This time, I barely had to reach for his magic before the row of buttons on his tailcoat started popping open. Kyrion shrugged out of the coat, then yanked off the frilly shirt underneath, which, thankfully, was button-free.

He tossed both garments aside, then stepped out of his pants and undergarments, so that we stood naked before each other.

My fingers itched with the urge to explore the hard planes of his body, but I merely arched my eyebrow at him again.

"Reward?"

"Hmm. Let me think."

Kyrion circled around behind me again. His breath tickled the back of my neck, and I balled my hands into fists to keep from reaching for him.

"I can feel you back there, looming behind me."

"I thought you enjoyed my looming." Kyrion snaked his hands around my body, reaching up to cup my breasts. "Or was I wrong about that?"

Pleasure spiked through me, and I gasped and arched back, giving him better access. "I do rather enjoy your looming."

"Mmm." His satisfied murmur rumbled against my skin. "I thought so."

His fingers moved up, squeezing and tweaking my nipples. More pleasure spiked through me, sizzling through my veins and liquefying into molten heat that pooled between my thighs.

Kyrion nipped and licked and kissed my neck, still caressing my breasts all the while. My hands dropped down and clutched his thighs.

"Sometimes I hate you for teasing me," I grumbled, arching into his touch even more.

His hands stilled, although his fingers tightened, and he drew me a little closer. "I love the way you hate me," Kyrion replied in a hoarse voice. "It's so delightful."

I opened my mouth to respond, but he spun me around and lowered his lips to mine. I surged forward, tangling my fingers in his hair, my tongue darting out to meet his. Kyrion growled and lifted me off my feet. He took a few quick strides, set me down, and pressed my back up against the permaglass wall. Then he broke off our kiss and went down on his knees.

Kyrion gave me a wicked grin, then leaned forward and

kissed the inside of my right thigh, then my left. My entire body trembled with anticipation, and I flattened my hands against the glass wall.

Kyrion's grin widened, then he leaned forward and put his mouth on me. I gasped again, and my entire body arched out to meet his touch. His tongue, his fingers, his breath skimming against my skin. Fire boiled through my veins, and it was too much and not enough at the same time.

"Yes . . . Kyr . . . *more* . . ." All I could do was mindlessly moan his name, my hands sliding against the glass wall in time to his quick strokes and slow licks.

Kyrion growled low in his throat, his own pleasure vibrating along the bond to me. Just when I thought he was going to push me over the edge, he surged to his feet and picked me up off my feet again.

Kyrion's eyes were almost completely black with desire. "Vesper . . ." he rasped. "I want . . . I *need* . . ."

I looped my arms around his neck and locked my legs around his waist, drawing him closer. Kyrion shuddered and put my back against the glass wall again. His gaze locked with mine, and he thrust inside me.

He groaned, and I nipped the side of his neck with my teeth. Kyrion rocked his hips forward again and again, thrusting into me, while I clutched his shoulders, my nails digging into his skin and urging him on.

"Ahh . . . Kyr . . . *yes* . . ."

That molten heat became hotter still, until I was gasping from the intense, crackling pleasure. Through the bond, I could feel an orgasm building inside Kyrion, keeping time with my own burgeoning desire.

Kyrion thrust into me again, deeper than before, and all that heat and energy and sensation erupted, flowing from me to him and back again in a cascade of white-hot pleasure.

"Vesper," Kyrion murmured against my neck. "Vesper."

I clutched him tighter, and once again, we both forgot everything else—except for each other.

Sometime later, Kyrion and I made it over to the bed and fell asleep. Sometime after that, I started to dream.

The castle, the library, the stairs down to the round room of my mindscape, with its doors, blue-moon peonies, and sapphsidian eyes. I walked through it all and stepped into the waiting darkness beyond. Once again, I wound up at my psionic nexus, and the eye-shaped sapphsidian altar was the same as always, right down to the lunarium eyes and arrows floating on the surface.

The last time I'd been here, I'd grabbed one of the eyes and hurled it into the darkness, and it had zipped back to the table like a boomerang. I had no desire to injure myself in my own mindscape, so this time, I gently, carefully, picked up one of the eyes and cupped it in my palms.

The opalescent lunarium sparked with color, and the stone itself gave off a pleasant, tingling warmth. I reached out with my magic, tightened my grip, and stared down at the eye, willing it to move, twitch, vibrate, maybe even fill me with some great wisdom or show me a startling new insight . . .

Nothing happened.

The eye just sat on my palms, shimmering with color and warmth. Was that all it did? If the nexus just sat here in the heart of my darkness, then what was the point of it being in my mindscape at all?

Disappointed, I dropped the eye back down onto the table, and the lunarium piece plopped into the sapphsidian like a raindrop hitting a lake. The shimmering eye disappeared below the dark blue surface for a moment before bobbing back up to the top.

More disgust surged through me. Why did I keep coming here and wasting my time?

I spun around on my heel, left the nexus and the darkness behind, and returned to the round room of my mindscape.

*Useless child* . . . Nerezza's voice hissed from its usual doorway.

I glanced at the memory, but it didn't ignite as much heartache as usual. My mother's long-ago insult was an old wound, and right now, I was much more concerned with the new wounds the Zimmers might inflict on me—

A door to my right flung itself open, and images started playing on the other side—my talk with the Zimmers earlier in the library. I hesitated, not wanting to relive that memory since it was so painfully fresh, but I stood in front of the door and watched the whole conversation again.

Beatrice's explanations. Wendell's pleas. Zane's quips.

My gaze lingered on Zane. Instead of crowing about how he'd supposedly helped Kyrion and me escape from Crownpoint, Zane had downplayed his role, and he'd cut off Wendell when his father had started to offer up more examples of Zane's supposed aid.

Yet again, that annoying spark of hope flared in my chest. If Zane really had helped Kyrion and me even before he'd known I was his sister . . . then maybe, just maybe, my brother wasn't the villain I thought he was. Maybe he actually had some tiny bits of decency buried deep inside his arrogant exterior. Maybe he really did care about me, at least as much as one could care about the sister they'd only known about for a few weeks.

That spark of hope burned a little brighter, but I was determined not to be fooled again. So I decided to approach the situation the way I would test a new brewmaker in the R&D lab.

Hope, but verify.

I went around my mindscape, waving my right hand, opening and closing first one door, then another, then another . . .

until I found my memories of the midnight ball.

I stood in front of the open door and watched it all play out. My confrontation with Nerezza. Holloway taking some of Kyrion's magic. My yanking the butterfly dagger out of my hair and stabbing Dargan Byrne with it. Kyrion and me unleashing our truebond. Our psionic lightning crackling through the throne room like a violent electrical storm. Then Kyrion and me running through the palace, boarding the *Dream World*, and zooming away from Crownpoint . . .

A frustrated growl rumbled in my throat. I'd already seen everything that had happened from my point of view. I wanted to know what *Zane* had done.

Wait. I was a seer. Why *couldn't* I do that? My magic often surged up and showed me things I hadn't witnessed in person, like Esmina shoving Micah off the bridge at Stardrop Falls. So why couldn't I do the same thing now? When I actually *wanted* to?

I stalked over to the door that featured the large stylized *Z* of House Zimmer—Zane's door. "Show mc Zane."

Nothing happened. The door remained shut, and the blue opals and sapphsidian pieces that made up the *Z* sigil glimmered at me like mocking eyes.

"Show me Zane," I called out again, my voice louder and more insistent.

Once again, nothing happened, although the jewels glimmered a little more brightly.

"Show me Zane!" This time, I snarled the words, putting as much effort, force, and magic into the command as possible.

But for the third time, nothing happened . . .

A gust of wind howled through my mindscape, whipping the blue-moon peonies back and forth on their long black vines. The jewels on the door burned so brightly I thought they might catch fire. Then the door flung itself open, hitting the wall behind it with a loud *bang*.

Images started playing, still showing the midnight ball, but this time, Zane was front and center.

Zane in a shadowy corridor, passing the jeweled butterfly dagger to Inga, the palace servant who'd done my hair and makeup for the ball. Zane in the throne room, watching Kyrion and me trying to reach each other, despite the Imperium soldiers attempting to drag us apart. Zane discreetly flicking his fingers, his pale eyes glowing just a bit. A tiny wave of telekinetic power snaking off him and slithering in between first me and then Kyrion and the soldiers attempting to pin us to the floor. Then Zane and Kyrion fighting, and Zane dropping his sword a fraction of an inch so Kyrion could wound him . . .

Shock punched into my heart, and I staggered back a few steps. Zane really *had* helped us. He'd given the butterfly dagger to Inga and slowed the soldiers' pursuit, just as Wendell had claimed. But the most surprising thing was that Zane had used his *own* telekinesis to knock the soldiers aside so Kyrion and I could finally reach each other.

Ever since I'd first met them at a Regal ball a few months ago, I'd had a nagging sense that the Zimmers were going to be a problem—that *Zane* was going to be a problem. But the cold, hard truth was that Kyrion and I would never have been able to unleash our truebond without Zane's help. We wouldn't have been able to escape the palace, and we probably would still be trapped in Crownpoint to this day . . .

As soon as that thought popped into my mind, images of the midnight ball melted away, and a large permaglass cell appeared. The cell was divided into two sections, with me on one side and Kyrion on the other. Both of us were sitting on the floor and slumped up against the center wall, our backs together, even though we couldn't touch each other through the thick glass.

A man stood in front of the cell, watching us both with a cruel, satisfied grin. Brown hair with a few silver threads, tan skin, and bronze eyes that gleamed as brightly as noontime suns with the magic he'd just stolen from us. Power rippled off Callus Holloway and washed over me out in my mindscape, and the sensation made me sick to my stomach.

Holloway snapped his fingers at a scientist wearing a white lab coat and clutching a tablet. "How long until they are ready for me to drain them again?"

This must be the future that would have happened if Zane hadn't helped us. I shuddered. Holloway taking our magic over and over was even more horrific than I'd thought. I didn't know how much time had passed in that version of the future, but Kyrion and I were both obviously on the brink of death, and yet Holloway still wanted more of our power. Greedy, sadistic bastard—

Kyrion murmured something in his sleep, shattering my connection to my mindscape. He rolled over and drew me into his arms, the warmth of his body soaking into my own.

My eyes snapped open. I was back in the real world in our bedroom at the Collier estate. I tried to go back to sleep and return to my mindscape, but I couldn't drift back into my dream world.

Kyrion had been right. Zane had done everything in his power to help us escape from Holloway. An unexpected bit of happiness pulsed through me, although it was quickly drowned out by my simmering anger at Beatrice for abandoning me.

I didn't know how to reconcile my brother's recent aid with my grandmother's dismissal all those years ago. And worst of all, I couldn't shake this nagging sense of dread that no matter what I did, or how I tried to protect myself, Zane, Beatrice, and Wendell would still end up breaking my heart sooner or later.

# TWENTY-TWO

## VESPER

Despite my best efforts, I only managed a few more snatches of sleep. Eventually, I slipped out of bed, took a shower, and got dressed. Kyrion was still snoozing, so I called for some food, and a servant brought several breakfast trays to our suite.

Thick, fluffy buttermilk pancakes served with a sweet but tart orange-cranberry syrup. Stewed apples sprinkled with cinnamon. Hearty oatmeal studded with blueberries and topped with slivers of toasted almonds. The food was delicious and filling, and I ate seconds and thirds of everything.

I checked my tablet, but neither Daichi nor Tivona had messaged with any new information. I also called up the sites for the Erzton gossipcasts, but to my surprise, Kyrion and I weren't mentioned. The gossipcasts' main focus was on the marriage mart, along with the attack at the House Collier mineral exchange. Leland was in several interviews, and he seemed to enjoy speaking to the reporters and spinning the story as an industrial accident still under investigation.

I drummed my fingers on the table. Esmina, Pollux, and their Serpens Corp mercenaries were the biggest, most immediate threat, especially given Esmina's desire to destroy House Collier. Ever since Esmina and Pollux had confronted me on Tropics 44, I'd had more questions than answers. Well, it was time to get those answers.

It was time to start playing offense instead of defense.

Footsteps sounded, and Kyrion strode into the sitting room. He too had showered and put on fresh clothes. He skimmed his hand across my back, then sat down across from me.

While he ate, I told him my plans. "I want to go to Asterin's workshop and see if I can figure out why Esmina and Pollux targeted the House Collier mineral exchange. Maybe I can find some clue to their ultimate plot and what they want with me."

Kyrion nodded. "Good idea. I'll ask Siya and Rigel if they have any leads on where Esmina and Pollux might be hiding. The mercenaries must have a base of operations somewhere on-planet, maybe even in the city."

He hesitated. "What do you want to do about the Zimmers?"

My heart plummeted into my stomach like a runaway elevator about to crash into the ground. "Esmina and Pollux are the most serious danger we're facing right now. I'll deal with my unwanted family later."

Kyrion's face softened with sympathy, and he squeezed my hand. "Meet me back here for lunch?"

I squeezed his hand back. "It's a date."

Kyrion and I went our separate ways. Asterin had some business with Aldrich and Verona, so she gave me the code to her workshop and promised to meet me later. She also arranged a transport for me, complete with some House Collier guards.

The transport dropped me off in front of Asterin's workshop

and returned to the estate, but the House Collier guards took up positions at the end of the street. More guards patrolled the shipping yard, mineral exchange, and public square. Too little, too late. Esmina and Pollux weren't stupid enough to return to the scene of their crime, and the mercenaries wouldn't show themselves until their next attack.

I just needed to figure out when and where that might be.

I entered the workshop, shut the door behind me, and turned on a terminal. Asterin had given me her password, so I accessed the House Collier servers and reviewed all the reports about Esmina and Pollux's attack. I looked at every photo, watched every video, and read through the interviews with the captured Serpens Corp mercenaries.

An hour later, I rocked back in my chair and massaged my throbbing temples. All this information, and I still didn't know any more than when I had started. I let out a tired, frustrated sigh and slowly spun my chair around, eyeing the shelves with their precise rows of hammers, laser cutters, and other tools. Asterin was as obsessively neat as I was messy. Even though this wasn't my workshop, I could still find anything I needed, thanks to the labels on every object.

My gaze locked onto the shelves filled with items Asterin had collected from the mines she'd worked in. An idea popped into my mind, and I spun my chair back to the terminal. Leland had compiled a list of every item the mercenaries had tried to steal from the House Collier mineral exchange. I pulled up a hologram of the list, then grabbed the corresponding stones from the shelves. I had always been a visual person, and laying the actual, physical items out on the table helped me *see* them much better than just scanning the list.

Aquamarine, blue diamond, chalcedony, indocolite, lapis lazuli, sapphire, sapphsidian, topaz, tourmaline, turquoise . . .

I put the samples in alphabetical order, hoping that would help me solve the mystery, but it didn't, so I rearranged the samples in reverse order. Still nothing. I tried several different variations, including size and weight, but no answers popped into my mind.

"Why did you want to steal these items?" I asked, the workshop walls soaking up my question. "Why these gemstones? Why not lunarium or something more valuable?"

A knock sounded, startling me. The door creaked open, and I spun around in my chair. "Asterin! I'm stuck on something, but maybe you can help me figure it out—"

My words died on my lips. Asterin wasn't standing in the workshop—Wendell Zimmer was.

"What are *you* doing here?"

He grimaced at my sharp tone. "Lord Aldrich, Lady Verona, and Lady Asterin are giving Beatrice a tour of the shipping yard and mineral exchange, so House Collier and House Zimmer can continue their negotiations about a potential alliance."

So that was the mysterious business Asterin had this morning. She was probably even more unhappy about the Zimmers being here than I was.

"They didn't need me for the negotiations, so I decided to go exploring. Lady Verona mentioned you were in Asterin's workshop. The door was unlocked, so I thought I would see if you needed some help." Wendell's gaze skittered away from mine, and he turned around in a slow circle, examining the workshop.

"A bit small, but the obsessive organization makes it feel much bigger than it truly is." A wry look flickered across his face. "My workshop isn't *nearly* this neat and tidy. The House Zimmer lab techs say it's a wonder I can find anything amid all the clutter."

"My Quill Corp workshop is a bit cluttered as well," I admitted.

Wendell gave me a small smile of commiseration, but it quickly wilted away. "Well, you look busy. Forgive me for interrupting. I'll leave you to your project."

He turned toward the door. I thought about my conversation with my unexpected family last night. Beatrice might have jettisoned me from House Zimmer like a piece of junk purged into the black void of space, but Wendell hadn't known about me. Neither had Zane. For that, they were blameless.

Once again, that tremulous spark of hope flickered in my heart, and for the first time, I decided to nurture it instead of squashing it.

"Actually, I could use some help," I said in a tentative voice. "If you have the time."

Wendell spun around, his face lighting up. "Really? Are you sure?"

I wasn't sure, not by a long shot, but I gestured for him to step over to the table. He listened while I explained everything that had happened during Esmina and Pollux's attack at the mineral exchange.

Wendell picked up one stone after another, hefting them in his hand before setting them back down. "The mercenaries certainly targeted an odd assortment of items. Most corporations don't care much about gemstones, since there is far more money to be made in iron, wood, coal, and the like."

"Exactly! I don't understand why professional mercenaries would try to steal these specific items. The gemstones are all readily available, and you could get them in any quantity you wanted, if you had enough credits."

Wendell stroked his chin, deep in thought. "Perhaps it's not the quantity that's important. Perhaps it's the quality or the wide assortment. Some of these gemstones are rare, if not all that valuable. Or perhaps it has something to do with the properties of the stones themselves . . ."

He threw out a few more theories that we debated back and forth. No answers presented themselves, but talking to Wendell was actually *fun*. He was a spelltech, someone capable of infusing psionic energy into weapons, so his magic was different from mine, but at heart, he was an engineer, an inventor, just like I was. I'd always wondered where that part of my personality had come from, why I'd always been so curious about how things worked. It was . . . nice to realize I'd inherited that piece of myself from Wendell.

"Perhaps if we run some simulations, an answer might present itself?" he suggested.

So that's what we did. We called up databases about each type of gemstone, but nothing obvious jumped out. Each stone could be used in a variety of ways, from making jewelry to being carved into statues to even providing glow-in-the-dark lights when crushed and mixed with the right chemicals.

After about an hour, Wendell sighed and looked up from the terminal at the table next to mine. "There are just too many variables. We need to know more about *how* the mercenaries wanted to use the gemstones. Do you remember anything else they said or did?"

"No. I didn't follow Esmina and Pollux into the mineral exchange, so I didn't hear any orders they might have given their mercenaries."

"Well, I suppose we'll just have to keep working until we figure it out." Wendell smiled at me, and I found myself smiling back.

The workshop door banged open, and Asterin stomped inside. She stopped, her gaze zipping back and forth between Wendell and me.

"Vesper, are you okay?" she asked in a sharp voice.

"I'm fine. Wendell was just trying to help me figure out why Esmina and Pollux tried to steal all these gemstones from the mineral exchange." I swept my hand out over the table. "Any ideas?"

Asterin shot Wendell another suspicious stare, but she stepped over to us. She picked up one stone after another, setting them all down in a precise row and rearranging them by color, putting the lightest piece of aquamarine first, all the way down to the darkest piece of sapphsidian.

My eyes narrowed. I hadn't noticed it before, but the gemstones were all some shade of blue. I peered at the list Leland had compiled. The mercenaries had tried to steal roughly equal amounts of every single stone on the table. Why would they need so many different blue stones?

Unless . . . you wanted to test *every* known blue stone for some reason.

My gaze locked onto the piece of sapphsidian, and a chill swept down my spine. "What if this is about the Techwave cannon? What if that's why Esmina and Pollux tried to capture me? Because they want me to fix the weapon?"

Asterin's eyebrows shot up in surprise. "You think Esmina and Pollux figured out the Techwave cannon needs a stabilizing agent to keep it from overheating?"

I nodded, dread flooding my stomach, along with a sinking sense of certainty.

"But Esmina and Pollux don't appear to be working for General Orion Ocnus," Asterin pointed out. "Otherwise, they would be using Black Scarab troops instead of their own men. So who else could know about the Techwave cannon?"

"Even the Techwave is riddled with spies," Wendell replied. "Perhaps one of the Techies leaked the information to a corporation to score a hefty payday. New weapons are big business across the galaxy, and if a corporation managed to develop a weapon that could cut through psionic and other shields . . ."

All the color drained from Asterin's face. "Then Esmina and Pollux could use those weapons against House Collier."

The three of us fell silent, contemplating that horrible possibility.

Asterin frowned. "But why would Esmina and Pollux target you, Vesper? I thought Harkin Ocnus was the only one who knew you had figured out what was wrong with the cannon."

"Maybe I was wrong about that."

I thought back, remembering my fight with Harkin Ocnus on Tropics 33, inside the lunarium mine at the Regenwald Resort. I'd crowed to Harkin that I knew what was wrong with his design, and then I'd killed him a few minutes later. All the other Techwave soldiers had also been killed, along with their mechanized Black Scarab troops. So who else could have learned about my discovery?

"Maybe someone is just fishing for information," Asterin said. "The Techwave kidnapping you is common knowledge, thanks to the gossipcasts."

Someone, probably a Quill Corp guard, had leaked the information about my abduction to the gossipcasts, which had broadcast countless stories about it, along with my escape from Crownpoint with Kyrion. The information was out there, and if someone had gotten their hands on a Techwave cannon, then I was the main thing they needed to finish perfecting the design.

"Wait. Are you talking about *that* cannon?" Wendell pointed at a nearby table.

With everything that had happened yesterday, I'd forgotten I'd left the Techwave cannon in Asterin's workshop.

"Zane recovered a cannon just like that from Silas, the Techwaver who infiltrated the summer solstice ball, although I haven't had a chance to examine it yet," Wendell said.

He glanced back and forth between me and Asterin, clearly confused, so I filled him in on why the Techwave had kidnapped me. I skimmed over a lot of the details, though, including Harkin Ocnus brutally torturing me. I didn't want to spill my guts to a father I barely knew, especially since I wasn't sure if Wendell could be trusted. Esmina and Pollux weren't the only ones who could benefit from the Techwave cannon—it would also be a great asset to House Zimmer.

I told Wendell how the cannon kept overheating and frying itself. I also pulled out the weapon's magazine, popped off the clear outer casing, and showed him how the Techwave scientists had threaded tiny bits of lunarium onto the standard solar wiring to make the cannon much more powerful than similar weapons. I didn't mention I thought sapphsidian was the key to stabilizing it, though. He didn't need to know my theory, especially since I wasn't sure what he would do with the information.

Wendell examined the magazine. "How unusual! I've long thought lunarium could have other, more practical applications than being used in stormswords and other simple weapons, but this is ingenious. And this cannon is based on your design?"

I couldn't stop myself from preening at the admiration in his voice. "Yes, the cannon is based on my original design, although Harkin Ocnus and the other Techwave scientists changed several things and added the lunarium-filled magazine." My pride vanished. "I never intended for the cannon to be such a deadly, destructive weapon. I designed it to stun people, not cut through psionic shields and turn guts to goo."

"Unfortunately, as inventors, the only thing we have control over is our product design. What people do with that design is up to them, and even the most innocuous product can be used to hurt others." Wendell shook his head. "Plenty of people have done awful things with my inventions, especially since House Zimmer manufactures cameras and other recording equipment."

"You mean spy cameras," Asterin said in a wry voice.

Wendell shrugged. "Yes, spy cameras. At first, I made them so House Zimmer spies could keep an eye on our enemies, but the tech was so valuable that I started selling it to support my House. You can do lots of horrible things with something as simple as a camera. Eavesdropping on conversations, snapping unwanted pictures, secretly recording videos of people in compromising positions to use as blackmail or sell to the gossipcasts."

Wendell gestured at the stone samples arranged on the other table. "So your theory is Esmina and Pollux tried to steal all these stones because they think one of the gems is the key to stabilizing the lunarium magazine? Why focus on gemstones instead of something more obvious like iron, copper, silver, or gold? Or some plastic polymer?"

I shrugged. "Maybe Esmina and Pollux have lab rats who've been experimenting with the lunarium and solar wiring combination. Maybe they've already tried metals and plastic polymers and have decided to focus on gemstones next. Maybe Esmina's magic whispered it to her, or maybe it's just a blind guess. Maybe Esmina and Pollux just wanted to hurt the Colliers, and this was what they decided to steal."

Wendell studied the hand cannon again. While he was distracted, I sidled over, slid the chunk of sapphsidian off the other table, and slipped it into my pocket. Asterin raised her eyebrows at me in a silent question, and I shook my head. The fewer people who knew sapphsidian might be the key to fixing the Techwave cannons, the safer we would all be.

Wendell straightened up and rubbed his hands together. "Well, let's test the mercenaries' theory and see if any of these stones work. What do you say, Vesper?"

I froze, not sure how to respond or why my heart was suddenly pounding with a mix of worry, dread, and longing.

Wendell's eagerness dimmed like a solar light that had used up its charge. "That is, if you want to. I understand if you don't." He cleared his throat. "I've already taken up enough of your time. I should go check on Beatrice."

He forced a smile onto his face, then backed away and headed toward the workshop door.

"Wait!" I said.

Wendell stopped and looked at me. I wasn't sure what had prompted me to call out to him. Maybe it was that tremulous spark of hope still flickering in my chest. Despite my best efforts to keep my distance from Wendell, that spark was burning brighter and stronger than ever before and was threatening to flare up into an actual flame of forgiveness.

"I would like that," I said in a tentative voice. "To work on this. Together. With you."

Wendell perked up with fresh enthusiasm, and he rubbed his hands together again. "Then let's get started."

He went back over to the table, picked up the lunarium magazine, and placed it on the holoscreen. Several scans popped up, and Wendell flicked through the holograms, muttering to himself.

I had done those same things a thousand times before when I was working on a tricky design. My pounding heart slowed, soothed by the easy familiarity. Wendell turned to me, that eager look still on his face, and I found myself getting swept up in his contagious enthusiasm.

I still didn't know what kind of relationship I wanted to have with my father, but this was a start. I just hoped for once that I was putting my trust in the right person—and that Wendell wouldn't break my heart like Nerezza always had.

# TWENTY-THREE

## VESPER

Wendell, Asterin, and I worked the rest of the morning.

Even though I thought sapphsidian was the key to stabilizing the hand cannon, I helped Wendell test all the other gemstones. I wanted to make sure sapphsidian was the only thing that might work, and my theory was correct. All the other stones failed, and every simulation ended with the lunarium and solar wiring in the magazine overheating and frying the hand cannon after a few blasts.

After we finished the final test, Wendell frowned. "We've tried all the stones, but I feel like we're missing something."

Asterin gave me a pointed look, and I shook my head at her again.

"I don't think so," I lied. "Maybe Esmina and Pollux stole something from the mineral exchange that wasn't on Leland's list."

Wendell shrugged, letting it go, and I let out a quiet sigh of relief.

Asterin's tablet chimed with a message. "Aldrich, Verona, and Beatrice are ready to return to the estate. My presence is requested," she muttered. "Beatrice is also asking about you, Lord Wendell."

"I'll catch up with you," he said.

Asterin looked at me, another silent question on her face. I nodded, and she left the workshop, shutting the door behind her.

I faced Wendell and crossed my arms over my chest, as if the simple motion would shield me from whatever he was about to say.

His gaze traced over my face, and a small, sad smile played across his lips. "You look so much like your mother."

Shock punched into my heart. Not what I'd expected him to say. Even more surprising was his gentle, almost wistful tone. Everyone knew Nerezza, but no one had anything good to say about her. Even if she hadn't abandoned me, I still would have been ashamed she was my mother, given how she used and manipulated people with her social engineering ability.

"You've probably wondered how I met Nerezza," Wendell said. "What our relationship was like."

"The thoughts had crossed my mind."

That was the understatement of the century. When I was a kid, I'd constantly wondered who my father was and especially why he wasn't around, but Nerezza had never answered any of my questions. Neither had Liesl.

"You probably know Miriol, my wife, Zane's mother, died shortly after giving birth to him. That was a very dark time for me."

Wendell's shoulders drooped, and he grabbed the table, as if he needed its support to hold himself upright. Even more telling, a wave of heartache and longing washed off him, but I didn't need Kyrion's telempathy to know Wendell had loved his wife very, very much.

"I was angry and grieving and panicked at the thought of raising a baby by myself," Wendell continued. "Of course, I had the full support of House Zimmer, and Beatrice helped as much as she could, but it was all so *overwhelming*. Every time I looked at Zane, I thought about how Miriol would never get to see him grow up and how Zane would never have a mother."

For the first time, I realized Zane and I had something else in common besides our DNA: we'd both grown up without a mother. His had been taken away, while mine had never wanted the job, but we'd both always had that same gaping hole in our lives. Uncomfortable needles of sympathy and commiseration pricked my heart.

Wendell cleared his throat. "Despite Miriol's death, I still had my Regal duties. The Imperium keeps chugging along, no matter what personal grief, heartache, or tragedy someone might be experiencing. One day, I went to a party. I was angry and brooding, so I grabbed a bottle of wine and plunged into the garden to drink my pain away." He paused. "And that's when I saw Nerezza."

My seer magic surged to life, and an image appeared in the air next to Wendell: a young Nerezza wearing a gauzy pink gown and strolling through a garden, trailing her fingertips across a bed of bloodred roses.

"I started to return to the party, but Nerezza waved me over," Wendell said. "I had seen her at various Regal events, but I had never talked to her before, and she was delightful. Smart and funny and so very sympathetic."

Another image appeared, showing Wendell and Nerezza sitting on a bench together. My heart squeezed tight. My mother did seem delightful, far more delightful and charming than she had ever been to me.

"Nerezza and I drank the bottle of wine and talked long into the night, and then . . ."

"What happened?"

"I kissed her," Wendell said, his pale eyes hazy with memories. "I'm still not quite sure how it happened. If it was all the wine I'd drunk or my grief or some combination of the two. But I kissed her, and it was the most wonderful thing. Fizzy and bright and beautiful. Nerezza giggled and ran off, but I called out, asking if I could see her again, and she told me to find her at the next party."

"And you did," I murmured.

He nodded. "Talking to Nerezza was the first time I'd felt alive since Miriol had died. The dark, heavy cloak of grief lifted from my shoulders, just for a little while, and I wanted more of that freedom. I sought out Nerezza at the next party, and then the one after that and the one after that. Soon I was spending all my free time with her. Beatrice didn't approve, of course. Even back then, she could see what Nerezza was scheming. But I was in love, and I was alive again, and I didn't care about anything else."

More images flickered in the air. Wendell and Nerezza smiling at each other, strolling hand in hand, even kissing in a passionate embrace. I blinked and shoved my magic away. I had no desire to see *that*.

"What happened? How did it end between the two of you?"

"I was supposed to meet Nerezza in Promenade Park for a picnic, but I was so eager to see her that I arrived early. Nerezza was already there, talking to another woman. I think it was your cousin, Liesl. She looked like Nerezza's sister."

Wendell shook his head. "Anyway, I heard Nerezza bragging about how she had finally snagged a Regal lord, and not a minor noble but one from a major House. One with enough power, money, and influence to support her ambitions. And that's when I realized Nerezza was just using me to get what she truly wanted: a way into House Zimmer. I was devastated."

More images appeared, showing Wendell's eyes widening in surprise and then his body sagging as Nerezza talked and laughed and thoroughly crushed all his love for her. My own heart squeezed in response. I knew that feeling all too well.

"I was just . . . *numb*," Wendell confessed in a low, strained voice. "I pulled out my tablet and sent Nerezza an excuse that I couldn't make it. She read the message to her friend, then laughed. I can still hear her laughter to this very day."

He closed his eyes, and I too could hear the echoes of Nerezza's merry, mocking laughter ringing through my ears.

After a few seconds, Wendell opened his eyes. "I returned to Castle Zimmer and told Beatrice what had happened. Beatrice said she would make sure I never had to deal with Nerezza again. I was so embarrassed, ashamed, and heartsick that it was a relief to let Beatrice get her hands dirty while I focused on Zane and my lab and my projects. I didn't see Nerezza again until she came back to Corios several years later."

"Have you ever talked to Nerezza?" I asked. "Since she returned to Corios?"

Wendell shrugged. "She's climbed up through Regal society, so we've been at dozens of events together. Every time I see her, Nerezza will smile and nod, and she will even engage me in polite conversation from time to time. Although I always got the sense that she was mocking me, as if she knew some great secret I didn't." His gaze flicked over to me. "The night of the midnight ball, I finally found out what that secret was."

"Me."

He nodded. "You. And I was *horrified*. Nerezza had never told me she was pregnant. I was in Beatrice's library at Castle Zimmer, railing about the unfairness of it all, when I realized exactly how quiet Beatrice was being. That's when I realized she had known about you all along and that she had forced Nerezza to leave Corios."

Wendell drew in a breath, then let it out, along with a rush of words. "I don't know who I'm angrier at—Nerezza for never telling me about you and then abandoning you to climb the

Regal ladder or Beatrice for making Nerezza leave Corios and hiding you from me."

His hands clenched into fists, and his pale eyes blazed with fury. More needles of sympathy and commiseration pricked my heart. Nerezza had used Wendell and tossed him aside just as she had done to me, and we were both victims of my mother's unending thirst for riches, power, and control.

"Ever since the midnight ball, I've been searching for you, although I'm not nearly as good at being a spy as Beatrice and Zane are," Wendell said. "When Zane told us that you and Kyrion were coming to Sygnustern, I knew I had to come too and explain about Nerezza and everything else." He hesitated. "That maybe you wouldn't hate me so much if you knew the truth."

"I don't hate you," I replied in a soft voice.

Nerezza was to blame for much of this messy situation, as was Beatrice. The two women had been engaged in a vicious power struggle, and Wendell and I had been the victims of their grim choices.

"I know you have no reason to like me or care what I think, but working with you today . . ." His voice trailed off for a moment. "Well, it was everything I hoped it would be. I know Beatrice and Zane have both hurt you, Vesper, and that I have hurt you too by turning my back on Nerezza, but I want to . . . well, I would say *fix things*, but you are not a weapon in need of repair—you are a person with wants and needs and feelings."

He shook his head, and a bitter laugh came from his lips. "Who am I kidding? There is no *fixing* how Beatrice hid your existence and Nerezza left you as a child. I wouldn't blame you if you never wanted to see or speak to me, Beatrice, or Zane ever again."

Wendell was right. Nothing he said or did would ever fully heal the wounds my grandmother and mother had inflicted. But I didn't want those scars to define me either, or worse, keep me from something that might be good.

"What do you want?" I asked.

Wendell straightened up like a soldier snapping to attention. "You are my daughter, and I would very much like the chance to get to know you better. But the decision is yours. I just hope you will consider it."

I didn't know what to say. As far as apologies went, his was pretty good, but I was still wary, and I could still hear Nerezza's voice hissing through my mind. *Useless child.*

What if I let Wendell into my life, my heart, and he didn't like what he discovered? What if he turned his back on me the way Nerezza had? What if he thought I was as useless as she had?

A tense, awkward silence dropped over the workshop. Wendell kept staring at me, but the more seconds that ticked by, the more the hope dimmed in his eyes. My own chest twisted in response. I hated hurting him, but I didn't want to get hurt again either.

"Well, Asterin and the others are probably wondering where I am," Wendell said. "I will leave you to your work. Perhaps I'll see you later at the estate?"

I didn't trust myself to speak, so I gave him a short, sharp nod.

Wendell bowed to me, then left the workshop. The door shut behind him with a soft *snick*, and the sound ignited an ember buried in the cold depths of my heart that I'd thought was long extinguished—the fragile hope that I still might have a real family someday.

I stayed in the workshop for several minutes, staring at nothing. Finally, I roused myself out of my turbulent thoughts and started putting things away. All the gemstones I'd grabbed from the shelves, all the tools we'd used, all the doodles and theories we'd scribbled on pieces of plastipaper.

If I'd been in my makeshift workshop on the *Dream World*, I would have left the mess exactly where it was, but Asterin would probably get twitchy if everything wasn't stored in its proper place. Besides, the simple motions soothed me. By the time I finished, I felt a smidge better, or at least well enough to put on a calm face, grab the Techwave cannon, and leave the workshop.

The House Collier guards were still stationed on the street, and they summoned a transport and escorted me back to the estate. I went to my suite and set the Techwave cannon on a table. I knew Kyrion could sense that I had returned to the estate through the bond, the same way I could sense that he was here, but I still messaged him on my tablet. I was waiting for a reply when a knock sounded on the open door, and a servant stuck her head inside the sitting room.

"Lady Beatrice has arranged for tea on the south terrace. She asked if you would join her, Lady Vesper."

The last thing I wanted to do was see Beatrice, but I had to face my grandmother sooner or later, and I might as well get it over with.

I followed the servant through the corridors, across a bridge, and out onto the south terrace where I'd had lunch with Asterin and Kyrion two days ago. Once again, an impressive spread of food had been laid out, including scones, tiny cakes, and cucumber sandwiches.

Beatrice was sipping her tea at a small, round table. A faint floral note of raspberries curled through the air, along with the sharp tang of the lemon slice she'd squeezed into the hot brew. She gestured at the empty seat across the table, as though I was just another Regal lady joining her for a pleasant snack.

I yanked out the chair, sat down, and regarded her with a cold expression. Beatrice arched a silvery eyebrow at my rudeness, but she kept right on sipping her tea.

A charged, hostile silence filled the air. I crossed my arms over my chest and leaned back against the cushioned seat. Beatrice had summoned me here, so she could explain herself.

Finally, after about three minutes of stony silence, she set down her empty cup.

"I see you are just as stubborn as Zane and Wendell are," she said.

"Maybe it's a family trait." I shrugged. "Or maybe not. I didn't grow up being part of House Zimmer, so who knows? Nature versus nurture is always a fascinating debate among galactic scholars."

Beatrice's mouth pinched into a flat line. Then she sighed, her ramrod-straight posture cracked, and she slumped back in her chair.

"I am sorry about what I did, Vesper. It was never my intention to hurt you. Only to protect my House and family from Nerezza." She sighed again, the sound longer, deeper, and full of aching regret. "And I am especially sorry about how Nerezza treated you. I thought having a child might change her for the better. At least a little bit. For your sake."

"Well, it didn't," I replied in an icy voice. "I was just another tool for Nerezza to use. And when she found out she couldn't use me the way she wanted, she threw me away like a piece of trash and never gave me a second thought. Just like you did."

Beatrice flinched as though I had slapped her. "I deserve every ounce of your anger, scorn, and derision. I am painfully aware of my own shortcomings."

She straightened up and lifted her chin, once again morphing into an elegant, unflappable Regal lady and the head of a powerful House. "But I am prepared to remedy that."

She picked up a black folder I hadn't noticed before, set it on the tabletop, and pushed it over to me.

"What is this?" I asked.

"Your trust fund. I started it the day you were born, just as I did Zane's. This money is yours, independent of House

Zimmer, just as Zane's trust fund is his to do with as he pleases." Her lips puckered. "Although your brother tends to spend his credits on inane things like new Arrow uniforms and ridiculously expensive tailcoats that get ruined within minutes of him donning the garments. I hope you will be a bit smarter than that."

Curiosity got the better of me, and I dragged the folder closer, opened it, and scanned the document inside. The staggering number of credits almost made my eyes pop out of my head, but suspicion surged through me.

I closed the folder and shoved it back toward Beatrice. "Let me guess. This isn't a trust fund so much as it is a bribe for me to disappear and keep my mouth shut about being Wendell's daughter."

Beatrice shook her head. "No. Wendell loved you as soon as he learned about you. The credits are yours to do with as you please. Callus Holloway is still hunting you, and he won't stop until either you or Kyrion is brought back to Corios. You need that money to escape from him and all the bounty hunters."

"And if there wasn't a bounty?" I challenged. "Would we still be having this conversation? Or would you still be pretending I don't exist?"

Beatrice shrugged. "I honestly don't know. You may not believe me, but when Liesl claimed you had died . . . well, it was a burden I carried every day until I learned you were alive. Always wondering if my own selfishness led to the death of my granddaughter. If things would have been different, if only I had brought you to House Zimmer where you belonged."

Her face remained smooth, her voice steady, but regret rippled off her, and more needles of sympathy and commiseration pricked my heart. At this point, my chest felt like a blasted pincushion.

"Ever since I realized you were still alive, I've been paralyzed with fear," Beatrice continued. "Fear that you would find out the truth. That Nerezza would sell the story to the gossip-casts. That Holloway would discover our connection and kill Wendell and Zane to draw you out. So much bloody *fear*." She snarled out the last word.

As much as I hated to admit it, she had a point, and all those awful things could still happen simply because I existed. "And now?"

Determination blazed in Beatrice's pale eyes. "I am tired of being at other people's mercy—or lack thereof. I will *not* fear Nerezza or Holloway or anyone else in the galaxy." Her face softened. "And I will not fear you any longer either, Vesper. You are my blood, which is a fact I've hidden for far too long. I hope you can forgive me someday. Or if you can't forgive me, that you can at least forgive Wendell. He desperately wants to be part of your life."

A sad smile played across my grandmother's lips. "I always thought Wendell's tender heart was a weakness, especially when he got involved with Nerezza." She sighed. "But now I think it is far better to have a tender, hopeful heart than an old, bitter, jaded one like mine."

I understood everything she was saying, everything she had done, but her explanation and reasoning didn't lessen the sting of her ruthless actions. Beatrice had been playing a game of Regal chess with Nerezza, and she'd sacrificed me, an unknowing pawn, so she could remain a queen and hold on to her own power. In that way, my grandmother and my mother were *exactly* alike.

Well, I was through letting them hurt me, and *I* would not fear Beatrice and Nerezza. Never again.

I had started to tell Beatrice exactly where she could shove her apology and her hush money when her empty teacup rattled on its saucer. For a moment, I wondered if we were having an earthquake or a rockslide, but in the distance, a faint buzzing sounded, quickly growing closer and louder.

Beatrice and I both surged to our feet. What was that noise? Where was it coming from?

Suddenly, a large transport zoomed up out of the enormous chasm at the edge of the estate. The transport quickly dropped down, as though it was going to crash into the energy shield that protected the grounds, but then the air shimmered, and the shield evaporated like fog. Shock pulsed through me. Why had the defenses gone down?

A flicker of movement caught my eye, and I glanced up. Leland was standing on a terrace higher up on the main castle, clutching his tablet. The chief of staff's dark gaze met mine, and even from this distance, his sly satisfaction punched into my chest like a spear.

*Leland was my father's business partner, and he lost everything too,* Asterin's voice whispered through my mind, quickly followed by Leland's words at the marriage mart. *Although some Houses fall farther and faster than others. Even as the people in them rise and rise again.*

More shock pulsed through me. Leland had apparently decided to rise again by betraying the Colliers and disabling the estate's defensive shield. I'd been so busy worrying about Esmina and Pollux that I hadn't spotted the rotten, jealous heart already lurking inside House Collier.

Leland's lips drew back into a thin smile, his teeth glinting like white razors in the sunlight. He saluted me with his tablet, then disappeared into the castle.

The transport zipped over and landed on the lawn next to the central topiary garden. A door on the side slid back, and mercenaries clad in black polyplastic armor rushed out of the vehicle like scorpions spewing out of a nest. Each merc was wearing a helmet and carrying a blaster or a large hand cannon, and a sick sense of déjà vu swept over me. This attack was eerily similar to the one at the mineral exchange yesterday.

The mercenaries moved forward, their weapons up and

ready to fire as they established a protective ring around the transport. One of the men waved his hand in an all-clear sign, and two more people got off the transport—Esmina and Pollux.

Esmina was clad in a long red cloak, while Pollux was wearing the same black polyplastic armor as the other mercenaries. He was also clutching a large hand cannon, and two war hammers dangled from his belt as usual.

A chill swept through my body, and I stood there, frozen in place, completely in the open, and utterly exposed.

Esmina looked up, and her gaze locked with mine, despite the distance between us. A smile curved her lips, and she dropped her gaze back down to the mercenaries gathered around her.

"Spread out!" she yelled, her voice drifting up to me. "Find him! Now! Along with the secondary target!"

She jerked her head, and she and Pollux strode across the lawn and plunged into the garden. The other mercenaries quickly followed them. Surprise shot through me. Instead of trying to capture me like they had in the shipping yard, Esmina and Pollux were moving in the opposite direction. For once, I wasn't their target. Why not? What had changed?

"Where are they going?" Beatrice asked. "What do they want?"

*Him.* The word pounded into my brain. Esmina had said *Find him*, which meant the mercenaries were searching for a man, but who? And why would they go into the garden? If the mercenaries were here to kill Aldrich, then they should have stormed into the main castle. But instead, Esmina and Pollux had gone in the other direction as if their target was someone in the guest wing . . .

"Wendell," I whispered, another chill sweeping through my body.

If Esmina and Pollux wanted someone to help fix the Techwave cannon, Wendell would be an excellent choice, since he was a well-known and respected spelltech. My stomach dropped. I still didn't know how I felt about my father, but I didn't want the mercenaries to capture him.

"What?" Beatrice asked in a sharp voice. "What did you say?"

I yanked my stormsword off my belt. "Get inside! Find cover! Go! Now!"

Beatrice bobbed her head, picked up her long skirt, and headed toward the nearest door. I sucked in a breath and started running.

# TWENTY-FOUR

## KYRION

After Vesper headed to Asterin's workshop, I prowled through the Collier estate, once again checking on the guards and making sure everything was as it was supposed to be. I eavesdropped on some servants and learned that Aldrich, Verona, Asterin, Beatrice, and Wendell had gone to the mineral exchange to discuss more specifics about a potential alliance between House Collier and House Zimmer.

Beatrice and Wendell being that close to Vesper worried me, so I checked on her through the bond, but a familiar hum of happiness surged back to me. Vesper was working on some project, and the Zimmers didn't seem to be bothering her, so I didn't send a thought to her. After everything that had happened last night, I was glad she had found some peace.

I just wished I could do the same.

Talking about my mother had dredged up even more old memories, and my dreams had been filled with images of my younger self shouting at Desdemona. Even when I was unconscious, I couldn't escape that shameful moment.

I wanted to know if Siya had any news about Esmina or Pollux, so I went to the training ring. Siya, Rigel, and the other Hammers were sparring again, this time with long spears, and they had a new audience member. Zane was leaning a shoulder against the castle wall, checking messages on his tablet.

I stopped beside him and crossed my arms over my chest. "You're still here."

"I can hear the word *unfortunately* on the end of that sentence," Zane chirped, scrolling through more screens. "Really, Kyrion, do you *have* to be so dour? So doom and gloom *all* the time? You're like a storm cloud, always raining on my parade. It's a beautiful day, the sun is shining, and we are at a fabulous estate. What more could you want?"

"You on a spaceship back to the Imperium. Or at the bottom of one of the mountain chasms, never to be seen or heard from again. I'm not particular."

My tablet buzzed, distracting me from Zane, and I pulled it out. Vesper was back on the estate. Good. I'd sensed her arrival through the bond, but I still appreciated the message.

"Is that my dear sister?" Zane asked.

I ignored his prying gaze and slid the tablet back into my pocket.

*Ding!*

A shrill chime erupted from Zane's tablet, making him grimace. I leaned forward just like Zane had so I could see the sender. Callus Holloway. Of course.

"Keeping an eye on Vesper and me for your boss?" I asked in a snide tone.

Zane shoved his tablet into his pocket. "Some of us don't have the luxury of throwing caution to the wind and running away from our responsibilities."

"If I didn't know better, I would say you were jealous."

"I'm absolutely *jealous*." Zane spat out the words. "Do you know what a gigantic bloody *mess* you've left behind? The awkward, dangerous position you've put me in? All because you had to go and fall in love with my sister."

I stepped toward him, my chest inches away from his. "The position I've put *you* in? What about the position you've put *Vesper* in? All you've done the last few weeks is brag about how you're going to drag us back to Corios."

Zane huffed. "You should know by now that I don't mean half the things I say on the gossipcasts."

"And yet you say them anyway. Why is that?"

"You wouldn't understand," he muttered.

"Try me."

Zane opened his mouth, but Siya stepped over to us, a spear propped up on her shoulder. "Would you boys care to settle your differences in the training ring?"

"I would love to, but I doubt Kyrion has the guts for it." Zane held his hand up beside his mouth as though he was about to reveal a secret to Siya. "The great Kyrion Caldaren doesn't like it when I kick his ass."

"You have *never* kicked my ass."

Zane tapped his index finger on his nose. "You're forgetting how thoroughly I broke your nose during the marriage mart last night."

My eyes narrowed. "You ambushed me in the dark. That's hardly a fair fight."

He grinned and gestured toward the training ring. "Then let's go find out who the better warrior really is."

Siya rolled her eyes. "Are the two of you going to fight, or are you just going to talk all day?"

I had opened my mouth to tell Zane that I was going to enjoy grinding his face into the dirt when a faint tremor swept through the ground. "What was that?"

"What was what?" Zane asked. "Quit stalling, Kyr."

I stepped away from him and glanced around. Two Hammers sparring, the other warriors watching them, servants and guards moving along the bridges and stairs that connected the main castle to the rest of the estate buildings. Everything was normal, but my psionic senses kept pinging. I turned around, trying to find the source of the disturbance.

Something was wrong.

"What are you doing?" Zane asked in an annoyed voice. "You're spinning around and around in circles like a child's toy that's been wound up too tight."

I ignored him and stretched out with my telempathy, scanning the training ring in front of me. Nothing unusual there, so I stretched even farther out with my power . . .

Dozens and dozens of presences flared to life, all zooming this way. Before I could shout a warning, a buzzing sound filled the air, quickly growing closer and louder, and a violent wind current shrieked, whistled, and battered up against the estate's energy shield.

"What is going on?" Zane yelled over the roaring noise.

A transport zoomed up out of the chasm a few hundred feet away from the training ring. The transport hovered in midair, then dipped down. For a moment, I thought it might crash into the energy shield, bounce off, and tumble back down into the chasm. But then the shield dimmed, flickered, and vanished altogether, and the transport zoomed to the right and dropped down onto the lawn beside the garden where I'd had breakfast with Lady Verona yesterday.

The transport thumped to the ground, flattening a couple of topiary hedges, along with some peony bushes, and green needles and blue petals whipped up into the air like shrapnel. A door on the side slid back, and mercenaries clad in black polyplastic armor spewed out of the vehicle. Each man was clutching a blaster or a hand cannon, and shock batons and other weapons dangled from their belts.

"Fuck," Siya muttered. "Those are Serpens Corp mercenaries. Hammers, Hammers, to me!"

She spun away to rally the other warriors, but I kept watching the mercenaries. The enemy fighters formed a protective ring, then stopped, and two more people hopped off the transport.

Esmina and Pollux looked around as though they were a queen and king surveying their future home. Esmina glanced up at something, and a smile spread across her face. Then she shouted a command I couldn't quite make out over the transport's continued roar. She and Pollux strode forward, with their men spreading out in all directions.

"Where are Lord and Lady Collier?" Siya yelled into her tablet. "Secure them immediately! Estate security has been breached! We are under attack! Repeat. We are under attack!"

Siya grabbed a war hammer from a hoverpallet of weapons, crossed the training ring, and sprinted forward, trying to cut off the mercs before they reached the main castle. The other Hammers followed her, but Zane and I stayed by the training ring.

*Pew! Pew! Pew!*

The Serpens Corp mercenaries snapped up their blasters and hand cannons and fired at the Hammers. Siya ducked down behind a low stone wall for cover, as did Rigel and the other warriors.

"What is going on?" Zane repeated. "Who are those people?"

I ignored his questions and watched the battle. Siya used the lunarium head of her war hammer to deflect a blaster bolt back into the chest of a mercenary, who screamed and tumbled to the ground. Rigel and the other Hammers did the same thing with their own weapons, dropping one enemy after another. The Serpens Corp mercenaries would take heavy losses trying to breach the main castle—too many losses to justify such a brazen, reckless charge—so what were the mercs really doing here? What was the point of this attack?

In the distance, Esmina and Pollux broke away from the main group of mercenaries. Dozens of men followed them, and they all sprinted toward the guest wing.

Zane spotted them too. "Where are they going?"

Once again, I ignored him, my mind racing. If Esmina and Pollux were here to destroy House Collier, they should be storming the main castle with the other mercs in hopes of killing Lord Aldrich and Lady Verona. So why were they headed toward the guest wing?

As soon as I asked the question, the answer came to me, and icy dread flooded my body. They weren't here for the Colliers. All the mercs were just a distraction so that Esmina and Pollux could capture their true target, the person they'd been after all along: Vesper.

For a moment, I stood there, frozen in place. Then my mind kicked back into gear, and I stabbed my finger at Esmina and Pollux.

"Vesper!" I yelled at Zane. "The mercenaries are here to kidnap Vesper!"

Siya and the other Hammers were still deflecting blaster bolts back at the mercenaries, but I yanked my stormsword off my belt and sprinted in the opposite direction.

Zane let out a curse. At least, I think he did. Hard to hear anything over the roar of my heart in my ears, but his footsteps slapped on the stones, and he surged up so that he was running alongside me.

*Do you have any sort of plan?* he yelled in my mind.

I growled back at him, *Kill everyone between me and Vesper.*

Zane's annoyed huff rippled through my mind, but I shut out the distraction and kept running, moving from this stone walkway to another one—

*Boom!*

Green cannon fire ripped through the air. I darted to the side, and the energy blast slammed into the wall beside me instead of into my chest. Chunks of stone flew out in all directions, and dust choked the air, making it hard to see and breathe, but I kept running. Zane cursed and slowed for a moment, but he quickly caught up to me.

The dust billowed away, revealing a mercenary standing at the end of the walkway, his finger already curling back on the trigger to fire his cannon again.

I flung my hand out, and my telekinesis ripped the merc off his feet and tossed him back into a nearby wall hard enough to crack his polyplastic armor. The merc flopped down onto his belly, a low groan escaping from his lips. He tried to get back up onto his hands and knees, but I kicked him in the head, then rammed my stormsword into his back for good measure. The merc screamed and collapsed to the ground, blood pooling under his body.

*Boom! Boom! Boom!*

My head snapped around, and I looked through an archway. Serpens Corp mercenaries had crossed the drawbridge and were firing hand cannons at the House Collier guards defending the courtyard in front of the main castle. Esmina and Pollux had sent men to infiltrate the estate from multiple sides to do as much damage as they could as quickly as possible. Smart.

"We have to get to Vesper!" I yelled at Zane. "Now!"

Zane scooped up the dead merc's hand cannon, and we started running again.

I didn't know exactly how many mercenaries Esmina and Pollux had at their disposal, but a veritable army of them had invaded the estate. Everywhere I turned, another merc popped into view, and streaks of cannon and blaster fire zipped through the air like fireworks. Stone walls exploded, while permaglass windows shattered, and the resulting pieces of debris *tink-tink-tinked* across the walkways like old-fashioned piano keys playing a merry, lively tune.

Servants ran everywhere, trying to escape from the mercenaries, who calmly strode forward and cut people down as though they were firing at plastipaper targets. Screams and shouts tore through the air, and the coppery stench of blood mixed with the acrid aroma of fried flesh and the electric burn of the blaster and cannon fire.

It was chaos, confusion, and carnage.

I cut down any merc who got within sword's reach and used my lunarium blade to send blaster bolts shooting right back at the people who'd fired them. Beside me, Zane wielded his stolen hand cannon with expert efficiency, coolly pulling the trigger and dropping one enemy after another.

Despite our mutual hatred, Zane and I had fought together countless times as Arrows, and we worked as an efficient, deadly team, killing anyone stupid enough to attack us.

*Vesper? Vesper, where are you?*

Even as Zane and I fought our way from one walkway and archway to the next, I reached out through the bond, searching for Vesper. The velvety ribbon of her in my mind whipped back and forth with a combination of fear and fury, and I couldn't quite get a grip on it to locate her. Icy dread rushed through me, making Vesper seem as if she was even farther away.

Zane blasted another mercenary out of the way with his stolen hand cannon, and the two of us finally made it to the courtyard in front of the guest wing. Several House Collier guards were lying on the ground, black curls of smoke rising from their chests, their sightless eyes staring at nothing. My gut twisted, but these people were already dead, and I couldn't do anything for them.

I started to step into the courtyard, but Zane grabbed my shoulder. "Wait," he whispered. "Listen. Do you hear that?"

In the distance, screams and shouts still tore through the air, along with sharp staccato bursts of blaster and cannon fire. But this courtyard was eerily quiet, and the only sound was the crackle of energy bolts still eating through the skin, muscles, and bones of the dead guards.

"I don't hear anything."

"Exactly," Zane muttered, his gaze sweeping back and forth. "This screams trap to me."

He was right. It *did* seem like a trap, but for whom? And why bother to set a trap when you had already stormed onto the estate?

"I don't care. I have to find Vesper."

Zane stared at me for a moment, then jerked his head in agreement.

Together we entered the courtyard, weapons ready. Instead of rushing forward, like we had before, we moved slower, taking care to make our footsteps as soft as possible, although it was hard to do, given the stone rubble and broken glass that littered the ground like a carpet of diamond shrapnel—

*Crunch.*

Zane and I both spun toward the sound, which echoed out of a nearby archway.

"Show yourself!" I commanded.

"Yeah," Zane chimed in. "Before my trigger finger slips, and you have a tragic accident."

"Okay, okay!" a familiar voice called out. "Don't shoot me!"

In the archway, a hand appeared, clutching a small silver blaster. More footsteps crunched, and Asterin stepped into view.

Zane hissed out a tense breath and lowered his cannon. "We really have to stop meeting like this."

Asterin's eyes narrowed. "I rather enjoy having my blaster aimed at your chest."

Zane grinned. "Your murderous urges have been duly noted, my lady."

Asterin harrumphed, but she lowered her weapon and strode over to us. Her silver gaze flicked from one body to another, and fury, disgust, and sadness surged off her and punched into my chest like arrows. "The Serpens Corp mercenaries did this?"

I nodded. "Esmina and Pollux sent squads to attack the main castle, front and back, but they're just a distraction. Esmina and Pollux broke off with another squad of mercs and came here to the guest wing."

Asterin frowned. "Why would they do that? Verona and Aldrich are always in the main castle."

"Esmina and Pollux are trying to kidnap Vesper again," I replied. "We need to find her. Now."

Zane shook his head. "No, Esmina and Pollux aren't after Vesper. At least, not right now."

"How would you know?" I growled. "You didn't even see the mercs before they landed on the estate."

Zane hesitated. "I just . . . have this feeling. I don't have time to explain it right now, but for once in your bloody life, trust me. Okay, Kyrion? I don't know what Esmina and Pollux and their men are doing here, but they are *not* targeting Vesper."

I had opened my mouth to growl that we were wasting time when a couple of quick, crunching footsteps rang out, quickly followed by dozens more, all headed in this direction.

There was no time to run for cover, so I snapped up my weapon and whirled around, as did Asterin and Zane. In an instant, the three of us were standing back-to-back-to-back in a loose triangle in the center of the courtyard.

One merc appeared in a nearby archway, then two more popped into sight in another archway. Then three more . . . four . . . five . . . six . . .

A dozen mercenaries flooded the archways and streamed into the courtyard. More footsteps crunched, and another dozen mercs appeared on the second level, all armed with hand cannons pointed at me, Zane, and Asterin.

"Fuck," Zane muttered.

We were surrounded and outgunned, and the three of us had no choice but to lower our weapons.

One of the mercs touched the comms device nestled in his ear. "Target acquired and courtyard secure, just as you predicted."

More footsteps crunched through the rubble. Pollux strode into the courtyard, clutching a hand cannon, and Esmina followed him, her long red cloak rippling around her body like a river of blood. Something silver glinted in her hand. For a moment, I thought it was a weapon, but then I realized it was an injector. What was she going to do with that?

Esmina stopped in front of us. Her green gaze flicked over Zane and Asterin before settling on me. A cruel smile spread across her face, and my gut twisted with dread.

Zane was right. For once, the mercs weren't after Vesper.

"Hello, Kyrion," Esmina purred. "I've been waiting for you."

# TWENTY-FIVE

## VESPER

"Vesper!" Beatrice yelled. "Be careful!"

I sucked down another breath and kept running. I didn't have time to be careful. Wendell was in trouble. I *knew* he was. My seer magic kept whispering it to me over and over like a rolling drumbeat warning of danger.

*Boom! Boom! Boom!*

*Pew! Pew! Pew!*

The mercenaries fired their cannons and blasters, while the House Collier guards did the same with their weapons, trying to stop their enemies from breaching the main castle. Bright green and red energy bolts zipped through the air, and the battle began in earnest. Walls exploded, permaglass shattered, and yells and screams boiled up into the air.

"We are under attack!" I thought I heard Siya's voice, but the continued cannon and blaster fire drowned her out.

So far, all the fighting was on the ground level. Beatrice's tea had been on the third-story terrace, and the mercs hadn't managed to get this high. Since no one was firing at me, I kept going, running as fast as I could, my stormsword clutched in my hand.

*Kyrion? Kyrion! I'm heading toward the guest wing! I think the mercenaries are targeting Wendell!*

I called out to Kyrion through the bond. The sticky cobweb of him in my mind pulsed with icy fury, but once again, the emotion blotted out everything else, and I couldn't tell where he was.

I growled in frustration, sucked down another breath, and picked up my pace. Thanks to my O2 enhancement, I didn't need as much oxygen as other people, but running from one bridge to another and then going up and down the stairs in between was still taking a toll. I felt like someone had clamped a metal vise around my chest and was slowly cranking it tighter and tighter and squeezing all the air out of my lungs, but I kept going.

There was no other option. Not if I wanted to save my father.

And I *did* want to save him. I still didn't know how I felt about Wendell, Beatrice, or Zane, but I didn't want them to die before I had a chance to figure it out.

More blaster bolts zinged through the air, along with the answering *boom-boom-boom* of cannon fire. I couldn't tell if the mercenaries had breached the main castle or if the Hammers and House Collier guards were turning them back, but that wasn't my fight, so it didn't matter right now.

*Kyrion? Kyrion!*

I called out again, still trying to figure out where he was, but all I got was a sense that he was trying to find me as desperately as I was searching for him. As difficult as it was, I released the bond. I needed to focus on the here and now, not all the thoughts and emotions rattling around in my mind and heart.

I finally reached the guest wing and forced myself to slow down. Running blindly forward and getting shot by a mercenary wouldn't do me any good, much less save Wendell.

Cannon and blaster fire continued to boom through the air, punctuated by sharp shrieks of pain, but most of the fighting seemed to be around the main castle. Looking and listening for any hints of danger, I raised my stormsword into an attack position, then stepped through the archway.

I crept from one corridor to the next, moving as quickly as I dared. The guest wing was eerily quiet, and I didn't encounter anyone, not even a servant who'd ducked into a room to hide. I didn't want to get trapped in an elevator in case the mercs cut the power, so I headed for the closest set of stairs and quietly tiptoed down them to the ground level.

The lower I went, the more signs of battle appeared. Blaster fire had scorched many of the walls, while cannon blasts had blown out big chunks of stone and glass, decimating entire rooms. The acrid stench of electricity hung in the air, mixing with the nauseating aroma of burned flesh and singed hair.

I rounded a corner and stumbled over the body of a servant sprawled across the floor. Smoke was still curling up from the blaster wound in her chest, which now resembled a slab of charred meat. Bile rose in my throat, and I shuddered and looked away from the awful sight.

I tiptoed down the corridor until I reached the Zimmers' suites. I cautiously eased through an archway, but no mercenaries were waiting on the other side. Doubt and unease tickled my spine like hot, needling fingers, but I kept going, making my steps as soft and silent as possible, despite the broken stone, glass, and other debris that littered the floor.

" . . . no . . . please . . . wait . . ." a man's voice said, the muffled words coming from up ahead.

I quickened my pace, eased up to an open door, and peered into the suite beyond.

A Serpens Corp mercenary was in the sitting room. The merc's cannon was pointed at Wendell, who had his hands up and was backing away. But the mercenary followed Wendell step for step, as though the two of them were doing a painfully slow dance.

"It's nothing personal," the merc said. "You're just being used to send a message."

Wendell kept easing backward. "What message?"

"No idea. But I have my orders, and I get a bonus for killing you, so it's time to die, Lord Zimmer." The merc grinned, his finger curling around the trigger.

White-hot rage roared through me, blotting out everything else. I churned my legs, sprinted across the room, and barreled into the merc's side.

*Boom!*

The cannon blast went wide, slamming into the stone fireplace instead of Wendell's chest.

"Vesper! Look out!" Wendell yelled.

The mercenary swung his cannon toward me, but I lashed out with my stormsword, driving him back. The man tipped over a low table and fell on his ass. His hand banged into the floor, and the cannon slid out of his grasp.

I snarled, raised my sword, and charged forward, but the merc kicked out, sending the table skittering across the floor. I tripped over it and went down on my hands and knees. My stormsword slipped out of my fingers, and I scrambled forward, still on my hands and knees, trying to reach the weapon.

The merc grabbed my ankle and yanked me back toward him. My hands squeaked across the floor, but I couldn't get a grip on the slick stone. I kicked and flailed, but the merc must have had a strength enhancement, because he easily dragged me over to him.

I rolled over onto my back and flung my hand out, trying to use Kyrion's telekinesis to toss the man aside. Nothing happened. Frustrated, I tried again, with the same useless result.

The merc laughed and dragged me even closer. His hand

darted up, and he locked his fingers around my throat and pinned me to the floor.

"Hold still," he growled, plucking a silver injector off his belt. "The boss told me this wouldn't happen, but I came prepared, and I'm going to collect the bonus for you too. And then Esmina will have a matched set—"

*Boom!*

A blast of cannon fire punched into the merc's back. He screamed and reared back.

*Boom!*

Another blast of cannon fire hit the merc, and his screams abruptly cut off. His hand fell away from my throat, and I raised my foot up between us and kicked him away. The merc tumbled over onto his side, and the injector slipped out of his fingers and rolled across the floor.

"Vesper! Vesper, are you okay?" Wendell crouched down beside me, the merc's still-smoking cannon clutched in his hand.

My father had just saved my life.

I'd never thought that would happen, but I didn't have the time to unpack the emotional implications of Wendell's actions right now. Instead, I grunted, scuttled forward, and grabbed my stormsword from where it had landed. Then I surged up and onto my feet and spun toward the open door.

I raised my weapon, expecting more mercs to hear the cannon blasts and pour into the room.

Ten seconds ticked by. Twenty seconds . . . thirty . . . forty-five . . .

The seconds turned into a minute. Shouts and screams ripped through the air, along with more cracks of cannon and blaster fire, but the fighting never got any closer, and no footsteps pounded in this direction.

I lowered my sword. No one else was coming for Wendell, so why target him in the first place?

"Vesper?" Wendell asked, still clutching the cannon. "What's going on?"

"No idea, but I'm going to find out."

I headed toward the open door. My foot hit something, and a silver cylinder skittered across the floor. I froze. For a split second, I thought someone had lobbed a solar grenade into the room, but then I realized it was just the injector the mercenary had tried to use on me.

*I'm going to collect the bonus for you too. And then Esmina will have a matched set.*

Matched set? My blood turned to ice. This whole thing had been nothing but a giant distraction. The attack on the main castle had drawn the Hammers and House Collier guards to that area, leaving the Serpens Corp mercs free to storm into the guest wing. Killing Wendell had been one of their objectives, but his death hadn't been the mercenaries' main goal.

No, Esmina had a different objective in mind, and it was far more sinister than anything I could have imagined.

"Stay in here! Lock the door behind me! Shoot anyone who tries to enter!" I yelled at Wendell, then sprinted out of the suite.

"Vesper, wait!"

But once again, I didn't have time to wait. This had never been about Wendell or me or even destroying House Collier.

No, Esmina had another target in mind all along: Kyrion.

I raced out of the suite and sprinted down the corridor. I also reached out with my magic. For once, the truebond worked, and I could sense exactly where Kyrion was—and just how much danger he was in, given the anger and frustration surging through the bond.

Every scrap of my seer magic was screaming that I needed

to move faster, so I barreled through the first archway I came to, then another one, then another one . . .

*Kyrion! Hold on! I'm coming for you!*

*No, Vesper!* he shouted back through the bond, and for once, I heard him loud and clear. *Don't! It's a trap* . . .

His voice trailed off. A small sting pricked my neck, then something cold, slick, and oily flooded the bond. The sensation was so strong, so very *wrong*, it made me recoil in shock and disgust. My boots slipped on some loose stones, and I almost lost my footing. My right shoulder banged into a broken wall, but I bounced off and used the momentum to regain my balance and keep going.

Once again, that metal vise clamped around my chest, but this time, it wasn't because of a lack of oxygen or how hard I was running. No, this time, the sensation was my own fear, squeezing out everything else. My heart roared in my ears, but I sucked down another breath and forced myself to run even faster.

"No! Stop!" Asterin's voice ripped through the air, panic ringing through her words. "Leave him alone!"

That horrible, horrible fear squeezed my chest a little tighter, and I ran faster still, my arms pumping by my sides, my stormsword swinging up and down in a sharp, dizzying motion.

I veered past a pile of smoking rubble. The guest wing courtyard appeared up ahead, and I finally forced myself to slow down and slip behind an archway. I drew in a breath to try to slow my racing heart and peered around the side of the stone.

Several mercs surrounded Zane and Asterin, who had their weapons lowered to their sides. A few feet away, two mercs were propping up Kyrion, who was sagging between them, his body limp, his stormsword lying on the ground.

My heart seized, and for one awful, terrible moment, I thought he was dead.

But then his head lolled to the side, and he mumbled something I couldn't hear.

Esmina was standing next to Kyrion, a silver injector in her hand, with Pollux lurking nearby. Esmina tossed the injector aside, and the spent cartridge tumbled over the rubble in the courtyard. That must have been the phantom sting in my neck I'd felt, and whatever drugs Esmina had given Kyrion must also be interfering with our bond.

A snarl rose in my throat, but I swallowed it, not wanting to give my position away. Esmina froze, then spun around and looked directly at me, despite my hiding spot. Once again, her precognition had told her exactly where I was.

"Let's go!" Esmina yelled. "We got what we came for! Kill those two! Now!"

The two mercenaries dragged Kyrion backward. Pollux went with them, along with several other mercs. Four men stayed behind, stepped forward, and took better aim at Zane and Asterin.

My gaze darted back and forth between Kyrion and my friends. As much as I wanted to save him, I couldn't let Zane and Asterin be killed.

Esmina smirked at me. The arrogant bitch already knew what I had chosen.

"Kill them!" she yelled again, backing out of the courtyard.

I sprinted toward the closest mercenary and flung my hand up, hoping, hoping, hoping that this time I could tap into Kyrion's telekinesis . . .

But once again, nothing happened.

The cold, oily sludge that coated the truebond made it impossible for me to get a grip on Kyrion's magic. I snarled with frustration, but I kept running forward.

One of the mercs swung his cannon in my direction. I snapped up my stormsword, but I doubted I would be able to swat away a blast from a weapon that powerful—

A violent burst of telekinesis ripped through the courtyard, throwing the mercenary back into another man and knocking them both down to the ground. Zane thrust his hand forward, then pulled it back. Another burst of telekinesis surged off him and yanked a third merc forward.

Zane snapped up his hand cannon and slammed the butt of the weapon into the merc's forehead. A sickening *crunch* sounded, and the man dropped without making a sound. The other two mercenaries yelled and scrambled back onto their feet. Zane flipped his cannon around and shot one in the chest, while I came up behind another man and sliced my stormsword across his back.

The last merc cursed. His cannon wavered between Zane and me before he focused on Zane. The merc's finger curled around the trigger—

*Pew! Pew! Pew!*

Asterin shot the mercenary three times in the chest, and he joined his dead friends on the ground.

My gaze zipped back and forth, but the rest of the mercenaries had retreated with Esmina and Pollux, and no more enemies were left to fight. I tightened my grip on my stormsword, scooped up Kyrion's weapon from the ground, and ran past both Zane and Asterin.

"Vesper, wait!" Asterin called out.

But yet again, I didn't have time to wait, and I kept running. Zane's and Asterin's footsteps pounded on the ground behind me, but I didn't slow down. I had to reach Kyrion, even though my seer magic was screaming that it was already too late.

I left the guest wing courtyard behind and sprinted forward. More rubble appeared, along with more and more bodies, showing where the mercs had carved a swath of destruction and death through this part of the estate. I veered around a crumbled archway, and the central topiary garden popped into view.

I plunged into the garden and raced along the center path. My body brushed up against one of the peony bushes, and blue petals swirled through the air like spearmint-scented snowflakes. The aroma reminded me of Kyrion, and I forced myself to run even faster.

Through the topiary trees and hedges, I could see the mercenaries racing through the garden. But instead of heading back to the transport they had landed in, Esmina, Pollux, and their remaining men veered in the opposite direction.

Where were they going?

A familiar buzz sounded, and in the distance, I caught sight of rotors whirling around and around. My heart plummeted into my stomach, but I kept running.

Finally, I made it to the edge of the garden. Another, much smaller transport was waiting on the lawn here. This transport was painted House Collier green, and Leland was already on board. He waved at Esmina, Pollux, and the two men dragging Kyrion along with them, urging them to move faster. Not only had Leland lowered the protective shield around the estate, but now he was helping the mercenaries escape. Fucking traitor.

Esmina jumped up into the open side of the transport, then whirled around. She barked out a command, although I couldn't hear her words over the buzzing rotors.

Pollux stepped forward and aimed his cannon at me. Once again, my heart seized in my chest, but I lifted my stormsword to deflect as much of the energy as I could.

Pollux grinned at me, then lowered the weapon and pulled the trigger.

*Boom!*

A blast of green cannon fire slammed into the ground three feet in front of me. Grass and dirt flew into the air, and the shock wave threw me back. I hit the ground hard, losing my sword and Kyrion's weapon, but I shook off my daze, scrambled back up onto my feet, and started forward—

Strong arms closed around me from behind, pinning my own arms to my sides.

"No!" I yelled, trying to break free. "Let me go! Let me go!"

"No!" Zane yelled back. "It's a trap! They're trying to get you too!"

He was right. Several mercs rushed around the side of the transport. They must have been waiting for me to get close enough so they could surround me. A couple of the men raised their cannons and headed in our direction—

*Pew! Pew! Pew!*

Asterin stepped up beside me and Zane and fired her blaster, driving the mercs back.

"Let's go!" Pollux's voice roared out. "Move, move, move!"

The mercs retreated to the transport. Helpless, I watched as two men dragged Kyrion on board. They dumped him onto the floor, and he didn't move a muscle.

"Kyrion!" I yelled. "Kyrion!"

No response.

The last of the mercs leaped into the transport. Pollux followed them, and the vehicle lifted off the ground.

Pollux leaned down and punched Kyrion in the face a couple of times. He and the mercs disappeared inside the ship's dark depths, dragging a clearly unconscious Kyrion along with them, but Esmina hung on to a strap beside the open door. The transport picked up speed, and the wind whipped her long scarlet cloak around her body, making her look like an undulating viper. She had already sunk her poisonous fangs deep into my heart and ripped away the man I loved.

*See you soon, Vesper.* Esmina's voice slithered through my mind, and she lifted her free hand to her lips and blew me a mocking kiss.

The transport's thrusters fully engaged, and it shot up into the sky before dropping down into the chasm on the back side of the estate.

Zane finally released my arms. I elbowed him aside and rushed over to the permaglass barrier that cordoned off the lawn from the steep drop below.

The transport was zipping through the chasm, moving farther and farther away with each passing second. The ship zoomed around a corner and disappeared, and a hard truth punched into my heart, stealing my breath.

Kyrion was gone.

# PART THREE

## RESCUES

# TWENTY-SIX

## VESPER

"Thirteen dead, and more than three dozen injured," Aldrich growled. "The estate's defensive shield is still down, and Esmina, Pollux, Leland, and the mercenaries have vanished."

He tossed a tablet down onto his desk and started pacing back and forth, his wing tips snapping out a quick, furious rhythm. Verona stood nearby, her hands clasped together, her gaze never leaving her husband.

Siya and Rigel were also in the library, standing stiffly at attention in front of the lord's desk, while Beatrice and Wendell were sitting in chairs off to the side. Zane was leaning a shoulder against the wall, while Asterin was lurking a few feet away from him. I was cloistered in the corner all alone.

Two hours had passed since the mercenary attack on the Collier estate. The wounded were being tended to, as were the dead, and we had all gathered in Aldrich's library to figure out what to do next. Well, everyone else had gathered here to figure out what to do next. I already knew exactly what I was going to do: find and rescue Kyrion.

I'd already sent Daichi all the information about the attack, and I was hoping he could figure out where Esmina and Pollux were headed. He *had* to figure it out.

I had to find Kyrion before it was too late.

Zane looked over at me, and I glared right back at him. It was his blasted fault I hadn't been able to save Kyrion. Zane quirked an eyebrow as if he knew exactly what I was thinking.

A soft chime rang out.

Everyone glanced around, and Verona raised her tablet. "It's mine. We've just received a video-chat request—from Leland."

Verona swiped her finger across the screen, and a hologram of Leland popped up and flickered in the air.

"Hello, Verona, Aldrich," he said in a smug tone. "In case you haven't guessed, I'm contacting you to formally tender my resignation."

Aldrich stepped forward, his hands clenching into fists. "Why did you lower the shield? Why did you betray House Collier?"

"Betray House Collier?" Leland sniffed. "I didn't betray you, Aldrich. I simply got tired of swallowing the table scraps of power you deigned to dole out. I should have been running my own House instead of toiling away as your chief of staff. I *would* have been running my own House, if not for Urston Armas's mistakes. That idiot cost me everything."

Asterin jerked forward, her body tense. "What do you know about my father?"

Leland sniffed again. "I know he was a grand fool, just as you are, my dear."

Asterin started to ask another question, but Verona laid a hand on her daughter's arm and shook her head.

Leland looked at Aldrich again. "Consider this my last duty as your chief of staff. Who knows? Perhaps our paths will cross again someday. But in the meantime, I'm going to enjoy a much-needed vacation funded by my new friends."

Leland grinned, then disappeared. For a moment, the hologram went dark, but then another familiar face appeared: Esmina.

"Greetings to House Collier. I hope you all enjoyed my little surprise party," she purred. "I certainly did, watching the House of Collier take such a great fall. It reminded me of old times."

Aldrich's fists clenched a little tighter. "What do you want?"

"I have Kyrion Caldaren, and if you want him back, you will follow my instructions exactly," Esmina continued. "Bring one hundred million credits on unmarked currency cards to the designated location at sunset. Otherwise, I'll start cutting off pieces of Kyrion and delivering them to you."

The hologram flickered, and Kyrion appeared. His head was slumped down, and he was clearly unconscious, but his body was propped upright, and his chest was encased in some sort of stone that anchored him to a wall. Given the oily sludge coating the bond, I hadn't been able to sense if the mercenaries were hurting Kyrion, and seeing that he was more or less okay unwound a tiny knot of tension in my chest.

Still, I couldn't help but wonder *why* the mercenaries had kidnapped him. Esmina had plenty of credits, power, and influence as the head of Serpens Corp, and she had no financial need to ransom Kyrion back to anyone. What was this really about?

Esmina held up a finger. "One more thing. Vesper Quill has something I want—the solution to fix a powerful new weapon. Vesper will bring that solution to me, or Kyrion dies. Vesper will come alone. If I see any Hammers or House Collier guards, Kyrion dies. Basically, if any of you do anything I don't like, Kyrion dies."

I could hear what she wasn't saying: Kyrion was going to

die anyway, even if we all did exactly what she said.

"But let's go back to the beginning. I've made my demands absolutely clear, so let's hope there are no messy mistakes on your end and that history doesn't repeat itself," Esmina said. "The ransom site has been geotagged in this message. If I were you, I'd get busy. See you soon, Vesper."

She grinned at the camera, then slashed her hand across her throat. The feed cut off, and the hologram winked out.

Aldrich spun around to me. "What weapon is she talking about?"

I sighed, but the time for hiding the truth was over. Esmina had made sure of that. "When I was working at Kent Corp, I designed a new hand cannon, but Rowena Kent secretly turned my idea over to the Techwave."

"So what?" Siya asked. "Every corporation, Imperium and Erzton alike, is always designing new weapons."

"The Techwave scientists modified my original design, and they've created a new hand cannon that is strong enough to cut through defensive energy shields. But the true value of the weapon is that it can wound—kill—even the most powerful psions, Arrows and Hammers alike."

A stunned silence dropped over the room.

Aldrich raked a hand through his hair. "Our spies had heard the rumors, but we were hoping they weren't true."

"Believe me," Zane muttered, rubbing a hand over his heart, "the Techwave cannons are very, very real."

Siya looked at me. "Do you have one of these cannons?"

"Yes. I grabbed one of the weapons when I escaped from a Techwave production plant on Magma 3 a few weeks ago."

At my confession, Aldrich jerked his head at Rigel, who rushed out of the library. Where was he going?

"What's wrong with the cannon design?" Verona asked.

"After a few blasts, the cannon overheats and fries itself, rendering it useless."

"And Esmina thinks you know how to fix that problem. Is she right, Vesper?" Siya demanded.

The weight of everyone's gaze settled on me like a spaceship about to land on and crush my chest. "Wendell and I worked on the cannon in Asterin's workshop earlier today, but we didn't come up with a solution."

That was as much of the truth as I was going to share, and I wasn't about to mention that I thought sapphsidian was the key to stabilizing the weapon. I glanced over at Asterin, who also knew about my sapphsidian theory. My friend chewed on her lower lip, her gaze flicking between her mother and her stepfather, both of whom were frowning at me.

Aldrich clasped his hands behind his back, then started pacing back and forth behind his desk again, as though the quick steps were helping him formulate a plan of attack. No one else moved, and more than two minutes ticked by in charged silence.

Footsteps sounded, and Rigel rushed back into the library carrying the Techwave hand cannon I'd left in my suite earlier.

Anger surged through me, along with a growing sense of dread. "You broke into my suite? And went through my things?"

"Technically, it's Lord Aldrich's suite, and the cannon was lying in plain sight on a table." Rigel placed the weapon on Aldrich's desk.

The lord studied the cannon, then shook his head. "It doesn't matter if Vesper can fix the cannon or not. We can't afford to let it fall into Esmina's hands. You saw what she and Pollux did with their mercenaries. If they ever got their hands on more advanced weapons that can cut through defensive and psionic shields . . ." His voice trailed off, but we all knew how devastating that could be.

"What do we do?" Verona asked.

"We ambush her," Siya replied in a grim voice. "Esmina

told us when and where to meet her. We get there early, wait for her to arrive, and then move in with enough Hammers to take her down. It's long past time we brought her to justice for her crimes."

Aldrich looked at Rigel, who nodded.

"It's our best option," Rigel agreed.

I stalked over to the desk, my hands balling into fists. "No. Esmina will kill Kyrion if she even *thinks* the Hammers are closing in on her location. You won't surprise her with an ambush. Not with her precognition. She'll be expecting you to attack, and she'll find some way to escape—or worse, kill everyone you send after her."

Aldrich stiffened with anger. "I am well aware of the dangers, but the other Houses already view everything that's happened to House Collier over the past few days as a sign of weakness. Once word gets out about today's attack on the estate itself, our position will be even more precarious. We must strike now." He nodded at Siya and Rigel. "Go. Prepare the guards, along with the Hammers. I want you ready to leave as soon as possible."

Siya and Rigel both bowed and hurried out of the library.

I looked at Verona, hoping she would convince Aldrich to listen to reason, but she shook her head.

"I'm sorry, Vesper," she said, an apologetic note in her voice. "I know what you are at risk of losing better than anyone, but we must protect House Collier."

Verona went over to Aldrich and slid her arm through his in solidarity.

No help there, so I looked at Asterin, who was still standing in the open space between Zane and her parents, a no-man's-land if ever there was one. Asterin bit her lip again, clearly torn, and I swallowed my plea. My friend had already done so much for Kyrion and me. I wasn't going to ask her to side against her family too.

Besides, Aldrich and Verona weren't completely wrong, even if their actions might end up costing Kyrion his life—and destroying mine in the process.

"*Fine.*" I ground out the word. "While the Hammers and House Collier guards ambush Esmina and Pollux, I'll figure out some way to find Kyrion and save him myself."

Aldrich shook his head. "No, the stakes are too high. You will stay here at the estate, in your suite, until further notice."

White-hot fury raged through my body, and my fists clenched even tighter. The lord was treating me as though I was a naughty child who needed to sulk in the corner and think about her actions.

"I don't belong to your House," I snapped. "And I'm not a member of the Erzton. I am a Regal lady, an Imperium citizen, and *you* have no authority over *me*."

Aldrich's face hardened, and anger flared in his hazel eyes. "As long as you are under the protection of my House, then *you* will do as *I* say."

"Then I reject the protection of your House." I spat out the words. "I would rather die trying to save Kyrion than sit here and twiddle my thumbs while the lot of you blunder straight into Esmina's trap."

Verona's face paled, and Asterin sucked in a breath. Beatrice and Wendell were also shocked by my harsh words, but Zane nodded, as if I'd done exactly what he'd expected.

Even more anger flared in Aldrich's eyes, and he straightened up to his full height and peered down his nose at me. "If that is what you wish," he said in a cold, clipped voice. "Consider the protection of House Collier revoked." He stabbed his finger at me. "But if you try to interfere with Siya, Rigel, and the Hammers in any way, you will be taken into custody, and I will ship you back to the Imperium and Callus Holloway the first chance I get."

It wasn't an idle threat, and he meant every word he said.

Well, me too. Esmina was playing yet another deadly game with the Colliers, even if they were too stubborn to admit it. I might only have the smallest chance of saving Kyrion, but I had to try.

"Very well," I replied, my voice just as cold as Aldrich's. "I will return to my suite and pack my things. I'll be gone within the hour."

"No," he replied. "You will stay in your suite until the Hammers apprehend Esmina and Pollux. Then you can do whatever you want. Is that understood?"

"Understood, Lord Collier." I tipped my head to him one scant inch. "Good luck with your hunt, even if it is a fool's errand."

I glared at him a moment longer, then whirled around and stormed out of the library.

I didn't even get halfway down the corridor before a couple of House Collier guards appeared. I marched past them, but the two men followed me, their hands on their shock batons, ready to subdue me if I did anything they didn't like.

I ignored my watchers and strode from one corridor to the next, leaving the main castle. I entered the guest wing, went to my suite, and locked the door behind me.

The first thing I did was whip out my tablet and message Daichi and Tivona, telling them what was happening. But my friends were on the other side of the galaxy, and there was nothing they could do to help me.

I would just have to help myself, the way I always did.

I didn't believe for one second that Esmina would be at the geotagged location she'd sent the Colliers. She was too smart for that, but she still wanted me to find her and bring her the fixed Techwave cannon. Esmina had to have left some clue behind in her crowing confrontation with Aldrich in the library, and thanks to the spy camera hidden in the House Caldaren sigil in my jacket, I had a recording of the whole thing.

I stripped off my jacket, placed it on a holoscreen embedded in the table in the corner, and downloaded the camera footage. I played the recording, but I didn't see any hidden clues in Esmina's words, just her mocking derision and supreme confidence that she had already won. I also studied the image of Kyrion, but he was anchored to a stone wall that could have been anywhere.

I paced back and forth, watching the video again and again. No new information revealed itself, but the answer to where Esmina wanted to meet was in the footage. I *knew* it was, although it wasn't going to do me any good if I couldn't figure it out. And if I didn't figure it out, Kyrion would die anyway, no matter what Siya, Rigel, and the Hammers did.

My heart seized at the thought, but I forced myself to turn off the footage. Whenever I was stuck on a project in the R&D lab, it always helped to take a break and return to a problem with fresh eyes, so I went over to the permaglass wall that overlooked the topiary garden. Many of the trees and hedges had broken branches, scorched leaves, and other battle damage, but I looked past them, studying the chasm that dropped away from the edge of the estate.

I don't know how long I stood there, staring at the landscape without really seeing it, but Esmina's voice started whispering in my mind, and I thought of all the odd little things she'd said to Aldrich—things that had no place in a ransom demand.

*Watching the House of Collier take such a great fall . . . It reminded me of old times . . . Let's go back to the beginning . . . Let's hope there are no messy mistakes on your end and that history doesn't repeat itself . . .*

I thought Esmina had just been mocking Aldrich and Verona, but what if there was another meaning to her words? But what would House Collier and great falls and history repeating itself have to do with where she was holding Kyrion?

*House of Collier . . . great fall . . . history . . .* Esmina's smug voice whispered through my mind again, although this time, it was followed by Aldrich's regretful tone. *She lured Micah to the waterfall where he had saved her and shoved him off a bridge . . .*

My eyes widened. I knew *exactly* where Esmina wanted to meet. Of course. She had been camped out under the Colliers' noses all along, and I could have smacked myself for not seeing it sooner.

Esmina was at the underground mining museum, at Stardrop Falls, where she'd killed Micah, severed their truebond, and taken his magic all those years ago.

Leland must have told Esmina that I knew what had happened at the waterfall, which was why she'd dropped all those little hints into her mocking message. With her precog magic, Esmina had known just what to say for me to figure out her location.

According to Asterin, the mining museum had long been abandoned, making it the perfect place to hide. Esmina probably appreciated the irony and loved thumbing her nose at the Colliers, even if they didn't realize she was doing it.

New determination blazed through me, and I marched into the bedroom and sorted through the gear Kyrion and I had brought to the estate. My stormsword was hooked to my belt like usual, and I grabbed Kyrion's sword and a few other things I thought might come in handy, then stuffed them all into my duffel bag.

Five minutes later, I was ready to leave, but I couldn't go out through the main suite door, since the two guards were waiting outside. So how was I going to get from this level down to the ground?

My gaze zipped over to the bed. I went over and shoved

the mounds of unnecessary pillows aside, revealing the thick blankets and fine sheets. A grin spread across my face.

"The classics never go out of style," I quipped, then got to work.

I stripped all the blankets and sheets off the bed and knotted the ends together. Next, I tied one end of my makeshift escape rope to a heavy wooden nightstand. I jerked on all the blankets and sheets several times, making sure the knots would hold, then opened a glass door and stepped out onto the balcony. No one was watching my suite, so I tied my duffel bag to the end of my makeshift rope and lowered the bag to the ground. Then it was my turn.

Staring down at the fifty-foot drop from this angle made me dizzy. Kyrion was right to be worried about falling from great heights. My heart ached at the thought of him, but I grabbed hold of the rope, swung my legs over the balcony railing, and climbed down.

Well, I didn't climb so much as slide from one knot to the next, but I made it down to the ground. I glanced around, but this section of the estate was empty, and no one had seen my improvised escape—

"I thought climbing down bedsheets to be reunited with their true love was something people only did in ridiculous romance serials," a familiar voice drawled.

I whirled around. Zane pushed away from one of the columns, stepped out of the shadows, and sauntered over to me. He'd changed into a fresh Arrow uniform, and his stormsword was dangling off his belt, but my gaze zoomed in on the large cannon strapped to his back—the same kind of Techwave cannon Rigel had taken from my suite.

"Where did you get that?" I demanded.

Zane smoothed his hands down his pale blue jacket. "This old thing? Fergus, the House Zimmer tailor, makes uniforms for me in bulk. The poor man. I'm probably responsible for every one of his gray hairs, given all his exquisite clothes I've ruined over the years."

"The cannon," I growled. "Where did you get the blasted *cannon*?"

He gave an airy wave of his hand. "Oh, I took it off the Techwaver who infiltrated the summer solstice ball. I thought it might come in handy one day, even if I'm afraid to fire it for fear of blasting off my own hand. Why? Do you need it for something?"

Zane knew—*he knew*—I needed that cannon to save Kyrion. No doubt my brother wanted me to beg for the privilege, but I wasn't about to play his stupid mind games.

I huffed out an aggravated breath, grabbed my duffel bag, and stalked away, heading around the side of the guest wing.

I mentally reviewed the estate layout in my mind. Around the next corner, a path skirted around a small topiary garden and ran right by the transport garage. With a little luck, I could break into the garage, steal a vehicle, and leave the estate before anyone realized what I was doing.

Footsteps sounded, and Zane fell into step beside me. We walked in silence until we reached the garden path.

I stopped and whirled toward him. "What do you think you're doing?"

"Isn't it obvious? Helping you save dear Kyrion."

"You hate Kyrion. Why would you want to save him?"

"*Hate* is a strong word. Perhaps *despise* is better."

I snorted. "*Despise* is just a fancy and polite way of saying *hate*."

Zane shrugged, neither agreeing nor disagreeing. I didn't have time for this. I didn't have time for *him*.

I poked him in the chest. "What are you really doing here? Why are you following me? And how did you even know I would climb down my balcony?"

He shrugged again. "Because it's what I would have done.

And I'm following you because you're going to get yourself killed if you take on Esmina and Pollux alone."

Anger spurted through me, and Esmina's voice whispered through my mind. *You're the weak link.*

I crossed my arms over my chest. "So you think I need a babysitter."

"No, I think you need help."

"Would you still be saying that if Kyrion was here and I was the one who'd been abducted?"

"Absolutely," Zane snapped, frustration creeping into his voice. "Kyrion wouldn't want you to be reckless, and Kyrion certainly didn't rescue you from Crownpoint all by himself. Asterin, Daichi, Touma, Tivona, and Leandra helped him do it. Back then, Kyrion knew he couldn't save you alone, and I think deep down, you know you can't save him by yourself right now."

As much as I hated to admit it, he was right. Esmina would let me walk straight into her trap, snap it shut behind me, and then Kyrion and I would *both* be caught. But I still felt like there was more to Zane's sudden benevolence than met the eye.

"Why are you *really* doing this?" I asked in a sharp voice. "Why do you want to help me? And tell me the *truth*, not some stupid quip about how you want to lord your prowess over Kyrion by rescuing him."

Zane sighed. "Because it will break my father's heart if you go rushing off without any backup and get yourself killed." He paused, an uncomfortable look on his face. "And it would greatly vex me as well."

"It would *vex* you? Seriously?" I rolled my eyes and spun away from him.

Zane reached out and touched my arm. Wary, I faced him again.

"This hasn't been easy for me either," he said. "Realizing

what Beatrice did to you. Trying to come to terms with the fact that she kept you a secret from my father and me for all these years. Remembering my own shitty behavior when you first came to Corios. I've been angry and regretful about *all* of it, including my own actions. More than you know."

I let out a bitter laugh. "Yes, being cast aside like a piece of trash by my grandmother and then repeatedly mocked by my brother has greatly *vexed* me as well."

Zane sighed again, the sound a little louder and deeper. "Beatrice's machinations aside, the simple truth is this: I can't *un-know* that I have a sister. Like it or not, the two of us are connected. Our father already loves you as much as he does me. Wendell has since the moment he learned about you."

For once, he was being completely serious, which was shocking in and of itself. Even worse, his words made that annoying spark of hope flare up in my chest, but I forced myself to ignore it.

I threw my hands up into the air. "See? That's the problem. You and me and Wendell never had a *choice* in any of this. Beatrice and Nerezza made their own choices and took away ours in the process. Well, I have a choice now, and I'm going after Kyrion—alone."

Zane stepped a little closer, a dangerous light flaring in his eyes. "You either take me with you, or I'm going to make enough noise to get every guard on this estate to come running. Siya, Rigel, and the rest of the Hammers will stuff you right back into your suite, and you'll *never* get to Kyrion."

Even more anger pulsed through me, along with a tiny bit of grudging admiration. Zane might pretend to be an arrogant idiot, but he was also clever and ruthless.

"You would actually blackmail me into taking you along?"

"Absolutely." He grinned. "Now, what do you say, sis? Shall we play the part of the cavalry and ride to dear Kyrion's rescue?"

My hands balled into fists. Zane was absolutely *infuriating*, but I was going to need all the help I could get against Esmina, Pollux, and their mercenaries. Zane was a strong psion and an Arrow with years of battle experience, and he just might mean the difference between my saving Kyrion and both of us dying.

"*Fine*," I growled. "But if you do anything to endanger Kyrion or me, or if this is all part of some elaborate trap to drag us back to Corios, then I will kill you myself."

Zane lifted his hand and snapped off a cheeky salute. "Whatever you say, sis. Now, let's go rescue your beloved Kyrion." He paused. "Before I change my mind and leave the broody bastard to rot."

I rolled my eyes again and headed toward the small garden. Zane fell into step beside me.

For the first time in my life, I had backup in the form of my brother. I still wasn't sure how I felt about that, but I would figure it out later—after we rescued Kyrion.

# TWENTY-SEVEN

## KYRION

For a long time, I knew nothing but darkness. Then I was dimly aware of voices muttering and hands hauling me from one location to another and then, strangely enough, propping me upright . . .

I woke with a start. My eyes snapped open, revealing a large, jeweled, sapphsidian eye staring right back at me. I jerked to the side, but my mind cleared, and I realized where I was: lying on the floor of Vesper's mindscape.

I slowly sat up. Pain erupted in my jaw, my head spun around, and it took me several seconds to shove all that hot, throbbing discomfort to a distant corner of my mind and wall it off behind a psionic shield. Slowly, the pain died down to a more manageable level, and the familiar eyes, flowers, and doors snapped into focus.

Why had I woken in here? In the past, I had only been able to enter Vesper's mindscape when she was in trouble and reaching out for me. A rueful grunt escaped my lips. Perhaps the truebond had pulled me in here because it knew *I* was the one in trouble this time.

I grabbed hold of a black vine and pulled myself to my feet. The blue-moon peony on the vine bobbed up and down, as if it was a Regal lady bowing to me. I released the vine and turned around in a slow circle, but the room was just as I remembered from all the other times I'd been here. I still didn't know why I was here, but perhaps I could get a message to Vesper.

I went over to a large door with an upside-down sapphsidian eye embedded in the dark gray stone. I'd gone through this door before, when Vesper had almost suffocated to death on the *Dream World*. Back then, the door had been standing wide open, but right now, it was closed. I ran my fingers all over the door, exploring the eye, along with the crescent moons and stars carved into the stone, but I didn't find any triggering mechanism, and the door remained firmly shut.

I drew back and glared at the upside-down eye, which twinkled with a knowing light, as if it could sense my frustration and was openly mocking me.

"Bloody seer power," I muttered.

The eye just twinkled again, a little more brightly than before, as though laughing at my cursing its existence.

I spun away from the unblinking eye. Perhaps I could open a different door and send a message to Vesper that way, although asking her not to try to find me was pointless, since I would have ignored any such message from her. No, Vesper was going to try to rescue me, and I needed to give her as much information about our enemies as possible.

I prowled around the room, hoping to get a glimpse of Esmina and Pollux or at least discover a clue about where they were holding me through the other doors, many of which were open. Memories played in several spaces, including Nerezza Blackwell calling Vesper a *useless child*. I grimaced. I'd seen that memory before, and I had no idea how Vesper endured such a vile thing constantly playing in her mindscape like a hologram that refused to be shut off.

I moved past the memory of Nerezza and studied the images flickering in the other open doors. Vesper taking part in the Techwave battle on Magma 7 . . . Vesper fighting Julieta Delano in the weapons lab at Quill Corp . . . Vesper and me kissing in the training room on the *Dream World* . . .

A smile curved my lips. I liked being in Vesper's memories, especially the happier ones, although the knowledge wasn't helpful right now.

Since none of the open doors held any clues, I tried the closed doors, but none of them budged. Either Vesper needed to be here to open the doors, or I just didn't have the necessary power right now, given that I was still unconscious from Esmina's chemicals and Pollux's punches.

I ended up in front of a door that featured the House Caldaren sigil of an arrow streaking upward through a cluster of stars. I'd forced my way through this door the night I'd saved Vesper from suffocating, but it was once again closed. It probably wouldn't budge either, but I tried it anyway.

To my surprise, the knob turned easily, and the door swung open with a low, ominous *creak*.

For a moment, darkness filled the space, but then a light flared, and a memory flickered to life. In the doorway, my mother sat on a bench in the Castle Caldaren garden, carefully pruning blue-moon peonies and then sliding the flowers into a crystal vase. Desdemona was pale and weak, and she had to stop every few minutes to rest, but she doggedly snipped one flower after another.

Shock rippled through me. This wasn't one of Vesper's memories—it was one of *mine*.

I'd seen this same image of my mother when I'd been having breakfast with Lady Verona in the topiary garden yesterday, and then again when Vesper and I had been talking in our suite last night. But why would Vesper's mindscape show me one of my own memories? Even though we were bonded, I had never been able to use her seer abilities with any success. Most of the time, Vesper's power flared like a bright silver star before abruptly winking out. Perhaps the chemicals Esmina had dosed me with were impacting our bond.

The memory kept playing, and I watched my mother prune peonies until she had a beautiful bouquet. Footsteps crunched on the crushed-shell path, and a thirteen-year-old boy came into view—me.

I grimaced. This was the day I'd yelled at my mother for not fighting back against Holloway. At first, I'd stomped away, but I'd been so ashamed of my actions that I'd returned to apologize.

Sure enough, teenage Kyrion tiptoed over to the table. A wicked gleam of black appeared, and a scorpion scuttled out of some peonies that were lying on the table. Kyrion darted forward and used the wooden sword he was clutching to smash the scorpion.

"Bloody scorpions," I muttered, my words perfectly in sync with those from my younger self.

"You should go inside. You might get stung again." Teenage Kyrion looked at the flowers on the table, anger flaring in his eyes. "Or better yet, get rid of the peonies, and plant some flowers that don't attract scorpions."

A few days earlier, Holloway had siphoned off my mother's magic, leaving Desdemona weak and shaking, but she'd still insisted on picking some fresh peonies, and she'd gotten a nasty sting. The scorpion's venom had further weakened her, and I'd been terrified she was going to keel over and die in the garden.

"The scorpions love the peonies as much as I do," Desdemona replied. "The scorpions will always be a danger, and they could always sting me."

"But?" Once again, I spoke along with my younger self.

"But you can't be afraid of the possibility," Desdemona said in a serious voice. "You have to let go of your fear, Kyrion. I let go of mine about being stung. Otherwise, I wouldn't have been able to pick this wonderful bouquet. Doesn't it smell divine?"

She nudged the crystal vase over to his side of the table. Even out here in Vesper's mindscape, I could still smell the peonies' spearmint scent. Bittersweet longing washed over me. I had spent so much of my life remembering how horribly my mother's had ended that I had all but forgotten about moments like this. Even then, with the shadow of Crownpoint looming over her in the distance, my mother had still found joy and beauty.

"Besides," Desdemona continued, "scorpions aren't the only things attracted to blue-moon peonies."

She tilted her head to the side. A mammoth butterfly was now flitting around the bouquet, its black-and-blue wings flickering and flashing with a beautiful iridescent light. But the strangest thing was that I felt like my mother was talking about something else entirely, something far more serious than getting stung by a scorpion. After a few seconds, Desdemona's head turned to the side, and I could have sworn she was staring right at me, as though she could actually *see* me standing in Vesper's mindscape.

"You have to let go of your fear, Kyrion," my mother said again, still staring at me. "Otherwise, you'll drown in the darkness and never embrace the light."

In the doorway, my younger self frowned and glanced in this direction, although I got the sense that he couldn't see me and was only viewing the rest of the garden as it had been that day. "Who are you talking to?"

Desdemona turned back to him, a soft smile on her face. "You'll see one day. Now, help me get these flowers inside. Your father will be home soon, and I want to brighten up the library for him . . ."

The memory flickered and faded away, and the door slowly swung shut. I stood there, rooted to the floor, staring at the House Caldaren sigil. One by one, the stars winked with light, then the arrow itself. I blinked, and the light vanished.

Why had Vesper's mindscape shown me this memory? And why had my mother seemed to realize exactly what was going on? Had Desdemona *known* I would be standing in this very spot one day, thinking about her truebond with my father?

Something jabbed into my neck, and hot chemicals zipped through my veins. Vesper's mindscape melted away, replaced by muttering voices.

Once again, my eyes snapped open, and Pollux's face swam into view.

The former Hammer lightly slapped my cheek, reigniting the pain in my jaw from where he had punched me earlier. "Welcome back, Arrow."

I growled and surged forward . . . but I couldn't move.

My body was in an upright position, with my back against a rough rock wall and my arms down and slightly out to my sides. Plasticuffs anchored my neck and wrists to the wall, and gray bricks had been stacked over my chest and most of my legs, as though I was being entombed.

I surged forward again, but the solid bricks didn't move. I reached for my psion power, intending to smash the stones to pieces with my telekinesis, but once again, I couldn't quite get a grip on my abilities.

"It's no use struggling," Pollux said. "I walled you up myself. It's an old Hammer trick. Interrogate your enemy and slowly brick him up in a wall if he doesn't cooperate. Most folks scoff at first, but by the time you start covering their faces and cutting off their air, they are all too happy to cooperate."

He grinned and slapped my cheek again. "Lucky for you, Esmina wants your pretty face out in the open. At least until your girlfriend shows up and gets a good look at you."

I swallowed a growl. The bricks over my arms, chest, and legs were heavy and solid, and I was too weak to break through them, so I stopped struggling and studied my surroundings.

I was anchored to a wall in an enormous underground

cavern. The wall curved to the left and the right, but the chamber in front of me was wide open. Thick stalagmites jutted up from the uneven ground, while even larger, thicker stalactites dropped down from the ceiling.

Soft white lights embedded in the ground, wall, and ceiling brought out the dark purple stones that glinted here and there among the dull gray rock. Permaglass stairs and walkways connected one level of the cavern to another, looking like icicle ramps that had frozen underground. The cavern was cool, bordering on chilly, and my breath frosted faintly in the air.

On the far side of the chamber, a permaglass bridge ran past an enormous waterfall that tumbled down the surrounding rocks. Several lights were trained on that area, and more purple stones glimmered along the waterfall's frothing edges, giving it a dark, amethyst tint.

In some ways, the area reminded me of the lunarium mine Vesper and I had toured on Tropics 33. But this space seemed abandoned, and a thick layer of dust coated everything, including the permaglass walkways, which were streaked with grime.

"What is this place?" I asked.

Footsteps clacked on the stone, and Esmina stepped into view beside Pollux. "It's the place where people come to die, Kyrion."

She gestured to the side. Just beyond a permaglass barrier, the cavern floor abruptly dropped away, plummeting into a steep chasm lined with razor-sharp rocks at the bottom.

"I would tell you to watch your step, but you can't go anywhere, can you?" Esmina let out a merry laugh that echoed around the cavern, bounced off the rocks, and slapped me across the face.

"Why are you doing this? What do you want with me?"

"I don't want anything from *you*, Kyrion. I simply realized I was going about things the wrong way. It happens from time to time, even when you're a precog and can see exactly how everyone is going to act and react."

Pollux playfully poked her in the shoulder. "You owe me a hundred credits. I *told* you grabbing the Arrow and using him as leverage was the smartest play."

Esmina grumbled under her breath, but she pulled a tablet out of her pocket and hit a few buttons. An answering chime rang out from Pollux's tablet, and he tipped an imaginary hat to her.

A sick feeling flooded my stomach. "You kidnapped me to get Vesper to come here—"

Esmina waggled a finger, cutting me off. "Please. Save your breath, Kyrion. I already know *exactly* what you're going to say—that my plan won't work, that your precious Vesper will find some way to outsmart me, and blah, blah, blah, blah. Do you know what the problem with truebonded couples truly is?"

She answered her own question. "One of them *always* has a driving, undeniable compulsion to save the other, even if such a foolish, reckless action will just doom them both."

"Is that what Micah had? An undeniable compulsion to save you? Because that didn't work out so well for him."

Esmina retained her relaxed posture, but a muscle ticked in her jaw, betraying her anger. "Leland said Lord Aldrich and Lady Verona had been sharing stories about me. Well, let me tell you something that's *not* in the House Collier files."

She leaned forward, her eyes as cold and empty as green glass. "Micah was a fool for me, just like Vesper is a fool for you, Kyrion. And Vesper is going to die for you, just like Micah died for me."

Esmina stared at me a moment longer, then drew back and strolled away. Pollux slapped me across the face yet again, then followed her. The two of them rounded a corner and disappeared, although Esmina's words kept echoing in my ears.

She was right. I was nothing but bait, and Vesper was going to walk straight into the mercenaries' trap.

# TWENTY-EIGHT

## VESPER

The Hammers were busy getting ready to go after Esmina and Pollux, while the House Collier guards and servants were still assessing the damage and cleaning up the mess from the mercenaries' attack. Everyone was distracted, and it was surprisingly easy for Zane and me to sneak into the transport garage. I hot-wired a hoverbike, which he insisted on driving. My big brother had some deep-seated control issues.

Gossipcasters had already gathered at the end of the drawbridge, so Zane steered the hoverbike into the woods and skirted around the cameras. No one saw us, and we went down the mountain and made it back to the city without any problems.

Zane maneuvered the bike into an alley, then stopped. "Now what? Do you know where you're really supposed to meet Esmina? Because she's obviously not going to be at the geotagged location she gave to the Colliers."

I might have been forced to let Zane come with me, but this was the moment when things got serious, and I had to decide whether to trust my brother—or not.

But once again, I didn't have a choice. Not when Kyrion's life was in danger. And maybe it was weird, but part of me *wanted* to trust Zane. I wanted to believe in someone and be proven right for once in my life, instead of Nerezza always proving me wrong.

"You're right. The meeting location Esmina sent the Colliers is a distraction, a way to get rid of the Hammers, so she can get what she really wants." I gestured at the weapon slung across Zane's back. "Esmina has been after the Techwave cannon all along, so I'm going to give it to her."

Zane's eyebrows shot up. "Earlier in Aldrich's library, you said you didn't know how to fix the cannon."

"I still don't know how to fix it, not exactly, but I have to try—or Kyrion is dead."

We left the House Collier hoverbike in the alley. This time, I took the lead, and we moved from one street to another until we reached the antiques emporium. I skirted around the emerald-green dome, and a few minutes later, we reached the street where Asterin's workshop was located.

No guards were posted outside, but the door was cracked open.

Zane noticed it too, and we both drew our stormswords. His blade shimmered like an icy moon, while mine blazed with dark blue fire. Zane nodded at me, and I yanked the door back so he could rush into the workshop. I barreled in behind him into the dark space—

A light snapped on. Zane and I both spun in that direction. A shadowy figure was sitting at a table, a silver blaster glinting in their hand.

Zane stepped in front of me and lifted his sword. "Who are you?"

The figure got to their feet and stepped into the light. Asterin grinned at Zane, her silver eyes bright and her blaster leveled at his chest. "I'm really starting to enjoy meeting like this."

"You just want to shoot me," he countered.

"Absolutely," she agreed.

The two of them stared at each other for several long, tense seconds. Then Asterin huffed out a breath and lowered her blaster.

"Maybe one day I will actually get to shoot you," she said.

Zane's head tilted to the side, and a bit of magic sparked in his eyes. "Perhaps you will. But today is not that day."

"What are you doing here?" I asked.

Asterin shrugged. "I spotted you climbing out of your suite. I knew you would come here to try to figure out how to fix the Techwave cannon, and I want to help."

"But what about your mother and stepfather?"

"Verona and Aldrich are wrong to shut you out, Vesper. Esmina is obviously setting a trap for the Hammers, even if Siya and Rigel are too stubborn to admit it." Asterin's face softened. "Besides, I know how much you care about Kyrion, and not just because of the truebond."

She was right. Ever since Kyrion had been taken, I hadn't given the bond one blasted thought. His magic and the bond and our combined power didn't matter to me. Not really. No, I loved Kyrion Caldaren for *himself*—for the caring, considerate person he was, for all the ways he listened, supported, and comforted me when I needed it most.

Deep down, I had known the truth for a while, but I hadn't wanted to admit it. I hadn't wanted to give Kyrion the ability to break my heart the way Nerezza had so many times in the past. For as much as I trusted Kyrion, I hadn't trusted *myself*.

Nerezza had abandoned me, and Beatrice had ignored me. If my own mother and grandmother wouldn't—or couldn't—love me, then who in the galaxy ever would? But over the past few days, I'd realized loving someone was a choice. I wasn't being influenced by the truebond. Not in the slightest. Even if the bond and our psion power and all the rest of it vanished,

I would still feel the exact same way about Kyrion. It was a choice—my true choice—to love Kyrion, and it was the easiest decision I'd ever made.

Zane's eyes narrowed, as if he could hear my whispered thoughts with his telepathy. "You actually love the broody bastard, don't you?"

"With all my heart."

I should have told Kyrion that I loved him and wanted to be with him no matter what dangers the galaxy threw at us. But once again, all my old issues with Nerezza—and my new ones with the Zimmers—had held me back. Well, no more. I was going to save Kyrion, and then I was going to tell him exactly how I felt.

But first, I had to give Esmina what she wanted, so I turned to Zane. "Hand over the Techwave cannon."

"You've only been my sister for a few weeks, and you're already making demands of me? Typical for a Zimmer." Zane let out a long, loud, dramatic sigh, but my brother's lips quirked up into a smile as he slid the cannon off his back and passed it over to me.

Strangely enough, I was smiling too.

My mind and especially my heart were still churning with worry, dread, and fear about everything that could go wrong. The Colliers realizing what I was doing. Siya, Rigel, and the other Hammers storming into the workshop. Esmina growing impatient and killing Kyrion before I figured out how to fix the cannon.

But worries were as useless as wishes, as Liesl used to say, so I laid the weapon on a holoscreen. I also fished Kyrion's stormsword out of my duffel bag and set it on another table. Then I got to work.

The first thing I did was set an alarm on my tablet, counting down the time until Esmina's deadline. I had roughly three hours to fix the Techwave cannon and figure out how to defeat the mercenaries.

No pressure.

I pulled up all the 3D scans of the cannon I'd made over the past few weeks, along with the failed simulations Wendell and I had run earlier today. Asterin pulled up her own notes and experiments on another holoscreen, but no matter what calculations we tried, the simulations kept failing, and the cannon kept overheating.

Zane leaned his hip against another table, swiping through holograms. Asterin had reluctantly given him access to the House Collier archives, and he was studying images and blueprints of the Stardrop Falls mining museum.

"This place is a death trap," he grumbled. "Esmina and Pollux could have multiple squads of mercenaries tucked away on the various levels, or even hiding in the bloody gift shop, and we won't know until we stumble right into the middle of them."

I rubbed my aching head, staring at yet another failed simulation. "You're not helping."

"Just making an observation. I don't want the two of you to blame me later for not adequately mentioning the absurd amount of danger we are putting ourselves in."

"Oh, I'm sure we'll have plenty of other reasons to blame you," Asterin muttered, swiping through her own failed simulation at another table.

Zane rolled his eyes, but he went back to plotting how we could best slip into the museum. I focused on the cannon again.

Back on the *Dream World*, I had fixed the Techwave cannon enough so that it would fire, so long as the user popped in a new solar magazine on a regular basis. Rigel had confiscated that cannon from my suite, but he, Siya, and the Colliers didn't know about the solar magazines, so that cannon wouldn't work for more than a few blasts.

Asterin and I still thought sapphsidian was the key to stabilizing the cannon, so I rummaged through my duffel bag and pulled out the chunk of sapphsidian I'd taken from the dead Serpens Corp mercenary during the attack on the mineral exchange. I hadn't had any sapphsidian to work with on the *Dream World*, so I hadn't been able to properly test my theory.

I handed the chunk of sapphsidian to Asterin, who used a laser cutter to slice it into smaller, usable pieces. Once that was done, I threaded a few tiny bits of sapphsidian onto the solar wiring in the cannon's magazine. I ran one simulation after another, adding different amounts of sapphsidian to the lunarium and solar wiring, but nothing worked, and the cannon kept overheating.

Frustrated, I swiped away the latest failed simulation and started pacing through the workshop.

"Our father does the same thing whenever he runs up against a tricky problem in his lab," Zane said. "Some of the similarities between the two of you are rather uncanny."

I shot him an aggravated look and kept pacing.

"On the bright side, if we fail to rescue Kyrion, I'm calling dibs on his stormsword," Zane said, tracing his finger along the blade, which was still lying on a table. "I've always wanted a second weapon."

A snarl rose in my throat, but before I could tell him to stop coveting Kyrion's sword, Zane turned the blade to the side. The bright workshop lights hit the large arrow-shaped sapphsidian jewel in the hilt, making it wink at me like a mocking eye.

My own eyes narrowed, and my gaze darted over to the stormsword belted to Zane's waist. It too featured sapphsidian jewels, just like my own sword did.

"Give me that." I snatched Kyrion's sword away from Zane, then held out my other hand. "And your sword too."

Zane grumbled, but he passed me his weapon. I laid all three stormswords on a holoscreen and made 3D scans of them. Then I studied the resulting holograms, which listed the parts, pieces, and components of the three weapons. The swords were all slightly different shapes and sizes, but they all had one thing in common: the ratio of sapphsidian to lunarium was *exactly* the same.

Of course. I could have smacked myself for not seeing it sooner. I'd literally been carrying the answer around on my belt this whole time.

"Vesper?" Asterin asked. "What have you figured out?"

"I'm not sure yet," I replied in a distracted voice.

I was dimly aware of Asterin coming over to stand beside me, with Zane hovering on my other side. I quickly assembled a new magazine, adding what I thought was the correct amount of sapphsidian to the lunarium and solar wiring. Now came the moment of truth.

I laid the magazine on the holoscreen, hit some buttons, and ran the same simulation I'd performed a dozen times before.

*Testing . . . testing . . . testing . . .*

The holoscreen repeated the words over and over again. I clutched the edge of the table, my breath stuck in my throat.

"How long is this going to take?" Zane asked.

"Shh!" Asterin replied.

Zane shot her a dirty look, but he fell silent. The holoscreen flickered once, twice, three times . . .

*Testing complete. Simulation successful. Predicted rate of success is 98.3 percent.*

I pumped my fist in the air in triumph.

"You did it," Asterin whispered. "You figured out how to fix the cannon. Way to go, Vesper!"

She held her hand up, and I gave her a high five. But my triumph quickly faded away, and my arm plummeted to my side. "It's just a simulation. It would still need to be rigorously tested before the cannon could be mass-produced."

"But?" Zane asked.

I blew out a breath. "But we still don't know what Esmina and Pollux want with the weapon."

"You mean besides destroying House Collier?" Asterin muttered.

"Tearing down House Collier and replacing it with her own House is one of Esmina's goals, but I still feel like something else is going on. Like there's some *other* player in this game we don't know about. Someone had to tell Esmina about the cannon in the first place."

Zane leaned an elbow down on the table. "Like the Techwave? Perhaps Esmina and Pollux are working for General Orion Ocnus. I'm sure he'd love to get his hands on you."

Asterin shook her head. "If the Techwave were involved, General Ocnus would have sent Black Scarabs to attack the estate, just like he did to my lunarium mine on Tropics 33. Not common mercenaries."

"There was nothing *common* about those mercenaries," Zane replied. "They were some of the best fighters I've ever seen. If Esmina and Pollux are working for someone, that person must have credits to burn, especially given all the attacks the mercs have launched over the last few days."

His words made me think back over everything that had happened. Esmina and Pollux had tried to kidnap me on Tropics 44, but Kyrion had stopped them. Two days later, they broke into the Collier mineral exchange to steal gemstones to try to fix the Techwave cannon themselves. Trying to capture me again in the shipping yard had been a last-minute addition after I'd destroyed their transport. And finally, earlier today, the mercenaries had stormed the Collier estate with the goal of kidnapping Kyrion, to make me fix the cannon and deliver it to them, and they had succeeded.

Those were all logical, rational steps—for someone who

knew I might be able to fix the weapon. But Asterin was right too. There had been no sign of Black Scarabs, and I couldn't imagine General Ocnus sending anyone but his own troops after Kyrion and me.

Who else knew the Techwave cannons were faulty? Who else would want to use the weapons against their enemies? I felt like the answer was right in front of me, but I couldn't quite see it—and I desperately needed to see it if I had any chance of saving Kyrion.

My hands moved over the stormswords, sliding the weapons back and forth in time to my turbulent thoughts. I found myself studying Zane's sword, which featured tiny *Z*s representing House Zimmer. The same sigil adorned the pommel of my own sword.

I traced the symbol with my index finger, my skin sinking into the grooves in the silver. For months, I'd thought the sigil was an *N* and an unfortunate reminder that Nerezza was my mother, but I supposed the hard truth was the symbol represented both halves of my family, for better or worse.

"Vesper?" Asterin asked. "What are you going to do?"

I dropped my hand from my sword. "No idea. I fixed the cannon to have something to bargain with, but I can't just hand it over to Esmina and Pollux."

"Not even to save Kyrion?" Zane asked.

Tears pricked my eyes, and my heart squeezed tight. "No, not even to save Kyrion. Esmina and Pollux will use the weapon to hurt—*kill*—more innocent people. We all saw what they did at the estate with standard weapons. If Esmina and Pollux give the Techwave cannons to their men, there will be no stopping them."

A tense silence dropped over the workshop as we all contemplated that horrible possibility.

Someone cleared their throat. "Perhaps I can be of some assistance."

Asterin drew the blaster from her belt, while Zane and I grabbed our stormswords. We all whirled around, weapons up.

Wendell froze, his eyes wide as he looked at first one weapon, then another.

I hissed out a breath, lowered my sword, and set it back down on the table. "How did you find us?"

Zane cursed and glanced down at his jacket. "You planted a tracker in one of my buttons? Again?"

Wendell bobbed his head. "I thought it prudent with everything that was going on."

Zane let out a rueful laugh, then glanced over at me. "Our father likes to keep an eye on things, even if that means planting his own spy gadgets on family members."

"I wouldn't have to resort to such extreme measures if my children weren't so determined to always sprint headlong into danger," Wendell quipped.

*My children.* He said the words naturally, without hesitation, as if he'd known he had two children his entire life. My heart squeezed. I'd come so close to losing Wendell when the mercenary had tried to kill him at the estate . . .

Wait. *Why* had the mercenary tried to kill Wendell? He was a well-regarded spelltech. If anything, the merc should have tried to kidnap Wendell in the hope that he might be able to fix the Techwave cannon in case I couldn't. But the merc had said he would get a bonus for taking out Wendell, so who would want my father dead? And why now?

I chewed my lip and tapped my fingers on the edge of the table hard enough to make my stormsword vibrate with the motion. The sigil on the pommel glinted in the light, while the sapphsidian eyes in the hilt winked at me . . .

I froze, my fingers stuttering to a halt, although a sick realization bloomed in my mind. I'd been right before. There *was* another player in this deadly game. Of course. I should have realized who it was before. Maybe I would have if I hadn't been so busy trying to escape Esmina's traps.

A bitter laugh spewed from my lips. Then another one . . . then another one . . . The loud, harsh sounds startled Asterin, Zane, and Wendell, who all exchanged worried glances.

"Vesper?" Wendell asked. "What's wrong?"

My laughter finally died down. I opened my mouth to tell him what I'd figured out, but at the last second, I clamped my lips shut. The information would only hurt his feelings, which was the last thing I wanted to do right now.

"Everything's wrong," I muttered.

"Well, I'm here now," Wendell said in a gentle voice. "Perhaps we can figure out a solution together. How can I help?"

Once again, my heart squeezed at his words, but I hesitated. I still wasn't sure if I could fully trust Zane and Wendell, especially with a weapon that could so greatly benefit House Zimmer, but Zane had already seen me fix the cannon, and Wendell was bound to figure out how to do the same thing. So I showed Wendell the lunarium and solar wiring inside the magazine and explained how adding the right amount of sapphsidian was the key to stabilizing the cannon's power source.

His face brightened. "Of course! I should have thought of that myself, especially given all the stormswords I've examined over the years."

"But now I have another problem. I can't give the cannon to Esmina and Pollux."

Or their partner in crime, although I didn't mention that. I needed some time to think about the person pulling the mercenaries' strings—and figure out how I could use the information to my advantage.

Wendell's gaze flicked over to the cannon, then up to the holograms still hovering in the air. "You're wrong, Vesper. You *can* give the cannon to Esmina and Pollux."

"What do you mean?"

He stabbed his finger at my last simulation, the one that had finally been successful. "You give the weapon to them—and then you take it away."

Wendell swiped his fingers through the hologram, removing the sapphsidian pieces and leaving behind the original magazine—the one that would only fire a few times before it overheated and fried the cannon.

"You could even add a little something extra to the cannon." He tapped some keys, running another simulation that had a very interesting result.

Asterin nodded. "That's brilliant."

Wendell shrugged. "I have my moments. If Vesper thinks it will work? It is her design."

"Asterin's right," I replied. "It's brilliant."

A sly grin spread across my father's face, and I found myself grinning back at him.

"I hate to break up the father-daughter bonding moment, but we have another problem," Zane said. "Esmina and Pollux will let Vesper walk right into the mining museum, but they won't be so kind to Asterin and me. The mercs will shoot us on sight."

Wendell squared his shoulders. "I'm coming too."

"*No*," Zane and I replied in unison.

The two of us looked at each other, then Zane focused on Wendell. "You've done your part, Father," he said. "Fixing things is what you do best. Well, fighting is what I do best, so leave it to me."

After a few seconds, Wendell gave a reluctant nod.

"Zane is right," Asterin chimed in. "We need to find some way to sneak into the museum, but how? The mercenaries are sure to have the latest scanners and equipment."

"Actually, I have an idea about that." Zane pulled up his jacket and shirtsleeve, revealing a wide silver band circling his left wrist.

My eyes narrowed. "Is that Jorge Rojillo's temperature-shielding wristwatch? How did you get one of those?"

"I stole it," Zane replied in a cheerful voice. "Lord Jorge tossed it across his workshop in a fit of temper the night of the summer solstice, and I thought it might come in handy."

Asterin frowned. "How will climate-control tech help us sneak past the mercenaries?"

Zane grinned at her. "I'm glad you asked, although you just answered your own question."

Asterin and Wendell exchanged confused looks, but the longer I stared at the wristwatch, the more my mind started to churn. Suddenly, I could see *exactly* what Zane was talking about.

"The watch lets the wearer set the ambient air to their preferred temperature," I said. "But if you set it to the *actual* air temperature, then a scanner would just read you as a blank space—not a person with body heat that would ping thermal imaging."

Zane shot his thumb and forefinger at me. "Exactly."

Grudging admiration filled me. "You really are quite clever."

"I have my moments." Zane repeated his father's words, then pointed at another table. "And I also spy another one of Lord Jorge's devices right over there. Your handiwork, I presume, my lady?"

"Actually, it was a team effort," Asterin replied. "I made the watch, but Vesper modified and improved it. Here, let me show you."

She strapped the watch around her wrist, then turned the knob on the side, making sparks of electricity zing out of the device. Zane jerked back to keep his eyebrows from getting singed off. He scowled at Asterin, who gave him an innocent smile in return.

*Beep-beep.*

An alarm blared out of my tablet, startling us all.

I shut it off, although my stomach quickly tied itself into worried knots. "We have an hour to get to the museum."

Asterin nodded. "Then we need to gear up."

She started grabbing blasters and other weapons from the racks on the walls. Zane and Wendell helped her, but I stayed where I was. My gaze dropped to Kyrion's stormsword, and I traced my fingers over the large sapphsidian arrow embedded in the silver hilt.

"I'm going to save you," I whispered.

Maybe it was my imagination, but the arrow glittered brightly for a moment, almost as if Kyrion could hear me through our bond. I added his sword to my weapons belt, then headed over to help the others get ready.

# TWENTY-NINE

## KYRION

The minutes ticked by and turned into an hour, then two, then three.

Esmina and Pollux moved through the cavern, along with their mercenaries. In the back of the chamber, the mercs had set up a mobile command center, complete with open crates full of blasters, cannons, and other weapons and portable holoscreens that showed security feeds of the outside of Stardrop Falls, the abandoned mining museum. This wasn't a secret base so much as it was a staging area. Despite their heavy losses at the estate, Esmina and Pollux still had more than enough men to capture Vesper, and they were obviously preparing to attack the Colliers again.

My gut clenched with dread. I reached out through the bond as I'd done countless times over the past few hours, but once again, I couldn't sense Vesper. Whatever chemicals Esmina had given me were still disrupting our connection, which meant I couldn't warn Vesper about just how many mercenaries were in the cavern. Of course, Vesper would know she was walking into a trap, but she would come here anyway, just as I would have come for her even if she'd been on the other side of the galaxy.

But the most curious thing was that the mercs weren't alone in their underground base. Every few minutes, Esmina would round a corner, disappear into another section of the cavern, and speak to someone in a low voice. Even more curious, the other voice sounded familiar, as though I had heard it somewhere before. I was tilting my head to the side, trying to listen to their latest conversation, when Pollux strutted over to me.

"Not so tough bricked up in a wall, huh, Arrow?"

I surged forward, but the stones shellacked over my chest held me fast. "Let me out of this rock, and I'll show you *exactly* how tough I am."

Pollux smirked. "As fun as it would be to beat you to death with my hammers, Esmina has other plans."

"What did she do to me? Why can't I feel my truebond with Vesper?"

Pollux tapped his finger on the plasticuff around my neck. "This cuff delivers a low dose of chemicals to your body through your skin. That's why you can't use your precious bond. The Serpens Corp scientists have been working on how to block psionic powers for a long time, and they finally concocted just the right formula."

A frustrated growl rose in my throat. The cuff scraped against my neck, and an oily sensation oozed against my skin. Pollux was telling the truth. The cuff really was dosing me with chemicals, and I had no way to remove it.

Pollux shook his head. "It's a shame. A warrior like you shackled to someone so weak."

"Vesper is not *weak*. She's the smartest, strongest person I know, and she's going to help me kill you and Esmina and all your men."

Pollux laughed and poked his finger into the cuff, zapping

me with another dose of chemicals. "Keep telling yourself that, pal. Esmina's seen it all play out with her precognition, and you and Vesper are both going to die screaming in this cavern."

Esmina stepped back into view and went over to speak to one of the mercs, who showed her something on his tablet. Esmina studied the device, and psion power surged off her like a tidal wave—so much *power*. Even with the chemicals dampening my own abilities, I could still feel exactly how strong she was.

I'd always thought Callus Holloway was the strongest psion I'd ever encountered. Well, Esmina was just as powerful—perhaps even more so, since her power was her own to command and not constantly stolen from other people like Holloway's was.

"You're a smart guy," I said, focusing on Pollux again. "You know Esmina will eventually betray you."

I didn't believe for one second that I could sway Pollux to my side, but perhaps I could plant a small seed of doubt in his mind. Something that might make him hesitant later, even if it was only for a second. Holloway had waged similar psychological warfare on my parents for years, and right now, this was the only battle I could fight.

"Esmina *will* betray you," I repeated. "As soon as you're not useful anymore, she'll find someone else to take your place. Someone stronger, faster, younger, more powerful."

Pollux shrugged. "Maybe she will, maybe she won't. We've been together a long time, Esmina and me. We've been through a lot of shit together, and in some ways, we're connected just as tightly as a truebonded couple."

He glanced over at her, admiration filling his face. Pollux might be a stone-cold killer, the same as me, but he really did care about his partner. I just had to figure out how to use that concern against him, the way Holloway had used my parents' love against them.

Pollux faced me again. "Esmina and I built Serpens Corp out

of *nothing*, taking any dumb, dangerous job that came our way. As soon as she heard about the Techwave's new hand cannon, Esmina knew it could change everything for us. And thanks to her planning and precognition, we're about to get everything we've ever wanted."

"What *do* you want?"

"First, we're going to finish tearing down House Collier. Once that happens, the other major Houses will have no choice but to officially recognize Serpens Corp as a new House." Pollux's shoulders squared, and his chest puffed up with pride. "It might take a few years, but eventually, Esmina and I will be running things on Sygnustern, and the rest of the Erzton will finally bow down to us."

"So you want revenge," I said. "How typical."

Pollux's nostrils flared with anger. "Not revenge—*retribution.* When Esmina and I decided to free ourselves from the shackles of our truebonds, we did something the Erzton nobles didn't approve of, something they were too bloody *weak* to do, and they exiled us for it. Well, fuck them and their stupid rules. Truebonds aren't these wonderful, magical things the Erztonians make them out to be. House Collier and everyone who supported them is going to pay for what they did to me and Esmina all those years ago, more than they ever dreamed."

A fervent light gleamed in his eyes. He truly believed every word he said, and he wanted to burn House Collier to ashes.

"Do you know how many people end up with truebonded partners who hurt them? Abuse them in terrible ways?" Pollux's face darkened with fury. "When my sister Derissa and I were in a transport crash, we were trapped in the wreckage, and we were both unlucky enough to bond with two other survivors. I got saddled with a sickly old woman named Lorna, while Derissa was bonded with a guy our age named Haron. Derissa thought forming the bond was true love, destiny, and all that other shit, so she married him a few months later."

"What happened?"

Even more fury darkened Pollux's face. "Haron beat my sister—and worse. Derissa hid it from me for a long time, but eventually, I figured out what was going on."

"And you killed him for it."

"Damn right I did," Pollux snarled. "Caved his skull in with one of my hammers. I didn't even give Haron a chance to beg for his miserable life."

"But killing him also killed your sister," I guessed.

"I told Derissa everything Esmina had discovered about truebonds, and I even showed her how to take her husband's power for her own, just like I had taken Lorna's power. I gave my sister a chance *and* a choice, which was more than Haron and their bloody truebond ever did." Pollux's nostrils flared with disgust. "But she didn't want to do it. Despite all the times Haron had hit and burned and kicked her, Derissa still loved the cruel bastard, and she didn't want to go on without him. She just gave up, shriveled up, and died like a cut flower."

Even more fury blasted off him and scorched up against my telempathy, despite the chemicals still dampening my abilities. I understood his fury. I'd felt the same way when I'd realized what Holloway was doing to my parents, and just like Pollux, I'd been helpless to save my family.

"Nothing in the galaxy is perfect, especially not a bloody truebond," Pollux continued. "I'm going to teach House Collier that very painful lesson, and they're going to suffer just as much as my sister did."

He glared at me a moment longer, then stalked over to the mobile command center. Pollux's words echoed in my mind, and I thought of my parents again. He was right. Truebonds weren't perfect, just as the people involved in them weren't perfect.

When I'd first formed a truebond with Vesper, I'd been worried she would get herself killed and thus kill me too. Later

I'd been worried Holloway would capture us both and turn us into his psionic batteries. Ever since we'd escaped from Crownpoint, I'd been worried about protecting Vesper from Zane, the other Arrows, and the bounty hunters. And now I was worried that I'd failed her by getting captured.

Determination surged through my body, and my inner monster roared in response. Vesper was coming here, and I was going to do everything in my power to help her, starting with figuring out how to escape my brick-and-plasticuff prison.

I jerked my arms, but the cuffs remained tight against my wrists, as did the one around my neck. I growled and flexed my fingers, trying again and again.

Something scraped up against my skin. What was that?

I glanced down. A tiny bit of stone was sticking out of the cavern wall beside my left wrist. Hope surged inside me, and I stretched my fingers out as far as they would go. I couldn't quite grab the stone, but it bumped up against my cuff. I shoved my wrist forward, then started moving it up and down as much and as fast as I could. If I could use the stone to saw through the plasticuff, perhaps I could free myself from the rest of my prison—

"She's here!" one of the mercs called out, and everyone in the cavern snapped to attention. "Vesper Quill is here!"

He swiped his fingers across a portable holoscreen, and a hologram popped into the air. The feed showed Vesper standing on a street outside a pair of closed, locked doors. Vesper looked up at the security camera and hefted the object in her hands—the Techwave cannon.

Esmina examined the hologram. "Let our guest inside, and escort her down here."

The merc nodded and hurried away, as did several others.

Esmina turned to Pollux. "Anyone else on the feeds?"

Pollux swiped through several more security feeds on his own tablet, then shook his head. "No one is showing up, and

I'm not getting any thermal readings on the sensors. Looks like she came alone."

Esmina tilted her head to the side, and her green eyes glowed with power.

"Something wrong?" Pollux asked.

The power faded from Esmina's eyes, and she shook her head. "Too soon to tell. But have everyone on high alert. Vesper probably has a few tricks up her sleeve."

Pollux nodded and started barking orders at the other mercenaries. Most of the mercs spread out across the cavern, although several climbed a set of permaglass stairs to the second level. Every merc was armed with either a blaster or a hand cannon.

More frustration surged through me. Vesper was walking straight into a trap, and there was nothing I could do to help her.

One minute passed, then two, then three. A tense silence dropped over the cavern. None of the mercenaries moved or spoke, and the only noise was the steady cascade of the waterfall.

Then, in the distance, footsteps scraped across the stone, quickly growing louder and closer.

Once again, I tried to reach out with my psion power, and once again, I couldn't get a grip on it. The chemicals were still dampening my abilities, and I needed to get out of these cuffs if I had any chance of helping Vesper. So I redoubled my efforts, rubbing the plasticuff on my left wrist up against that jagged bit of stone over and over again . . .

Vesper entered the cavern, trailed by a couple of mercenaries. She was carrying the Techwave cannon in her arms, and her stormsword dangled off her belt, along with my sword.

She glanced around, looking at Esmina and Pollux standing in the middle of the open space, with their mercenaries arrayed behind them and more enemies stationed on the second level.

Finally, Vesper's gaze met mine. Her eyes blazed with determination, the silver flecks burning like pinpoint stars in her dark blue irises. For a moment, I could feel her through the bond, and I stared back at her, trying to tell her so many things just with the force of my gaze.

Vesper stared at me a heartbeat longer, then strode forward and stopped in the center of the cavern.

"I see you fixed my hand cannon," Esmina purred. "Excellent! Pollux was right. Taking Kyrion properly motivated you."

Vesper hefted the cannon a little higher in her arms. "I don't need any motivation to kill you."

"It's nothing personal. And it's certainly not *my* fault *you're* so weak in your psion power. Jealousy does not become you." Esmina clucked her tongue in mock sympathy, and Vesper flinched.

*I am* not *a weak link.* Vesper had said that after our skirmish with the Hammers in the antiques emporium, but for the first time, I realized just how much Esmina had made Vesper doubt her own abilities. Once again, I cursed the cuff around my neck, because if I could have used my telepathy and telempathy, I would have told Vesper *exactly* how strong she was and let her feel every ounce of my unwavering belief in her.

Esmina stepped forward and held her hand out. "Give me the cannon."

She didn't say anything about letting us go, and I knew she wouldn't. So did Vesper, judging by the way her jaw clenched.

"Nah, I'm going to hold on to the cannon for now," Vesper said. "After all, I haven't met your boss yet, and I'm just *dying* to talk to them."

Boss? What boss? Who were the mercenaries working for?

Esmina's hand plummeted to her side. "I don't know what you're talking about."

"Sure you do," Vesper replied. "The person who told you about the Techwave cannon and hired you to come after me in the first place. Your boss is here, right now, in this very cavern. They wouldn't leave such an important moment to chance, especially since you haven't been very successful in carrying out your missions so far."

Esmina stiffened, and for the first time, a bit of uncertainty flickered across her face.

"I know you're here," Vesper called out, her voice ringing through the cavern. "So you might as well come out and face me, instead of hiding like the coward you are."

For several seconds, nothing happened. Then more footsteps scraped against the stone. A figure rounded one of the stalagmites and stepped into view. A long dark blue cloak covered their head, along with the rest of their body, and I couldn't tell if it was a man or a woman.

"Come on," Vesper called out again, her voice even more mocking than before. "There's no need to hide any longer."

The figure huffed in annoyance, then tossed back the hood of their cloak, revealing familiar features—long dark brown hair, pale skin, and eyes that were the same dark blue as Vesper's.

The mercenaries' boss was Nerezza Blackwell.

# THIRTY

## VESPER

"Hello, Mother," I drawled, my voice as cold as the air wafting through the cavern.

Nerezza strode forward and stopped beside Esmina, who looked back and forth between us. I had surprised the precog by figuring out she was working for my mother, but it hadn't been too difficult. Nerezza craved power more than anything else, and getting her hands on the Techwave cannon was one way to improve her own position.

"I figured it was you."

Nerezza arched an eyebrow. "How?"

I gestured at Esmina and Pollux. "Because you always send other people to do your dirty work."

Nerezza held her arms out wide. "I'm right here in the thick of things, doing my own dirty work."

"Sure," I replied. "*After* the actual hard, bloody work is done, like letting the mercenaries attack the Collier estate instead of doing it yourself."

Esmina and Pollux looked at each other. My mother ignored

the mercenaries, so she didn't see the acknowledgment flicker across their faces.

"I've been wondering where you slithered off to after the Regal midnight ball. I just didn't think you'd wind up on Sygnustern."

A smile split Nerezza's mouth. "What can I say? I have friends across the galaxy."

"I think you mean marks instead of friends. You told me all about your social engineering talent, remember?"

"Social engineering?" Pollux asked.

"Oh, yes. My mother is quite proud of her little magic trick. How she can figure out *exactly* how to manipulate someone to get what she wants."

I looked at Esmina. "It's just another form of our seer magic, and my mother is a master at it. Even you, with all your precognition, didn't realize what she was truly doing, did you? How she was subtly moving you around like a pawn to further her own goals." I clucked my tongue in mock sympathy just as she had earlier. "Now who's the weak link?"

Esmina's face remained smooth, but her eyes glittered with anger. I didn't know what Nerezza had promised her, but she'd fallen for at least some of my mother's lies, just as so many other people had.

I turned my attention back to Nerezza. "After you fled from the Imperium, I'm guessing you went straight to General Ocnus. You pretty much had to, after I outed you as being a Techwave spy."

Nerezza's lips pressed into a thin, angry line. That was her only visible reaction, but I didn't need Kyrion's telempathy to realize how much she hated me for ruining her position in Regal society.

My own mother hated me.

The knowledge stabbed deep into my chest, and for a moment, I couldn't breathe. Even now, after all the horrible things

Nerezza had done, a sliver of my heart still hoped she might have a shred of concern for me, that I might be the one person she cared about, in her own diabolical way.

But my mother had never cared about me, and she never would, and I might as well have wished for a Frozon moon to plummet out of the sky and drop into my lap. I drew in a breath, steadying myself. The hurt didn't fade from my heart, but I could bear it now.

"I bet General Ocnus didn't like you spying on him for Callus Holloway, but I'm guessing you used your social engineering ability to talk your way out of trouble."

Nerezza's eyes crinkled with amusement. "People tend to listen to me."

"I'm guessing General Ocnus didn't listen so much as he commanded."

Nerezza's amusement vanished, and the dark, petty part of my heart thrummed with satisfaction at wiping the smug smirk off her face. "What do you think Ocnus commanded me to do?"

"Find me, capture me, and force me to fix the Techwave cannon." I hefted the weapon in my arms, and Pollux and the other mercenaries tensed. "This cannon. Without it, General Ocnus can't kill enough Arrows and soldiers to topple the Imperium."

I lowered the weapon, and Pollux and the mercenaries relaxed. Idiots. They should have killed me and pried the cannon out of my cold, dead hands the second I'd arrived, not let me stroll into their lair. But Esmina, Pollux, and Nerezza thought they'd already won, and they wanted to taunt me with their victory.

"How did you know it was me?" Nerezza asked, circling back to her original question. "That I hired the mercenaries?"

"I didn't know—at first. But Esmina and Pollux weren't interested in turning me over to Holloway to collect the bounty.

Then they broke into the House Collier mineral exchange. At first, I thought they just wanted to hurt the Colliers, but then I realized the mercenaries had stolen a variety of gemstones, as if they needed them for something specific. Like, say, figuring out how to fix a broken weapon. That's when I started thinking about the Techwave cannon."

Once again, I hefted the cannon in my arms, causing the mercs to flinch, but that was okay. The more they focused on me, the easier it would be for Asterin and Zane to slip into the cavern.

"But I didn't figure out you had hired Esmina and Pollux until one of the mercenaries tried to kill Wendell at the Collier estate. None of the mercs knew about my connection to Wendell, so there was no reason to target him. Unless someone had told Esmina and Pollux that Wendell was my father, and the only other person who knew that information was you. But I'm guessing you had your own reasons for wanting him dead."

"I never cared about sweet, foolish Wendell, and he was always just a means to an end," Nerezza said. "But since he was stupid enough to follow you to Sygnustern, I thought it would be amusing to kill him, especially since the Black Scarabs I sent to the summer solstice ball failed to do the job. Even Beatrice Zimmer would mourn the loss of her precious son."

"You still want revenge on Beatrice? You certainly know how to hold a grudge, Mother."

Nerezza jerked forward, her hands clenching into fists. "That bitch ruined everything! If not for her, I would have taken my rightful place in the Imperium long ago. *I* would have been the head of House Zimmer instead of having to waste my time climbing the Regal ladder. Beatrice cost me *years*, and she's going to pay for that."

Hate twisted her face, and rage boiled up off her like heat bursting out of an exploding sun. But just as quickly, the emotion dropped off Nerezza like rain rolling down a window, and she was calm once more. "But you're right about one thing, girl."

I flinched. Nerezza had never bothered to give me a real name, and she had always called me *girl* when I was young. I hated that blasted word almost as much as I despised her.

"I *did* engineer all of this," Nerezza continued, throwing her arms out wide, her voice swelling with pride. "It took longer and cost far more men and credits than I expected, but I have you and Kyrion *exactly* where I want you."

I looked over at Kyrion, who stared back at me. His expression was calm, and the belief shining in his eyes took my breath away. Even now, when we were surrounded by enemies, he still trusted me to save us both.

I faced Nerezza again. "Do your friends know about your master plan?"

Once again, Esmina and Pollux glanced at each other, then at Nerezza.

"And what is my master plan?" Nerezza drawled, a clear challenge in her voice.

"You're going to cut out all the middlemen."

She blinked, but that was her only reaction. Just like Esmina, my mother hadn't expected me to figure out her plot.

"You were *never* going to turn the Techwave cannon over to General Ocnus. You were always going to keep it for yourself." I waved the weapon around the cavern. "You've already hired an army of mercenaries. With them and the cannon, you can kill Ocnus and take control of the Techwave."

"Not just the Techwave," Nerezza said. "Callus Holloway was foolish enough to put a bounty on my head. He's going to pay for that, along with the rest of the Imperium."

My seer magic surged to life, and an image of Nerezza appeared, flickering in the air. The other Nerezza was wearing a glittering crown and sitting on a massive throne, looking every inch like the Regal queen she was so determined to be. No, not just a Regal queen but the empress of the whole blasted galaxy—and the weapon in my hands could help make that vision a reality.

"Enough," Esmina cut in, her voice brimming with impatience. "It won't be long before the Hammers find the surprise Pollux and I left at the geotagged location. We need to be in position to attack the Collier estate before then."

Pollux stepped forward. "Hand over the weapon, or I'll crush your hands with my hammers."

Nerezza smiled. "Yes, Vesper, do be a dear and hand over the weapon you so thoughtfully fixed for me."

Esmina and Pollux heard Nerezza's *me* as clearly as I had. The two mercenaries glanced at each other, engaging in some telepathic conversation I couldn't hear. But now that they knew the full scope of Nerezza's plan and how she tended to betray the people she was working for and with, they would turn on Nerezza as soon as possible, no matter how many credits she was paying for their supposed loyalty.

I was counting on it.

"Hand over the weapon," Pollux demanded again. "Right bloody *now*."

I stepped forward and held the cannon out to him—

"Stop!" Esmina barked out.

I froze. All the mercenaries aimed their weapons at me again, and Kyrion tensed inside his stone prison along the wall.

"What's wrong?" Pollux asked.

Esmina tilted her head to the side, the gold flecks in her gaze glowing with her seer magic. "It's a trap. Vesper's rigged the weapon in some way."

Nerezza looked at me, and magic flickered in her eyes as well, making them burn like blue torches. "She's right. My darling daughter is up to something."

Once again, I flinched. *Daughter*. I couldn't ever remember Nerezza calling me that, and my mother couldn't even be bothered to say the name I'd chosen for myself. White-hot fury shot through me, but I throttled the emotion.

"Fire it," Esmina ordered.

Pollux glanced at her. "What?"

Esmina kept staring at me. "Fire the cannon, Vesper. Or Kyrion dies."

Half of the mercenaries swung around, aiming their blasters at Kyrion. His eyes narrowed, and he glowered at first one enemy, then another.

I pointed the cannon at Esmina, who laughed. "Please. As much as you would love to shoot me, we both know you won't risk your precious Kyrion's life."

A couple of mercs stepped forward and took a little better aim at Kyrion, who growled in response. His entire body strained, but he couldn't break free of the bricks that encased him.

Kyrion stared at me again, then deliberately looked down and flexed the fingers on his left wrist, as though trying to tell me something.

I reached out with my magic and studied the stone around him, trying to find any weakness I could exploit. A faint silver light flared about ten feet away from Kyrion, near the bottom of the wall. My eyes narrowed. There. That might be something.

It *had* to be something. I only had one shot to make this work—literally—or Kyrion and I were dead.

"I could always shoot Nerezza." I swung the cannon in her direction. This time, I had the satisfaction of making her flinch.

"Don't be so dramatic, girl," Nerezza retorted.

She was so busy sneering at me that she didn't see the hopeful look that Esmina and Pollux exchanged. They wouldn't care if I shot Nerezza. I was tempted—so very *tempted*—but I released the trigger. Killing Nerezza wouldn't help Kyrion and me escape.

"Fine," I muttered. "What do you want me to shoot to prove the cannon works?"

Esmina waved her hand. "Whatever you like. We're far enough underground that no one is going to hear or feel the blast, if that was your hope. No one is coming to rescue you, Vesper."

I ignored her insult and turned around in a slow circle, as if pondering what to shoot. The mercenaries eyed me with obvious wariness, but I had a far more important target in mind. I finally stopped and aimed the cannon at the spot in the wall my magic had highlighted earlier.

"Fire it," Esmina commanded. "Right now. Or my men will drop you where you stand."

The time for talking and stalling was over. Now I just had to trust that Asterin and Zane were in position, so I took a little better aim and squeezed the trigger.

*Boom!*

A blast of green fire shot out from the cannon, zipped across the cavern, and slammed into the wall. Huge chunks of stone blasted apart, and dust billowed up into the air in a thick, hazy cloud. But even more curious—and alarming—was the fact that the green energy blast pulsed around the massive crater it had created, as though it was a fire feeding on more and more of the surrounding wall.

My gaze locked onto the tiny cracks that were slowly but surely creeping through the stone in all directions, including over to where Kyrion was still trapped. Bull's-eye.

"By the stars." Pollux breathed out the words in an awed voice. "That cannon does *exactly* what you claimed."

"I told you how powerful it is," Nerezza replied.

Pollux moved forward and held out his hand, an eager look on his face. Reluctantly, I passed the cannon over to him. The mercenary stepped away from me and ran his hands over the weapon.

"Lightweight, compact, easy to aim and carry." He let out a low whistle of appreciation. "It's an impressive weapon."

"Nerezza was right. Even weak links are good for something on occasion." Esmina sneered at me.

Once again, I bristled at her words. All my old doubts surfaced, whispering in my ears, but I ignored their idle chatter.

Nerezza snapped her fingers. Several of the mercs scurried forward, forming a loose circle around me.

"I gave you what you wanted," I protested, even though I had been expecting the betrayal.

"Yes, you did, but we both know I was never going to release you or Kyrion. But the problem is you are both far too valuable to kill, which means I need to find another use for you." Nerezza smiled. "Luckily for me, an opportunity has already presented itself."

Horror swept through my body. Maybe it was my seer magic, but I knew exactly what she was going to say.

"You were right at the midnight ball, Vesper. I *do* enjoy playing both sides against each other to get what I want." Nerezza's smile widened. "And Callus Holloway's thirty-million bounty for you and Kyrion will go a long way toward funding production of my new hand cannons. Why, turning you both over might even convince Callus that I've seen the error of my ways and wish to return to the Imperium."

My stomach roiled with nausea. Even though I'd been expecting Nerezza to once again use me to my fullest, foulest potential instead of killing me outright, I couldn't stop an arrow of hurt from shooting through my heart. Just when I thought my mother couldn't get any crueler, she sank to a bitter new low and showed her true cold depths.

"Holloway's bounty would be a nice bonus, but he's not stupid enough to trust you again," I replied. "And the bounty doesn't matter anyway, because you're never going to get the chance to collect it."

I jerked my chin to the side, and Nerezza looked over at Pollux, who was pointing the hand cannon at her.

Esmina stepped up beside the other mercenary. "All your talk about bounties is quite interesting, Nerezza. I wonder how much Callus Holloway would pay for you *and* Vesper *and* Kyrion."

Fury stained Nerezza's cheeks a bright red, and her hands clenched into fists, her knuckles standing out against her skin. "We had a deal!"

Esmina shrugged. "Deals change. You should know that better than anyone."

Once again, all the fury abruptly sluiced off Nerezza. Her fists loosened, and a knowing smile spread across her face. "You're right. I do know that deals change, better than anyone."

She puckered her lips and let out a loud whistle. All the Serpens Corp mercenaries spun around and aimed their weapons at Esmina and Pollux.

"Bloody traitors!" Pollux growled, pointing his cannon at the closest man.

"I'm not the only one with a bounty on my head," Nerezza said. "When you and Esmina told me how much you wanted to destroy House Collier, I did a little digging. The Erzton Houses have a sizable reward for your capture, dead or alive—and dead is just fine with me."

Pollux let out another angry growl. Esmina eased a little closer to him, although she kept her icy gaze on Nerezza. The other mercs kept their weapons trained on Pollux and Esmina, but many of the men shifted on their feet or swiped the sweat from their foreheads. A tense silence dropped over the cavern.

I glanced to the right. Kyrion was still bricked to the wall, but the energy blast from the cannon was slowly but surely eating away at the stone, and more and more cracks were creeping in his direction like spiders scuttling along and dragging black webs through the rock wall.

My gaze met Kyrion's, and I deliberately looked over at the cracks spreading in his direction. He gave me the tiniest nod in return. We might not be able to send telepathic thoughts through the bond right now, but we could still communicate. Even more important, I trusted him, and he trusted me, and the same could not be said for anyone else in the cavern.

"Fuck this, and fuck you, traitors!" Pollux snarled, stepped forward, and pulled the trigger on the Techwave cannon . . .

*Click.*

Nothing happened. No sparks of energy, no blast of power, no incinerating green fire.

Pollux growled and pulled the trigger again. And then again . . . and again . . .

*Click. Click-click. Click.*

Nerezza's smile widened. "Looks like you were right about Vesper tampering with the cannon. I was certainly expecting it."

Once again, my stomach roiled with nausea. Maybe I truly was the weak link, at least when it came to being a seer, because both Esmina and Nerezza had seen right through most of my lies. Or maybe they were just better at double-crossing people than I was.

Nerezza waved her hand, and the mercenaries crept a little closer to Pollux and Esmina.

Pollux kept pulling the trigger, still trying to get the cannon to fire. Suddenly, he stopped, a puzzled look on his face. "Why is it getting . . . hot?"

Esmina's eyes widened. "Drop it! Drop it now!"

She lunged forward, slapped the weapon out of Pollux's hands, and kicked it away. Then she whirled around and hunkered down on the cavern floor. Pollux followed her lead, the way he always did, but Nerezza and the other mercs hesitated, not understanding what was happening.

The cannon spun to a stop at Nerezza's feet. A red light flashed on the side, and a shrill warning whistle cut through the air, screaming like a brewmaker about to boil over.

Nerezza also whirled away from the cannon. She shoved a mercenary between her and the weapon, then darted behind a large stalagmite.

All the mercs were focused on the cannon, so I sprinted toward the wall where Kyrion was still trapped.

"Vesper!" he yelled. "Vesper, get down—"

*BOOM!*

The cannon exploded, drowning out his words, along with everything else.

I couldn't give the Techwave cannon to Esmina, Pollux, and Nerezza, but I couldn't *not* give it to them either, not if I wanted to save Kyrion. So with Wendell's help, I'd done the next best thing: I'd booby-trapped it.

I'd coded the cannon to my DNA so only I could fire it. Anyone else who pulled the trigger would get no response and activate the explosives Wendell and I had packed into the solar magazine. Pollux had pulled the trigger far more times than I'd expected, causing the explosives to heat up faster than I'd intended, but the end result was still the same.

Vesper 1, mercenaries 0.

I hadn't wanted to blow Kyrion or myself up with our enemies, so the explosion wasn't nearly as large as I would have liked, but the shock wave still threw me forward five feet. I slammed into the wall beside Kyrion and bounced off, landing on my hands and knees. The rough stone scraped my palms, but that was a minor sting compared with the intense ringing that filled my ears as though I was standing in front of a drummer who was beating his instrument for all it was worth.

"Vesper? Vesper!"

Dimly, I became aware of Kyrion shouting, although his voice sounded muffled and far away.

"Vesper? Vesper!"

Kyrion's voice sounded again, a little louder and clearer. I shook the rest of the ringing out of my ears and scrambled back up onto my feet.

The exploding cannon had created a large crater in the cavern floor, and smoke was still boiling up into the air. The mercs who'd been the closest to the blast were dead, their mangled bodies lying in burned, crumpled heaps, while the injured men were screaming, shouting, and trying to crawl away from the epicenter. I didn't see Esmina, Pollux, and Nerezza.

My balance was off, but I staggered over to Kyrion. The spiderweb cracks had finally spread over to his left side, and he snarled and jerked his arm forward. The plasticuff around his left wrist snapped. He reached up and yanked on the cuff around his neck, but he couldn't pull it free of the stone, and I couldn't cut the plastic without cutting him.

I grabbed my stormsword off my belt and hammered away at the wall beside his neck. "Hang on!"

I swung the weapon with all my might, but I just wasn't strong enough to chip away the stone as fast and as much as I needed to. Shouts and yells sprang up behind me, and I knew that I only had seconds to free Kyrion before the mercs targeted us again—

Kyrion's eyes widened. "Vesper! Behind you!"

I whirled around. A mercenary was stumbling in my direction, his blaster aimed at my chest. I stepped in front of Kyrion and snapped up my stormsword, even though I knew I would be too slow to deflect the bolt back at the mercenary—

*Pew! Pew! Pew!*

Blaster fire punched into the merc's back, and he screamed and toppled to the ground. I tensed and lifted my sword higher, looking for the source of the shot.

Across the cavern, Zane lifted his blaster to his forehead, saluting me with it. Then he lowered the blaster, and his eyes narrowed in concentration as he aimed the weapon in our direction.

*Duck!* Zane's voice sounded in my mind.

I scrambled out of the way.

*Pew!*

Zane's bolt punched into the rock right beside Kyrion's neck.

*Pew! Pew! Pew!*

Zane shot the rock next to Kyrion's right hand, then both of his ankles, as though he was a sharpshooter showing off his skills for a cheering crowd. Kyrion let out a loud, fierce roar and surged forward, tearing his neck and right hand out of the cracked stone and loosened plasticuffs. Kyrion roared again, and a wave of telekinesis surged off him, smashing the bricks across his chest and legs flinging them away.

I yanked Kyrion's stormsword off my belt and tossed it over to him, then sprinted in his direction. Kyrion easily caught the blade and raced toward me.

We met in the middle. Kyrion grabbed me around the waist and yanked me toward him. I stood up on my tiptoes and kissed him. The second my lips touched his, the bond roared back to life in my mind, stronger than ever, and the sticky cobweb of him pulsed with energy, emotion, and awareness.

The kiss lasted only an instant, but it jolted and jumpstarted everything inside me, as though I was a machine that had just gotten a brand-new solar battery. I drew back and stared into Kyrion's eyes, which were blazing like dark blue stars. He grinned at me, then spun away, his stormsword glowing with the same fierce light as his eyes. I grinned and spun the other way, lashing out with my own weapon.

*Pew! Pew! Pew!*

*Pew! Pew! Pew!*

More mercenaries scrambled to their feet, and blaster fire zipped through the cavern. So many people were firing so many weapons it was hard to tell who was targeting whom.

Through the swarm of bodies, I spotted Pollux swinging his two hammers and crushing the arms, legs, and skulls of any mercs who were stupid enough to engage him. Esmina was a few feet away, moving back and forth as though she was dancing through the mercs. Every time an enemy shot at the seer, she whirled away at exactly the right moment so that the bolt punched into the chest of another merc instead of wounding her.

"Vesper! Behind you!" Kyrion yelled again.

He rushed forward, putting himself between me and a mercenary, even as I turned to deal with the threat—

*Pew!*

The merc fired his blaster, and Kyrion barely raised his sword in time to deflect the bolt at another merc, who screamed and fell to the ground. I ran over to help Kyrion, but a merc took a swing at me, making me scuttle back.

The fight only got worse from there.

Every time I tried to reach Kyrion, an enemy got in my way, and every time he tried to reach me, Kyrion opened himself up to more blaster fire. A merc managed to punch me in the stomach before I swiped my sword across his chest, while another one tripped me and sent me staggering into a stalagmite jutting up from the cavern floor.

Not only did the pain of my own wounds pound through my body, but the echoes of all the hard blows Kyrion was taking also rippled through the bond, and I felt as though I was getting attacked and hit from multiple sides at once. A frustrated growl tumbled from my lips, but the sound was lost in the screams, shrieks, and continued blaster fire.

It was the same problem we'd had when we fought the Hammers in the antiques emporium a few days ago. Kyrion was trying to protect me at the expense of protecting himself, and I wasn't trusting my own skills enough to be as decisive as needed. Only this time, we were surrounded by enemies who wanted to kill us, and if we didn't figure this out, we would both die.

Kyrion glanced at me, worry creasing his face, and the sticky cobweb of him pulsed with the same stomach-churning emotion. He could feel it too. We were once again out of sync, and I had no idea how to fix it—

Wait. Maybe *that* was the problem. Maybe my trying to fix things the way I always did and Kyrion trying to protect me the way he always did *was* the problem. Maybe we were both holding on too tight when what we should be doing was just . . . *letting go*.

I'd once told Kyrion a truebond was about trust. I just hadn't realized that trusting in *myself* was part of the process.

I wasn't the awesome fighter Kyrion was. Oh, I could hold my own against most people, but I would never cut through enemies like they were made of plastipaper the way he did. And for the first time, I realized that was okay. I wasn't a broken brewmaker or a faulty cannon or something else that needed to be fixed. Not being on Kyrion's level as a warrior didn't make me a weak link, as Esmina had claimed.

It just made me, well, *me*.

I looked at Kyrion, opening myself up to him through the bond, letting him feel the newfound confidence I had in myself, and him too, and especially the two of us together.

Even when we were apart.

Kyrion stared at me, and an answering pulse rippled through the bond. Cool, calm acceptance flooded my body, along with a rush of softer, warmer emotions that brought tears to my eyes.

Kyrion and I stared at each other a heartbeat longer, then whirled around in opposite directions, focusing on the enemies in front of us instead of the bond at our backs.

My world narrowed to ducking blaster fire and cutting down one mercenary after another. Instead of trying to reach Kyrion,

I held my ground, protecting my own little patch of space, even as I searched for more enemies to fight. A shadow moved out of the corner of my eye, and I whirled in that direction.

A merc was running toward me, a shock baton clutched in his hand, white-hot electricity crackling on the end—

*Pew! Pew! Pew!*

Three blaster bolts punched into the merc's back, and he tumbled to the ground. My head snapped up, and I spotted Asterin on the second-story balcony, coolly spinning around and shooting another merc who was charging at Zane down on this level.

*Pew!*

Asterin dropped that merc as well. Zane gave her a showy little bow, then rushed forward to fight another enemy. Asterin rolled her eyes and did the same thing on the second level.

I kept hacking and slashing my way through one enemy after another. I didn't see Nerezza anywhere, but Esmina and Pollux were still in the thick of the fight. I sliced my sword across the chest of another mercenary and headed in their direction.

"Now, Pollux!" Esmina yelled, sidestepping another round of blaster fire. "Now!"

With a loud, bellowing roar, Pollux leaped into the air, using his telekinesis to propel himself at least twenty feet off the ground, close enough that his blond hair brushed the bottoms of some stalactites jutting down from the ceiling.

Just as quickly, Pollux started to drop, and psion power erupted in his hammers, the lunarium heads blazing a bright neon green. The hammers whistled downward in vicious arcs toward the crater created by the cannon explosion, and I realized what he was going to do.

"Brace! Brace! Brace!" I screamed, but my warning came too late.

*BOOM!*

Pollux slammed his hammers into the ground. Thick, wide cracks zipped through the stone, and a concussive shock wave ripped through the cavern. The force was much, much stronger than the explosion caused by my booby-trapped cannon, and it knocked me off my feet.

For several seconds, the world spun around in crazy loops, as though I was on a blitzer that was spiraling through the air, and I lost my balance. My hands and knees smacked into the ground, and my brain rattled around inside my skull at the hard, vicious impact.

The entire cavern bucked and heaved, and enormous chunks of stone broke off from the ceiling and crashed down onto this level, crushing several mercenaries. I had to roll to the side to keep from getting impaled by a falling stalactite, but Esmina kept up her graceful dance, smoothly moving from left to right, as though she was skating on ice instead of careening across solid stone.

Pollux let out another roar and slammed his hammers into the ground again.

*BOOM!*

The previous cracks he'd created zipped outward and then merged into one enormous chasm that widened and deepened with every passing second and each bit of ground it chewed up. One merc after another dropped into the growing, gaping chasm, all flailing and screaming as they fell to their deaths.

Pollux roared and hit the ground a third time with his hammers.

For an instant, everything slowed down, as though I was watching a video one frame at a time. I could *see* the magic moving through Pollux's body and down into the hammers and then the lunarium weapons amplifying his power ten, a hundred, a thousand times over and turning it into something truly devastating—

*BOOM!*

Pollux's blow ripped through the cavern, stronger and louder than the others. No one was fighting anyone anymore, and all I could do was hunker down on my hands and knees and try not to get tossed into the chasm by the rapidly splitting ground . . .

Sometime later, the quaking and shaking finally stopped.

A cold wind whistled into the cavern, bringing with it a misty kiss of the waterfall spray and clearing out the thick, billowing clouds of dust. Tears streamed down my face, and my chest spasmed with coughs, but I tightened my grip on my stormsword and slowly climbed to my feet. Moans and groans rang out through the cavern, but they were soft sounds compared with the roaring in my ears.

I crept forward and peered down.

Pollux had used his hammers to punch all the way through the cavern floor, revealing a honeycomb of chambers underneath. Despite its sturdy appearance, this whole place was made of pockets of air, and Pollux had cracked it all open like it was as fragile as an eggshell.

Even now, the psionic echoes of his power scraped across my skin like someone was rubbing my face in a bed of broken glass. I shuddered in revulsion. No one should have that much power. In his own way, Pollux was even more dangerous than Esmina. She was a laser, narrow and focused, but Pollux was, well, a hammer, a broad, blunt instrument with only one purpose: destruction.

Pollux climbed to his feet, clutching his weapons. The lunarium hammers were still burning with that bright, intense, eerie green light, and another shudder rippled down my spine. A blow like that should have depleted even the strongest psion's magic, but Pollux was as powerful as ever, thanks to his stolen truebond.

Kyrion and Zane also got to their feet. They had both managed to hang on to their stormswords, but they were swaying back and forth, trying to shake off the shock of Pollux's blows. Me too. I felt as though I'd developed a sudden, severe case of vertigo, and everything was just a little off-balance.

"Excellent," a voice purred. "Pollux caused even more damage than I expected."

I turned around. Esmina was standing several feet away, and she stalked toward me. One of the mercenaries reached up and tried to grab her ankle. She didn't even look down as she sidestepped him, then drew her foot back and kicked him in the head. Esmina put some of her magic into the blow, just as Pollux had done, and the merc's skull caved in with a sickening *crunch.*

I whirled around and stepped forward, but instead of solid stone, my boot sliced through empty air, and I had to windmill my arms to propel myself backward. Pollux had broken the floor wide open, and a thirty-foot chasm now separated the two halves of the chamber.

My head snapped up. Kyrion and Zane were on one side of the chasm, along with Asterin, Pollux, and several mercenaries, and I was on the other side with Esmina, who was wading through and killing the remaining mercenaries, drawing closer to me all the while.

I was trapped—and on my own.

# THIRTY-ONE

## KYRION

I scrambled to my feet. Beside me, Zane groaned and did the same thing.

"An earthquake?" he muttered. "No one told me there would be a bloody earthquake!"

I ignored his complaints and rushed over to the edge of the chasm Pollux had created. He was strong—much, much stronger than I'd realized—and he'd cracked open the floor like it was a child's toy and he wanted all the candy inside. So much dust clouded the chasm I couldn't even see the bottom—or all the bodies lying down there.

My gaze lifted. On the opposite side of the chasm, Vesper stopped short, waved her arms to regain her balance, and lurched back from the jagged edge. She looked at Pollux, then Zane, then me, her worry pulsing through the bond. In the distance, Esmina drew a long lunarium dagger off her belt and moved forward, going from one injured mercenary to the next and quickly, ruthlessly cutting their throats.

I backed up, trying to give myself as much of a running start as possible. I had to reach Vesper before Esmina did—

Zane grabbed my arm, stopping me. "Don't be a fool! You'll never make it!"

He was right. Even if I used my telekinesis to propel myself up and out, I doubted I could leap across a thirty-foot chasm. And if—*when*—I missed, I would fall to my death.

"I can't reach you!" I yelled.

"I can't reach you either!" Vesper yelled back. "But that's okay!"

Okay? It wasn't *okay*. Being able to see Vesper but not being able to help her—protect her—was my worst nightmare come to life.

Vesper stared at me, and our gazes locked and held. *It's okay, Kyr. I trust you, and I need you to trust me right now.*

*I* do *trust you—more than anything.*

A grim smile curved her lips. *And I trust you more than anything. But it's also time we started trusting* ourselves. *It's the only way our bond is ever truly going to work. We can't save each other all the time. Sometimes we both need to save ourselves.*

The air at Vesper's side flickered, and an image of my mother appeared, showing her arranging flowers just as she had been doing in the Castle Caldaren garden.

*The scorpions will always be a danger, and they could always sting me*, my mother's voice echoed in my ears. *But you can't be afraid of the possibility.*

Desdemona hadn't been talking about scorpions. Not really. No, she'd been talking about Callus Holloway. Despite how many times the siphon had taken my parents' power, my mother had still hoped the next time would be different, that she and my father would figure out a way to stop Holloway, that she and my father would finally be *free*. Somehow, in the garden all those years ago, she'd known I would need to hear those words and remember her lesson.

Holloway might not have captured Vesper and me, but I had still let him lock me in a prison of my own making. All I had done the past few weeks was worry, and I was tired of it. I should be celebrating my truebond with Vesper and reveling in my love for her, not living in constant dread and fear of the worst happening. Perhaps I would have been able to do that, if not for Callus bloody Holloway.

Well, no more. The siphon wasn't going to control me through fear the way he had controlled my parents.

My inner monster roared in denial, but for once, I shut out the sound. I smiled back at Vesper, although my lips twisted more into a resigned grimace. *Then go save yourself and come back to me, seer. That's an order.*

Her eyes brightened. *You do the same, Arrow. Because I'll come over there and kill you myself if you don't survive this.*

*And I'll do the same to you. Tried and true, remember?*

*Tried and true*, she repeated.

We stared at each other a heartbeat longer, so many thoughts and feelings rippling through the bond from me to Vesper and back again. Then, at the same time, we spun away from each other and faced our enemies.

Turning away from Vesper was one of the hardest things I'd ever had to do, but she was right. I couldn't protect her now, and she couldn't rescue me, so we would just have to save ourselves.

Looking away from Vesper didn't lessen my fear. The emotion would always be there, waiting to sting me like a vicious scorpion, just like my mother had said. But the hope was there too, waiting to blossom into something beautiful. Now Vesper and I just had to make that hope a reality.

*Pew! Pew! Pew!*

On the balcony above, Asterin had gotten back on her feet and started firing at the mercenaries on that level, but my eyes were fixed on the enemy in front of me.

Pollux.

He swung his two war hammers in a furious rhythm, bashing in heads and breaking the bones of the remaining mercenaries with quick, ruthless efficiency. His lunarium weapons were also spitting out large balls of fire, burning and further terrorizing his victims.

Zane stepped up beside me, twirling his stormsword around in his hand. "How in all the bloody stars does he still have so much psion power?"

"Pollux was part of a truebonded pair," I responded, twirling my own sword around, my motions mirroring Zane's. "Until he decided he didn't want to share his power."

"Let me guess. He killed his bonded partner and took their power for his own."

I glanced at him in surprise.

Zane shrugged. "I've been reading a lot of books about truebonds. I wanted to know exactly what you and Vesper are capable of in case I couldn't reason with you and the two of you tried to kill me."

"And what *are* we capable of?"

For once, Zane was completely serious. "For two people who love each other as much as you and my sister do? Any bloody thing you can possibly imagine."

He was right. I loved Vesper, and I hoped that she loved me. And that emotion was stronger than anything, even the fear that would always be lurking in the cold depths of my heart.

"Now, what do you say we kill this guy?" Zane said, his voice returning to its usual sardonic drawl. "Because I have no desire to die in this bloody cave."

Zane held his sword out as though we were teammates wishing each other luck before a big game. I rolled my eyes, but I tapped my blade against his, making shards of ice spit out of my sword and flashes of fire spew out of his. Then, together, we lifted our weapons and firmed up our fighting stances.

Pollux swung his hammer again, catching another merc in the chest, lifting him up, and flinging that man into the chasm. The merc screamed, his voice growing thinner and fainter, until . . .

The merc's wail cut off, replaced by the sickening *splat* of his body hitting the bottom.

Pollux caught sight of Zane and me. We were the only two people still alive on the cavern floor, although Asterin was firing her blaster at the mercenaries on her level. She was also using some watchlike device on her wrist to shock the enemies who got within arm's reach.

Pollux twirled his hammers around in his hands as though they were as light as feathers instead of heavy, substantial weapons. The glow of the lunarium hammers matched the gleam of psion power in his dark eyes. "I've killed more than a few Arrows but none of your calibers."

"You're not going to be killing us either," I called out.

Pollux grinned. "We'll see about that."

He looked at me a moment, then his gaze flicked over to Zane. The three of us stood there, frozen in our own little bubble of danger.

Then, with a collective roar, Zane and I rushed toward our enemy.

I swung my stormsword at Pollux's head, but he easily ducked the blow, along with the one Zane aimed at his chest. In an instant, he spun away from us both. Not only was he strong, but he was also *fast*. Before I could recover, Pollux spun right back around and lashed out with his war hammer.

I barely managed to snap my sword up in time to block his blow. Even then, the force of it reverberated all the way through my arm. For a moment, I thought my fingers were going to go numb, and I was going to lose my grip on my sword, but I gritted my teeth and threw up a psionic shield in my mind, walling off the stinging sensation.

Pollux pressed his advantage, leaning down and forcing me to fall to one knee just to keep my sword between us. "I'm going to enjoy grinding your body into dust," he hissed, leaning down even more.

My muscles were already shaking from the effort of keeping him at bay, and I didn't have the breath for a reply. My arm started to buckle, and I couldn't hold him back any longer, so I ducked down and threw myself forward, rolling away from him . . .

*Boom!*

Pollux's hammer slammed into the ground where my body had been, and a green fireball shot off the lunarium weapon, scorching the stone.

I used the momentum of my roll to propel myself back up and onto my feet. Zane darted in to attack Pollux's blind side, but the other warrior sensed the coming blow and twisted out of the way, and Zane's stormsword only whistled through empty air.

Pollux lashed out with his hammers in retaliation, but Zane spun away from him, and I stepped up beside my old rival. Together we charged forward.

*Clang!*

*Clang! Clang!*

*Clang!*

Back and forth, Zane and I swung our swords at Pollux, who whipped his hammers from side to side in a quick rhythm, easily blocking our attacks. Frustration surged through me. The rogue Hammer was knocking our stormswords aside as though they were made of wood instead of lunarium. We weren't even wearing him down, even though the two of us were moving as fast as possible.

Finally, after a particularly furious exchange, Zane and I fell back. Sweat streamed down my face, his too, and we were both breathing hard.

"How are we supposed to kill this guy?" Zane wheezed. "He's not even winded!"

I didn't have the breath to respond, nor did I have an answer.

"Aw, are you boys tired already?" Pollux sneered. "I thought Arrows were supposed to be the best of the best. You two are bloody disappointments."

"Now he's just being mean," Zane wheezed again.

Pollux grinned, then drew his arm back and threw one of his hammers at us. The weapon zipped through the air, glowing a bright, vivid green. Zane and I dove in opposite directions, hitting the ground. The war hammer shot between us and plowed into the wall.

*Boom!*

Stone exploded, dust billowed up, and cracks zigzagged out from the hard, smacking impact. Pollux flicked his fingers, and the hammer wiggled out of the stone and zipped right back over into his hand again. Zane and I both got back onto our feet.

My eyes narrowed, and my gaze locked on Pollux's hammers. "Do you trust me?"

"Never."

I glowered at Zane.

He huffed. "Fine. I suppose I can make an exception this one time to keep from dying. What do you have in mind?"

I stabbed my stormsword at Pollux. "Separating that bastard from his hammers, and then his head from his shoulders."

Zane's eyes brightened. "Just like that maneuver Julieta and I pulled off on Magma 17 last year?"

"Just like that."

Zane's eyes dimmed, probably at the mention of Julieta, who had been his best friend until she had betrayed us by working with Rowena Kent to crash Imperium ships. But after a few seconds, he perked up. "Fine. But you're the bait."

Before I could protest, he let out a loud yell and charged forward. Pollux stepped up to meet Zane's seemingly reckless charge.

At the last moment, right before Zane would have plowed straight into Pollux's hammers, he dropped into a slide and used his telekinesis to spin himself around, zipping right past Pollux and coming up behind the other warrior.

I charged forward, but Pollux was expecting the move, and he tossed one of his hammers at me, even as he turned to block Zane's attack with his other weapon.

The first hammer zipped straight toward me, propelled by Pollux's telekinesis. This time, instead of trying to avoid the blow, I spun to the side, braced myself, and let the weapon slam into my left shoulder.

*Thwack!*

Pain exploded in my shoulder, zinging up into my neck and all the way down into my fingertips, and fire boiled up, singeing my jacket and burning my skin. The stinging, burning blow knocked me back, but I managed to stay on my feet, even as I swallowed a growl.

Fuck. That had *hurt*.

But the hammer had hit its target, having won its battle with my battered shoulder and blistered skin, and the weapon clattered to the ground.

Pollux swung his other hammer at Zane, making the Arrow twist to the side to avoid getting the sharp spike rammed into his stomach. Then the mercenary whirled around in my direction and snapped out his hand. A wave of telekinesis surged off him, and the hammer at my feet slid across the rocks in his direction.

At the last moment, right before the hammer lifted off the ground, I threw myself down and out and latched onto the hilt with my left hand.

Pollux growled and stretched out with even more of his telekinesis, but I was a lot bigger and heavier than his hammer, and he wasn't prepared for the added weight. He hesitated, giving Zane enough time to dart forward and slice his sword across Pollux's left arm.

The mercenary howled and staggered back. Zane kept right on attacking, swiping his sword across Pollux's body and inflicting deep wounds on the mercenary's right arm, right thigh, and left calf.

Pollux fully turned his attention to Zane, swinging his remaining hammer back and forth in a desperate effort to keep the Arrow from cutting him to pieces. Since he was distracted, his telekinetic grip on the other hammer broke, and the weapon finally clattered to the ground.

My arm was still burning, and my fingers were still stinging from Pollux's previous attack, but I gripped the hammer's hilt and got to my feet. I hefted the hammer in my left hand, getting a feel for its weight, shape, and balance. Then I drew my arm back as far and as high as I could.

"Hey!" I yelled. "You arrogant bastard! Catch this!"

Pollux lashed out with his weapon, making Zane stagger back, then the merc spun toward me. I snapped my hand forward and used my telekinesis to throw the war hammer at Pollux the same way he had thrown it at me.

I put as much psion power into the throw as I could, and the hammer picked up speed as it flipped end over end, whistling straight toward the merc's head . . .

Pollux cursed and jerked to the side, and the hammer flew past him—just like I wanted it to.

*Smack!*

Zane reached up and snagged the hammer out of midair.

The hilt slapped up against his palm, and he caught the weapon as easily as a child would catch a hoverball in a schoolyard game.

For a moment, Zane stood there, holding the hammer high, and the lunarium weapon glowed an icy blue in a reflection of his psion power.

"Show-off!" I yelled.

Zane grinned and lowered the hammer to his side, twirling the weapon around in his hand with easy familiarity, almost as if it was his weapon instead of Pollux's.

Zane advanced on Pollux, his stormsword in one hand and the merc's hammer in the other, both weapons sending out flashes of fire. I also advanced on the merc, my stormsword glowing a dark blue and spitting out sharp shards of ice.

Pollux backed up so he could see us both, and for the first time, uncertainty crinkled his face. The merc growled and charged at me, swinging his remaining hammer at my head, but I spun to the side, avoiding the blow. Just as quickly, Zane moved in, swinging his own hammer in response.

Pollux saw the blow coming, but for once, he was too slow, and Zane slammed the hammer into the merc's right forearm. Pollux's bones broke with audible *crack-cracks*, and the remaining war hammer slipped through his fingers and clattered to the ground.

Zane stepped forward and kicked the hammer in my direction. I waggled my fingers, and the hammer flew up off the ground and settled into my left hand. The lunarium weapon started glowing a dark blue with my psion power, spitting out shards of ice just like my stormsword was still doing.

"Not so tough without your toys, are you?" I taunted.

Pollux's gaze flicked between Zane and me, then past us. In the distance, I could hear Vesper and Esmina fighting. I didn't dare turn to see what was happening, but Pollux glancing in that direction told me everything I needed to know.

"Esmina can't save you now," I snarled.

Grudging agreement flashed across his face, but Pollux snapped up his hands, wave after wave of telekinesis surging off him.

Pollux picked up rocks, blasters, cracked pieces of armor, broken tablets, and the other debris littering the cavern floor and threw it all at Zane and me. Zane lifted Pollux's hammer, letting the lunarium weapon absorb part of the barrage and knock aside some of the flying debris. I did the same thing, crossing the hammer I was holding with my stormsword and reinforcing them both with my own telekinesis, creating an invisible psionic shield in front of my body.

Pollux growled and redoubled his efforts, sending out more waves of telekinesis and debris, but I growled right back at him and stalked forward, eating up the distance between us.

"Kyr? What are you doing?" Zane yelled. "This wasn't part of the plan!"

I had a new plan now, and all that mattered was killing this enemy. I kept stalking forward, ignoring the sharp shrapnel that slipped past my psionic shield and sliced across my hands, arms, chest, and legs.

Pollux charged forward. I dug my boots into the ground, then sprang forward and launched myself at him. The instant my body crashed into the mercenary's, I lashed out with my own telekinesis and shoved him away as hard as I could. My psion power lifted Pollux off his feet and tossed him back.

*Smack!*

Pollux punched into the wall hard enough to make chips fly out of the stone. More jagged cracks also zipped up and outward through the wall, and I followed the cracks with my gaze the same way I always followed the ribbon of Vesper in my mind.

*There.* That's what I was looking for.

Pollux slumped to the ground, stunned from the vicious blow.

He blinked a few times, but a second later, he was climbing back to his feet. The tough bastard wasn't going to quit unless I *made* him quit.

"Kill him!" Zane yelled. "Kill him now, Kyr!"

I could feel Zane rushing up behind me, but I didn't need his help. Not for this. I drew my hand back and threw Pollux's hammer. The mercenary ducked, but once again, I wasn't aiming for him.

The hammer smacked into the ceiling twenty feet above Pollux's head, plowing into the middle of all the cracks he'd created and shearing through a stalactite. The stalactite broke off the ceiling and zoomed down. Pollux dug his boots into the ground, trying to lurch out of the way—

*Splat.*

Too late. The long, jagged chunk of stone punched into Pollux's chest, slamming him to the ground and impaling him as cleanly and neatly as a stormsword would. The mercenary let out a strangled scream, although the sound quickly cut off.

I picked the hammer up off the ground, then walked over and stared down at Pollux. Blood had already covered his chest, creating a wide ring around the stalactite, like a dark gray arrow that had found its target in the center of a scarlet bull's-eye.

Pollux thrashed around for a few seconds, although his arms and legs quickly stilled. He lifted his head off the ground and glared up at me. "Bloody fucking Arrows . . ."

The rest of his breath escaped as a raspy sigh, and his head dropped down. He twitched a few times, then was still. His eyes remained open and focused on me in a familiar, silent accusation, even though the mercenary was dead and was seeing something far beyond the stars now.

Zane came over and nudged Pollux's body with the toe of his boot. When he was satisfied the merc was dead, Zane raised his arm and used the sleeve of his jacket to wipe the sweat and dust off his face. “That bastard did not go down easy.”

I had opened my mouth to agree when a bloodcurdling scream ripped through the cavern.

“Vesper,” I whispered.

I dropped Pollux’s hammer next to his body, then whirled around and started running.

# THIRTY-TWO

## VESPER

Across the cavern, the sounds of weapons crashing together rang out, and the echoes of magic reverberated through the air. As much as I wanted to turn around and see how Kyrion and Zane were doing against Pollux, I had my own battle to fight.

By this point, Esmina had killed most of the mercenaries on this side of the chasm. Only one man was left, and he raised his shock baton high and charged straight at her. Idiot. He was already dead. He just didn't know it yet.

Esmina flicked her fingers, using her telekinesis to send the merc flying through the air. He dropped into the chasm, his screams becoming fainter and more frantic the farther he fell. I scrambled away from the edge of the chasm, still clutching my stormsword. She wasn't going to kill me that easily.

I looked around, but there was nothing useful on this side of the cavern, just dead mercenaries, piles of rubble, and the permaglass bridge that ran by the waterfall. Despite Pollux cracking open the cavern floor, the water was still tumbling down the rocks in a steady, frothy stream.

Esmina advanced on me, and I ran across the bridge. I sprinted into the next chamber, but it was more of the same, and another permaglass bridge ran past this side of the waterfall before ending in a circular balcony.

I bit back a curse and whirled around. I had to make a stand, and I had to figure out how to kill Esmina—or I was dead.

Footsteps scraped across the stone, and Esmina stepped into the chamber. She walked toward me, her pace steady and unhurried, as though she had all the time in the galaxy. Given her precog abilities, she probably already knew exactly how long it would take to kill me.

She stepped onto the bridge and trailed her fingers across the glass. Her short, dark purple nails scraped out a shrill, screeching tone.

Esmina stopped and gestured over at the waterfall. "Do you know why I bought this place? Why I decided to use Stardrop Falls as my base? Because of all the memories it holds."

"What memories?" I asked in a wary voice.

"This is where Micah and I formed our truebond the day I fell exploring the waterfall. Later on, he proposed to me in this very spot." Esmina's fingers stroked the railing, almost as if she was petting the permaglass. "And this is where I took control of my own future and pushed him over the side."

A chill swept down my spine. I knew she'd killed Micah in the cavern, close to the waterfall, but I hadn't realized she'd done it in this very chamber.

My magic surged to life, and suddenly, I could see it all playing out. Micah dropping to one knee, a ring in his hand, looking at Esmina with such love, hope, and devotion. Her letting him slide the ring onto her finger, then rise to his feet. Esmina planting her hands against Micah's chest and shoving him back, making him flip up and over the side of the bridge. His screams ringing out, followed by the loud *crack* of his body hitting the rocks below. Then Esmina quickly descending a rope to the bottom of the cavern, her dagger in one hand. The lunarium blade glowing as she leaned over, cut Micah's throat, and took his power for her own . . .

"Do you believe in destiny, Vesper?" Esmina asked.

Her voice broke the spell of my magic, and the images vanished. She took a few more steps toward me, and I backed away, matching her move for move, as though we were doing an elaborate Regal dance.

"No, I didn't believe in destiny—until I met Kyrion."

Her eyebrows shot up, and she let out a mocking laugh. "You think *he's* your destiny? How very quaint."

"Then what would you call it? Kyrion and me finding each other out of all the billions of people in the galaxy? Us forming a connection, a truebond?"

"Random chance? Luck of the draw? An unfortunate accident? Anything but *destiny*." A fierce light flared in Esmina's eyes. "No matter how strong or weak they are, people make their own destinies, whether they realize it or not. After all, what is choice if not a part of destiny?"

Maybe it was strange, but in a way, she was right. I wouldn't be here right now without choices. All the grim choices Beatrice had made to exile Nerezza from Corios. All the easy choices Nerezza had made to abandon me to climb the Regal ladder. All the complicated choices Kyrion and I had made about our truebond.

Grim, easy, complicated. Some of them were mine, and some of them belonged to others, but all those choices, all those actions, had led me here, to this moment, and I still couldn't help but feel like some of them were destiny too.

"What choice are you going to make now?" I asked. "Nerezza betrayed you and Pollux, your own mercs turned against you, and it's only a matter of time before the House Collier Hammers show up."

Esmina shrugged. "Nerezza betraying us was always a strong possibility. You were right about one thing, Vesper. Your mother doesn't like to get her hands dirty. Nerezza fled from the cavern as soon as the fighting started. I'm sure she's already on her way to a spaceport, planning to get off-planet as fast as possible. I'm counting on it."

A chill swept down my spine. "What did you do?"

"Pollux and I planted bombs on Nerezza's ship," Esmina replied. "It will explode a minute after takeoff."

My heart squeezed at her words. Nerezza might deserve such a vicious death, but I couldn't say the same about other passengers on her ship, and people on the ground might get hurt by the falling debris. And even though Nerezza had never been my mother in any way that truly mattered, I still couldn't stop mourning the loss of something I'd never had.

"You were counting on Nerezza betraying you? Why?" But as soon as I asked the question, the answer came to me. "You were *always* planning to double-cross Nerezza. You and Pollux were going to kill her and keep the Techwave cannon for yourselves."

"Of course we were. We were also going to turn you and Kyrion over to Callus Holloway to collect the bounty. I could see it all playing out so clearly, but things haven't happened the way I expected." Esmina's lips puckered in thought. "I'm not quite sure when or how things went wrong. You've done something no one has in a long time, Vesper. You managed to surprise me. Perhaps you're not as weak as I thought."

"Is that supposed to be a compliment?"

Esmina shrugged again. "I don't care what you think it is. All that matters is you're still not as strong as *me*."

She twirled the dagger around in her hand. The hilt gleamed a wicked gold, while the blood of all the mercenaries she'd killed dripped off the blade. Esmina tightened her grip on the dagger, and the lunarium blade sparked with bright gold flecks.

"What about the bounty?" I asked, trying to buy myself some more time to come up with a plan—any plan—to defeat her. "I thought you wanted to turn me in for all those sweet, sweet credits."

"As you said, the Hammers are probably on their way here right now, so that's no longer an option." Esmina gestured back toward the other chamber filled with dead mercenaries. "I never leave enemies alive behind me. It's your unlucky day, Vesper. If only you had managed to be on the other side of the chasm, you might have lived a few minutes longer."

She tilted her head to the side. In the distance, several loud yells rang out, along with the sharp *bang-bang-bang* of weapons. "At least until Pollux finishes killing your friends."

Kyrion's anger, frustration, and worry surged through the bond. I could feel how hard he was fighting, and my heart iced over at the thought of him being killed. Zane too, but I couldn't help them right now, and something about Esmina's words nagged at me.

"If you're so strong, then why are you hiding in this cavern instead of toppling House Collier? Leland disabled the estate's defensive shield, so why didn't you go ahead and wipe out the Colliers? When your men were attacking the estate earlier today, why didn't you go after Aldrich and Verona?"

"All in good time," Esmina replied, but her voice wasn't quite as confident as before.

I eyed her. What did Aldrich and Verona have that Esmina didn't? But as soon as I asked the question, the answer came to me. "It's because the Colliers are a truebonded pair. Together they're still stronger than you, aren't they?" My eyes narrowed. "Which means *I'm* still stronger than you are too."

Esmina scoffed. "Please. Your bond hasn't even solidified yet. Even if it had, you're still flailing around in the dark, trying to figure out what you can do with your own seer power." She gestured around at the empty chamber. "Kyrion isn't here to thwart my plans like he did in the junkyard. Face it, Vesper. Your magic is weak, and no one is coming to save you."

Her mocking words stung, but I lifted my sword a little higher. "You're right. I don't know all the ins and outs of my magic yet, and no one is coming to help me—but I don't need anyone to *rescue* me. I was on my own a long time before I met Kyrion, and I managed to survive."

"Surviving is not *winning*," Esmina snarled.

"Is that what you've been doing all these years? Just surviving?"

Agreement flashed across her face before she could hide it.

"What does winning look like to you?" I asked, genuinely curious.

Esmina's jaw clenched, and her eyes glimmered with unmistakable longing. "Tearing down House Collier. Establishing my own major House." She hesitated. "Finally coming home."

Once again, my seer magic stirred to life, and another image flickered in the air: Esmina relaxing in a comfortable chair, a mug of Frozon hot chocolate in her hand, flames crackling in a nearby fireplace.

I blinked, and the cozy image vanished, along with the peace and warmth it inspired. "You're *homesick*? That's what this is really all about?"

Surprise flickered across her face, but it quickly boiled up into anger. "You're damn right I'm homesick. Thanks to Aldrich Collier and the other Houses putting a bounty on my head, I haven't spent more than a few days at a time on Sygnustern in *years*."

I stabbed my sword at the spot on the bridge where she had pushed Micah over the side. "Because you murdered your friend!"

"Micah thought our truebond meant he got to stick to my side and suck off my power like a bloody leech for the rest of our lives. I *never* wanted that. I never wanted *him*." Even more anger boiled up in her eyes, turning them more gold than green. "Micah made his choice, and I made mine—and I chose to set myself *free*."

Part of me understood her desire to be free. When my true-bond had first formed with Kyrion, I'd been horrified that I was connected to one of the most notorious killers in the galaxy, and I'd even thought about killing Kyrion to protect myself when he'd menaced me after the Techwave battle on Magma 3. But I hadn't taken that drastic action. Not because I was soft or weak, like Esmina claimed, but because I'd been strong and patient enough to explore other options, to consider other choices—and loving Kyrion was the best choice I'd ever made.

"You could have chosen something else, gone somewhere else. You didn't have to kill Micah."

"Why should I have to leave *my* home?" Esmina replied. "Why should *I* be shackled to someone and forced to endure all their thoughts and feelings? Why should *I* let someone else's weakness drag me down and potentially put *my* life in danger?"

"So you took Micah's life instead? And then took his magic?" I shook my head. "That's not power—that's fear."

Esmina jerked back as though I had slapped her. The anger in her eyes burned hotter still, morphing into crackling fury. She stabbed her dagger at me. "Surrender now, and I'll make your death relatively quick, Vesper. That's far more mercy than I showed Micah."

"Mercy? You don't know the meaning of the word."

Esmina shrugged. "Have it your way."

Without warning, she charged forward and slashed her dagger through the air, aiming at my chest.

Once again, time slowed down, and I spotted one tiny detail after another. Esmina's hair streaming out behind her like a rippling red river. Her lips drawing back into a feral smile. And most of all, the lunarium dagger in her hand, the golden glow of her psion power burning away all the blood speckled on the sharp blade . . .

Time snapped back to its normal flow. I snarled and stabbed out with my sword, aiming the blade at Esmina's chest . . . and she smoothly stepped aside, spun past me, and lashed out with her dagger.

I didn't even see her cut me, although a hot line of pain zipped across my upper left arm. I hissed, whirled around, and snapped my sword up into a defensive position. Blood welled up out of the slice and trickled down my arm.

Esmina grinned and crooked her finger in a clear challenge. I rushed forward.

Thrust. Parry. Spin. Dodge.

My sword clashed with Esmina's dagger over and over, creating a quick, sharp chorus that echoed off the cavern walls. I fought as hard as I could, swinging my sword faster than I ever had before, but Esmina easily avoided my blows. Every time I attacked, she simply moved to the side and swiped her dagger across whatever part of me she could reach.

My right forearm. My right hip. My left thigh. My left calf.

Esmina moved up and down and glided back and forth as though her body was made of liquid instead of muscles and bones. I couldn't even nick her with my sword, and she was slowly but surely killing me.

I tried yet again, driving my sword toward her leg in an attempt to at least hobble and slow her down, but once again, Esmina avoided the blow. This time, she stepped in close and sliced her dagger across my stomach.

A shriek of pain ripped out of my throat, and I lurched back and clapped my hand over the burning, stinging wound. Hot blood spurted out between my fingers and dripped down my skin. A chilling realization swept through my bones. If she'd wanted to, she could have gutted me—killed me—with that attack.

"You can't beat me, Vesper," Esmina crowed. "I can literally see every move you make before you make it."

Frustration shot through me. She was right. Her precog magic gave her a huge advantage, and the other seer was waltzing around me the same way she had done with the mercenaries earlier. Esmina was just playing with me the way a Tropics tiger would play with a mouse it had spied in the rain forest.

I always hated being the mouse, and I had never felt more like a toy in my entire life.

Even when Callus Holloway had siphoned off my magic, I had been able to fight back, or at least try to block his power, but that wasn't the case with Esmina. How did you defeat someone who always knew when and where and how you were going to attack?

"Come on, Vesper," Esmina said. "Isn't it time to admit I've been right all along?"

"Right about what?" I asked, keeping my sword up and tracking her movements as she circled around me, even as I tried to think of some way to kill her.

"That being part of a truebond isn't some great and glorious destiny. That it's nothing but a giant *mistake*. A pair of magical shackles that usually gets not one but two people killed."

Her lips curled back in disgust. "It's a shame a psion as powerful as Kyrion Caldaren is bound to someone who can't even access the full potential of her own seer magic. What a laughable failure you are." She shook her head. "And now Kyrion's going to die because of you. What a bloody waste of his potential."

My stomach clenched. I had been calling up all of Kyrion's sparring lessons, using everything he had taught me about being a warrior, and it still wasn't enough.

Esmina was right—I *was* a failure.

She must have sensed my thoughts, because another cruel smile curved her lips. "I was right about you all along, Vesper. You truly are nothing but a weak link, and I've already broken you." She tilted her head to the side, the gold flecks in her eyes flaring with magic. "I wonder how long it will take for your precious Kyrion to die. Perhaps he'll be so stricken with grief that his heart will just give out, and his death will happen quickly. Or perhaps he'll try to hang on because that's what you would want him to do."

Her smile widened. "I hope it's the latter. Perhaps I can collect on Holloway's bounty after all. It will be easy to capture Kyrion in his grief-stricken state, and he's worth more than you are anyway."

Dread flooded my heart like an icy river. The bitch was going to wait until I was dead, then take Kyrion back to Corios. Holloway would do his best to keep Kyrion alive as long as possible, which would be a fate worse than death.

I couldn't let that happen. I would not *let* that happen. Not to Kyrion. But how could I stop it? The other seer was well on her way to killing me, just like she said.

Esmina raised her dagger. I tensed and lifted my sword, even though I already knew it wouldn't do me any good against her vicious swipes.

Suddenly, Esmina stopped and blinked, and her magic flared even brighter in her eyes, as though she was seeing something else instead of me standing in front of her.

"Pollux," she whispered. "He's . . . *dead.*"

Esmina's eyes widened, and she reached up and clutched her chest with her free hand. I eyed her warily, but I didn't get the sense she was acting. She and Pollux might not have been bonded, but she was feeling . . . *something.*

But instead of going mad with grief, as Adria Byrne had when she had lost her brother Dargan, Esmina let out a small sigh. She shook her head and dropped her hand from her chest.

Then her gaze cleared, and she was calm once again.

"Your friend is dead," I said.

"Yes."

And that was all she said. That one simple word. As though she had accepted the fact that Pollux was gone, and she had already returned to the problem at hand: how to amuse herself until she finally decided to kill me.

I'd known Esmina was ruthless, but for the first time, I realized how *empty* she truly was. The only thing Esmina had ever loved in the cold depths of her heart was herself. The other seer was remarkably similar to Nerezza in that regard.

"Pollux being dead might be for the best," Esmina said in a thoughtful voice. "He reached his full psion potential a long time ago, and he's been stagnant ever since. After I kill you, perhaps I'll kill Kyrion and see if I can take his power. Increasing my own psionic abilities would eliminate my need for someone like Pollux."

Another image shimmered in the air: Esmina cutting Kyrion's throat and watching him bleed out on the rocky ground.

My heart froze in my chest. Somehow I knew that would be even more painful than Holloway siphoning off our magic. Esmina would pull the magic, life, and energy out of Kyrion all at once, just as she had done to Micah so long ago, and she wouldn't care how much Kyrion suffered in the process.

I growled and rushed toward her, trying to take her by surprise, but Esmina just laughed and slid to the side the way she'd been doing all along.

"Haven't you learned anything yet?" she called out in a mocking voice. "You can't beat me, Vesper."

For the first time, I realized *I* wasn't trying to beat Esmina—*Kyrion* was. Or at least, the part of me that he had trained as a warrior was trying to beat her.

Kyrion's fighting skills clearly weren't working, and more and more blood oozed out of all the cuts on my body every time I tried to attack Esmina. It was time to change course and try something different.

It was time to use my own magic.

Esmina might have the power of a truebonded pair running through her veins, but in the end, she was still just a seer, just like me. No two seers were alike, and we all saw things differently, both with our eyes and our other senses and especially with our magic. All I had to do was see something she didn't, just like I'd been able to fix the Techwave cannon when no one else had.

I'd told Kyrion to believe in my ability to keep myself safe. Now I needed to do the same thing—to trust in myself and especially in my magic.

I kept my sword up, but I backed away from Esmina, moving farther across the permaglass bridge and closer to the waterfall.

Esmina shook her head. "Running away won't save you, Vesper. You don't have anywhere to go."

She was right—and wrong. I didn't have anywhere physically to go, since the balcony was the end of the line in this chamber. But I could go anywhere I wanted to with my magic.

I kept staring at Esmina, but in my mind's eye, I was in the round room of my mindscape. I ignored the memories and images flickering in the archways and sprinted straight into the Door filled with darkness. In an instant, I moved through the blackness, a silver light appeared, and I skidded to a stop beside my psionic nexus, the eye-shaped altar that was the heart of my magic.

*Come on*, I thought, staring down at the altar. *Do something! Show me something! Anything to stop Esmina and save Kyrion!*

The nexus remained still as always, although the lunarium eyes and arrows winked up at me from the sapphsidian table like silver stars. I was two minutes away from dying, maybe less, and I still couldn't figure out how the blasted nexus worked or what, if anything, it actually *did.*

Fury roared through me, and I slammed my fist onto the table. To my surprise, the lunarium eyes brightened in response, and sparks shot off them like fireworks, matching the heat raging through my body.

I frowned and pulled my hand back. Verona had said my magic was a white-hot star, while Kyrion's was a cold blue moon. Our powers ebbed and flowed, just like our emotions did, but our magic was always lurking inside us.

Maybe *that* was the purpose of my psionic nexus, to be a visual reminder that my magic was always a part of me, always steady and sturdy and waiting here in the dark depths of my mindscape. Maybe I didn't need more magic, more emotion, right now. Maybe I just needed to tap into what I *already* had, what I'd *always* had.

Instead of focusing on the lunarium eyes and arrows, I plunged my hands into the dark blue sapphsidian, as though I was trying to reach down and touch the very bottom of the table. A comforting coolness swept up my arms, and I pushed my hands even deeper into the table, letting more and more of that soothing sensation flood my body. For the first time, I recognized the sensation for what it was: calm, cold calculation.

In front of me, out in the real world, Esmina's eyes narrowed. "What are you doing, Vesper? Trying to call up even more of your seer magic to use against me?" She laughed, the mocking sound even louder than the gush of the waterfall. "How sad and desperate you are. I have far more power than you've ever *dreamed* of, even with your precious truebond."

I ignored her taunt and looked past her, still holding on to my psionic nexus in my mind's eye.

One by one, colors sparked in my field of vision. The frothy white blur of the waterfall. The dull gray shimmer of the rocks. Even the transparent sheen of the permaglass bridge. I saw all those colors and a dozen more. Not just color but strength and energy and substance.

Esmina clutched her dagger a little tighter. The other seer practically burned with color, and a miasma of green and gold swirled around her head like jeweled comets spinning around and around. The same shades shot off her lunarium dagger, which was glowing so brightly it hurt my eyes to look at it.

I squinted past the harsh glare, still holding on to my magic. I still wasn't quite sure what I was searching for, but I needed to stop overthinking and worrying and debating things to death. Trusting my own instincts and taking immediate action was the only way I was going to cancel out Esmina's precognition, and right now, my instincts were whispering that the answer to defeating the other seer was somewhere in this cavern. I *knew* it was, just like I knew I could always fix whatever broken appliance crossed my desk in the R&D lab.

The waterfall, the rocks, the bridge. I looked at them all again, but it wasn't just colors I saw—it was also the absence of them.

Like the clear, tiny tendrils that were slowly snaking through the permaglass bridge.

And just like that, the answer came to me. Of course. I should have realized it sooner. I was always so focused on fixing things—broken appliances in the lab, the overheating Techwave cannon, even my truebond with Kyrion—that I never considered the other side of my power.

As a seer, I could fix things—but I could also destroy them.

"You're right about one thing," I called out, still holding on to my psionic nexus in my mind's eye.

"What's that?" Esmina asked.

"People do make their own destinies."

She gave me an amused look. "If you're trying to lure me into a trap by agreeing with me, it won't work. You don't have anywhere else to go, Vesper."

She was wrong about that. I *did* have one more place to go.

It was just the one place no one in their right mind would go, which was probably why she hadn't thought of it and why her magic hadn't whispered a warning about it yet.

I laughed, and the sound bounced off the cavern walls. Esmina frowned, but she slowly closed the distance between us. She was so focused on what I was doing that she never looked down, so she never saw more of those spiderweb cracks zigzagging through the bridge with every step we both took.

*That's it*, I thought. *Keep coming this way. Just a few more feet. That's all I need . . .*

Esmina stopped, wary of a trap. Her frown deepened, and she brandished her dagger at me. She knew I was up to something, but she still wasn't looking down, so she hadn't seen the real threat yet. I kept my sword up, even as I subtly rocked back and forth on my feet. The vibration caused even more spiderwebs to appear in the glass, although the rush of the waterfall masked the cracking sounds.

I rocked back and forth again, and one of the spiderwebs snaked into another, and they spiraled out, zipping faster and faster through the permaglass. I stopped moving. There. That should do it.

"Do you know what your problem is?"

"What?" Esmina snapped, still suspicious.

I grinned. "Even with all your magic, you can't fly any more than I can."

Confusion creased Esmina's face. Then magic sparked in her eyes, and she lunged toward me. "No! Don't!"

Her dagger arced straight toward my heart. She wasn't playing around anymore. She knew exactly what I was plotting, and she was determined to stop me.

But this time, I was ready. I sidestepped Esmina's attack, dropped to my knees, and slid across the slick glass. I made it back to the center of the bridge and stopped, right in the middle of all those clear, tiny cracks. Through the glass, below the bridge, I spotted a stone ledge sticking out from the side of the waterfall. Hope rose in my heart. Maybe I could actually survive this after all.

Esmina screamed with frustration, whirled around, and rushed toward me.

I ignored her frantic charge, wrapped both hands around my stormsword, and raised it up as high as my arms would go. In my mind's eye, I plunged my hands even deeper into the sapphsidian pool of my psionic nexus, gathering up as much of my magic as possible. Then I drove my stormsword down into the bridge.

Flames exploded out of the tip of the lunarium blade and rushed through all the cracks, and for a moment, the dark blue burn of my magic lit up the entire bridge.

Then, with a thunderous roar, the permaglass shattered, and the bridge collapsed.

# THIRTY-THREE

## KYRION

I ran to the right, trying to sprint into the next chamber where Vesper was fighting Esmina. Pollux's blows hadn't shattered the floor here, but the cavern tunnel had collapsed.

"You're not getting through that," Zane said, stopping beside me, a worried note in his voice.

I growled, snapped up my hand, and reached for my telekinesis. I'd fling every bloody rock in this place aside to reach Vesper—

"Hey!" a voice called out. "Up here!"

My head lifted. Asterin was still on the second level, clutching a blaster. "This level is still intact! We can get to the other chamber this way!"

I glanced around. So did Zane. But if any stairs or ramps had been in this section, they'd crumbled away during Pollux's attacks. So I ran over to the largest pile of rubble and started climbing. Zane also started climbing. Together we scrambled up to Asterin's level, which was littered with dead mercenaries.

"Come on!" she said. "This way!"

Zane and I ran after her. The three of us rounded a curve and made it into the next chamber. No mercenaries were alive in here, so no blaster fire zinged through the air.

My gaze zoomed over to Vesper, who was standing on a permaglass bridge close to the waterfall. She was bleeding from several deep cuts, and her face was pale and sweaty. The instant I saw her, the pain of her wounds surged through the bond, and stinging lines zipped across my own skin from my arms to my stomach to my legs. Esmina had cut her to pieces.

"How do I get down there?" I asked.

Asterin's head snapped back and forth. "Zane, help me find some stairs!"

The two of them moved deeper into the chamber, but I stayed where I was, staring down at Vesper. Helplessness surged through me, but all I could do was watch.

Vesper backed all the way over to the far end of the bridge, which arced out into a balcony. She blinked, and magic exploded in her eyes, making them burn more silver than blue.

Through the bond, I could feel the power surging through her, first white-hot, although it abruptly shifted to ice-cold, as though Vesper had flipped some psionic switch deep inside her. The velvety ribbon of her stilled, and satisfaction rumbled through the bond.

"Do you know what your problem is?" Vesper called out.

"What?" Esmina yelled back.

Vesper's eyes burned a little brighter, and a knowing grin curved her lips. "Even with all your magic, you can't fly any more than I can."

I frowned. What did she mean by that?

Esmina must have figured it out, because she lunged forward and lashed out with her dagger, but Vesper ducked the blow, dropped down, and slid back across the bridge.

Vesper rose onto her knees, lifting her sword high overhead.

Then she slammed the lunarium blade into the bridge.

*BOOM!*

A wave of pure, raw psion power surged off Vesper, zipped down into her sword, and exploded out of the lunarium like a star being born. A bright light flared, so intense I had to look away. But in the next instant, the light winked out, and the bridge shattered, taking Vesper and Esmina along with it.

"Vesper!" I screamed.

I leaned over the railing and stretched my hand out, along with my telekinesis, but there was nothing I could do. Vesper was falling, falling, falling, and I couldn't catch her . . .

*Smack!*

Vesper landed on a long ledge jutting out from the side of the waterfall. Pain spiked through the bond, but before it could reverberate through me and bounce back to Vesper, I threw up a psionic shield, pulling as much of her hot, pulsing pain into my body as I could.

Esmina also landed on the ledge, which was about ten feet below where the bridge had been. She shook off the hard fall and got back up onto her feet, her dagger still in her hand, but Vesper didn't move. Esmina slowly turned around, her gaze locking onto Vesper.

*Come on*, I thought. *Get up, Vesper.*

No response. Vesper didn't move. Esmina took a wobbly step in her direction, then another one, then another one . . .

I ignored the other seer and focused on Vesper. I was too far away to help her, and she had to get up—or she was dead.

*Vesper!* I roared in my mind. *Get up! Get up now!*

Vesper's body jerked, as though my words had shocked her back to life like a defibrillator in a medtable, and she pushed herself up onto her elbow. It took her a few more seconds, but she staggered onto her feet. Somehow she'd managed to hang on to her stormsword, although the lunarium blade was barely glowing.

I hissed out a breath. As long as Vesper was awake, she still had a chance to kill Esmina.

"Kyrion!" Asterin yelled. "Over here!"

She waved at me, then hurried down a set of stairs I hadn't noticed before. Zane followed her, and I also sprinted in that direction.

I just hoped we weren't already too late to help Vesper.

# THIRTY-FOUR

## VESPER

The bridge cracked away to nothingness under my feet. The glass plummeted down like raindrops falling from the sky, and I followed it.

Air rushed over my body, and everything spun around in dizzying circles. My arms and legs instinctively flailed, trying to grab onto something that would stop my fall, but I forced my mind to reach out for Kyrion's telekinesis. His power threatened to slip away, but I clung to it as tightly as possible and used it to propel myself toward the ledge that I'd seen through the bottom of the bridge—

*Smack!*

My left shoulder clipped a rock jutting out from the waterfall, then slammed into the stone ledge below. Pain exploded in my body, so intense and white-hot it blotted out everything else, and I couldn't even draw air into my lungs . . .

*Vesper . . . get up . . . get up now!*

Kyrion's voice roared in my mind, and my eyes snapped open. Some of the hot, agonizing pain receded, ebbing like a tide being pulled away from the shore, and I could breathe again. I blinked away the white stars flashing in my eyes, and the realization that I was still alive flooded my body.

My crazy plan had actually worked.

More sensations washed over me. The rough scrape of stone against my cheek. The cool mist from the waterfall gathering in my hair. The wind whistling up from the chasm below.

My fingers twitched, and the familiar weight of my storm-sword settled into my right palm. I propped myself up on one elbow, then dug the point of the blade into the stone like a crutch and hoisted myself upright.

My mind spun around, and I swayed back and forth on my feet for several seconds before everything settled into focus.

I was standing on a long narrow ledge that curved around this section of the cavern like a crescent moon. The waterfall was only a few feet away, and the mist had already soaked my hair and seeped into my clothes. My body was cold and numb, but that might be for the best, given my abrupt landing.

I glanced down, but the bottom of the chasm was hundreds of feet away and lined with sharp, jagged rocks, as though I was staring into the gaping maw of a monster. I shuddered and looked away. Next, I glanced up, but I'd done an excellent job of destroying the permaglass bridge, and nothing of it remained, except for some metal support beams that were out of reach. The cliff face itself was slick with water. Even if I'd had the strength to climb up, I wouldn't have been able to get any foot- or handholds on the wet surface.

Once again, I was trapped.

An angry snarl sounded behind me, making the hair on the back of my neck stand up. I slowly turned around.

Esmina had also landed on the ledge, and she was picking her way over to me. She was still clutching her dagger, and the lunarium blade blazed a little brighter with each step she took.

"You crazy bitch!" she yelled. "You almost killed us both!"

"That was the idea! I'd rather be dead than let you hurt Kyrion!"

Esmina growled and lifted her dagger. I snapped up my sword. Esmina took another step toward me, and I braced myself for her attack—

*Crack.*

*Crack-crack.*

*Crack.*

Beside us, bits of stone tumbled down, and the cliff started splintering. Jagged openings appeared, and water seeped into the empty spaces, pushing more bits of stone out of its way.

My stomach sank. The ledge had been weakened by the bridge debris battering it, as well as the force of Esmina and me landing on it. Now the waterfall was going to finish the job and wash the rest of the stone away—and us along with it.

Esmina spun toward the cliff face. She stabbed her dagger deep into the stone and tried to hoist herself up, but even more of the stone crumbled away, and she slid right back down onto the ledge.

Her eyes widened, and she stared at the rocks as if she couldn't believe what was happening.

"What's wrong?" I called out in a mocking voice. "Didn't see this coming?"

She shot me an angry glare and stabbed her dagger into another spot, once again trying to hoist herself up. I didn't bother doing the same thing with my sword. I didn't have the strength to drive the blade deep enough into the stone, much less pull myself up. Instead, I glanced around, searching for another way off the ledge.

Out of the corner of my eye, I spotted several flickers of movement. Somehow Asterin had gotten into this chamber and was running down a set of stairs. Zane was following along behind her, with Kyrion right on his heels.

The three of them reached the bottom of the stairs, rushed forward, and skidded to a stop at the edge of the chasm.

"How can we reach her . . ."

"Why didn't someone bring a rope . . ."

"So sorry I forgot to pack that in my bag of spelunking supplies, my lord . . ."

Asterin and Zane sniped at each other, but I only had eyes for Kyrion. Blood, cuts, and bruises covered his face and hands, and he looked as battered and exhausted as I felt, but he was still alive.

His gaze locked with mine, and our thoughts and feelings flowed back and forth through the bond more easily than they ever had before.

*I assume you have a plan for getting off that ledge before the water washes it away?* Kyrion asked.

*I do now that you're here—but you're not going to like it.*

A wry grin tugged up the corner of his mouth. *Do I ever like your plans?*

I grinned back at him, then focused on Esmina again. The other seer was still trying to pull herself up, but her frantic motions made even more of the cliff face crumble away. Water was gushing out in spurts now, and the ledge started cracking under our feet.

I slid my stormsword back into the slot on my belt. "You know what your other problem is?"

Esmina turned her angry glare to me.

I smiled. "You don't have anyone to catch you when you fall."

She snarled and lunged toward me, her dagger whistling through the air in a deadly strike. I waited, waited, waited—and then stepped back.

A burst of water gushed out in the spot where I had been and hit Esmina in the side. She shrieked in surprise and stumbled toward the edge. Her right foot slipped off the ledge, and she frantically windmilled her arms trying to regain her balance.

Her gaze locked with mine, and the gold flecks in her eyes sparked with magic. Panic and fear blasted off her, and I knew exactly what she was seeing, because I could see it too.

Her death.

Esmina sucked in a breath to scream, but even more water rushed out of the cracks in the rocks. The blast of water hit her square in the chest and knocked her off the ledge.

Grim satisfaction filled me. I might still die in this cavern, but at least I'd taken her down with me.

The water gushed out faster and faster, washing away more and more of the ledge. The rest of the stone disintegrated under my feet, and I too started to fall.

"No!"

"Vesper! Vesper!"

Asterin and Zane shouted, and air and water rushed over my body again, but I wasn't afraid. Sometimes you needed to save yourself, and sometimes you needed to let other people help you. I trusted in myself and my abilities—and I also trusted in Kyrion's.

I plummeted downward, the bottom of the chasm rushing closer and closer. Five more seconds, and I would be splattered all over the rocks.

*Five . . . four . . .*

*Three . . . two . . . one . . .*

At the last instant, a telekinetic wave of magic grabbed me, as though a giant hand had snatched the back of my jacket. The abrupt motion jerked me to a stop, making my mind rattle around inside my skull again.

Below me, Esmina kept on falling. Her mouth opened in a silent scream, and her arm stretched up as if she was trying to use her telekinesis to grab hold of me, even though she was rapidly running out of time and distance—

*Splat.*

Esmina hit the jagged rocks below, and her body bucked and heaved. My seer magic surged to life, and an image, a memory, flickered right beside Esmina: Micah hitting the rocks like she just had. I didn't know if it was my magic at work or the last thought running through her mind, but a moment later, the image vanished, and Esmina stilled.

She was dead. I closed my eyes, but a few tears snuck out from beneath my lashes and trickled down my cold, numb face.

A jerk jolted my body, and I realized I was going down instead of up. Kyrion might have caught me with his telekinesis, but he was losing his grip on his power—on *me*—and I was too exhausted to try to shore up his power with my own magic.

I dropped a foot. Then two. Three. Five. Every downward jolt came a little quicker and lasted a little longer, and before I knew it, I was plummeting toward the jagged rocks again—

A second wave of magic dove down to meet that first one, as though another, different hand had also latched onto me. Together those hands hoisted me up, one taking over whenever the other faltered, and I slowly started to rise.

I wasn't sure how much time passed. A minute, two, maybe even three or four. But I steadily rose higher and higher into the air as though I was as light as a feather, although I could feel the combined effort it took to lift me up.

Eventually, I reached the top of the chasm. Those invisible hands hoisted me over the rim and flung me forward. I landed on my hands and knees, and I had never been so glad to feel stone scraping my palms.

"Vesper! Vesper!"

Kyrion grabbed me around my waist and set me on my feet. I pulled him closer, or maybe he pulled me closer. I didn't know, and it didn't really matter. In an instant, we were locked together. His frantic gaze searched mine, and I drank in the sight, feel, and strength of him.

Kyrion's body slowly relaxed, although his fingers clutched my waist a little tighter. "You were right. I despised your plan." He arched a chiding eyebrow. "If letting yourself get washed off a ledge into a chasm is actually a *plan*."

A laugh burst from my lips. "I love you."

He froze for a heartbeat, but then heat flared in his eyes, and a soft smile spread across his face. "I love you too."

I curled my fingers into his jacket. Kyrion leaned down and rested his forehead against mine, both of us just soaking up the warmth, love, and comfort of each other's presence.

Someone pointedly cleared his throat. "As touching as your reunion is, you're both still bleeding. You might want to fix that before it gets any worse."

Kyrion growled, but a smile curved my lips.

I drew back and looked over at Zane. "I didn't realize you were so pragmatic."

My brother shrugged. "I didn't go to all this trouble to help you save Kyrion, and then help him save you, just to watch you both slowly bleed out."

"Zane is right," Asterin chimed in. "The two of you both need multiple skinbonds. Here. I have some."

She plucked a couple of injectors off her belt, stepped forward, and jabbed one into my shoulder. Then she turned and did the same thing to Kyrion.

Zane stepped in front of her. "And what about me?"

Asterin gave him a sweet smile. "You can suffer, preferably in silence, although I know how difficult that will be for you."

He sniffed. "No one *ever* suffers in silence, especially not someone as loquacious as me."

Asterin opened her mouth to snark back at him—

In the distance, footsteps thundered, and yells rang out.

Kyrion drew his stormsword and stepped in front of me, as did Zane, while Asterin raised her blaster.

A few seconds later, Siya and Rigel ran into view on the chamber's upper level, along with more than a dozen Hammers. They quickly pounded down the stairs and spread out. Siya snapped her hand up into a fist, and Rigel and the other Hammers skidded to a stop.

Siya's gaze shot over to the shattered bridge, while Rigel peered over the side of the chasm. He let out a low whistle and gestured for Siya to join him. Her eyes widened when she spotted Esmina's broken body lying at the bottom.

Siya whirled around and stabbed her finger at me, Kyrion, Zane, and Asterin. "What in all the bloody moons happened here?"

I sighed and exchanged a knowing glance with Asterin. Once again, we had a lot of explaining to do.

# THIRTY-FIVE

## VESPER

More Hammers arrived, along with Aldrich and Verona. The Hammers secured the scene, making sure all the Serpens Corp mercenaries were dead, along with Pollux and Esmina. There was no sign of Nerezza, but that didn't surprise me. She had more lives than a cockroach, and she always managed to scurry away when the fighting started, even when she was the cause of it.

Eventually, Kyrion, Asterin, Zane, and I were escorted back to the Collier estate. Beatrice was seated in a chair in Aldrich's library, while Wendell was pacing back and forth in front of the fireplace.

"Thank the stars!" Wendell said.

He rushed forward and enveloped Zane in a tight, bone-crushing hug. Then, to my surprise, he did the same thing to me. I just stood there, my mouth gaping, my eyes wide, my arms hanging limply by my sides.

I glanced over at Zane, who rolled his eyes. *Have you never been hugged before?*

The uncomfortable truth was that yes, I never had been hugged before. Not by a parent.

Zane's face softened with understanding. *Well, don't ruin the moment. Hug him back, you idiot.*

I glared at him over Wendell's shoulder, but my arms crept up, and I returned my father's hug. It felt . . . nice, safe, comforting. Everything I had always thought a father's embrace would be. Everything that had always been missing my entire life. Tears pricked my eyes, but I blinked them away.

Wendell hugged me a second time, and I glanced over at Beatrice, who nodded at me. After a moment, I returned the gesture, my chin scraping against my father's shoulder. I still didn't know how I felt about Beatrice, but I could at least be civil to her for Wendell's sake.

"Sorry," Wendell said, clearing his throat and dropping his arms. "I didn't mean for that to go on quite so long."

Zane clapped his father on the back. "It's okay, Father. I think Vesper has realized you're a hugger."

An embarrassed blush tinted Wendell's cheeks a bright pink, but a grin crept across his face.

"At least some of us are getting hugged," Zane added in a low voice only Wendell and I could hear.

I followed his gaze across the library. Verona was clasping Asterin's hands, but her eyes were cool, and her face was unreadable. Aldrich was staring at his stepdaughter, a tense line creasing his forehead. Guilt spiked through me. The last thing I had wanted was to cause any friction between Asterin and her family.

I glanced at Kyrion, who nodded back. Together we went over to the Colliers. Verona dropped Asterin's hands and stepped back beside her husband. Aldrich regarded us both with an icy expression.

I squared my shoulders. I wasn't going to apologize for going after Kyrion. I would have done the same thing again right this very second. But I could at least try to smooth things over for Asterin.

"You should know that Asterin found me in her workshop trying to fix the Techwave cannon. She tried to stop me, tried to get me to call the Hammers and tell them what I was doing, but I refused. I forced her to let me go to the cavern."

Zane stepped up beside me. "And I helped. I trussed up Asterin like a ham just waiting to be baked for winter solstice dinner and dragged her along with us."

Asterin glared at him, her left eye twitching in obvious fury, but she didn't refute his lies.

"Is this really true?" Aldrich stared at me. "Or is it just a convenient story?"

"More or less," I replied. "I'm happy to give you all the details about how Zane and I snuck out of our suites and off the estate."

Zane snapped his fingers. "And we should tell them where we stashed their hoverbike. The one you hot-wired and I drove right out of their transport garage."

Siya sucked in a breath and opened her mouth, but Rigel touched her arm and shook his head, and she swallowed her angry words.

Aldrich kept staring at me, and I looked right back at him.

"I don't approve of your reckless actions," he said in a stern voice. "You disobeyed your host's orders, escaped from custody, stole House Collier property, and commandeered House Collier resources."

"But . . ." Verona prompted in a gentle voice.

Aldrich blew out a breath. "But House Collier owes you a great debt. Without you confronting Esmina and Pollux, we never would have found their base and realized just how close they were to launching another attack."

The Erzton lord didn't say anything else, and that was as close to an apology as I was getting. I was okay with that. I was alive, and so were Kyrion, Zane, and Asterin, and that was all I cared about right now.

Aldrich gestured over at a couple of chairs close to his desk. "I'd like to debrief you both. We already have teams combing through what's left of the cavern, but I want to know everything Esmina and Pollux said. They might have had other allies we don't know about."

I looked at Kyrion, who nodded. Together we stepped forward and sat down.

Kyrion and I told Aldrich, Verona, and the others everything that had happened. While we talked, Hammers, guards, and servants came and went, bringing updates along with them, as well as food, drinks, and more skinbonds.

By the time we were done, it was well past midnight, and yet I wasn't tired. Maybe it was funny, but everything that had happened made me feel more alive than ever before. One by one, the others left the library to get some sleep, although Aldrich and Verona remained behind.

Kyrion and I were the last to leave, and on our way out of the library, Verona stopped me and touched my arm. Kyrion raised his eyebrows in a silent question, and I nodded, telling him to go ahead. He strode down the corridor, leaving me alone with Verona.

"Congratulations," she said. "You and Kyrion solidified your bond."

I blinked. I hadn't thought about the bond in hours, not since Kyrion had used his telekinesis to fish me out of the chasm, along with Zane's help. But Verona was right. The bond felt different now—stronger and sturdier—and Kyrion's magic and mine flowed alongside each other like twin streams of power in a way they never had before. Somehow I knew I could dip my hands into his stream of power and use it just as easily as I could use my own seer magic.

"Did you know what was wrong with us? How we were both so worried about letting the other person down that it was interfering with the bond?"

"I suspected as much. Aldrich and I had a similar problem when we bonded. But our problem wasn't worry." A shadow passed over Verona's face. "It was guilt."

"Because you were both moving on and finding happiness again?"

She nodded, her hands twisting together. "I felt so much guilt over Urston's death, and Aldrich felt the same about Opal. It impacted our bond for a long, long time. And of course, it still impacts other people to this day."

I knew she was talking about Asterin and Siya, but I didn't say anything.

Verona's hands stilled. "But we can't live our lives in the past. We only have the present and the future we hope to make for ourselves. Once Aldrich and I accepted that, our bond finally solidified." She looked at me with a serious expression. "Just because you are part of a truebond, even one as strong as yours and Kyrion's, doesn't mean you stop being an individual person or that all your fears, worries, and guilt vanish."

"Then what does it mean?"

"A true partner makes your strengths stronger and your weaknesses easier to manage." A genuine smile lit up her face. "And whatever else you want it to mean. You'll figure it out, Vesper."

I nodded. "With Kyrion. Together. Tried and true."

"Tried and true," she echoed, then slipped into the library and shut the door.

Still thinking about Verona's words, I went through an archway and stepped onto a bridge that connected the main castle to the guest wing. To my surprise, Zane was standing in the shadows and leaning against the railing. I glanced down, wondering what had caught his attention.

In the garden below, Siya and Asterin were facing off, their arms crossed over their chests. Their heated voices drifted up to me.

" . . . can't believe you did something so reckless . . ."

" . . . Vesper and Kyrion needed my help . . ."

" . . . you put House Collier at *risk* . . ."

" . . . I helped *save* House Collier . . ."

I walked over and stepped into the shadows with Zane. "I never took you for an eavesdropper."

Zane straightened up and let out a low, rumbling laugh. "Oh, my dear sister, I wouldn't learn anything or be privy to such juicy gossip if I didn't eavesdrop. Why, eavesdropping is a skill every Regal develops practically as soon as they can walk. We really must expand your education. We have a lot of work to do to catch you up on everything you've missed while you've been away from House Zimmer."

His tone was breezy, but a serious undercurrent rippled through his words. My heart squeezed with longing.

"Is that what you want? For me to actually become part of House Zimmer?" I paused. "Even though it's already crystal clear *I* will be Wendell's favorite?"

"Teasing me already? How delightful! I've been the favorite for the last thirty-eight years. I think I can share the spotlight with you." He paused. "For a while. Until I decide to take back the favorite-child crown."

Even though I was the one who'd started the teasing, an exasperated huff escaped from my lips. "Can you never be serious?"

"Where's the fun in that?"

I tried again. "I felt your magic in the cavern. You used your telekinesis to help Kyrion haul me up out of the chasm. He wouldn't have been able to do it by himself. You saved my life, Zane."

He shifted on his feet. "Yes, well, you'd gone to so much trouble to kill Esmina. It seemed a shame to let you plummet to your death after all that bloody effort."

"You can't even say it, can you?"

"What?"

"That you were concerned about me." I poked my finger into his shoulder. "That you, Zane Zimmer, actually *like* the idea of being a big brother and having me for a sister."

He arched an eyebrow in a challenging look, then poked me right back in my own shoulder. "That depends. Can *you* say it?"

"Say what?"

His eyebrow arched even higher. "That you were just as concerned about me as you were about Kyrion when we were fighting Pollux. That you would have been devastated if I had been killed."

I hesitated. Despite everything that had happened, all my old fears arose once again, but this time, I swatted them aside. Verona was right. We only had the present to live in, and I was done letting Nerezza's cruel actions dictate anything about my life. In the cavern, I had trusted my magic, and now it was time to trust my instincts about Zane.

"I know what you did for me and Kyrion the day of the midnight ball," I said in a soft voice. "I saw it all from your point of view in my mindscape."

His lips puckered in a sour expression. "Bloody seer magic. Seems you have a much easier way to eavesdrop than I do."

"Kyrion and I wouldn't have reached each other in the throne room if not for you. Kyrion and I wouldn't have been able to unleash our truebond magic, and we wouldn't have escaped from Crownpoint. We would still be sitting in a cell, forced to let Holloway take our power." I shuddered. "I saw that future too, and it was more horrible than I ever imagined. So thank you, Zane, for saving us."

He didn't say anything, but emotions flickered in his pale eyes. Wariness, worry, and just the faintest bit of hope. That spark of hope ignited the one that had been flickering in my chest ever since I'd learned that Zane was my brother, and for the first time, I let it ignite into a flame of caring.

"When I was a kid, especially after Nerezza abandoned me, I would daydream about what my father was like, what his family was like. But in all my daydreams, I never thought I would have a brother like you."

"Like me?" Zane asked in a guarded voice.

"Someone so cocky and arrogant and overall infuriating."

He nodded. "Those are some of my best qualities."

"And someone so fierce and loyal and devoted to his family." I had to stop and swallow the knot of emotion in my throat. "Even the sister he never even realized he had until a few weeks ago."

Zane blinked, as if he was having trouble understanding my words. He opened his mouth, but I shook my head and cut him off.

"Don't ruin the moment. Hug me, you idiot."

He blinked again, then stepped forward and slowly, tentatively put his arms around me. I hugged him back just as tightly as Wendell had hugged me.

We stayed like that for several seconds, then broke apart. Zane cleared his throat. I did the same and swiped a tear out of the corner of my eye.

Then Zane's face brightened, and he slung his arm across my shoulders as though he'd been doing it for years. "Well, now that we've got all those pesky emotions out of the way, the first thing we need to talk about is your horrid taste in men. Kyrion Caldaren? Really, sis? You couldn't pick someone more suitable?" He shook his head. "I've been stuck with that broody bastard my whole life, and now you've made him part of our family."

*Our family.* My heart squeezed tight. I loved the way that sounded, and as weird as it seemed, I loved Zane's teasing. In that instant, I felt like we had known each other our whole lives instead of just a few months.

I lightly jabbed my elbow into his side. "Well, if you want to talk about horrid taste, look no further than your shampoo commercial. Galactic Suds for Studs? Really, bro? I'm *never* going to forget the image of you bare-chested, splashing around in a bathtub surrounded by bubbles and rubber duckies."

Zane gave me a sour look, but it quickly melted into another arrogant smirk. "You wouldn't be making fun if you knew how many credits Galactic Suds paid me to hawk their product. And then, of course, there is the lifetime supply of shampoo . . ."

He proceeded to tell me exactly how many credits it was, along with all the other inane details of the commercial shoot and how he had already promised to do another one, this time for conditioner.

It was fantastic.

Zane practically talked my ear off as we walked over to the guest wing. We finally went our separate ways, and I returned to my suite. Kyrion had already gotten cleaned up, and I did the same, taking a long, hot shower to wash away the grime, dust, and blood of the cavern fight.

The memories would be much harder to slough off. I would have nightmares about Esmina attacking me for a long, long time, but I would manage them—with Kyrion's help.

I got dressed, then went into the sitting room. Kyrion was standing beside a holoscreen, updating Daichi and Tivona on everything that had happened. A gossipcast was also flickering over the table, although Kyrion had muted the sound.

"What's your next move?" Daichi asked.

Kyrion shrugged. "Lord Aldrich has agreed to let us stay here as long as we like. We'll probably take a few days to regroup and see if we can find any trace of Nerezza."

"Do you think she died when her ship exploded?" Tivona asked.

My gaze flicked over to the gossipcast, which featured an excited reporter pointing at the sky, along with footage of a ship exploding into an orange fireball.

The news had broken while we'd been in Aldrich's library. A ship had taken off from a private spaceport at the edge of House Collier territory. Sixty seconds into flight, the ship had exploded in spectacular fashion, although it was unclear whether anyone had been on the transport. According to the gossipcast, the cause had yet to be determined, but I knew it was thanks to the bombs Esmina and Pollux had planted on board.

"Even if Nerezza survived, her scheme still failed," I replied. "She didn't get her hands on the Techwave cannon."

"No one did," Daichi replied in a dry tone. "Since you blew it up."

"Sometimes destruction is the best course of action," I quipped back.

Daichi rolled his eyes, while Tivona laughed.

Kyrion and I promised to check in with our friends again in the morning. We all signed off, although the news about the ship explosion kept playing on the holoscreen.

"Vesper?" Kyrion asked in a soft voice. "Are you okay?"

"No," I replied, jerking my chin at the footage. "If Nerezza was on that ship, then she's dead. I should feel relieved, but instead, I just feel . . . empty."

Kyrion wrapped his arms around me. "It's all right," he murmured. "It's all right."

I clung to him, resting my head on his shoulder and soaking up all the care and comfort he so freely offered. Behind him, the ship continued to burn on the holoscreen, and a few tears trickled down my cheeks. I wasn't sure if they were tears of relief that Nerezza might be out of my life for good—or tears of worry that she might come back and hurt me and Kyrion yet again.

# THIRTY-SIX

## KYRION

The next morning, Vesper and I woke up early. We took a long, hot, pleasurable shower together, then got dressed. Zane and Asterin were having breakfast on the south terrace, studiously ignoring each other.

Vesper filled a plate with food and sat down next to Asterin. Zane swaggered over to me at the breakfast buffet.

"You're looking well this morning," I said.

"And I could swear you almost have a smile on your face, despite the fact that you are chronically allergic to happiness." Zane shuddered. "Love. I hope I never catch such a foul disease."

The two of us might be connected through Vesper, but Zane was still the same arrogant jackass, and I resisted the urge to punch him in the face and break his perfect nose again.

*Ding!* Zane's tablet chimed with a shrill, familiar tone.

"Holloway?" I asked.

"Of course," he muttered, not even bothering to look at the

message. "I never considered you a saint before, Kyrion, but you could apply for such exalted status just for putting up with that demanding bastard all these years."

"What *are* you going to tell Holloway?"

Zane shrugged. "That I used my family's trip to Sygnustern as an excuse to chase down leads on you and Vesper and Nerezza Blackwell. That someone bombed Nerezza's ship, although it's unclear if she survived. And that, of course, I kept Nerezza from getting her hands on Vesper and the Techwave cannon."

"Do you really think that will work?"

He shrugged again. "I might not have captured you and Vesper, but Holloway doesn't want the Techwave getting to you first. I can spin it as a modest victory."

"Or Holloway will execute you for yet another defeat."

Zane smirked. "My dear Kyrion, it almost sounds like you're worried about me." He pressed a hand to his heart. "I'm touched. Truly."

"Concerned about you? *Never.*" I sighed. "But Vesper would be upset if something happened to you."

Zane glanced over at Vesper with a gentle expression I would have never thought him capable of. "Agreed. My sister has grown quite fond of me already, but then again, how could she not, given how magnificent I am?"

I rolled my eyes. "I'm just thankful arrogance doesn't run in your family."

Zane looked at me again. "I came over here to say one thing and one thing only. Truebond or not, if you ever hurt my sister, I will carve your heart out with my stormsword and squish it between my fingers like it's a bloody stress ball." His voice was cheerful, but his eyes were ice-cold as he pantomimed the motion with his fingers.

"By the stars, you are insufferable," I muttered again.

His grin widened. "Oh, my dear, Kyrion. I have not yet

*begun* to be insufferable toward you. At least, not where Vesper is concerned."

I groaned.

Zane was just as insufferable as he promised, but Vesper enjoyed his teasing, so I contented myself with glowering at him during breakfast. Which, of course, delighted him to no end.

Vesper and I had just finished our food when Siya stepped onto the terrace, along with Rigel. Siya's gaze flicked over to Asterin, who bristled. Vesper had told me about their argument last night. I thought the two stepsisters were too stubborn to admit how worried they'd been about each other, but Siya and Asterin would have to work out their conflicting loyalties and friendship for themselves.

Siya turned toward me. "The Hammers need to get in some training before we go deal with the mess the four of you left behind in the cavern yesterday. Care for a rematch?"

I glanced at Vesper, who nodded. "Absolutely."

Everyone headed down to the training ring. Vesper and I armed ourselves with wooden practice swords, as did Siya and Rigel, along with the rest of the Hammers.

I arched my eyebrows at Siya. "Two against a dozen?"

She shrugged, but a smile snuck across her face. "Verona thought you and Vesper might need more of a challenge today. Now that your bond has solidified."

I glanced up. Verona was now standing on the terrace, along with Aldrich. I bowed to her, and she waved back.

I held my sword out to Vesper, who lightly tapped her blade against mine, and the soft *clack* sounded like music to my ears. Together we stepped into the middle of the training ring. Vesper and I stood side by side, raised our swords, and faced the Hammers.

Siya gave the signal, and she and Rigel rushed forward, along with the other warriors. I didn't worry about protecting Vesper at all costs, and she didn't wonder if she was a weak link. Instead, we just *moved*, flowing from one attack to the next, battling our own opponents but moving to guard each other's backs when necessary.

It was *amazing*.

One Hammer fell. Then another . . . then another . . . until only Siya and Rigel were left.

The two of them battled hard, but eventually, Vesper sliced her wooden sword across Rigel's chest, mock-killing him, while I poked my blade into Siya's back, doing the same thing to her. In an instant, Rigel and Siya were both on their asses, with slightly stunned looks on their faces.

I started to head over to Vesper, but a translucent shimmer of black and blue caught my eye. A mammoth butterfly was hovering over one of the peony bushes, its fluttering wings making the flowers bob up and down, almost as if they approved of our victory.

Memories of my mother flooded my mind, and bittersweet longing washed through me. Desdemona had been right about a lot of things, and I was glad I'd been able to remember some of her advice, instead of just the agony and aftermath of her death.

I went over and picked one of the blue-moon peonies, inhaling its sweet spearmint scent. Then I walked back to Vesper, bowed low, and presented her with the flower. "I love you."

A grin spread across her face, and she took the peony and tucked it behind her right ear. "You're just saying that because we mock-killed all the Hammers."

"Absolutely," I agreed. "And because it was my turn to say it first. You beat me to it in the cavern."

She leaned forward, her eyes bright, as though she was sharing a conspiratorial secret. "Then I will say it last this time. I love you too."

A laugh burst from my lips, and I wrapped my arm around Vesper's waist, bent down, and kissed her.

"Will the two of you quit snogging each other?" Zane called out. "I just ate breakfast."

Vesper laughed, but I raised my hand and flipped him off. Zane chuckled, but even he couldn't ruin this moment.

Siya got back to her feet and picked up her practice sword. "Best two out of three?"

Vesper and I stared at each other. Then, with one thought, we broke apart, raised our swords, and turned toward our opponents.

I grinned at Siya. "It would be our pleasure."

# EPILOGUE

## NEREZZA

"Your mission was a complete and total failure," General Orion Ocnus said, a sneer in his voice.

He tossed his tablet down onto his desk and shook his head, as though I had greatly disappointed him. The motion made his short dark brown hair gleam like needles stuck into his ruddy scalp.

The two of us were in Ocnus's office, if you could call it that. The only pieces of furniture were the chrome desk and matching chair he was currently ensconced in. Ocnus didn't even have a chair for anyone else to sit in, which forced me to stand in front of him like I was one of his common soldiers. The lack of courtesy made me despise him even more.

"I wouldn't say that," I replied, spinning my own story. "I learned a great deal about the Erzton, including the fact that they're not nearly as strong and united as we thought. There is just as much infighting with the Erzton Houses and nobles as there is with the Regal ones."

Ocnus flapped his hand, dismissing my words. "I didn't

send you to Sygnustern to spy on the Erzton. I sent you there to capture Vesper Quill or at least get a working prototype of my hand cannon, and you failed to accomplish either objective. Not to mention the fact that you also tried to start your own coup on the planet by bribing the Serpens Corp mercenaries to work for you. Which, of course, was another massive failure on your part."

"A calculated risk," I countered.

"Let me guess—it all would have worked out *exactly* the way you intended except for Vesper Quill and Kyrion Caldaren, who once again managed to foil all your carefully laid plans." Ocnus eyed me. "Your daughter is becoming quite the thorn in my side, Nerezza."

*Daughter.* He said the word as if it would—or should—stir some deep-seated emotion in me. Ocnus didn't understand me at all, and that was going to be his downfall, sooner than he realized.

"Then perhaps Harkin should have done a better job of breaking Vesper when he was torturing her in his charming medical lab," I said. "Seems as though we've both been disappointed by our children."

Ocnus's black eyes narrowed, but I maintained my serene smile. He had cared as little for his son, Harkin, as I cared for Vesper. To Ocnus and me, children were simply tools to be used to achieve our goals, but he took such reminders personally, and my jab was far more effective than his.

"We did learn some useful things on Sygnustern about the new hand cannons," I continued in a more reasonable and less cutting tone. "Esmina Reston's theory that the lunarium and solar wiring magazines need a stabilizing agent is promising. I've already got some of the scientists working on a possible solution."

Ocnus dipped his head a fraction of an inch, acknowledging my point. "True. As was the information you discovered about how truebonds can be broken, and the resulting psionic power absorbed, if the circumstances are right. But that information doesn't outweigh your many failures."

"Esmina and Pollux deviated from my orders," I replied, trying to keep the anger out of my voice. "Instead of grabbing Vesper like I told them to, they decided to kidnap Kyrion. Everything unraveled from there."

"Then perhaps you should have convinced the mercenaries to follow your plan," Ocnus snapped back. "Instead of antagonizing them to the point where they bombed your ship and blew even more of our resources out of the sky."

I ground my teeth to hold on to my benign expression. The bombs on my ship had been particularly nasty, although not much of a surprise. Esmina and Pollux hadn't been as subtle or clever as they'd imagined, and I'd expected them to betray me from the moment I'd hired them.

Then again, I always expected everyone to betray me. People were only useful until they weren't, including Ocnus.

"I have other things to worry about today besides your failures, Nerezza. Dismissed!" Ocnus barked at me as though he was still a real Imperium general and not the head of a terrorist organization.

"Of course," I murmured, ignoring the urge to use my telekinesis to fling him into the nearest wall and snap his neck.

Thanks to the rumors Beatrice Zimmer had started when I was younger, Ocnus thought my psion power had faded away long ago. I was going to enjoy showing him just how strong I really was, but sadly, now was not the time.

Soon, though. Very, very soon.

"Of course what?" Ocnus barked out again.

I barely restrained myself from rolling my eyes at his pettiness. "Of course, sir."

He jerked his head, satisfied for the moment. "Get out of my sight, and get back to work."

Ocnus picked up his tablet again, ignoring me. I tipped my head to him again, then left his office.

I moved through the Techwave base, nodding and smiling at everyone I passed and cataloging the expressions I received in return. Most of the scientists ignored me, far more concerned with their work than with being polite.

But one man blushed and almost dropped his tablet. I memorized his face. He might be useful later, especially since Ocnus was growing more and more impatient for me to deliver all the things I'd promised.

I returned to my suite. Unlike Ocnus's sterile office, my chambers were comfortable in the extreme, with cushioned chairs, velvet settees, and other fine furnishings.

I went over to a table along the wall and poured myself a glass of apricot sangria, which I cooled to just the right temperature. The Quill Corp logo mocked me from the top of the beverage chiller as I picked up my glass, reminding me of perhaps my greatest failure.

My long-lost daughter.

I'd been wrong all those years ago. My daughter hadn't been as useless as I'd thought. Looking back, I could see how easily I'd been fooled. How Liesl had hidden the truth and made it seem as though the girl didn't have enough magic to fill the palm of my hand, much less enough to help me force my way into House Zimmer.

And then, of course, Liesl had taken things a step further and claimed the girl had been killed in an accident. Apparently, she'd told Beatrice Zimmer the same lie, and the old crone had been as shocked as I had by Vesper's familial revelations at the midnight ball.

I'd already killed Liesl, shot the blackmailing bitch out of the sky, and I would find a way to exact my revenge on Beatrice as well. It was a pity the mercenaries hadn't killed Wendell at the Collier estate like I'd wanted. That might have finally broken Beatrice, but part of me was looking forward to doing that myself. I sipped my sangria and indulged in a daydream of stabbing Wendell in the stomach while Beatrice watched in helpless horror.

The thought brought a genuine smile to my face and lightened my mood. I wandered over to a settee, sat down, and studied the plastipapers on the low table in front of me. While Vesper and her friends had been fighting Esmina, Pollux, and their mercenaries, I had hacked into the Serpens Corp servers and downloaded all the data and experiments Esmina's lab rats had conducted on the Techwave cannon.

A Techwave scientist in my thrall had scanned the information and declared it unimportant, but I was going to study every word, line, and simulation. I didn't have Vesper's seer magic, but I knew something important was lurking in the plastipapers.

It might take some time, but I would figure out *exactly* how Vesper had fixed the hand cannon—and then I would use the information for my own ends.

My gaze wandered over to the wristwatch that was also lying on the table. The device was based on Jorge Rojillo's design. Ocnus still hadn't told me his plans for the temperature-shielding technology, but my Techwave scientist was quietly working on that as well.

Several other items were also laid out on the table, projects in various stages of development. Vesper might have slipped out of my grasp, but I'd learned a long time ago to hedge my bets, and I had my own weapons in the works.

I grabbed my drink, got up, and went over to the window. Down below, the Techwave scientists kept assembling one Black Scarab after another, putting arms and legs on headless torsos, but in my mind's eye, I was seeing my own schemes and plans slowly coming together.

It wouldn't be long before I took control of the Techwave. And then everyone in the Imperium would bow down to me, including the useless girl who called herself Vesper Quill.

Thank you for reading ***Only Cold Depths***.
Vesper and Kyrion will return
in another **Galactic Bonds** adventure.

Want to know more about Kyrion Caldaren?
Keep reading for a look at a bonus/deleted chapter from ***Only Cold Depths***, book 4 in the **Galactic Bonds** science-fiction fantasy series.

# BONUS CHAPTER
# ONE

## KYRION

This takes place after Chapter 25 in ***Only Cold Depths***.

Everything seemed to be happening in slow motion, like a bad dream that just kept getting worse and worse with each new action.

Esmina plunging the injector into my neck. The hot cascade of chemicals zipping through my veins. Pollux swatting my stormsword out of my hand. Two mercs dragging me between them as though I was a sack of potatoes they were hauling across the ground.

Then my gaze locking with Zane's, his eyes bright with worry as the mercenaries aimed their weapons. The other Arrow stepping in front of Asterin, trying to shield her from the deadly cannon fire that was coming their way.

I blinked, and the scene changed. Now the mercs were dragging me through a garden. I tried to move, dig my heels into the dirt, do something, *anything*, but my arms and legs simply wouldn't work, as though I was an action figure a child was playing with, with no free will or movement of my own.

In the distance, bright flares of light caught my eye. Vesper was running this way, her stormsword and mine clutched in her hands, both blades burning a dark blue with her psion power. Zane and Asterin were also sprinting in this direction.

*No! Stay back! Don't come after me!*

I tried to send the thought to Vesper, but I couldn't quite grip my telepathy through the hot chemicals still cascading through my body. Frustration spiked through me. I'd never felt so bloody *helpless*. Even when Vesper had been taken to Corios to face Holloway, I'd still had my psion power. Without it, I didn't know how to fight back.

The mercenaries reached the edge of the garden, crossed a lawn, and headed toward a waiting transport.

Vesper kept running in this direction. The stormswords in her hands whipped up and down, and peony petals swirled around her like blue snowflakes.

"Wait until she gets close enough, then break cover and grab her," Pollux growled into the comms device attached to his shoulder.

My chest squeezed with dread. Vesper being captured was my worst nightmare, but I knew she wouldn't give up, and she was going to run right into Pollux's trap.

Pollux stepped forward and fired his cannon in Vesper's direction. The blast knocked her down, and the stormswords slid out of her hands, although she quickly scrambled back up onto her feet.

"Get ready to move!" Pollux yelled.

Vesper headed toward the transport again, but Zane put on an extra burst of speed, surged forward, and wrapped his arms around her. Vesper struggled, but Zane was stronger, and he held her back.

My gaze met his across the distance separating us. *Thank you. No matter what happens to me, keep her safe.*

Zane blinked, as though he'd heard my telepathic thought. I didn't see how that was possible, given how weak and distant my power felt right now, but Zane tightened his grip on Vesper and kept her from coming any closer.

"Don't worry about it!" Esmina called out. "She'll come to us!"

Pollux nodded, then reached for his comms device to issue another order. "Let's go! Move, move, move!"

The two mercenaries hoisted me up and into the vehicle. They released my arms, and my body thumped to the floor. The chemicals were still pumping through my veins, and I couldn't even lift my head off the grimy metal.

Pollux and the rest of the mercenaries also retreated and hopped onto the transport. Pollux made a circular motion with his index finger, telling the pilot to take off.

"Kyrion! Kyrion!" Vesper screamed, but I couldn't so much as grunt in response.

The thrusters roared even louder. The transport surged up into the sky, making my stomach zoom up into my throat. The motion also slung me over onto my back and banged my wrist up against the metal wall. Pain spiked through my hand, and I managed to twitch my fingers. The chemicals were finally wearing off. Perhaps I still had a chance to escape—

A shadow dropped over me, and Pollux leaned down and sneered in my face. "Not so tough now, are you, Arrow?"

"Knock him out," Esmina ordered. "I don't want any problems before we get back to base."

Base? What base? Where? Thoughts tumbled through my muddled mind one after another, but I couldn't focus on any of them.

Pollux grinned. "With pleasure."

He cracked his knuckles, then slammed his fist into my face. Pain exploded in my jaw, and white stars winked on and off in my eyes like the lights on a blitzer warning of an imminent, unavoidable crash. Once again, I struggled to focus, and my thoughts turned to Vesper.

*Don't come after me . . . Don't fall into Esmina and Pollux's trap . . .*

I had no idea if Vesper had heard me, and she probably wouldn't listen even if she had, but that was one of the many things I loved about her.

*Vesper, please . . . save yourself . . .*

Pollux growled and punched me again. More pain exploded in my jaw. Those white stars in my eyes darkened to gray, then bled to black, and I knew nothing more.

# About the Author

Jennifer Estep is a *New York Times*, *USA Today*, and internationally bestselling author who prowls the streets of her imagination in search of her next fantasy idea.

Jennifer is the author of the **Galactic Bonds**, **Section 47**, **Elemental Assassin**, **Crown of Shards**, **Gargoyle Queen**, and other fantasy series. She has written more than forty-five books, along with numerous novellas and stories.

In her spare time, Jennifer enjoys hanging out with friends and family, doing yoga, and reading fantasy and romance books. She also watches way too much TV and loves all things related to superheroes.

For more information on Jennifer and her books, visit her website at **www.jenniferestep.com** or follow her online on Facebook, Instagram, X (formerly Twitter), Amazon, BookBub, and Goodreads. You can also sign up for her newsletter: www.jenniferestep.com/contact-jennifer/newsletter/

Happy reading, everyone!

# Other Books by Jennifer Estep

**THE GALACTIC BONDS SERIES**

*Only Bad Options*
*Only Good Enemies*
*Only Hard Problems* (Zane Zimmer book)
*Only Cold Depths*

**THE SECTION 47 SERIES**

*A Sense of Danger*
*Sugar Plum Spies* (holiday book)

**THE ELEMENTAL ASSASSIN SERIES**
FEATURING GIN BLANCO

**BOOKS**

*Spider's Bite*
*Web of Lies*
*Venom*
*Tangled Threads*
*Spider's Revenge*
*By a Thread*
*Widow's Web*
*Deadly Sting*
*Heart of Venom*
*The Spider*
*Poison Promise*
*Black Widow*
*Spider's Trap*
*Bitter Bite*

*Unraveled*
*Snared*
*Venom in the Veins*
*Sharpest Sting*
*Last Strand*
*Stings and Stones* (short story collection)

**E-NOVELLAS**

*Haints and Hobwebs*
*Thread of Death*
*Parlor Tricks*
*Kiss of Venom*
*Unwanted*
*Nice Guys Bite*
*Winter's Web*
*Heart Stings*
*Spider and Frost* (crossover novella)

**THE CROWN OF SHARDS SERIES**

*Kill the Queen*
*Protect the Prince*
*Crush the King*

**THE GARGOYLE QUEEN SERIES**

*Capture the Crown*
*Tear Down the Throne*
*Conquer the Kingdom*

**THE BLACK BLADE SERIES**

*Cold Burn of Magic*
*Dark Heart of Magic*
*Bright Blaze of Magic*

**THE BIGTIME SERIES**

*Karma Girl*
*Hot Mama*

*Jinx*
*A Karma Girl Christmas* (holiday story)
*Nightingale*
*Fandemic*

**THE MYTHOS ACADEMY SPINOFF SERIES**
FEATURING RORY FORSETI

*Spartan Heart*
*Spartan Promise*
*Spartan Destiny*

**THE MYTHOS ACADEMY SERIES**
FEATURING GWEN FROST

**BOOKS**
*Touch of Frost*
*Kiss of Frost*
*Dark Frost*
*Crimson Frost*
*Midnight Frost*
*Killer Frost*

**E-NOVELLAS AND SHORT STORIES**
*First Frost*
*Halloween Frost*
*Spartan Frost*
*Spider and Frost* (crossover novella)

**OTHER WORKS**
*The Beauty of Being a Beast* (fairy tale)
*Write Your Own Cake* (worldbuilding essay)

www.ingramcontent.com/pod-product-compliance
Lightning Source LLC
Chambersburg PA
CBHW030341310726
48979CB00001B/136

* 9 7 8 1 9 5 0 0 7 6 4 6 8 *